T0009666

Praise for the novels of Amanda Ske

The Medicine Woman of Galve

"A wonderful story about seizing second chances—
those? Amanda Skenandore has a keen eye for dev......
who transform while keeping the endearing, relatable qualities that
made us root for them in the first place. A charming cast of misfits and a
devastating hurricane were just the ingredients I needed to completely lose
myself in this book." —Elise Cooper, author of *Angels of the Pacific*

The Undertaker's Assistant

"Effie's community of freedmen and Creoles in Reconstruction New Orleans
is unforgettable. Skenandore's second novel is recommended for readers who
enjoy medical historical fiction reminiscent of Diane McKinney-Whetstone's
Lazaretto, and historical fiction with interpersonal drama." —*Library Journal*

"Readers who like complex characters amid a roiling historical setting
will be fascinated by Effie's quest. . . . Teen readers will empathize with
a young woman's search for identity and love." —*Booklist*

"Our immersion in that world—from the particulars of baking marble
cake to the grisly minutiae of embalming corpses to the messy and violent
politics of the Reconstruction South—is so complete that the reader never
doubts it once existed. That said, one of this novel's many virtues is how
it subtly conveys how many black citizens in the post-Civil War era took it
upon themselves to improve their own lives." —*Historical Novels Review*

Between Earth and Sky

"Intensely emotional. . . . Skenandore's deeply introspective and
moving novel will appeal to readers of American history, particularly
those interested in the dynamics behind the misguided efforts of
white people to better the lives of Native Americans by forcing
them to adopt white cultural mores." —*Publishers Weekly*

"A masterfully written novel about the heart-wrenching clash of
two American cultures . . . a fresh and astonishing debut."
—V. S. Alexander, author of *The Magdalen Girls*

"By describing its costs in human terms, the author shapes tension
between whites and Native Americans into a touching story. The title
of Skenandore's debut could refer to reality and dreams, or to love and
betrayal; all are present in this highly original novel." —*Booklist*

"A heartbreaking story about the destructive legacy of the forced
assimilation of Native American children. Historical fiction readers and
book discussion groups will find much to ponder here." —*Library Journal*

Books by Amanda Skenandore

BETWEEN EARTH AND SKY

THE UNDERTAKER'S ASSISTANT

THE SECOND LIFE OF MIRIELLE WEST

THE NURSE'S SECRET

THE MEDICINE WOMAN OF GALVESTON

Published by Kensington Publishing Corp.

THE
MEDICINE
WOMAN
OF
GALVESTON

AMANDA SKENANDORE

KENSINGTON
PUBLISHING CORP.

www.kensingtonbooks.com

KENSINGTON BOOKS are published by
Kensington Publishing Corp.
600 Third Avenue
New York, NY 10022

Copyright © 2024 by Amanda Skenandore

All rights reserved. No part of this book may be reproduced in any form
or by any means without the prior written consent of the Publisher, ex-
cepting brief quotes used in reviews.

All Kensington titles, imprints, and distributed lines are available at special quantity discounts for bulk purchases for sales promotion, premi-
ums, fund-raising, educational, or institutional use.

This book is a work of fiction. Names, characters, businesses, organiza-
tions, places, events, and incidents either are the product of the author's
imagination or are used fictitiously. Any resemblance to actual persons,
living or dead, events, or locales is entirely coincidental.

To the extent that the image or images on the cover of this book depict
a person or persons, such person or persons are merely models, and are
not intended to portray any character or characters featured in the book.

Special book excerpts or customized printings can also be created to fit
specific needs. For details, write or phone the office of the Kensington
Sales Manager: Kensington Publishing Corp., 119 West 40th Street,
New York, NY 10018. Attn. Sales Department. Phone: 1-800-221-2647.

Kensington and the K logo Reg. U.S. Pat. & TM Off.

ISBN: 978-1-4967-4169-1 (ebook)

ISBN: 978-1-4967-4168-4

First Kensington Trade Paperback Printing: June 2024

10 9 8 7 6 5 4 3 2 1

Printed in the United States of America

For Berry
And the light, love, and laughter you bring to the world

THE
MEDICINE
WOMAN
OF
GALVESTON

1

St. Louis, Missouri, 1900

Tucia's head whipped up at the sound—high-pitched and urgent. She swiped a greasy hand across her forehead, pushing aside straggly, sweat-dampened hair, and turned from the oily gears of the tempering machine.

The sound belonged to the new girl three stations down. She stood writhing and wailing beside her machine.

Tucia took a single step toward her before catching sight of the blood. The girl's sleeve had caught in the machine's gears. Her arm, or what was left of it, was twisted amid the metal, flashes of bone and muscle visible between bits of shredded shirtsleeve.

Tucia managed another step forward. A tourniquet was needed, high on the arm, until she could assess the extent of the girl's injury. A ligation, perhaps, judging from the pulsing splatter of blood. She'd need a blade in case she couldn't find the end of the vessel after exploring the wound. A needle and thread. Cauterization might be necessary . . . Tucia's feet had stopped. Stuck. Heavy. Cold. Her pulse sped. Her vision, only moments ago sharp, lost focus. The blood, she could still see it spurting, but the girl's cries grew distant.

Tucia closed her eyes and tried to breathe despite the tightness in her throat. When she opened them, the factory, with its steam-choked air and whirring machines, had vanished.

You've gone and nicked an artery thanks to your careless approach. Now what will you do? a voice said over her shoulder, loud enough for everyone in the room to hear. Tucia rattled her head—that voice, it wasn't real—but her hands, they were bloody, from the tips of her fingers to her elbows. Bloody and shaking. The smell of antiseptic blended with the stench of sweat and overworked gears redolent throughout the factory.

You'll never grasp the vessel if you can't still your hands.

But Tucia couldn't even find the vessel. She cast aside the scalpel and groped for a clamp and ligature. Her slick hands could barely hold onto them.

You're taking too long. How much blood can a patient lose before death is imminent?

When she didn't reply, he all but shouted. *How much blood?*

"Five pints."

Correct. And your blundering has cost her at least three. Dr. Seldon, check her pulse.

Tucia flattened her bloody hands over her ears. This wasn't real.

Weak, sir, and thready.

She sucked in a breath and tried again to find the vessel, but the woman's abdomen was quickly filling with blood. A cacophony of whispers rose through the operating theater. Tucia willed her mind to clear. What had the *Annals of Surgery* said about stopping hemorrhages? Gravity was used in cases of placental abruption. Elevating the pelvis above the head. Could such a technique be applied here? It might buy Tucia precious time to find the nicked artery. She called for the nurse's assistance, but a louder, gruff voice rose above her own.

Out of the way, you incompetent woman, you're killing her.

Tucia was pushed aside. As she stumbled forward, reaching out to steady herself, her hand landed on a rough wooden surface. A workbench?

The sights, sounds, and smells of the operating room faded. Rusty machines again surrounded her. Bare lightbulbs hung from above, and threads of afternoon light pressed in through the grimy windows. Tucia felt turned inside out, her heart still racing and her skin clammy. But she'd never been happier to be in this dingy factory.

Then she remembered the girl. Tucia's eyes darted to the machine where her arm had caught. Shreds of fabric and tissue hung from the gears, but the girl had somehow broken free and lay in a bloody heap at the foot of her work table. To Tucia's relief, the man who had brushed past her was the ambulance surgeon. The factory foreman followed at his heels but stopped several feet short of the girl, his face twisting into a grimace.

A crowd now filled the room. Workers from every department—spinning, stitching, hacking, cutting—pressed in among the machines. They gawked and murmured like they had in—Tucia scrubbed her hands over her face. They weren't bloody after all, only smeared with dirt and grease from the machine. How long had she been standing there?

The doctor set his physician's bag on the floor, careful to avoid the sprawling pool of blood, and rummaged inside it. After an achingly prolonged moment, he withdrew a stethoscope. He tiptoed to the girl as if more concerned with preserving his shiny shoes than saving her life. When he reached her, he inserted the earpiece into his ears and leaned over her, pressing the drum to her chest. Two fingers to her carotid would have yielded a quicker result, and even that could wait until a tourniquet was applied and the bleeding staunched. Tucia willed herself forward that she might assist him, but her legs were still too leaden to cooperate.

The doctor rose and removed the stethoscope from his ears.

"Shall I fetch your tourniquet?" she said, though her feet remained unyielding, rooted to the floor.

He shook his head.

"Have you suture thread in your bag? If you've got a quick hand, a ligation of the artery—"

He silenced her with another shake of the head. "Too late. With a wound like that, she hardly stood a chance."

"Are you sure? Perhaps—"

"Do you know how much blood a person can lose before they die?"

Tucia flinched. "Five pints," she muttered.

"Five pints," he said as if she hadn't spoken at all. "There's at least that here on the ground, wouldn't you say?"

Tucia's gaze flickered downward. In the operating theater, a basin of sawdust beneath the surgical table caught the majority of blood lost during a procedure. Here, it spread uncontained, dark and oozing, seeping into the floorboards.

She raised her eyes, the edges of her vision blurring again, and nodded at the surgeon. He replied with a knowing snort and tip-toed through the blood back to his bag. "I'll send an attendant over from the deadhouse to fetch the body," he said to no one in particular and left.

The foreman shooed the crowd of workers back to their jobs. But Tucia lingered until he called her out by name and threatened to dock her the day's pay if she continued to dally. Her feet, still stiff and heavy, obeyed.

It was the second person she'd let die.

2

As soon as the factory's horn blew that evening, Tucia hurried home, wending her way through the busy city. She muttered as she walked, counting the cracks in the sidewalk. People might think her mad, but Tucia didn't care. It gave her something in the here and now to focus on. Otherwise she might splinter apart.

The counting was a trick she'd picked up from an old army lieutenant who'd lived a few doors down when she first came to the city. A loud noise, and he was back at Chancellorsville with artillery booming and minie balls whizzing by his head. But if he could latch on to something in the present—the ticking of a clock or the number of petals on a flower—he might keep himself from slipping away.

Slipping away. That had been his term for it, and she'd thought it fitting. It called to mind losing purchase on the edge of a cliff or being caught in the undercurrent of a frozen river. One moment your handhold was strong, the ice beneath your feet solid, then— *crack*—you were slipping away. Falling. Gone.

The alienist had a different term. Hysterical attacks. She'd seen him only a few times after the incidents first began. Besides his blithe diagnosis and a rambling explanation of her innate female frailty, his only advice was to keep her mind—weak as it was—focused on the present.

Whatever the name, Tucia hadn't experienced one in years. She was careful, after all. Had whittled her life down to the bare necessities. She avoided hospitals and blood sports and even carbolic soap. But the old man had warned her the waking nightmares would return.

Now, she dared not stop counting, though it slowed her pace. A bone-deep exhaustion plagued her step, but her every nerve still crackled as if on high alert. The normal ebb and flow of traffic on the streets—the rattling streetcars and clanking carriages and jangling bicycles—now seemed a frightful source of danger. At any moment, they might collide or strike an errant pedestrian.

What then? Would she freeze like she had that afternoon? Watch as another person bled out in front of her?

She forced herself to stop by the bakery a few blocks from her flat and bought a loaf of day-old bread. Then to the deli for a wedge of cheese. The shops were crowded with workers like her, hoping to stretch what little money they had until payday. It was hot inside the deli and stuffy. A bitter taste of the summer heat to come. Today the line of tired workers seemed fiery and restless. Their sighs and grumbles louder. Their glances cutting and suspicious.

Absentmindedly, she plucked a hair from behind her ear and began twirling it between her index finger and thumb. A moment later, she realized what she'd done. She dropped the hair and groped along her scalp for bald patches, mussing her bun and upsetting her hat.

No. Please, no! Not again.

Her whole body heaved with relief when she found nothing on her head amiss. But the urge to pluck another hair was so strong she had to close her eyes and ball her fist to keep it at bay.

"Next!"

Tucia startled at the loud voice, her heart leaping and eyes popping open.

"Hey, lady, you're next."

She hurried to the counter, bought her cheese, then threaded her way through the crowd and out the door.

Her last stop was the A&P. She clutched the handles of her bag with both hands and counted seventy-nine sidewalk cracks before arriving. Another snaking line awaited her inside, causing her stomach to twist and breathing to quicken. She'd much rather skip the store for home, but she'd promised to stop.

Inside, cans and boxes and jars lined the floor-to-ceiling shelves. Coffee, tea, sugar, baking powder, condensed milk— nearly anything one wanted could be found here. Her eye snagged on the boxes of packaged tea. Orange Pekoe, India-Ceylon, English Breakfast. She'd been brewing the same leaves at home for a week now. But she couldn't justify the expense. Not even after a day like today. When she reached the counter, the clerk asked for her list. Tucia shook her head with a stab of embarrassment and pointed to the jar of penny candy. "One piece, please."

Before reaching home, she passed another dozen sidewalk cracks and twice caught her fingers twirling a newly plucked hair.

"Home" was really too grand a word for the two-room flat she rented on the fourth floor of a decades-old tenement in the lower quarter of the city. Especially considering the fine Italianate home she'd grown up in. Sometimes she'd think about it—the plush oriental carpets, the richly lit rooms, the soft upholstered furniture— as she trudged up the creaky stairs to her flat, swallowing a tinge of regret before opening the door. But tonight, the spare, drafty rooms with peeling wallpaper and rotting floorboards would be a welcome reprieve from the day's horrors.

She opened the door to near darkness, the last rays of evening's light retreating through the room's lone window. Tucia shuffled forward, feeling her way to the table, and lit the oil lamp. The flame flared, then settled into a weak but steady glow. A glance about the room revealed Mrs. Harsnatch seated in one of the two ladder-back chairs, her feet propped on a stack of Tucia's books, the daily paper draped across her lap. Her mouth gaped open, and her chest rose with the steady rhythm of slumber. Otherwise, the room was empty.

Panic flared inside her. "Toby!" She dropped her bag and wheeled around, crossing to the adjoining room. "Toby!"

The answering silence struck her like ice water. She stumbled in her haste, bracing herself on the door jamb. Her eyes swept the room. Nothing. Her breath hitched. Then, beside the bed, a flash of movement. Her son looked up from his building blocks and grinned at her.

Tucia hurried over and knelt beside him, wiping away an errant tear. Of course he was here, safe and sound. Where else would he be? How foolish of her to worry.

She brushed the hair from his forehead. "What are you doing playing here in the dark?"

"Making a house."

"Didn't you hear Mama come in?"

He shrugged and turned back to his blocks.

"You gave me quite the fright. The least you could have done is answered when I called." Her words came out sharper than she'd intended.

Toby's smile fell. He dashed the lopsided tower he'd been building, sending the blocks scattering. Tucia winced and pulled him to her. Though he was small for his age, as most children with his condition were, he barely fit in her lap anymore. "I'm sorry, darling," she said.

"I'm sorry," he repeated. He nestled his head against her neck, and Tucia wrapped her arms around him. For the first time since the accident that afternoon, she could fully breathe. He'd always been that way—her anchor, her joy. She held him close until he grew restless and wiggled free.

"Look what I've got for you." She pulled the small piece of candy from the watch pocket of her jacket.

Toby clapped and reached for it.

"Not until after supper." She kissed him on the nose and stood. "Wash up while I say goodbye to Mrs. Harsnatch."

Tucia returned to the main room to find Mrs. Harsnatch still snoring softly. If the woman could sleep through Tucia's shouting, who was to say she'd awaken if Toby called out in need? Thank goodness he hadn't.

She wished sorely she could sack the woman. But she'd never be able to find a replacement nanny willing to work for so little. Mrs. Harsnatch didn't drink. She didn't strike Toby or call him simple. She didn't go wagging her tongue about them to friends or neighbors. And that meant a lot. Tucia knew all too well how quickly rumors spread.

Still, it would be nice if the woman could at least manage to stay awake. Tucia drew close and cleared her throat. When that didn't work, she stomped her foot, sending a rumble through the worn floorboards. Mrs. Harsnatch startled, toppling the books at her feet and sending the newspaper fluttering to the floor.

"Good evening, Mrs. Harsnatch. I'm home."

She straightened and swiped at her eyes. "Ain't no mystery there."

"Toby was playing in the dark when I arrived. Unsupervised, I might add."

"You said to mind the oil."

"Yes, but I merely meant not to burn the lamp in the middle of the day when the window affords sufficient light."

Mrs. Harsnatch only grunted. She rose from the chair and grabbed her frayed shawl from the peg on the wall without bothering to pick up the newsprint or return Tucia's books to the makeshift shelf where Tucia kept them. "Them loan sharks came by again today." She jutted her chin at a letter on the table. Undoubtedly she'd read it, then folded it back up. "That ain't gonna affect our arrangement, is it?"

Tucia forced a thin-lipped smile. She knew without reading it what the letter said. Her debt—nearly seven hundred dollars—was coming due in eight days.

"No, certainly not," she said, though she had no means of paying such a sum. The salary lenders knew that too. It suited them just fine to renew the loan—at a higher interest rate, of course—and siphon off more of her weekly wages. She might not be able to afford her apartment, meager as it was, or even Mrs. Harsnatch's salary.

But for now, she could. She grabbed her bag from the floor and fished out a quarter.

As soon as the coin was in her hand, Mrs. Harsnatch scuttled out the door. Tucia fixed Toby a plate of buttered bread and cheese. She took half a slice for herself, unbuttered, and heated the kettle for a cup of weak tea. While waiting for the water to boil, she dusted off her books and returned them to the shelf. *Human Anatomy. The Principles and Practice of Medicine. Materia Medica. Disorders of Bones and Surrounding Tissues. Dissection and Pathology.* She hadn't read them in years. Mrs. Harsnatch put them to better use as a rest for her dirty feet than Tucia ever had. But even after all these years, she couldn't part with them.

Next, she gathered up the scattered newsprint. This, at least, would make a useful fire starter or stuffing for the bed. As she folded the pages, a headline caught her eye:

RENOWNED SURGEON TO LECTURE AT HAMBY HALL

Tucia needn't read on. That life was behind her. What good was there in knowing the latest advances in asepsis or a new technique for lithotomy operations or the best way to suture the fascia after an ovariotomy? She couldn't even manage to fashion a tourniquet when someone was exsanguinating right in front of her.

She shuddered but read on anyway, stopping a few lines in when she read the renowned surgeon's name: Dr. Archibald Addams.

3

Tucia stood outside the Hamby Lecture Hall, her stomach knotted with indecision. A dry lump sat in her throat, and her hands were cold, despite the day's lingering warmth.

She'd thrown up into her chamber pot after first reading the article. Toby had used it to relieve himself earlier that day, though he was supposed to use the shared water closet on the first floor, and stale urine had splashed into her face. After she'd emptied the pot and cleaned herself up, she balled up the newspaper and threw it into the corner to use in the stove the next day.

But before burning it, she'd read it again. And again, memorizing the date and time two days hence. By the time she stuffed it in the firebox, a dark, relentless curiosity had sparked inside her.

Now she was here, dressed in her Sunday clothes, her hat strategically pinned to hide the small patch of baldness newly exposed atop her head. She didn't remember plucking the hairs. It might have been in her sleep when nightmares haunted her dreams. Or at the factory, where the dark ring of the woman's blood still stained the floor. It might have been during the long debates she'd staged in her head about whether to attend tonight's event. A debate still raging. She itched to pluck one now.

People—mostly men—streamed around her into the hall. She'd paid Mrs. Harsnatch an extra ten cents to stay late. Money Tucia could scarcely afford to spend. Money she wouldn't be getting back whether she attended the lecture or not.

Tucia rubbed her hands together and swallowed. She might as well sate her curiosity and see the man. What damage could he do that he hadn't already done?

She walked up the short flight of stone steps and into the lobby, weaving through the crowd to a door at the far end. She'd forgotten how it felt to be around these sorts of men, their hubris and self-importance wafting off them like cologne. She'd been that way once, too, though everyone was quick to remind her how ill-suited the scent was on a woman. Now they were polite enough, tipping their heads as they moved aside for her. Now that she smelled only of soap and machine grease.

When she reached the door at the far end, a man in a silk-lined cape stepped in front of her. His eyes, a curious shade of blue—no, not blue but violet—momentarily stunned her.

"Allow me," he said, doffing his shiny top hat and bowing low before opening the door for her.

Tucia thanked him with a nod and a weak smile, then stepped inside. The choice seats at the front of the hall near the stage were already occupied. Those in the middle were filling up fast. If she polished up her smile, she might be able to persuade one of the gentlemen at the front to give up his seat to her. But Tucia had no desire to be that close. The vast hall felt too small as it was.

She found a seat in the very last row. The man who'd held the door for her seated himself across the aisle only a few rows ahead, though there were still dozens of better seats to be had. Something about him sent a prick tiptoeing down her spine, but she couldn't say why. His flashy clothes, perhaps? His too-polished manners? His strange eyes? It wasn't just their color but the intensity of his stare. He surveyed the growing crowd with keen interest but, thankfully, did not look back in her direction.

A bell chimed in the lobby, announcing the commencement of the lecture. The last of the seats were quickly filled, and Tucia fixed her attention on the stage. The voices in the hall quieted, and time seemed to slow, each second stretching longer than the last until Dr. Addams strode onto the stage.

Tucia's body tensed at the sight of him. His sharp features. His broad frame. His brisk, confident step. Only a man as well assured of his good looks and brilliant mind as he could exude such effortless supremacy. Its effect was palpable. Whispers ceased. Shoulders bowed. Chins dropped. Then, almost in unison, the audience leaned forward, each man tugged by an invisible string. Even Tucia felt the pull.

The dean of the local medical college introduced Dr. Addams, extolling his vast contributions to the field of surgery. Then he bowed and yielded the stage.

Dr. Addams spared no time arranging himself at the podium, neither fumbling with spectacles nor searching for misplaced note cards the way some men did. He lectured by memory, always had, grabbing the sides of the podium like an Olympian readying to mount a pommel horse.

He seemed unchanged as if the past eight years hadn't touched him. What had she expected? That time and hardship had ravaged him as it had her? No, he was the very same man, and she but a shadow of herself.

His voice carried easily through the hall. Tucia didn't register what he said, only the hauntingly familiar cadence and timbre of his words. Her pulse hastened at the sound, and her windpipe narrowed. The distance between them collapsed. He was no longer fifty yards away, a sea of people between them, but standing close. *Too* close. Always a bit too close. But locked within his orbit, you could scarcely pull away. Didn't care to pull away. You felt larger, grander, capable beyond your natural means. Until you weren't. Until he wasn't standing in front of you or beside you, but behind you, unleashing his venom in your ears.

Worthless. Incompetent. Careless. Imposter.

Tucia felt the hall and all its men closing in around her. Blurring. Warping. Receding, only to rush back at her. Then, suddenly everything was still, the hall, the men all back in sharp focus. Dr. Addams had paused his lecture and was looking right at her.

Miss—er—Dr. Hatherley, why don't you come forward and enlighten the audience about the vascularity of uterine tissues and the danger of hemorrhage during supravaginal amputation?

She stood abruptly, shielding her face with her hands, and rushed from the hall. He hadn't recognized her. Couldn't have recognized her.

She stopped halfway through the lobby to catch her breath, steadying herself against a wingback chair, but only a sip of air made it to her lungs. She'd been a fool to come. A fool! She reached up and violently plucked a hair at the base of her scalp. And then another. And another. Four. Five. Six. Seven.

"Miss Hatherley?"

Tucia stopped at the sound of the unfamiliar voice and glanced over her shoulder.

A man walking with a cane hurried over. "Miss Hatherley? It is you, isn't it? Are you quite all right?" He reached out to her, but she flinched and pulled away.

"Mr. Seldon," he said as if she ought to recognize the name. "We were interns together at Fairview Hospital."

Tucia blinked. Her breath was coming easier, but her mind still felt fuzzy, and she had no recollection of the man before her. "Don't you mean *Doctor* Seldon?"

"I'm . . . er . . . not practicing."

He stuffed his free hand into his pocket and flashed a sheepish smile. Perhaps she did recognize him. Vaguely. They were so alike, the other interns. Arrogant and ambitious. They'd thought her a novelty at first, each going out of his way to prove how gallant he was, how unperturbed he was by her presence. Until Dr. Addams asked them about gangrene and the treatment of postoperative suppurating wounds during their first week of surgical rounds.

Not one of the fools knew the answer. But Tucia had, and offered it readily.

After that, all pretense of gallantry disappeared. She'd become their collective enemy. They would laugh uproariously when she entered the room. Whisper taunts and lewd jokes whenever she was in earshot. Crowd around a bedside or dissection table, casually shifting this way and that to keep her on the periphery.

She glanced now at Mr. Seldon's cane. It wasn't just for show the way so many other foppish men's were. A fractured tibia that hadn't healed properly, judging by the way he walked.

"A horse accident, I'm afraid," he said. "Though that's not why I'm not practicing. Never really was my thing. My father, if you remember, was—is—a physician. He'd always been the one pressing me to attend."

A flush of anger prickled beneath Tucia's skin. She'd wanted to be a doctor her whole life. Had fought and scraped every step of the way. Had studied harder and longer than him or any of the other interns. And in the end, even that hadn't been enough. For him, it was just a dalliance, an appeasement to his father, and yet the path before him had been laid smooth as butter.

"I'm in town on business. Just passing through, really. But when I saw the advertisement for Dr. Addams, I extended my stay. I thought I might see someone from the old crew here, though I confess, I hadn't expected it to be you."

"Old crew?" Tucia straightened. "Mr. Seldon, you put the shriveled remains of a human penis in my medical bag, wore down the blade of my dissection scalpel so I couldn't slice through a cadaver's skin, intentionally spilled a patient's urine sample all over my dress—and that was just within the first two weeks of our arrival at Fairview." She straightened her hat and turned toward the door, saying over her shoulder, "I have no doubt you toasted my expulsion too."

She walked briskly toward the exit, but Mr. Seldon caught up and kept pace beside her. "I tried to dissuade the others from putting the—er—appendage in your bag. I did."

Tucia snorted and continued on. Her entire body still felt out of sorts, her heart thudding as if a wolf were stalking her. She wanted desperately to be home, alone and safe with her son.

Maddeningly, Mr. Seldon reached the door before she did and held it open for her. She stopped, scowled at him, and stepped through.

"We behaved like cads, Miss Hatherley. Worse than cads, and I'm sorry."

The earnestness in his voice struck her, and her feet slowed. She glanced back and saw a flash of regret in his eyes.

"You were far superior to us both in intellect and dignity," he continued. "We dishonored ourselves and the profession in the way we treated you. That day, in the operating theater . . ."

Tucia winced and looked away.

"Dr. Addams was wrong to put you in that position. I thought it then and think it still today. Why, it could have been any one of us who—"

"But it wasn't," Tucia snapped. "It was me, and I'm the one who's had to live with the consequences." She hurried down the stairs without looking back or bothering to bid him goodbye.

4

That night, Tucia dared not close her eyes for fear of meeting Dr. Addams again in her dreams. She held Toby close, counting each of his slow, steady breaths quietly aloud—two thousand four hundred and sixty-eight, two thousand four hundred and sixty-nine—to keep from hearing the doctor's voice.

The next night passed much the same. And the next. When she did sleep, her dreams were drenched in blood.

Three days after the lecture, Tucia rose early for work. With Toby still sleeping, she washed herself at the nightstand and dressed behind the moth-eaten screen. Her nerves felt like they'd been scrubbed raw with wool steel. She'd been fifteen minutes late to work yesterday. Half an hour the day before. The foreman, a troll of a man with beady, narrow-set eyes, had glowered at her each time, jotting her name down on his little clipboard so he could be sure to dock her pay. Today, she was determined to be on time.

Once dressed, she pulled back the flannel curtains from the small window, allowing the pale glow of dawn to light the room. Toby stirred but didn't wake. She watched him for a moment, his sweet face relaxed, the corner of his lips twitching with a grin. Tucia smiled, too, imagining what pleasant dreams he might be having.

The doctor who'd delivered him had grimaced when he first saw Toby. He laid Toby at the foot of the hospital bed and did a cursory examination, muttering words like *hypotonia*, *brachycephaly*, and *heart murmur*. Exhausted and breathless as she was, Tucia gasped. She tried to sit up and see better what the doctor was doing, but the nurse held her down.

"A rather sickly infant, I'm afraid," he said, at last addressing Tucia. "I don't expect he'll make it through the night."

At that, the stiff bed seemed to swallow her. Sickly in what way? What was the diagnosis? Her thoughts raced, one stumbling atop the other, warring with the fiery pain between her legs and a swarming weariness. But when the nurse swaddled Toby and placed him in her arms, all that vanished—her pain, her exhaustion, her ambivalence. She felt only love.

Toby did survive the night. And the next. Proving his stubbornness even then. Upon discharge, the doctor reminded her of Toby's weak constitution. Furthermore, he said, the babe had the look of a Mongol and would never be more than a feeble-minded idiot. Tucia, too, had read Dr. Down's work on mental afflictions and knew the prognosis. But when his eyes met hers, his gaze deep and curious, she'd known both men were wrong. Though the intervening years had not been easy, Toby had proven her correct a thousand times over and in a thousand different ways.

She watched him sleep a moment longer, then turned toward the small mirror hung on the far wall above the nightstand. Her dress was rumpled and speckled with lint. The buttons of her shirtwaist were misaligned. Had she looked such a mess yesterday? In truth, she couldn't remember so much as glancing at the mirror since leaving for the lecture.

Tucia fixed her buttons and brushed off as much lint as she could. She hadn't time to heat the iron, so the wrinkles would have to stay. As she combed her hair, she noticed with horror half a dozen new bald spots, her scalp scabbed and flecked with dried blood. No matter how she styled her hair or pinned her hat, a few patches remained visible.

She rummaged through her drawers for her hair switch. It had been years since she'd needed to wear it, and couldn't remember where it was hidden. When she finally found it tucked beneath her winter sleeping gown and a pair of booties Toby had long since outgrown, the brittle hairs all but crumbled in her hands. The costly piece had once been fine and lustrous, but time had whittled it down to a few snarled and fragile strands.

Now running late, Tucia tossed the switch to the ground. She tore off her hat and tied a scarf around her head instead.

She boiled water and made a quick gruel—no counting on Mrs. Harsnatch to do it—and left as soon as the woman arrived and Toby was up and eating. Nevertheless, Tucia arrived at the factory four and a half minutes after the morning work bell had rung. The foreman was waiting with his notepad and pen.

For the third day in a row, she was assigned to the spinning room. It was easier work than in the tempering room. No grimy gears and levers. No bloodstain on the floor. Instead of the hiss of steam and grind of metal, hushed chatter filled the room.

Tucia had never been good at idle chitchat. As a child, when other girls wanted to talk about dolls and ribbons, she'd wanted to discuss the frog skeleton she'd found in the garden or the fowl she'd seen born en caul. It wasn't until medical school that she had true friends.

Few medical colleges countenanced coeducation. No woman of true delicacy would be willing to attend medical lectures with men. Or so the logic went. Those who did shamelessly unsexed themselves. So Tucia's college, one of many newly founded to circumvent this stricture, taught only women.

Though Tucia had been disappointed to be barred from the more prestigious institutions, which taught only men, it had been a joy to be surrounded by women who'd shared her same peculiarities and aspirations. But after graduation, she and her classmates had scattered, keeping in touch through letters, until Tucia, envious and ashamed, stopped writing. She'd not made another friend since.

Today, Tucia largely ignored the women's chatter, counting the rotations of the large bobbin as she fed the coraline fibers into the winding machine. But she couldn't escape the feeling they were talking about her. She'd look up and catch two or three of them leaning over their machines, staring in her direction and whispering. Twice she caught women pointing. Was it her headscarf? Her quiet counting? Or was she just being paranoid?

When the lunch bell rang, Tucia was the last to leave her machine. She'd run out of time that morning to pack herself a meal. A pretzel or sausage vendor often parked his cart outside the factory this time of day, but she couldn't afford the expense. Not when her pay had already been docked three days in a row. Still, a bit of fresh air would be nice. She started for the main stairwell that led to the exit, but the foreman intercepted her.

"A word, Miss Hatherley. In my office."

Tucia reluctantly followed him through the factory. The day was warm and sunny, and most of the workers had taken their lunch pails to the lawn, leaving the vast rooms empty. She couldn't help but recall the late evenings after the other interns had been dismissed, following Dr. Addams through the sleepy wards of the hospital to his richly furnished office off the main hall. If she'd felt a nagging unease, as she did now, she'd thoroughly ignored it.

The foreman's office, by contrast, was a musty, closet-sized space with a grimy window overlooking the stitching room. She could imagine him peering out at the women as they worked, his greasy forehead pressed to the glass, his clipboard in hand, eager to catch the slightest misstep.

He sat behind a small desk cluttered with papers. His was the only chair, so Tucia stood.

"Close the door, Miss Hatherley."

Tucia hesitated. With the other workers gone on their lunch break, he needn't worry their conversation would be overheard. But she could see the impatience growing in his beady eyes and pulled the door shut. Clearly her recent spate of tardiness had irked him. Best not to add kindling to the flame.

"I'm sorry about my lateness this morning," she said, hoping to spare herself whatever lecture he had in store. "And yesterday."

"And the day before that."

"I promise it won't happen again."

The foreman leaned back in his chair and frowned.

"If you review my record, you'll see I've worked here nearly three years and not been late once."

"Ah, but you've four unexcused absences."

"My son, he has a weak heart and delicate constitution. What would be a simple cold for another child can quickly progress to pneumonia. I sent word by telegram explaining his condition each time. The previous foreman had—"

"What the previous foreman did is irrelevant." He steepled his hands and eyed her in a way that made her skin prickle. "If your boy is sickly, perhaps his father ought to get a better-paying job so you can stay home and look out for him."

Tucia's muscles clenched at his callousness. It was never that simple or easy. "His father is dead."

"I see." He stood and walked around to the front of his desk, leaning against the edge and crossing his arms.

Tucia glanced through the window at the empty workroom and shuffled back. Her hands itched for the strands of hair that had slipped free of her scarf, but she buried them in the folds of her skirt.

"I'm a reasonable man," he said in an oily voice. "I could, perhaps, overlook a few days' lateness. But the other workers have complained."

"On what account?"

He shrugged. "Some are complaining of lice. They say you pick at your hair and see nits covering your dress."

"I don't have lice," Tucia said. "And it's lint. Not nits. We work in a damn corset factory. There's lint everywhere."

"A few have even suggested you're mad, say you've been muttering to yourself ever since the unfortunate accident in the tempering room. You were there that day, weren't you? I seem to recall telling you to return to your station."

"She died right in front of me. I was . . . I was greatly disquieted by it, as I'm sure the other witnesses were."

"And yet, they manage to report for work on time. No complaints have been lodged against them." He sighed. "I'm afraid we have to let you go."

"Let me go?" The air in the cramped room grew thin. "But I'm not . . . you can't . . . the complaints are unfounded."

"I can, and I must."

"No, please, I promise I shan't be late again. And no more counting—I mean, muttering." She tore the scarf off her head. "And you can see for yourself, I don't have lice or any such thing."

His thin lips puckered as his eyes raked over the bald spots scattered across her scalp.

"Please," she said, her voice trembling. "I cannot lose this job. I promise not to be any more trouble."

As it was, her paltry wages were barely keeping her debtors at bay. Without them, she'd lose everything.

His gaze slid to the window, and his sour expression softened into something far more ominous. "I suppose we might be able to come to some arrangement."

As he unfastened his belt and began unbuttoning his trousers, Tucia realized what sort of an arrangement he had in mind.

She backed away, bumping into the wall. He closed the space between them, grabbing her hand and forcing it between his legs.

"Go on, then, we haven't got much time before the bell."

Tucia couldn't move. Her mouth was dry as day-old bread, and her pulse thudded in her ears.

The foreman huffed and covered her hand with his, forcing her fingers to close around him. He was hot, hard, and sticky with sweat. She gagged, choking back bile.

With a tight hold, he moved their hands up and down, letting his head loll back and eyes close. "There you go. I knew a girl like you would know plenty well what to do."

A sudden rage swarmed inside her, gathering with a terrific hum until it was all she could see, feel, and hear. Her free hand curled into a fist. She punched his eye with all the force she could muster. The foreman stumbled back, knocking into his desk. Papers scattered to the floor.

Tucia wasted no time in flinging open the door and fleeing from the room. She pushed past the workers returning from their lunch break, no longer caring if they stared or whispered. Lice, madness—let them think what they would. She just had to get out of there.

By the time she reached the street, that humming anger had begun to wane. She hurried to the nearest fountain and scrubbed her hand raw. Then she headed home. Exhaustion filled the void her anger left behind, a tiredness that settled in the marrow of her bones. She didn't count the cracks in the sidewalk or pluck her hair. She just walked.

When Tucia reached her flat, she found Mrs. Harsnatch reading the morning paper, oblivious to the mess Toby had made by turning out the ash bin onto the floor and dragging his soot-stained fingers across the wall.

A flicker of her earlier rage returned. She paid Mrs. Harsnatch her quarter—never mind that she'd only worked half a day and was due far less—and sent her away, telling her she was a useless old bag and needn't return. Not tomorrow or the next day or ever again. Mrs. Harsnatch huffed, muttered something about feeble-mindedness being a mark of God's curse, and stomped away.

Toby watched, his almond-shaped eyes going wide, then went back to his play. The smudges on the wall were drawings, he told her happily: a tree, a dog, a lopsided figure he proclaimed was her. It took the last of her energy to muster a smile. She shuffled into the bedroom, leaving the door open, and crawled into bed. She closed her eyes, welcoming whatever dreams or nightmares would come.

5

When Tucia awoke, sharp rays of light pierced the room. Squinting as her eyes adjusted to the painful brightness, she fished the watch from her pocket and checked the time. Ten o'clock, the tiny hands read. But that made no sense. How could there be light when the sun had set only a few hours ago? Moonlight, perhaps? She burnished the watch on her shirtsleeve and checked the time again. The hands remained stubbornly in place, the short one pointing at ten and the long one stretched toward twelve.

Tucia bolted upright. It wasn't night at all but the next day. She'd slept for over twenty hours.

"Toby!" she called, her gaze scouring the room.

He peeked in from the next room, a look of uncertainty on his face. He was clothed in yesterday's ash-stained shirt and socks. Tucia held her arms out, and he ran to her, climbing onto the bed into her lap. He smelled of soot and sour milk, but she hugged him close, rocking him side to side.

The events of yesterday came back to her with aching clarity. What was she going to do? No job, no nanny, hundreds of dollars of debt coming due. The weight of it paralyzed her. She rocked her son and closed her eyes to stave off tears. The urge to pluck her hair—just one strand—built inside her.

Tucia gave in. One hair. She sighed, twirling the strand between her fingers. Her relief lasted only a minute. Then the urge overwhelmed her again. She plucked another and another and God knows how many more until she opened her eyes and found her son looking up at her.

Dr. John Langdon Down believed children like him had dampened and defective emotionality. That the more advanced of them were merely mimics. And it was true Toby looked to her for emotional cues. He laughed when she laughed. Smiled when she smiled. Frowned when she was stern or upset. But it wasn't mere mimicry. He might not always have the words to express himself, but he had a sense—better than anyone she'd known—of what others were feeling. And he reacted to those feelings, sometimes in kind, sometimes with his own native emotions.

And now, that emotion was clear: concern.

"I made you breakfast, Mama," he said and crawled off her lap. He returned a moment later from the other room carrying the cook pot. Inside were a handful of uncooked oats swimming in a pool of cold water.

Tucia felt as if she might shatter. She was the adult. It was *her* job to take care of *him*. Never mind that she'd slept through supper and breakfast without any care for his needs. No, the truth was worse. She'd gone and lost everything.

But she sat as straight as she could and forced a smile, fishing a few oats from the pot and putting them in her mouth. "Thank you so much, darling."

Toby watched expectantly as she chewed and swallowed. "Why are you crying?"

She swiped her cheeks and smiled wider. "Because I'm so happy you made breakfast for me. These oats are delicious." She plucked a few more from the water and ate them. They crunched between her teeth and slid dryly down her throat.

Toby, his small hands still stained with ash, scooped up several oats before she could stop him and ate them. He frowned, seemingly confused why they were hard and crunchy.

"Here, let Mama make some more for you."

She took the pot and peeled herself from the bed. Her work dress clung stiff and scratchy to her body like a second skin. A mess greeted her in the next room. Not just spilled ash and smudged walls, but scattered oats and the whiff of something sharp—urine—coming from a pair of balled-up trousers in the corner.

But Tucia forbid herself to cry anew. For Toby's sake, she had to hold herself together. She took a steadying breath, then another, and got to work—cooking, cleaning, laundering, dressing. It kept her hands busy while she figured out what to do. The answer, of course, was simple—find another job—and by midday, she was ready and determined to do just that.

That afternoon and all the next day, Tucia crisscrossed the city in search of a new job. She hadn't anyone to watch Toby, so she scrubbed his face and dressed him in his Sunday clothes and brought him along. She hoped it might spark pity—a kindly woman with her sweet boy in tow—but one shopkeeper after the next dismissed her. She hadn't any better luck with factory foremen. Not even the meanest factories that belched foul-smelling smoke had a place for women like her.

They didn't trouble themselves to explain *why* she wasn't suited. It certainly didn't help that she hadn't any references. But she couldn't help but notice the way their eyes lingered on her carefully wrapped headscarf, as if they knew she was hiding something. Or the way their brows knit when she introduced her son. One even had the gall to suggest Toby ought to be in an asylum.

At day's end, they returned home to find another letter from her creditors stuffed beneath the door. She fed Toby his supper and tucked him into bed before opening it. He'd endured enough today with all the walking and standing and waiting, never mind the curled lips and sidelong stares. He didn't fully realize yet he was different, though he'd asked on their way home what an asylum was. A place for sick people was all she'd told him. Then he'd wondered aloud how the man knew about the extra sound his heart made. She couldn't protect him forever and dreaded the day when the world's ignorance and unkindness caught up with him.

Now, at least, she could protect him from the trouble at hand: their dwindling prospects and her harried nerves. By the light of the oil lamp, she read the loan agency's letter. She'd telegraphed them yesterday, requesting a small advance—just enough to buy food and pay the coming rent—and a week's forbearance. Surely by then she'd have another job and could renegotiate her wage assignment and pay whatever loan renewal fees they required.

But there was no bank draft enclosed within the letter. Her request for an advance had been denied. As had her appeal for a forbearance. Instead, the agency presented her with three options. She could pay off her loan in full—all six hundred and sixty dollars of it. Or she could agree to an immediate loan renewal fee of twenty-five dollars with a weekly wage assignment of five dollars and late fees of one dollar and twenty-five cents, respectively, for every day's delinquency. Should she fail to avail herself of one of these two options by close of business tomorrow, then she'd be left with option three wherein the agency would appeal to the justice of the peace for a complete and total liquidation of her assets.

Tucia flung the letter onto the table and crossed to the window. Smoky fog blanketed the night, and she wondered how long it had been since she'd seen a sky full of stars. She raised the window sash and leaned against the casement, hoping for a breeze. But the air hung heavy and still, scented with the stench of refuse from the alley below.

Life hadn't always been like this. She remembered a sky bright with stars and air perfumed with lilac and honeysuckle. She remembered a world filled with challenges, yes, but also replete with possibility. A world where even women could reach for life's dreams. Where a small loan seemed inconsequential when you had a diploma in hand and the letters *MD* behind your name. What had happened to that world? The challenges remained. But the possibility was gone. She'd give anything for a fresh start— just her and Toby, somewhere far away where the past couldn't find her.

Tucia shook her head and closed the window. No amount of dreaming would help her now. She sat back down at the table and considered the agency's terms. She hadn't anywhere close to the money needed to pay off her loan. A few times in the past, she'd been able to get a new loan to pay off her existing one and avoid renewal and late fees. But that had been when her debt was less than a hundred dollars. No loan agency in this city or beyond would give an unemployed, unwed mother the kind of cash advance she needed now. So option one was off the table.

Option three was a straight shot to the poorhouse. Tucia had passed by the dilapidated building many times and heard stories of the horrors within—dirty rooms and linen, rancid food, flies and mosquitos in the summer, frostbite in the winter, rats all year long. The stigma its residents faced was worse still. Poorhouse inmates were branded drunkards, idlers, and incorrigible sinners. Tucia had thought so herself before she'd learned how savage life could be.

She'd do anything to avoid the place. But not because of the deplorable conditions or stigma. Because she'd lose her son. Children were prohibited in the poorhouse. Instead, they were sent to orphanages or, as would be the case with Toby, to the state asylum for the feebleminded and epileptic.

That left only option two. But how would she find the money to pay the loan renewal fee without a job? Left too long, the late fees would pile up such that even once she found a job, the wage assignment the loan agency would require would leave her unable to pay rent or buy food.

Her gaze snagged on the medical textbooks arranged neatly on the shelf. She walked over and trailed a finger atop their well-worn spines. What promise they'd once held. During her medical school days, she'd spent countless hours engrossed in their pages. Some foolish part of her had believed she'd find a use for them again.

Regret burned like bile in her throat, and she recoiled.

In the end, Dr. Addams had been right. She didn't have the fortitude or strength to be a doctor. Even if she could escape somewhere far away, she was too broken to ever be able to practice. Her inaction during the factory accident had proven that.

She swept the books haphazardly off the shelf into her arms, then dumped them onto the table. The oil lamp rattled, its flame sputtering. She could probably get several dollars apiece for them at the pawnbroker's. That would be enough to pay the loan renewal fee.

All she'd need then was a job. Over the past two days, it seemed like she'd already inquired at every shop and factory in the city. She plucked a hair from her head and twirled it between her fingers. Surely there were shops she'd missed. And if not . . . She dropped the hair down the lamp's chimney, watching through the glass as it caught flame and burned. Then she plucked another. If she gave the foreman at the corset factory what he wanted, maybe he'd rehire her. The idea made her sick. And she knew from experience he'd come asking—no, not asking—demanding again.

There had to be another way. But what?

Tucia lowered the lamp's wick and blew out the flame. Tomorrow she'd search for the answer. Tonight, she hadn't oil to spare.

6

The pawnbroker offered her only a dollar for *Human Anatomy*. Two for *Materia Medica* and *Disorders of Bones and Surrounding Tissues*. And fifty cents for *Dissection and Pathology*. For *The Principles and Practice of Medicine*, the most valuable book of all, he offered only a quarter. It felt like parting with old friends, but Tucia reluctantly accepted, keeping only *The Principles and Practice of Medicine*. Twenty-five cents was far too paltry a sum for such an important work.

They passed the A&P on their way home, and Toby begged for a peppermint stick. It broke Tucia's heart to tell him no. He had such few pleasures, after all. She did go inside, however, to inquire if they had any positions in need of filling. She'd do anything, she told the old clerk—mind the counter, mop the floors, shelve merchandise. They were not in need, the clerk told her, before hollering for the next person in line. Toby, meanwhile, had crossed his arms and begun stomping his feet, his eyes still fixed on the candy jar. Tucia had to carry him out of the store.

When they got home, she searched the pockets of every piece of clothing she owned. She dumped out her bag and turned out the lining. She groped underneath the mattress and beneath the loose floorboard where she'd once stored her extra change. Toby, the peppermint stick now forgotten, followed her around, thinking it a game. He turned out his own pockets, adding a rubber ball, two marbles, five jacks, and several bits of lint to the small pile of coins and bills on the table. All together, including the money she'd gotten that morning from the pawnbroker, Tucia counted twelve dollars and ninety cents.

She set two dollars aside—Toby still had to eat—and put the rest of it in her purse. Hopefully, it would be enough to renew her loan and keep the agency from going to the justice of the peace. She pinned on her hat and checked herself in the mirror. There was no hiding the patches of missing hair now, but at least it wasn't as bad as in the months after Toby's birth when she'd plucked herself bald.

The urge to pull out her hair had started when she was twelve and harried her on and off over the years. Sometimes, it was just a hair or two a day. Other times, she might clear a quarter-sized patch in minutes. Try as she might, the urge never entirely left her. Instead, she'd learned to fluff and style her hair so it looked less scraggly. She bought switches and bangs and curly head toppers woven into vegetable lace—all made of real human hair the same chestnut shade as hers. Add a hat or bonnet and scarcely anyone could tell.

But after Toby's birth, the urge overwhelmed her. For all her medical knowledge, she had little practical experience caring for a baby. His muscle tone was greatly diminished compared to other infants, and he suckled weakly at the breast. Her thoughts were a constant stream of worry. Was he feeding enough? Was he too hot? Too cold? Was his skin too dry? Would his weak heart suddenly give way? When her hands weren't occupied changing his diaper or coaxing him to the nipple, they were at her scalp, plucking and picking.

Had she not been alone, it might have been easier. Seeking help from Toby's father or his family was entirely out of the question. But after three months of struggle, when the last pennies of her inheritance were gone, Tucia buried her pride and traveled to her girlhood home.

Her stepmother's circumstances were much changed since the last time Tucia had seen her four years before. The grand house was weathered and shabby. Much of its fine furniture had been sold, and the staff let go.

Her stepmother, however, had not changed. She refused to admit Tucia through the front door but shooed her around to the back, craning her neck to ensure none of the neighbors had spied them. In the cold, fireless kitchen, she leered at Toby, asleep in Tucia's arms, and said only, "Where's his father?"

"He doesn't know," Tucia said, regretting her honesty as a sneer spread across her stepmother's face.

"Ruined. I warned your father this would happen if he let you go to that silly school." She leaned closer and stared at Toby, whose eyes peeked open. "He's an odd-looking one. Do yourself a favor and leave him on the orphanage steps on your way out of town."

Tucia hugged Toby tighter. She choked back her anger and said, "I'd hoped we might stay."

"Here? You and your bastard son? Think of the gossip you'd invite!"

"If Father were alive—"

"Your father would die a second death from the disgrace of it. Why, he's probably turning in his grave as we speak. I told him not to . . ."

Her stepmother had gone on for another hour about Tucia's failings. Even the recent closure of the family's sawmill was somehow Tucia's fault. But her stepmother did let her and Toby stay the night on a pallet in the old cook's quarters, provided they were gone before first light.

On the way out, Tucia took the last of the silver—four spoons and a tarnished candlestick that had belonged to her *real* mother.

Now, with that silver long gone, Tucia inhaled a steadying breath. First to the loan agency and then, if she could screw her courage and keep down the bile already rising in her throat, to the corset factory.

But when she opened the door to leave, she was startled to find a man standing outside on the landing, his fist raised as if about to knock. Not just any man, she quickly realized. The man she'd met at the lecture. The man with violet eyes.

"Dr. Hatherley," he said, bowing with the same showy flourish as before. "Might I come in?"

Doctor Hatherley? No one had called her that in years. He must have assumed all the guests at Dr. Addams's lecture were physicians. But strange that he, a man, would make that assumption about a woman. He'd traded his tuxedo and cape for a well-tailored morning coat and matching trousers but still had the glossy top hat in hand. He stood with impeccable posture, neither rigid nor stooped, and though he was a small man—no taller than Tucia—he gave off the impression of one who took up great space.

"I seem to have encountered you on your way out," he continued. "I'd offer to call again another time, but I've an errand of much urgency. One, I assure you, you'd benefit much to hear."

His voice had a rich, hypnotic quality, and Tucia found herself nodding and stepping aside as he entered without knowingly deciding to do so.

"And this must be your son, Toby," the man said, bowing again. "How do you do, young lad?"

Hearing Toby's name brought her back to her senses. This man looked harmless enough, but he was a stranger after all. He'd squatted down in front of Toby and was holding out his hands as if to show they were empty. "Did you wash behind your ears this morning, young man?"

Toby nodded.

The man reached behind Toby's ear, then held out his hand again. A lemon drop now rested in his palm. At first, Toby looked puzzled, feeling behind his ear, then he squealed and grabbed the candy from the man's palm.

"Look, Mama! I had candy behind my ear."

"I see that, darling," Tucia said, stepping between them as the man rose. "Go eat it in the bedroom while this gentleman and I talk." She turned to the violet-eyed man. "Who are you, sir, and what's your business?"

"Forgive me. My name is Hugh Horn. Huey to my friends." He winked at Toby, who still lingered behind her, peeking around her skirt. "But most know me as the Amazing Adolphus."

His voice rose when he said the name, and he paused as if he expected her to recognize it. When she didn't reply, he continued, undeterred. "I'm a businessman of sorts, and I've come to offer you the job of a lifetime."

Tucia frowned. Despite his polish, there was something unsettling about this man. "Thank you, sir, but I already have a job."

"At the corset factory, yes, but we both know such work is a mockery of your true talents."

How did he know where she'd worked? And just what did he mean by *true talents*? Tucia's muscles tightened. Had the foreman been spreading rumors about her? Inflating what had happened between them? And even if he were, how should this man have heard them? She peeled Toby's sticky fingers from her skirt and shooed him into the bedroom. Once he was safely away, she squared her shoulders and said to Mr. Horn, "I don't know what talents you're referring to, but I'm afraid you are mistaken."

"You're not a medical doctor, then? There's a license registered in your name with the Illinois state board."

Tucia flinched. She almost would have preferred he call her a whore. That, at least, she could protest in good faith. But the claim he'd laid was the truth. "I completed medical schooling, yes. But I . . . er . . . I chose not to practice."

"Ah, I see. May I ask why?"

"No, you may not. How do you know so much about me?"

Mr. Horn smiled. It was a handsome, disarming smile, and Tucia felt her guard slipping despite herself.

"It's what I do, Dr. Hatherley. I'm an observer of people. A scientist, if you will, of life and human behavior."

"What does that have to do with my medical license?"

He gestured to the table. "May we sit?"

Tucia frowned again at the same time she found herself nodding. Mr. Horn swept around the table and sat in the far chair. Tucia sat opposite him, leaving the sudsy basin of soaking breakfast dishes on the table between them.

"I confess, you've been the subject of my study ever since I saw you at Dr. Addams's lecture. It is there I overheard your name and set out to learn more about you."

Tucia thought back to that evening, shifting uncomfortably in her chair. If he'd overheard her name, he must have followed her and Mr. Seldon out into the lobby. Had he seen the crazed way she'd pulled out her hair too? Had he heard Mr. Seldon mention the operating theater incident? Surely not, or he wouldn't be here offering her a job.

"I have not engaged the services of a lady physician before, but I've a hunch you're just the person I'm looking for."

"I told you, Mr. Horn, I'm *not* a practicing physician. I haven't picked up a scalpel or stethoscope in almost eight years." Just talking about it made Tucia's hands begin to tremble. She buried them in her lap and continued. "I'm afraid I can't help you."

"Ah, but you can. It's your license I care about. Those two little letters that fall so neatly after your name: *MD*. Not your skill or experience."

"I don't understand."

He flashed that dashing smile again. "I am a medicine man. My show is the most successful operation ever to crisscross this country. And I am in need of a doctor to travel with me. That is why I'm here."

It took Tucia a moment to process his words. "A medicine man? You mean one of those charlatans who stand on the corner and con passersby into buying their ridiculous cure-alls?"

"You speak of low pitchmen, Doctor. Fools and amateurs, the lot of them. *I* am a showman. A pitchman of the finest degree. My company of performers could play on the stages of America's top cities if they so desired. And my medicine could hold up against anything you'd buy from a druggist."

He spoke with such confidence Tucia half believed him. But he was still a medicine man. A huckster, a swindler—there was no other type. These were the sorts of men who sowed distrust in proper medicine and gave real doctors a bad name.

Tucia stood. "Mr. Horn, I'm afraid you have me mistaken, both in character and kind. I studied medicine to help people, not to harm them. And though I may be a doctor in little more than name, I still believe in the tenants of the profession."

"Yes, yes, *primum non nocere*. First, do no harm. I've read Hippocrates too. But tell me, Dr. Hatherley, is that always the case? How many patients suffer from the toxic drugs you prescribe? How many die from gangrene or pyemia after surgery? How many never make it out of the operating theater at all?"

Tucia's throat tightened, and her heart beat double-time. How did he know? He couldn't. But he knew so much else about her. Even if he were speaking only in generalities, he had to go. She crossed to the door and flung it open. "Out, sir. I want nothing to do with your medicine show."

Mr. Horn didn't rise. Instead, he crossed his legs and removed his gloves, laying them neatly on the table. The glint of two bejeweled rings—one on each of his hands—caught her eye. "You haven't heard my offer yet," he said.

"There's nothing you could offer that would make me betray my principles."

"Oh? I understand you're in quite a lot of debt."

Tucia flinched. "Why would you suppose that?"

"You've been the subject of my observation these past few days since our fortuitous encounter at the lecture hall."

"Nothing about that night was fortuitous," Tucia said.

"I also understand that you had something of an altercation with the foreman of the corset factory where you work. Or, previously worked."

Tucia's legs felt suddenly weak, and she steadied herself on the doorjamb.

"Please, have a seat. Hear my terms, and if you don't like them, I'll leave without another word."

Reluctantly, Tucia closed the door. She glanced into the other room where Toby sat licking the last of the lemony sweetness from his fingers, then returned to her chair.

"As I said, I'm looking for a doctor to travel with my show, and I believe you're perfectly suited for the job."

Tucia couldn't help but snicker. "Don't you profess to be a doctor? Isn't that the graft? What do you need me for?"

"Though some medicine men claim to be doctors of sorts, they are not the same. At least not in the eyes of the law."

"In the eyes of anyone with an ounce of sense."

"You'd be surprised how many senseless people there are in this world. But that is neither here nor there. I desire a physician for the show and am prepared to assume your debt if you agree to join me."

Tucia stared at him agog. "All of it?"

"Yes. All six hundred and sixty dollars."

It unnerved her that he knew the exact amount of her debt. But if he'd been following her, as he said, he could have bribed the messenger boy for a look at the loan agency's letter before he delivered it. Did Mr. Horn really have that kind of money on hand? She glanced again at his rings. She'd thought perhaps they were fake, cut-glass imitations he used onstage for his acts. But up close, they looked as if they could be real.

"You seem incredulous, Dr. Hatherley."

"Stop calling me that!" She reached for a strand of hair but stopped herself. "I'm not . . . I'm not a doctor anymore." She looked down at her trembling hands and could hardly remember a time when they'd been steady and sure. "I never really was."

"You needn't worry, *Mrs.* Hatherley. We have a saying in the medicine show business—never treat a man who's truly sick."

"What would I be doing, then?"

He leaned back in the chair. "This and that. Everyone helps out with the show. Why, even young Toby there could help look after the properties table. But the real money comes after. With the purchase of every bottle of medicine comes a ticket for a free examination. I have a fine tent we'll set up as a case-taking parlor. When people come with the ticket, we'll usher them inside, perform a quick examination, and send them off with our prescribed treatment: herbs, salts, salve—whatever's on hand to fit the need. For an additional fee, of course."

At the word *examination*, Tucia's breathing quickened as if her lungs were suddenly starved of air. "I cannot."

She wrapped her arms tightly around herself and crossed the room to the window. The warm sunshine and familiar view steadied her breathing.

"You needn't perform the examinations yourself or offer the diagnosis. Leave that to me. People will assume you are my assistant. We simply won't bother to correct them."

"But that's fraud."

"A judge would not see it that way. Especially not if we take a moment to consult before giving the diagnosis."

Tucia laughed bitterly. "And that's all that matters, isn't it? Avoiding trouble with the law."

She heard the creak of the rickety chair and pad of his footsteps as he came to stand beside her at the window.

"I am not the devil you think I am, Mrs. Hatherley. My show brings cheer and entertainment to towns that would otherwise have nothing. My medicine soothes the mind that needlessly worries of catarrh, worms, or consumption at no cost to the body. Join me and you will see."

Tucia kept her arms wrapped around herself and said nothing. Men seldom thought themselves the devils they were. No matter how he spun it, it was still a life of lies.

"Think of your son, Mrs. Hatherley. Think of the good the fresh air and adventure would do for him. So unlike the damp, unventilated wards of the asylum."

"I'd never let him go to such a place."

"Ah, but if the state were to find you insolvent, you wouldn't have a choice."

She glanced over her shoulder into the next room. Toby wouldn't last a year at such a place. Not with his weak heart. Even if she did manage to get her job at the corset factory back, how long would she be able to keep it? How long before the foreman grew tired of her and decided to repay her for the shiner she'd given him? What then?

"You said you would assume my debt?"

"Yes, in lieu of payment for your services. You needn't worry about room and board either. We have a first-rate cook who prepares all the meals, and you and the boy will have your own wagon." He paused. "We can go to the loan agency right now and have the matter settled."

Reluctantly, she turned around. "For how long? If I am to trade one debt for another, I must know the terms."

"I pay those in my service twenty-five dollars a week."

Tucia's breath caught in her throat. That was four times what she'd been making at the factory! "Fifty."

"Thirty."

"And you shan't charge interest or fees on my debt?"

"I shall not."

Tucia swallowed. "You have a deal, Mr. Horn."

His smile sent a chill tiptoeing down her arms.

"Please, as I said, my friends call me Huey."

7

Tucia found herself on a train with Toby and Huey, chugging away from the city that very evening. It hadn't taken long to pack their meager belongings. A few sets of clothing. A few secondhand toys. A quilt she'd inherited from her mother, now threadbare and faded. Huey had assured her the company already had a full set of cookware, so she left her chipped bowls and rusted teakettle. At the back of her wardrobe, hidden beneath a moth-eaten shawl, she found her old doctor's bag. Tucked inside were her stethoscope, otoscope, and ophthalmoscope, a thermometer, a tongue depressor, microscope slides, percussion hammer, syringes, tweezers, scissors, and a scalpel. It carried a few *real* medicines too. Morphine, atropine, strychnine, and digitalis. She wouldn't need any of it, of course. But, like *The Principles and Practice of Medicine*, she couldn't bring herself to leave it behind.

It took even less time to settle her debt. Huey wrote down the terms of their agreement on a crisp sheet of paper that they signed under the disinterested gaze of the city notary. Then they proceeded to the salary loan agency. Exerting the full force of his charm and persuasion—which, Tucia had to admit, was considerable— Huey explained he now owned her debt and was prepared to pay in full right then and there, provided they deduct fifteen percent off the principal balance. To Tucia's amazement, they agreed.

Then it was a quick trip to the department store, where Huey insisted on buying both her and Toby new sets of clothing, and, finally, off to the train station. Huey splurged for first-class tickets and two sleeper cars the last night of their two-day journey to . . . well, Tucia wasn't even sure where they were headed. He had mentioned the name of some small railroad town or another. It didn't matter. She'd made her bargain. And though she loathed the idea of working—of all the jobs!—in a medicine show, for the first time since the accident at the factory, she felt like she could fully breathe. Toby was safe and beside her. They were assured of food and shelter. That was all that mattered. And once she'd repaid her debt to Huey, maybe then she and her son could truly start over.

On the last morning of their journey, after a light breakfast in the dining car, Huey led them to the caboose. They exited onto an open-air platform that extended several feet beyond the car, circled by an iron railing. Toby delighted in watching the ground speed by beneath them, and Tucia welcomed the fresh air. She sat on a low-lying stool, holding onto the back of Toby's jacket as he pressed his face between the iron rails. Huey stood beside him, explaining how the train used steam to power its wheels. She liked that he didn't talk to her son as if he were incapable of understanding, the way so many people did.

"Can we see the front too?" Toby asked. He wore one of the suits Huey had bought for him, a jaunty outfit with knee-length pants and a sailor-collared jacket. The blue twill fabric brought out the color of his eyes. A handsome color, to be sure, but one that too closely matched his father's. Thankfully, that was the extent of their resemblance.

"Not this trip, lad," Huey said with a chuckle. "We're almost to our stop. Next time, I promise we'll get the fireman to show us the coal car and the locomotive. And, say, do you like horses? We've got a team of fine horses that pull our wagons . . ."

He continued to regale Toby with talk of the horses, but Tucia only half listened. So much had happened in the last week—the accident at the factory, Dr. Addams's lecture, the incident with the foreman, the return of her "hysterical attacks"—that she'd felt like she were drowning. Here, at last, she was on dry ground.

A few other passengers, including the head porter, milled about the platform with them. The train, almost imperceptibly, began to slow. Tucia was about to stand and usher Toby back inside when the wheels suddenly screeched to a jolting stop. Tucia's grip on Toby tightened. One of the other passengers on the platform shrieked, and everyone grabbed for the railing. Just as the jostling subsided, the stool flew out from beneath her. She landed with a thud on her rear. The next moment Huey was beside her.

"Are you hurt?" he asked loudly. "No, don't try to get up. Dear Lord, you could have been killed." He looked up at the porter. "Is there a doctor on the train? I fear she might have broken something."

The porter scurried off.

"I'm all right," Tucia said. She tried to rise, but Huey laid a heavy hand on her shoulder.

"Be still and say no more until the doctor assures us you're not gravely injured."

Gravely injured? She'd only fallen a few feet to the ground. At worst, she'd suffer a bruised tailbone. How had her stool gone flying anyway? She righted her plume-trimmed hat. It and the carefully styled hair switch beneath were other gifts from Huey.

A small crowd had gathered. Huey looked up at them. "Is anyone here a doctor?"

Tucia tried again to stand, but Huey pressed down all the more firmly on her shoulder, squeezing until she felt a jolt of pain.

What was going on? Tucia didn't need a doctor. She was perfectly capable of assessing her own injuries. A fact Huey knew well.

Standing beside her, Toby looked frightened, his bottom lip trembling as if he might cry.

"It's all right, darling. Mama's—"

"It's about damned time!" Huey said over her as the crowd parted for the porter. The train's conductor followed behind him. Huey stood and faced the conductor. Huey was the smaller man by far, but his puffed-up posture and commanding voice made it seem an even match. "Just what sort of a deathtrap are you conducting, sir? When you so hastily stopped, she was thrown from her stool to the ground. It's a miracle she landed here and not on the other side of the rail where I daresay she'd be even more grievously injured than she already is."

"There was a telegraph line down on the tracks, and we had to break, sir. It could not be helped."

"Not be helped! Isn't there someone watching for such hazards? Or did your man fall asleep at the watch?"

"I assure you, sir . . ."

The crowd watched enrapt as Huey and the conductor continued to argue, leaving Tucia to struggle to her feet alone. She brushed off her skirt and gloves. Her new lace-trimmed petticoat had offered some padding against the fall, but her rear was still sore.

At least she'd been the one to fall and not Toby. She took his hand and smiled down at him reassuringly. She'd stopped listening to what the men were saying but could tell by the pitch of their voices that Huey's point had landed, and the conductor was backing down and the crowd disbursing. The conductor pulled a pen and small pad from his jacket pocket. He scribbled something onto the top sheet of paper and handed it to Huey. "Take this to the ticket counter when we arrive, and they'll issue you a full refund." He turned then to Tucia. "Very sorry you were hurt, ma'am. I trust the accident won't cause you any lasting injury."

"Thank you, sir. I'm perfectly—"

"As you haven't a doctor aboard, the degree of her injuries has yet to be determined," Huey said.

The conductor glowered at him, his patience clearly wearing thin. Huey continued, his tone softening. "But this reparation shall suffice for now."

The conductor nodded to them and left the platform, leaving the three of them alone. Huey tucked the paper the conductor had given him into his pocket and smiled. "What a lucky turn of events."

"I hardly think—" Tucia stopped, pondering the moment her stool toppled . . . toppled as if someone had kicked it out from beneath her. "Did you orchestrate this whole fiasco on purpose?"

"We must seize opportunity where we find it, Mrs. Hatherley. That's the first rule of being a good businessman."

As he spoke, the train started up again. He opened the caboose door and held it wide for her and Toby. "Best get your things from the sleeper. We'll be arriving any minute."

Tucia hesitated, unease settling in her stomach. He hadn't answered her question. An honest man would protest the very idea of kicking out her stool and putting her in harm's way just to wrangle back a few dollars. But for all his charm and generosity, perhaps Huey wasn't as honest a man as he appeared.

Once they collected their luggage and Huey had pocketed the money the ticket clerk had begrudgingly refunded him, they waited on the plank sidewalk outside the station. For what or for whom, Tucia wasn't sure. Huey had told her only that the rest of the company had set up camp at a vacant lot just outside of town, attending their arrival.

As they waited, a flier posted on a nearby lamppost caught her eye.

TO-NIGHT!
The Amazing Adolphus
And his Traveling Medicine Co.
An unrivaled array of AMUSEMENT.
Featuring Grazyna the Dancing Giant,
Chief Big Sky, Cal Crip Caboo
& MORE!

The letters were printed in bright blue and bordered by red and yellow filigree. Handwritten at the bottom was the location of the lot Huey had mentioned, followed by the words, *Curtain Rises at 8 o'clock!*

Tucia glanced down the road toward the small cluster of brick-and-wood buildings that comprised the town. Fliers just like this one stamped every post and storefront in sight.

Tonight? She hadn't expected them to begin performing so soon. It was already afternoon, and even the luxury of a sleeper car couldn't erase two days of wearisome travel. At least there was no mention of a doctor on the flier. Hopefully her part in the charade wouldn't begin until the next town, giving her time to acclimate to this bizarre new life.

A few minutes later, an open, flat-bottomed carriage rumbled up to the station.

"Is it impossible for you to be on time?" Huey said as the driver slowed the horses and climbed down from the front seat.

The driver only shrugged. He stood a head taller than Huey, with broad, slumped shoulders. A cowboy sombrero, worn and weathered, was pulled low over his ears, shading his face.

He raised his chin and scanned the sidewalk. With his face now visible, Tucia could see why he kept his hat pulled so low. A scar ran from his left nostril to his lip, causing the lip to curve and pull upward. A cleft repair, she guessed, and not a good one, as little care had been taken to minimize scarring and avoid foreshortening of the lip. She wondered absentmindedly who had done the surgery—obviously one with little skill—and whether the man's palate had been cleft as well. It was certainly more common for both to occur together than a harelip alone.

His gaze slid past Tucia and Toby as he craned his neck to see inside the station. "Where's the boozer?"

"Right in front of you," Huey said with an impatient gesture toward Tucia.

The man's brown eyes settled on her, and he frowned. "A woman?"

The slight nasally resonance of his voice confirmed her suspicion that his cleft affected not only his lip but palate as well.

"Yes," Huey said. "And she's *not* a boozer."

This seemed to further confuse the man. He stared at her a moment more, then his gaze flickered to Toby. "And the boy?"

"He's my son," Tucia said, her hand tightening around Toby's. The man's serious eyes, imposing height, and permanently snarled lip gave off a menacing, unfriendly air. She wondered if he'd ever smiled a day in his life. "And you are?"

"This is Darl," Huey answered for him.

Tucia looked between them. "And . . . do you have a last name?"

"Just Darl." He dropped his head and gathered their luggage, heaving it onto the boot of the buckboard carriage behind the second bench seat. Huey, though he had twice as many bags as she and Toby, stood idly by while Darl loaded it all. She watched him as he made quick work of the baggage, taking less care with Huey's than he had with hers and Toby's. He looked a few years older than she, perhaps, the skin on the back of his neck sunbaked to a warm tan color.

Glancing again at the flier, she wondered whom among the listed performers he was. Certainly not Grazyna. Chief Big Sky, perhaps? He didn't much resemble an Indian, though. "What sort of act do you perform?"

He snickered, not bothering to look back at her as he shoved the last of Huey's luggage into the buckboard.

"Darl doesn't perform in the show," Huey said. He hoisted Toby in the back seat of the buckboard, then offered Tucia his hand. She took it reluctantly, remembering the incident on the caboose platform. Her rear still ached from the fall. No sooner was she seated beside Toby than Darl climbed onto the driver's bench and shook the reins. Huey cursed and scurried around to the opposite side, swinging himself aboard next to Darl just as the horses set off. Huey glowered at him.

"Just tryin' to make up for lost time," Darl said.

The buckboard rattled down the main thoroughfare through town. They passed a post office, a dry goods store, two churches, a bar, and a clapboard building with peeling white paint labeled TOWN HALL. A few shotgun houses hunkered nearby, and beyond that, farmland. Toby tented a hand over his eyes and stared at the vast tracks of sprouting cropland. His mouth hung open, the edges curving toward a grin. Tucia wished she shared his wonder at the newness of the landscape.

When he was smaller, she'd made a point of taking him to City Park each Sunday, believing the fresh air and sunshine would benefit his weak constitution. And it had. Growing boys needed space to run and play too. But a bout of pneumonia eighteen months back had relegated him to bed for weeks. He'd recovered, but Tucia's nerves had not. She came to see the city—the park included—as a cesspool of sickness and rarely permitted him outside the apartment.

Now she saw the damage she'd done. He was far too pale, for one. And not at all conditioned for the level of exertion this new life would require of them. She'd need to keep a close eye on him and the others of the company too. She might be indentured to Huey, but her son was not. Under no circumstances would she allow him to be pressed into work.

Up ahead on the road, several large carrion birds stood clustered around an animal carcass. They waited until the horses were nearly upon them before taking flight.

"Birds!" Toby said, tugging on her sleeve and pointing overhead. He watched with delight as they squawked and circled. Tucia's gaze, however, was drawn back to the carrion. It was impossible to tell what type of animal it had been. A wild dog, perhaps, or a coyote, judging from the size. The birds had picked clean most of its flesh and organs, leaving only tufts of fur and bloodstained bones behind.

8

A mile or so beyond the town, not long after they'd passed the buzzards and their lunch, the road curved around a thick stand of trees, and an overgrown field came into view. What Tucia imagined was once tidy rows of budding greens was now a maze of bushes and weeds, the dead shoots of winter tangling with spring's abundant growth. A split-rail fence paralleled the road, its wood weathered and rotting. Several of the rails were splintered and broken. Other parts of the fence had collapsed entirely, becoming fodder for mushrooms and grubs.

Amid the overgrowth and neglect, a swath of bright colors caught Tucia's eye. Several yards back from the road stood three hardtop caravan wagons parked in a semicircle around a raised stage. Behind them sat a cluster of tents.

Each of the wagons was a different color. The first, painted red, had a yellow roof and trim. *Free Show!*, and below it, *Sterling Entertainment!*, were emblazoned in white letters across the side. The middle wagon was royal blue with giant gold lettering. *The Amazing Adolphus Medicine Company,* it read amid a flourish of swirls. *Miraculous Cures!* and *Remedies for Everything!* were stamped across the green paneling of the final wagon.

They reminded Tucia of the tiresome posters pasted throughout St. Louis, advertising everything from sewing machines to cigars. Here in the country, though, the too-bright colors and shameless pandering seemed all the more garish.

In contrast, the tents were the dull white of undyed canvas. Two were simple wedge tents. The other two were wall tents—rectangular in shape with straight sides and tall, pitched roofs. A blue flag jutted from the peak of the largest tent, flapping languidly in the breeze. A horse and half a dozen mules had been turned loose to graze on the nearby weeds and bramble.

At a break in the fence, the buckboard turned off the road onto a short, rutted drive that led to the encampment. They stopped beside the wagons, and Huey and Darl climbed down.

"This was the best place you could find?" Huey asked, surveying the camp.

Darl began unhitching the horses without a reply.

Huey climbed a short flight of stairs at the far back corner of the stage, studying the site from this new vantage. "I suppose it will have to do."

It wasn't a large stage compared to those Tucia had seen in the city—perhaps a dozen feet long and half as wide. Nor was it particularly high, rising just above the tips of the surrounding switchgrass and weeds. Huey walked from one end to the other, pausing every few steps to stomp or jump, the thud of his feet atop the wooden planks echoing through the camp.

"Why isn't the backdrop up yet?"

"It's next on my list," Darl said.

"Why didn't it go up yesterday?"

"Rain."

Huey shook his head and leapt down from the stage, looking out toward the road. "When you're done hanging the backdrop, put a flag or two out on the fence post so the yokels can find us." He swatted at the grass. "And for heaven's sake, flatten all this down so they don't have weeds tickling their knees."

Darl replied with a grunt, not even looking at Huey as he removed the horses' harnesses and bridles. As Tucia watched him work, she realized he was the first person they'd encountered who seemed entirely impervious to Huey's charm. When the horses were free, he gave their withers a good scratching, then smacked them lightly on the rump. They trotted off to join the other animals in the field beyond the camp.

"Well, what do you think?"

Huey's voice startled her, and she turned to find him beside the buckboard, holding out his hand to help her down.

For the first time since leaving the city, Tucia felt the full weight of her decision. Never in her life had she been someplace so remote. The quiet stillness reminded her of the dissecting room. But unlike that room, where she could do her business and be gone, this place had no exit. It went on and on and on as far as she could see.

She realized that Toby had scooted closer to her—so close he was nearly in her lap. He, too, was looking at her expectantly, waiting for her to decide upon this strange place before venturing out himself. At that, Tucia swallowed her unease. However foreign and remote, it was far better than the life they'd left in the city. "It's more . . . pastoral than I imagined," she said, taking Huey's hand. "But I'm sure we'll be able to make do."

Huey lifted Toby down next, ruffling his hair after setting him on the ground. "Welcome to your new home, lad."

Home. The word sounded strange to her ears, especially when applied to a place such as this. But she managed a thin smile. "Isn't it wonderful, darling?"

Toby's gaze crept over the wagons and surrounding fields, his expression still uncertain. "No train?"

"The train's gone, darling. It never stays in one place for long. We'll see it again someday." Although when she didn't know. "But here we have wagons and horses instead." She pointed to the horses and mules in the field. At this, his eyes lit up, and a wide grin spread across his face. He'd never seen a draft animal separated from its conveyance before, she realized. He took an eager step toward them, but Tucia grabbed his hand. Who knew what else made a home of that field—snakes, hornets, badgers? Toby huffed and pulled against her hold.

"There will be plenty of time to see the animals later," she said. After she'd done a full accounting of the dangers.

Then a boy not much older than Toby rounded the wagons. He whistled as he walked—barefoot, she noticed—his head down and hands stuffed in his pockets. He wore dusty overalls, a flannel shirt with rolled-up sleeves, and a straw hat like a character from a Mark Twain novel. Toby's face brightened again, but Tucia stiffened. Huey hadn't mentioned other children.

The boy stopped whistling when he saw them. He eyed them a moment, then glanced at the buckboard as if expecting someone else to be with them. "Where's the new doc?" he said at last to Huey.

"This is her," Huey said.

The boy frowned, glancing back and forth between them. "A lady doctor?"

Huey nodded.

"Ain't never seen one of them before." Then, to Tucia, he said, "That your boy?"

"Yes, this is my son, Toby."

"How old is he?"

Tucia turned to her son. "Why don't you tell the boy how old you are, Toby?" But Toby had grown shy, looking down and nestling closer, so Tucia answered. "He'll be seven next month. How old are you?"

"Eight and a half." He cocked his head, staring at Toby, and Tucia braced herself for what he'd say next. How come his eyes are slanty? How come he's so small and got such a flat face? How come his mouth hangs open like that? Tucia had heard those questions before and worse. Instead, the boy said, "How come he's so scared?"

Tucia released a pent-up breath. "It's all very new to him. He's never been out of the city before."

"Never?" The boy seemed to contemplate this a moment, then he grinned, showing off several missing teeth. He walked over and extended his hand to Toby. "I'm Al. It ain't so bad here. Not once you get used to it."

Slowly, Toby reached out and let Al shake his hand.

"What do you say, darling?"

"Good to meet you."

"That's all the time we have for niceties, I'm afraid," Huey said. "We've got a show to prepare for. I'll introduce you to everyone else at supper." He turned to Al. "Fetch the flags from the supply wagon and hang them out there on the fence while Darl here shows Mrs. Hatherley to her wagon."

"See ya later, Toby," Al said, bounding away.

Toby waved goodbye, tugging against her hold again, eager to tag along. She'd have to watch him closely lest he wind up lost. Yet another danger of this strange new place.

Tucia reached for her hair but stopped, gathering up her skirt instead. She'd made her decision and was here now. There was no going back. Nothing in her old life to go back to. Maybe this was the new beginning she'd been hoping for.

"Take a few minutes to get settled," Huey said to her as he pulled a crate of clanking bottles from beneath the stage. He held one up and inspected it. "You'll hear the supper bell."

Huey put the bottle back into the crate and pulled out another. Dark liquid sloshed inside. A red label affixed to the glass read, *Revivifying Rattlesnake Oil.*

Rattlesnake Oil? Tucia blinked in the too-bright sunlight. Was that the so-called medicine they sold? Surely not. Perhaps it was a fancifully named hair tonic or cologne water. Or maybe—

Darl cleared his throat, interrupting her thoughts. She turned to see him waiting with their bags. "Ain't got all day," he said.

"Sorry. Lead the way."

When Huey had spoken of their lodging, he'd described a spacious wagon outfitted with every comfort. The animation in his voice stirred her imagination, and Tucia had envisioned something akin to the grand sleeper cars she'd seen in magazines with velvet drapes and polished wood, upholstered parlor chairs nestled around a tea table, and a richly dressed bed.

Now, as Darl stalked to the green wagon at the far end, she realized how foolish she'd been.

A short, rickety flight of stairs led to the entry. The steps groaned beneath Darl's weight as he climbed up and unlatched the door. It squealed open, its rusty hinges stiff. A swell of musty, putrid air spilled out such that even Darl grimaced. He stepped inside, set down their bags, and rummaged around. Tucia and Toby remained where they were, covering their noses with their sleeves. A few moments later, he emerged, holding a dead mouse by the tail. He flung it into the field and hopped down the stairs.

"You seen the stage. And that there's the cook tent." He pointed at the large tent with its drooping blue flag. "Reckon that's all the tour you need."

"What about the . . . er . . . water closet?"

He removed his hat and ran a hand through his dark hair. It looked like it could use a trim, curling this way and that at the ends, though Tucia was hardly one to judge. Besides, the mussed state of it suited him.

"We ain't got one of those," he said and jutted his chin toward the field. "Couple hundred feet yonder you'll find the latrine."

"And the smell?"

"Hold your nose, I guess."

Heat swept into her cheeks. "Not *there*. In the wagon."

"You're a doctor. Ain't you used to smells like that?"

"Not where I sleep."

"Open them windows. A few days it'll be gone," he said, then walked away.

Tucia didn't move. A few days! She'd seen her share of mice, of course. And once you'd spent an afternoon dissecting a body, the smell of putrefaction lost some of its bite. But it was one thing to encounter such odors in the deadhouse or in alleyways amid the trash bins and something else entirely when it was your living quarters.

This was only temporary, she reminded herself. Like Darl said, a little air and the smell would be gone. She sensed Toby waiting for her verdict, waiting to know if this truly was their new home. So she donned a brave smile and climbed inside.

The room was perhaps nine feet long and six feet wide. The plumes of her hat brushed the arched ceiling, but when she unpinned it, Tucia found she could stand straight in the center of the wagon with a few inches to spare above her head. A narrow bed stretched along the back wall. Above it sat a window, not much bigger than a dinner plate. It took several tries before she could jimmy it open.

With a weak cross-breeze now blowing, Tucia looked around. A shallow wardrobe and waist-high dresser lined one wall. Above the dresser was a boarded-up window. A wicker chair with a broken leg lolled against the opposite wall. Beside it was a rectangular board held flush against the wall by hinges at the bottom and a wood knob at the top. When Tucia turned the knob, the board sprung free, lowering like a drawbridge. A flap table. Rather ingenious, except the support beneath was broken and one of the hinges loose, rendering it altogether useless.

She found another window behind a dusty curtain above the broken table. It looked out onto the cluster of tents and the field beyond. One of the side-by-side casements swung open with ease. The other remained stuck, the hinge unyielding despite Tucia's best efforts to push it open. She gave up and sat on the bed, drawing Toby beside her. The mattress sagged beneath their weight as a flurry of dust motes took to the air.

"What do you think, darling? Cozy, isn't it?" she said, doing her best to ignore the cobwebs fluttering in the corners and the carpeting of dirt on the floor.

"I like it," he said with some hesitation.

"Me too," she lied, pulling him close so he wouldn't see the tears brimming in her eyes.

9

Tucia had only just begun wiping away the dust and cobwebs from their wagon when the supper bell rang. She coaxed Toby into letting her clean his face and comb his hair, then pinned her hat back in place. After two and a half days of travel, they both could use a bath, but for now, a dab of rose water and a freshly scrubbed face would have to do.

Outside, a nip of cold had stolen into the air as the sun dipped toward the horizon, and she pulled her shawl snugly around her shoulders. Darl had strung wide swaths of muslin between poles just beyond the wagons, blocking the view of the stage. But she could hear Huey stomping around, hollering about where to hang the lanterns and stake the lights. Otherwise, the camp was eerily quiet. Nothing like the ever-present din of the city.

She took a deep breath and released it slowly. Peaceful—that's what the quiet was, not eerie. A balm for her tender nerves. If she kept telling herself that, perhaps it would become true.

She turned her back to the wagons and stage, and took Toby's hand. The tents sat several yards on amid the grass and weeds, each spaced a generous distance from the other. The flaps of the largest tent were tied open, and light glowed from within. As they drew closer, the clink of tinware and the murmur of voices became audible.

Tucia hesitated a moment, then let Toby tug her onward. His earlier shyness was gone, and curiosity had sprung up in its place. She loved that about him, his wonder at the world, even as she worried it might one day lead him unwittingly to danger. It certainly had her.

Inside, a trestle table ran almost the entire length of the tent's interior, with benches flanking either side. Around it sat four people—Al, the boy they'd met earlier, and three adults—all of whom turned, sizing them up as they entered.

"The show ain't for another hour," one said. He was a small man of about forty, with a bulbous nose too big for his face. His skin had the look of a walnut shell—hard and furrowed. But his blue eyes were clear and keen. "You can wait by the stage, but, pardon my bluntness, you ain't welcome here."

The smile Tucia had pinned to her lips as they entered faltered. "Actually, we're—"

"That's the boozer!" Al hollered over her.

"Well, no, I'm not a b—"

"Told you she was a woman."

"Albrecht, don't interrupt," the woman seated beside him said with the faintest of accents. German, perhaps, or Swedish. "It's rude." She turned to Tucia. "You were saying?"

But Tucia was so struck by the woman's appearance she forgot what she was saying. A real giant. Or, more precisely, someone afflicted with gigantism. She towered over everyone else at the table. But it wasn't just her extraordinary height. Her hands were double the size of Tucia's—both in length and width. She wore her dark blond hair pulled back in a simple bun, making no attempts to hide her prominent forehead and large jaw.

As gigantism was extremely rare, little had been written in Tucia's textbooks about the disease. Most doctors, she recalled, attributed it to a super-functioning pituitary gland, but treatments, including attempts to extract the gland, had proved ineffective.

Did anyone else in her family suffer from the disease, she wondered, and at what age had her symptoms developed and—

The giant pursed her lips, and Tucia realized she was staring. "I only . . . that is . . . I was just saying that I'm not an alcoholic but I am . . . I'm a doctor." It felt like spitting out a mouthful cotton saying the words.

"You'll be a boozer before long," the big-nosed man said with a snort, turning back to his food. "If you outlast the week, that is."

"Sounds like a wager to me," the man sitting beside him said. Chief Big Sky, Tucia guessed. He had the russet skin and dark hair of an Indian but a Roman nose. A long black braid trailed down his back. He was the youngest of the bunch, excluding Al, perhaps a decade younger than herself. Twenty-one. Twenty-two. Certainly no more than twenty-five. But there was little trace of the boyishness she sometimes saw in the faces of other men that age. No lingering roundness about the jaw. No flush of youthfulness in the cheeks. His dark eyes, however, still held a glint of mischief.

He pulled a silver dollar from his trousers pocket and set it on the table. "Three weeks."

"Deal," the big-nosed man said.

"I want in," Al said.

"No, *mäuschen*," the giant said. "Gambling is for rogues and degenerates."

"But Pa—"

"Besides"—the giant glanced sidelong at Tucia—"she's bound to last at least a month."

Tucia felt like she was back at Fairview, surrounded by fellow interns hell-bent on showing her how unwelcome she was. She marched with Toby back to their wagon, grabbed a silver dollar—one of her last—and returned to the tent. They were laughing as she and Toby entered.

She slammed the dollar down on the table. "You're all wrong. Five and a half months and not a day longer." She'd done the calculation on the train. Twenty-two weeks at thirty dollars a week was just enough to cover her debt.

They all went quiet.

"Come along, Toby," she said. "Let's get our supper."

The silence held as she filled her and Toby's plates at the makeshift buffet at the back of the tent. Pork and beans and cornbread. Tucia wasn't hungry, but she'd eat every last bite to prove to the others that their antics didn't bother her.

She ushered Toby to the far end of the table, leaving a wide gulf between them and the others. Toby waved to Al, but Tucia lowered his hand, pressing a fork into his palm.

Three bites into her pork and beans, which, begrudgingly, she had to admit were quite good, and Huey strode into the tent. He'd changed out of his travel clothes into the shiny black tuxedo and cape he'd worn the night they first met.

"You found your way to the cook tent, I see," he said to her. "And did you meet the others?"

Tucia straightened, her gaze sliding to the opposite end of the table, then back to Huey. "Toby and I received quite the welcome, yes."

"Splendid!" He turned to the others. "See, I promised you I'd find a good one. Now, chop-chop! The show won't perform itself."

They stood, looking far more disgruntled than when Tucia had first entered the tent, and tossed their plates into the wash basin beside the buffet.

"You'll want to hurry, too, Mrs. Hatherley, lest you find yourself at the back of the crowd, too far away to see." With that, he winked at her and followed the others out of the tent, leaving Tucia and Toby at last alone.

10

Though Tucia had scant interest in watching Huey and his ragtag troupe perform, he'd seemed quite intent on her attending. Hopefully the show was a short one. The day's events had already left her weary, and a dull ache pressed against her skull. She doubted any of them had much talent. Otherwise, they wouldn't be performing for a bunch of roughnecks in the middle of nowhere.

When she and Toby finished their supper, they joined the waiting crowd in front of the stage. The grass had been tamped down as Huey insisted, and a few dozen townsfolk milled about. Most were men, but a few women and children had come too. Some wore their Sunday best for the occasion. Others looked—and smelled—as if they'd come straight from a long day in the field. A group of men toward the back passed around a jar of moonshine. Tucia steered clear of them, finding a spot at the far edge where Toby would have a good view.

It surprised Tucia how greatly the lot had changed since earlier that afternoon. Velvet bunting now skirted the stage, hiding the crates of bottles beneath, and a striped canvas awning hung overhead. The wagons had disappeared behind a curtain that stretched for several feet on either side of the stage. Frontier scenes decorated the fabric—miners panning for gold, covered wagons traversing green hills, Indians attacking a train. At the back of the stage, an ornate set of double doors had been painted onto the muslin. Above it, two-foot-high scrolling letters read, *The Amazing Adolphus and His Traveling Medicine Show.* Torches with a gasoline reservoir and pan-shaped burner cast everything in a bright glow.

She'd seen medicine shows before, albeit smaller in scale. Men who stood on street corners hawking their cure-all potions out of suitcases, a banjo plucker or blackface comedian occasionally on hand to attract a crowd.

She and her medical college classmates had been warned of these quack pitchmen. Snakes and imposters who besmirched the noble profession of medicine, one professor had said. A blight to humanity, another had lamented. It made her head throb all the more to think she'd joined one.

The crowd quieted as the big-nosed man slipped between a break in the muslin backdrop to the left of the stage and tottered up the stairs. He'd changed his drab workman's clothes for a brightly colored patchwork suit. In one hand, he carried a banjo. In the other, a bow and fiddle.

She'd noticed he was short when he'd gotten up to clear his plate in the cook tent and now realized why. Both of his legs bowed outward at the knee.

Cal Crip Caboo—she remembered the name from the flier she'd seen in town. Crip, as in *cripple*? Who had come up with such a nickname? It was catchy, yes, but also cruel.

He must have had rickets as a boy. A severe case, by the looks of it. She couldn't help but wonder what fool of a physician had treated him. If he'd been treated at all. Fresh air, a good diet, and a daily dose of cod-liver oil would have prevented such deformity.

His slow, rocking gait spurred a few chuckles from the crowd, especially in the back corner where the men continued to swig from their jar of moonshine. Tucia felt a stab of sympathy for the man, despite how rude he'd been in the cook tent.

If the snickering bothered him, he made no show of it. Without the slightest hurry, he set down his fiddle and bow and dragged a stool from the back corner of the stage to the center. The chuckles mounted as he sat down and readied his banjo.

"Get on with it!" someone yelled.

The bowlegged man ignored the heckler. He plucked a string on his banjo, paused, then plucked another. And another. Then, suddenly, his fingers were flying faster than Tucia could track them, picking out a lively tune.

The audience fell silent. Heads began bobbing and foots tapping. Somehow the rhythm sped even faster, each note ringing as clear and precise as the last. After a moment, it slowed enough for the audience to clap along. Beside her, Toby clapped, too, not quite in time with the tune, but with more than enough gusto to make up for it.

The song ended, and another began. This one was slower but required even more intricate finger work. Tucia watched the man, both dumbfounded and awed. In her youth, she'd attended her share of dances and symphonies and private parlor concerts. Never had she seen such a talented musician, one who played with such raw feeling and skill. It was a stark contrast to the sour man she'd met earlier.

A glance around the audience—many of whom stood agog— told her she wasn't alone in her amazement. What was a man with such prodigious ability doing here, performing for them in this vacant lot?

Next he played a few jaunty numbers on the fiddle. Then a graceful ballad on a harmonica he plucked from his pocket. A knot rose in Tucia's throat as the song ended. The woman standing next to her wiped away a tear. Several seconds passed before the awestruck crowd remembered to clap.

Cal Crip Caboo grabbed his instruments and stood, padding offstage without a bow.

Huey took the stage next, his dark suit as lustrous as oiled beaver skin in the flickering torchlight. Disabused of their skepticism, the audience greeted him with applause instead of chuckles. Huey doffed his top hat with a wide sweep of the hand and sank into a bow.

"Welcome! Welcome," he said as he rose. "Thank you for joining us for this very special show. You're in for a real treat tonight. From Cal Crip Caboo to Chief Big Sky to Grazyna the Dancing Giant, I guarantee feats and wonders you could live a hundred years and never see the likes of again."

His voice carried easily through the crowd, and he seemed as he had that day on the landing of her apartment—bigger and grander than he truly was.

"I am your humble host, Dr. Adolphus P. Aidenheimer, better known as the Amazing Adolphus." He paused for another round of applause. "Without further ado, let me call to the stage a savage plucked from the wilds of Indian Territory, a scout who served at the side of General Custer at the tragic battle of Little Big Horn, Chief Big Sky."

Murmurs of excitement rippled through the crowd as they waited for Chief Big Sky to appear. But for Tucia, the word "doctor" had shattered Huey's spell. He'd said it so quickly, so off-handedly, she guessed most in the audience hadn't even registered the word. *Doctor* Adolphus P. Aidenheimer. It was the exact sort of prevarication forbidden by law. But then, he hadn't claimed to be a *medical* doctor. She wasn't sure he'd claimed anything at all. It reminded her of this morning on the train when the stool suddenly flew out from beneath her.

Chief Big Sky's arrival interrupted her thoughts. He'd transformed from the plain-clothed man she'd met earlier into a character out of a dime novel, replete with buckskin pants, a porcupine quill necklace, and a feather headdress. He held a tomahawk in one hand and a dried gourd in the other, which rattled as he walked. After circling the stage, he came to stand beside Huey.

"Chief Big Sky, tell these good people of Custer's brave last stand," Huey said. But before the chief could speak, Huey turned and addressed the audience. "Patience now, he speaks but little English, so I must translate."

Tucia frowned. She'd heard him speaking at supper. His English was as good as anyone's. And he would have been an infant during the Battle of the Little Bighorn, if he'd been born at all.

Chief Big Sky began uttering strange sounds and words Tucia didn't recognize. He waved his tomahawk as he spoke, eliciting *ooh*s and *ahh*s from the audience. Beside her, Toby stood in open-mouthed awe.

After half a minute or so, Chief Big Sky paused, and Huey translated. They carried on like this for several minutes until the chief let out an ear-splitting war cry, pantomimed a few blows with his ax, then fell silent.

"The rest, my dear audience, you know all too well. After being felled by the great Sioux enemy's blade and rendered unconscious for some short minutes, he arose to find brave General Custer slain. Indeed, the entire cavalry lay dead, their scalps gone."

The men in the audience wagged their heads. The women clutched their cameos and crosses. After a moment, Chief Big Sky shook his rattle again, breaking the silence. He made another slow, mournful circle around the stage before descending the stairs and disappearing backstage.

Huey promised the chief would return later to awe them with his lariat, then introduced the next act: Grazyna, the Dancing Giant. The woman Tucia had met earlier emerged through the break in the backdrop, stooping to clear the overhead pole.

Several people in the audience gasped. Others chuckled nervously. Tucia wasn't sure whether it was Grazyna's costume or her height that stirred such reactions. It was hard to tell just how tall she was—tricks of lighting and perspective could fool the human eye—but Tucia guessed she was well over six feet, perhaps nearing seven. And for one of such great size, she wore very little. Her bell-shaped skirt of gossamer and tulle ended just below the knees, revealing pale pink stockings. Her bodice had an evening gown's deep neckline and short, puffy sleeves. Silk slippers, squared off at the toe, ensconced her enormous feet.

Tucia put her hand on Toby's shoulder, ready to pull him close and cover his eyes if the act proved to be a bawdy one. Several other mothers in the audience did the same while one of the men at the back whistled.

Grazyna wasn't just tall but broad-shouldered and large-boned. Yet she mounted the steps with surprising grace. Another hoot and whistle sounded as she readied herself center stage with her long arms curved at her sides, her legs together and feet out-turned. For a long moment, she stood perfectly still. Then Cal Crip Caboo appeared beside the stage with his fiddle and began a sweeping, classical tune.

The giant came to life with the music, sashaying, leaping, and twirling. She moved light as a bird, as if her bones were hollow and her limbs feathered wings. She flitted from one side of the stage to the next, balancing on the tips of her toes.

Ballet dancing, Tucia realized. She'd never been to a perfor-mance but had heard tell of it from those who'd visited Europe. Grazyna danced so beautifully, Tucia almost forgot the woman's giant size.

Almost.

Despite how light and airy her movements were, how nimbly she leapt and spun, the stage registered its protest, creaking and shuddering beneath her considerable weight.

The song ended, and Grazyna curtseyed low. Once again, the crowd was slow to clap as if still digesting what they'd seen. But once the first few started, the rest joined with hardy applause.

Grazyna exited with the same birdlike grace she had when she'd arrived, and Huey took the stage again. There was a pal-pable eagerness in the crowd now. Tucia noticed it in their still-ness and silence. In the way they readily drew closer to the stage at Huey's command. He promised more daring feats and amazing acts to come but first had something truly astonishing to share with them.

He beckoned the crowd even closer, and Tucia and Toby were swept forward with them. Once he was satisfied, Huey began his tale.

"I was orphaned at the tender age of five," he told them and pointed to a child near the front of the audience. "Not even as old as this fair lad. A fire took my parents, I'm afraid, and I was sent to stay with my great uncle, the ambassador to Siam. We lived within the King's Palace, a place so resplendent it rivals the fabled city of Xanadu."

Murmurs of awe sounded around her. The press of bodies and stench of sweat made Tucia uneasy, and she scooped Toby up into her arms in case things got unruly. She risked a tantrum picking him up, but, for now at least, he seemed happy to have a better view of the stage. The alluring timbre of Huey's voice certainly helped too.

And Toby wasn't the only one entranced with his words. Everyone around them listened enrapt.

"Servants waited on us day and night, and we feasted on the finest Siamese delicacies—tropical fruits, exotic game, sea creatures of every kind. Nevertheless, it was a lonely childhood. For you see, I was forbidden from playing with the king's children—of whom there were dozens, as he had many wives and concubines—for fear of a great pestilence. The dreaded Oun-yo-rah."

The crowd drew in a collective breath, but Tucia was immediately skeptical. *Oun-yo-rah?* She'd never read about any such illness in her medical textbooks, not even in Dr. Lanbee's *Compendium of Oriental Diseases.*

"Some of you may doubt such an illness exists. But you would not if you had seen the great suffering it caused these people. Inflammation of the liver. Softening of the bones. Boils the size of a goose egg. Nose bleeds that couldn't be stopped. To a man, anyone who caught Oun-yo-rah died and in the most excruciating way."

Members of the audience exchanged grave looks and shifted with unease. Mothers once again pulled their children close. Toby clung to her more tightly. But Tucia only shook her head. The cluster of symptoms he'd described didn't make sense and certainly didn't constitute any real disease.

"Being young and of good health," Huey continued, "I joined the Siamese healers' quest for a cure. For years we searched. In the dense jungles where tigers stalked our trail. Along the shore where waves—tall as church spires—fought to drown us. Among the crumbling ruins of cities where booby traps guarded ancient gold. At last, in a musty old cave, where bones of treasure-seekers littered the ground, I noticed an ancient drawing etched into the wall."

He paused, his violet eyes panning the audience. No one spoke or moved. Not even Tucia, though Toby had grown heavy in her arms. At last, someone whispered, "What was it?"

"What was it, you ask?" Huey said loudly enough to cause several people to jump. "A snake! But not just any snake. One with great fangs and a rattle at the end of its tail. This etching showed not only the snake but the process—by way of soaking the snake, once dead, in oil from the sacred jobaba-bean tree—to transform its venom into a potent cure.

"It took us many more months to find this particular snake. Its poisonous bite killed two of the Siamese healers before I managed to grab hold of it just below its powerful jaw and cut off its windpipe."

He pantomimed grabbing the snake in both hands and struggling to subdue it.

"When the snake was dead, we took it back to the palace and soaked it in jobaba-bean oil for the length of ten moons as the ancients had instructed." He paused again and straightened. "Now, it was with no small fear we presented this snake oil elixir to the king—for even though my uncle was the ambassador, the king would have our heads if the elixir failed. He called forth his second but favorite son, who'd just contracted the deadly Oun-yo-rah. We administered him a dram of the elixir and waited to see if he would be cured.

"I'll tell you, ladies and gentlemen, those were the longest hours of my life. But, by the very next morning, all traces of the Oun-yo-rah sickness were gone. The snake oil elixir had cured him!"

Applause broke out across the audience. Huey waited until it petered out before continuing. "The king was so grateful that he made me his honorary son. I was finally free to play with the other children, but by now, I was almost a man and had no interest in games. Instead, I continued to study with the royal doctors and healers, perfecting this miraculous elixir. Then I returned to America to replicate the process for my countrymen.

"I was but a lad of nineteen when I left Siam, and, as you can see, I am no longer so young. It has taken me years to find a snake of equal potency native to our land and several more to discover a plant oil powerful enough to transmute its venom into medicine. But, ladies and gentlemen, I have done it." He stomped his foot for emphasis. "I have done it!"

At that, the slit in the backdrop opened, and Al hurried out carrying a large glass jar. A rattlesnake was coiled inside in a bath of pale yellow liquid. Al climbed the steps and handed the jar to Huey, who held it up for the audience to see. The snake's mouth was open, revealing long, sharp fangs, and its rattle stood upright. Tucia shuddered, even though she knew it was dead.

After a moment, Huey handed the jar back to Al, who set it on the stool at the rear of the stage. "With careful study, I have determined this elixir to be even more potent than that discovered by the Siamese ancients. Just seven drops diluted in a bottle of the purest spring water cures everything. Catarrh, rheumatism, liver trouble, dyspepsia—it works on it all. Men, it will bring back the energy and vigor of your youth. Ladies, it will soothe your nerves and quiet even the most troubling of your feminine ailments."

While Huey spoke, Al hurried down the steps and pulled out a crate of medicine from beneath the stage. He tossed one of the bottles up to Huey, who caught it with barely a sidelong glance.

"Revivifying Rattlesnake Oil, ladies and gentlemen!" Huey said, holding the bottle up as if it were the holy grail. "Yours tonight for the very low price of one dollar."

Tucia had to hold back a laugh. An elixir that cured everything from cirrhosis to achy joints to aging. No medicine in the world could do that. Surely, Huey's claim was too ridiculous for even these countryfolk to believe. But no sooner had Huey finished speaking than a man in the audience held up a dollar. Al was at his side a moment later with a bottle. Another hand went up and another and another. Chief Big Sky and Cal Crip Caboo were suddenly among the crowd, though Tucia hadn't noticed them arrive, passing out bottles of medicine.

"Don't miss out, folks," Huey said over the rising clamor. "You won't find this amazing remedy anywhere else. Nothing in the drugstore can compare."

A sickening feeling overcame Tucia as more people in the audience succumbed to Huey's spiel.

"We're almost out, boss!" Al called, holding up the last two bottles from the crate. They quickly sold, just as another crate was conveniently discovered beneath the stage. The man beside her bought two bottles. Another in the back, three.

Huey now held up a small silver tin with a red label that matched the bottle. "For just twenty-five cents more, those of you who bought a bottle of Revivifying Rattlesnake Oil can have my Miraculous Corn-busting Salve. It sells alone for twice that price!" He went on to proclaim how it cured not only corns but any skin ailment from burns to itchy piles to ringworm to pimples.

Tucia didn't wait to hear what else this purportedly miraculous salve healed. She pushed through the crowd, holding tight to her son, even as he reached back and cried, "Me! Me. I want one too."

What sort of madness had she agreed to take part in?

11

Tucia didn't need nightmares to keep her awake that night. The show continued long after they left with more dancing, music, and another lengthy spiel about the wonders of rattlesnake oil and corn-busting salve. They could hear everything through the thin walls of their wagon, and Toby, overtired from the long, strange day, flung himself to the floor, kicking and hollering. Tucia's attempts to soothe him did little good, but eventually he cried himself to sleep, and she was able to scoop him off the floor and settle him in bed.

By then, the show had ended, and all that could be heard were crickets, field mice, and the lonely hoot of an owl. Tucia lay beside Toby on the small, lumpy bed and stared into the darkness. Revivifying Rattlesnake Oil? Miraculous Corn-busting Salve? What had she gotten them into?

She'd known that medicine pitchmen made ridiculous claims, preying upon those who were too uneducated to know truth from lie. But seeing it in action was different. The poor townsfolk who'd come tonight never stood a chance. And not because they were stupid—although certainly their understanding of the basic principles of medicine was gravely deficient—but because they'd been swept up in the thrill of it all. Even Tucia had lost hold of her senses for a moment.

She twisted a finger around her hair, winding her way up to the scalp, then began tugging out the strands one by one. She remembered feeling that way before—that subliminal thrill—during her short-lived internship at Fairview. Remembered how easy it had been to ignore her misgivings. And how dearly she'd paid for it after.

She snuggled closer to Toby and forced her fingers to still. The thought of taking part in the show—even if only in Huey's little case-taking tent—sickened her. But what could she do? A debt was a debt whether it was made with a loan agency or a showman.

Perhaps she could steer Huey and the show toward greater repute. Perhaps he didn't know the error of what he said. He wasn't a doctor after all. Tucia could educate him. He seemed like a reasonable man, after all, albeit a little bullish.

Of course, they would have to sell *something*. Soap perhaps. She'd heard of traveling showmen who sold scented soap packaged in pretty paper. And why not? Then Huey needn't lie at all. With a little schooling, he could expound for days on the health benefits of cleanliness and hygiene.

She let go of her hair and managed to settle into the mattress. Perhaps this little adventure needn't be so bad after all. Her lids drooped shut, and she thought of neatly wrapped cakes of soap until, at last, sleep found her.

The next morning, Tucia awoke to the shrill ring of the breakfast bell. Light spilled into the wagon through holes in the moth-eaten curtains. She roused Toby, and they dressed. Were it not for him, she'd skip breakfast, but a growing boy needed to eat. He was already small for his age on account of his condition. And the paltry sum she'd had to spend on food in the city hadn't helped. At least here he would be well-fed, even if the others didn't much like their company.

Toby struggled to fasten the new side-button boots Huey had bought him in the city, growing so impatient he flung one across the room. "No shoes!"

Tucia sighed. So he, too, had noticed Al walking around barefoot yesterday. She tried to explain the multitude of reasons why it was unsafe for Toby to go about shoeless, then gave up and stuffed his feet into the boots, buttoning them herself.

Everyone but Huey was already sitting down with a plate of food when she and Toby arrived at the cook tent. The group's conversation skidded into silence. Cal Crip Caboo scowled as if he'd hoped yesterday's cold reception would have been enough to scare her off.

The lengthening quiet and directness of their stares made her uneasy. But she squared her shoulders and led Toby across the tent to the food. She fixed them both a plate, then sat down with him at the far end of the table, leaving as much distance as she could between them and the others.

At first, no one spoke. The only sound in the tent was the clink of their forks and soft whoosh of Toby's swinging legs. A strained silence to be sure. Tucia had to sit on her free hand to keep it from drifting to her scalp. She didn't need these people gossiping about her the way the women at the factory had.

Finally, Chief Big Sky cleared his throat. "You gonna fix that loose board today?"

Tucia wasn't sure whom he was talking to until Darl grunted his assent. So he was the man responsible for upkeep around camp. Perhaps he could fix the broken table in her wagon too. But before she could ask, Huey's voice called cheerily from the mouth of the tent.

"Good show last night, good show." He spoke as if he were oblivious to the tension in the air, though Tucia suspected he was not. "What's for breakfast, Chef?"

"The usual," Cal said.

He was the cook? It surprised her that such a crabby man could produce such good food. And such good music.

Huey strode to the far end of the tent, poured himself a cup of coffee, then sat down at the opposite side of the table in the no-man's-land between Tucia and Toby and the others. "Darl, there's a loose board in the—"

"I know."

"Good. Get it fixed. And, Chief, your monologue's getting a little long again. Didn't you think so, Mrs. Hatherley?"

"Me?"

"Yes, you were watching the show last night, weren't you? What did you think of Chief Big Sky's monologue?"

"Monologue?" She didn't want to admit that she hadn't stayed for the whole show and hoped they were talking about the act recounting the Battle of the Little Big Horn. "I . . . er . . . couldn't understand what he was saying. But I venture that's for effect."

Huey slapped his hand down on the table. "See? The audience can't understand you, so you've got to keep your part quick. The longer you drone on, the more apt their attention is to wander."

The chief ate a forkful of grits and washed it down with a swig of coffee, not looking at either of them.

"And if their attention wanders?" Huey slapped the table again, this time with real force. Toby startled, dropping his fork. Tucia put her arm around him and pulled him close, a nervous jolt traveling from her core to her limbs.

"If their attention wanders?" he repeated loudly.

"We lose the sale," Chief Big Sky murmured.

"Precisely!" He turned back to Tucia, his everything's-right-as-rain smile filling her with greater disquiet. "What else did you think of the show?"

"It was . . ." She groped for the right words. She needed to let him down easily so he'd be receptive to her idea about soap. ". . . quite a spectacle. The audience seemed very amused, but—"

He turned his attention to the giant before Tucia could continue. "They must not have noticed your late entrance during the second act, then. I trust we can do better tonight."

Grazyna's lips flattened, and she nodded.

Tucia worried that was the end of it, that she'd lost her shot at telling him what she really thought of the show and how they could improve it. But thankfully, Huey's gaze swung back to her. "You said *the audience* was amused. Not you?"

"The music and dancing and storytelling—it was all pleasant enough."

Huey said nothing but continued to regard her with earnest curiosity, so she went on. "There were certain inconsistencies, medical and otherwise, when you spoke about your time in Siam. And it strains the imagination to believe that any remedy could cure such an array of ailments."

The tent had gone still while she spoke. Forks down and coffee going cold. Even Toby's legs had stopped swinging. All eyes were on her and Huey.

"I see," he said. "And what would you suggest?"

Tucia straightened. Here was her chance. "A less exaggerated approach. The benefits of sanitation and proper nutrition, for example, could improve these people's health to a far greater extent than any elixir or salve. Perhaps if—"

"You cannot sell fresh air and sunshine, my dear," he said. The others at the table chuckled.

"No, but I was thinking soap."

Darl snorted. He stood, shaking his head as he carried his plate to the washbasin. Tucia did her best to ignore him.

"I've heard some showmen sell it, do they not? Instead of that fictitious story about rattlesnakes and Siamese princes, you could lecture on the principles of cleanliness and good hygiene."

"Soap," Huey said, like he was trying the word out in his mouth. "Soap."

Hope stirred inside her. "Yes. We could scent it with rose or lavender and package it up quite attractively. I'm sure it would sell. And then you wouldn't need to . . . er . . . exaggerate so much."

For a moment, Huey said nothing, though he seemed to be contemplating her words. The others stared at their plates of grits and bacon, their laughter gone.

Then Huey scooted down the bench with his cup of coffee until he sat right in front of her.

"Are you enjoying the food here?" he asked. Though he'd moved close enough to whisper, he spoke in a voice everyone could hear.

Tucia shifted on the hard bench. What did this have to do with soap? "Yes."

"Nice to be able to feed your boy three square meals a day, isn't it?"

"Yes."

"And the new dresses I bought you, are you enjoying those too?"

A flush of embarrassment crept into her face. She hadn't asked for those dresses. He'd insisted. "Yes, but—"

"And the wagon? The others here sleep in tents. But you, you're a doctor, a position of some prestige, and I wanted to be sure you were comfortable."

Something told Tucia now was not the time to mention the dead mouse, lumpy mattress, or broken window and flap table. She glanced at the others who, one by one, grabbed their plates and padded toward the washbasin.

"Do you think you'd be afforded such luxuries if we sold soap?" Huey continued.

"I . . . I don't know. I'm sure if—"

"Al," Huey called over her. "How many bottles of rattlesnake oil did we sell last night?"

"Forty-five, sir," Al responded. "I counted twice to be sure."

"There's a good boy. And corn-buster?"

"Twenty."

Grazyna grabbed Al's hand and pulled him along toward the exit, shooting Tucia a cautionary look.

"Well, there you have it!" Huey said. "Fifty dollars on our first night. And we'll do better tonight. It's word of mouth that brings the yokels in, see?"

"Yokels?"

"The customers. Chumps, suckers, gills, rubes, simps—you'll

get the parlance down soon enough. And I'll tell you this, soap won't get them talking."

"Isn't that what the music and dancing are for?"

"All that ballyhooing helps, sure. But it's no replacement for a mysterious nostrum and a slick pitch."

Tucia could see that her reasoning hadn't worked. Despite the warning in the giant's eyes, she switched tactics. "Couldn't a *great* showman sell anything? Snake oil, soap, salve. Surely it's not the medicine that matters but the man who makes the sale."

The others lingered at the tent's entryway as if awaiting Huey's response. His face twitched, and eyes darkened. A smile followed, but one that made her breakfast turn sour in her stomach.

"My dear Tucia—I can call you that, right, seeing as we're all like family here? Perhaps you've forgotten the hundreds of dollars shelled out to liberate you from those loan sharks and the debt you owe me in return."

Once again he'd spoken loudly enough for all to hear, and she could only imagine what sort of lurid thoughts the others were thinking. Debt—even an honest salary loan—was always unseemly. Most especially for a woman. Her gaze dropped to the table as humiliation burned through her. Now everyone in the troupe knew of her low situation, and she was grateful when she heard them shuffle away. She was even more grateful that Toby had long since lost interest in the conversation and was now smashing the remainder of his grits with the tines of his fork in silent play.

"I didn't make that kind of money selling soap," Huey continued. "And I'm not about to change course now. A great showman knows what works and sticks with it. Understand?"

The tone of his voice brooked no further argument, and Tucia nodded.

"Good. But, to your point about ballyhoo, tonight you go on as Madame Zabelle, teller of fortunes and mind reader extraordinaire."

She looked up. "What?"

"Too much too soon?" he asked with an amused smirk. "All

right, we can hold off on the fortune-telling bit. For now, memorize this. In order."

He pulled a folded show bill from his pocket and handed it to her. On the back, he'd written two dozen items, each with a corresponding number.

"I don't understand."

"It's your act. Tonight I'll call you onto the stage and blindfold you. Then I'll move among the audience and find someone in possession of the first object on the list. I'll cue you, and you'll call out the item. Then we'll move on to the next item and the next. If I have to skip one, I'll clear my throat. The audience will think you have the gift of second sight and are reading their minds to decipher the object. We can work out a more elaborate code later, but for now it will do."

She glanced at the list again. They were common enough objects—necktie, hat, watch chain, handkerchief—and easy to find in a crowd, but that was hardly the point.

"I can't do this." She slid the paper back across the table. Huey didn't pick it up.

"You're telling me a woman who graduated medical college cannot memorize two dozen words in a day?"

"I'm not a performer. I'm a doctor." She was barely even that. But doctor, at least, was the role she'd agreed to play.

"Everyone does double duty around here. Chief looks after the animals, Crip cooks, and our resident giant sews the costumes. Why, even Al keeps count of how much medicine we have on hand. And they all perform. So will you."

Tucia turned to Toby. "That's enough playing with your food, darling. Take our plates to the washbasin, please."

He frowned but did as he was told.

"And don't forget to scrape them over the slop bucket first," she called after him. Then she turned back to Huey and leaned across the table, speaking in a hissing whisper. "I didn't agree to that. And I certainly didn't agree to that for my son."

Huey flapped a hand and continued to smile. "So long as he

doesn't get in the way of the show, I've got no designs on young Toby. You, however, will pull your weight around here like everyone else."

"I agreed to help out with the show. Not to perform in it."

"I'm afraid that's not how the terms of our little arrangement read." He felt around his jacket and pulled out another piece of paper—the contract he'd written back in St. Louis.

Had she agreed to such a thing? She tried to recall their meeting in her apartment. Her thoughts had been all ascramble that day, not to mention her nerves. The loan agency, the foreman, the prospect of losing her son. She'd been so focused on her debt and the terms of her repayment that she hadn't paid much attention to anything else.

She snatched the contract from him and reread it now, this time more carefully. Several lines down, after delineating the amount of her debt, to whom it was owed, and Mr. Hugh A. Horn's agreement to assume said debt, it read:

. . . to be repaid with services rendered, as determined by Mr. H. A. Horn, in support of the Amazing Adolphus Medicine Company.

At the bottom was her signature, alongside Huey's and the notary's seal. Tucia winced and handed the contract back to him. How had she agreed to such unrestricted and vague terms?

Huey slipped it back into his pocket and stood. "You best get to memorizing, my dear Madame Zabelle."

12

Tucia sat beside Toby on the bed. His secondhand school primer was splayed across his lap, and he fisted his pencil, messily copying down the letters of the alphabet. It was far from the ideal setting for his schooling, but with the table and chair broken, it would have to do.

Most saw little value in teaching children like Toby to read and write. Asylums and institutions favored a blend of work and play with little actual learning. Tucia disagreed. Practical skills and play were important, but so were the three Rs. His mind might wander, as young boys' minds were apt to do, but she wouldn't let someone else's preconceived notions limit what Toby could learn.

Today, however, it was *her* mind wandering. The list Huey had given her lay folded on the nearby dresser. He'd been right; it wouldn't take more than half an hour to memorize the words. But she refused to acquiesce to his harebrained idea. Madame Zabelle, mind reader extraordinaire! Who would believe such an act?

She glared at the paper, wishing it would spontaneously catch flame and burn. Her a mind reader? A grifter and charlatan, to be more precise. Eight years ago, she'd graduated top of her class from medical school, and now this?

Those three years at Woman's Medical College of Chicago had been among the best of her life. She'd hoped to go to Chicago Medical College, or College of Physicians and Surgeons, or perhaps even Harvard—but none of them accepted women. Though coeducational schools were more common now, in her day many still objected to educating the sexes together—or to educating women at all.

Even a few of her professors at the woman's college had felt that way. One, a doctor well into his sixties, gave only two lectures the entire term and spent the better part of both describing not the function of protoplasm within cells but the utter uselessness of teaching women.

Another professor, a well-respected surgeon, stated simply he didn't believe in female doctors, and they were greatly mistaken if they thought the world was waiting for them. He, at least, lectured weekly but spent much of his time telling trifling anecdotes and glancing at his watch.

Tucia and her classmates pressed on undaunted. They compared notes and studied for examinations together. They shared tips on how best to withstand the foul odors of the dissecting room. In addition to lectures, they attended weekly clinics at the nearby hospitals where patients with various maladies were brought forward and their cases discussed.

Despite a few naysaying professors and the occasional physician who refused to begin his clinic with women present, Tucia and her classmates graduated in high spirits, believing wholeheartedly in the future. Those who could afford it traveled to Europe for practical instruction in France or Switzerland. Those who could not sought work in women's hospitals or dispensaries here in America. A few set out as missionaries.

Tucia had been the lone, lucky graduate to score high enough on her competitive exams to secure an internship at the prestigious Fairview Hospital. The world, it seemed, *was* waiting for them.

How very different the world seemed now.

Tucia sighed and grabbed Huey's list from the dresser. She needn't like it, only do the work. The bare minimum that Huey required. And she needn't associate with the others either. Needn't become one of them. Toby certainly wouldn't benefit from their vulgar influence. They did this because they wanted to. Because they didn't mind taking advantage of people. Tucia was here because she had no other choice. As soon as her debt was paid, she and Toby would be gone.

Before she'd read the list all the way through, a loud knock rattled the wagon. Tucia straightened. Who would be knocking on their door? It wasn't yet noon, so they hadn't missed the call to dinner. The knock came again.

Tucia hesitated a moment before standing and crossing to the door. She jerked the latch and swung the door open. "Yes?"

Grazyna the Dancing Giant stood at the foot of the steps. Until that moment, Tucia had not appreciated the full extent of her height. Forget tricks of lighting. Tucia had never met anyone— man or woman—as tall, and it took conscious effort not to drop her jaw in wonderment.

Their eyes locked, and the woman pursed her lips as if she sensed what Tucia was thinking. "Huey wants you fitted for your costume."

Costume? He hadn't said anything about a costume. "I'm a doctor, not a circus sideshow. I'm sure my regular attire will suit just fine."

The giant flinched.

"Sorry, I didn't mean . . . that is . . ."

"You don't grow to be as tall as I am without also growing a thick skin. Now come on. Boss's orders."

Without fully thinking about it, Tucia reached up, feeling along the soft hairs at the nape of her neck before plucking one free. With few carefully prescribed exceptions, no respectable woman wore a costume. And this—a mind-reading act for a traveling medicine show—certainly wasn't one of those exceptions. But she didn't want to risk another row with Huey.

"Well, you coming?" the giant asked.

Tucia snapped the hair in two and let the pieces fall to the ground. "I haven't got much choice in the matter, have I?"

"Not if you want to stay on Huey's good side."

The side of himself he'd shown her that morning was a far cry from good, but no, she didn't want to meet his bad side either. "Can't we do the fitting here?"

"You think I'm going to fit in there without folding myself in two?"

"Oh," Tucia said. "Right."

The giant shook her head. "And here I thought you doctors were supposed to be smart." She turned and started to walk away, saying over her shoulder, "We'll do it in my tent. Let's go."

Tucia told Toby to set aside his book, and they followed the giant across camp to the second of the large tents, shuffling to keep up.

As bad as her cramped and run-down wagon was, living out of a tent would be far worse. She imagined a few bedrolls thrown down on the hard ground as wind rattled the flimsy walls and every sort of vile creature slithered in and out beneath the canvas.

But when the giant held open the front flap of her tent for them to enter, Tucia was struck by how spacious and homey it was inside. In the far corner sat two wooden-framed cots pushed close together, one considerably longer than the other. Thick mattresses rested atop each, covered with brightly colored bedclothes tucked in neatly at the corners. A smaller bedstead sat flush against the opposite wall. The weeds had been shorn, and a large rug covered most of the ground. Two large dresser trunks stood along the back and, beside them, a damask-paneled dressing screen.

She'd overheard Al call the giant "Ma" and Cal Crip Caboo "Pa" but had assumed those were nicknames like "Chief" or "Crip." She hadn't actually thought they were a family. She recalled from a lecture that disruptions in menses caused most women with gigantism to be infertile. But judging by the number of beds in the tent, they were a family, if not in blood, at least in practice.

The giant tied back the front tent flaps, brightening the room with sunlight. Then she nodded to a small round table with three folding chairs to the right of the entry. "There it is."

At first, Tucia didn't know what *it* was. Then she noticed the mountain of crepe heaped over the back of one of the chairs. "That's my costume?"

The giant picked it up and gave it a good shake. Dust billowed into the air.

"Undress, and we'll see how it fits."

Tucia seated Toby at the table, then undressed behind the screen. She draped her skirt, jacket, and shirtwaist over the top, and the giant handed her the dress. The shabby fabric had faded to a dark rusty color and reeked of must. Someone's widow's weeds, she realized as she threw the dress on over her head. Unlike to-day's fashion, the sleeves were straight and narrow, and fell several inches too long, while the bodice, which buttoned up the front to a high, unadorned collar, would barely fasten over her bust. As she made her way around the screen, Tucia had to hike up the limp, heavy skirt to avoid tripping.

The giant had placed an upturned crate in the center of the room and beckoned her over. Tucia climbed atop it. The giant circled her with narrowed eyes.

"The sleeves are a bit long," Tucia said. "And I fear if I take a deep breath these buttons will pop off."

The giant nodded. She grabbed hold of the skirt and held it out as if trying to determine how much fabric was actually there. "You'll need a cage crinoline."

"How old is this dress?" A steel-hooped underskirt was the sort of thing her mother and grandmother had worn decades ago.

The giant shrugged. "Who knows where Huey gets these things." She dropped the skirt and sighed. "I can't hem it properly without the crinoline, but I think there's one in the supply wagon. Don't move."

Tucia tried to remain as still as she could while the giant

stepped outside and hollered for her son. But the fabric itched and made her want to sneeze. Toby, meanwhile, had snuck off the chair and crept to a small box of toys stowed at the foot of the smaller bed. Tucia caught sight of him from the corner of her eye just as he pulled a wooden horse on wheels from the box.

"Toby, darling, no. Those aren't your toys." She started to step down, but the back of her dress caught on the edge of the crate. She twisted around and shook her skirt free. When she turned back, she saw the giant had gotten to him first.

Toby's eyes went wide, and his mouth gaped as the giant squatted beside him.

"Here you go, *liebling*," she said and emptied the box onto the ground. "Take your pick. That is"—her gaze flickered to Tucia—"if your mother approves."

They both looked at her expectantly.

"Yes, of course. Thank you," she said. "Toby, what do you say to . . . er . . . Mrs. Grazyna?"

"Thank you, Mrs. Graseena," he repeated, tripping over her name.

The giant laughed, a rich, full sound that startled Tucia. She patted Toby's head and stood. "Grazyna is my stage name."

"Oh, I'm sorry. I . . . I shouldn't have presumed . . ."

"Franziska Trout. You can call me Fanny."

"I'm Tucia."

Fanny nodded. She walked over to one of the dressers and opened a drawer. When she returned to Tucia's side, she held a pink velvet pin cushion trimmed with lace. It was far lovelier than any Tucia had owned. But then, the only sewing she'd been interested in was the kind done in the operating theater.

"Hold out your arm," Fanny now instructed her.

Tucia did as she was told. Fanny folded back the dress's too-long sleeve and began pinning.

"What about the others?" Tucia asked after a moment. "I'm guessing Cal Crip Caboo's a stage name too."

"Huey came up with that," Fanny said, snickering. "Thought it sounded musical. Calvin Trout's his real name, but everyone calls him Cal."

Tucia couldn't help her gaze from sliding to the two cots pushed together in the corner. "And you're . . . married?"

"Going on eight years." She slipped a final pin into Tucia's sleeve, then moved on to the other. "You?"

"Ah . . . widowed." Tucia felt a twinge of guilt at the lie, but widowhood was the only answer she could give without being branded a strumpet and Toby a bastard. Never mind the truth was rarely that tidy.

"Mustn't be easy raising a boy on your own. I'm grateful every day for my Cal. He's not as grumpy as he seems. We're all a little gun-shy around new folks."

"And the wager?"

"Sorry about that. So many of you have come and gone, we forget our manners."

"What happened to them all?"

Al arrived before Fanny could answer. She sent him to the supply wagon to look for the hoop skirt. He said a passing hello to Toby, not seeming to mind Toby playing with his toys.

Fanny got back to work pinning Tucia's sleeves. "Huey caught the last doctor drinking from the tapeworm jar when he ran out of booze."

"Tapeworm jar?"

"A show prop Huey uses from time to time. He'll go to a ranch or pig farm and get the biggest tapeworm he can find." She spread her giant arms. "At least this long and as fat as my thumb."

Though usually not squeamish about such things, Tucia grimaced.

"He throws it in a jar with some alcohol, puts it on display, and yokels start buying medicine like mad."

"And the doctor, he was drinking the preservative?"

"Yah. We lost two fine specimens that way."

Tucia shuddered at the thought.

"We had another doc who got so liquored up before the show he stumbled off the stage in the middle of his act and broke his leg. Another"—Fanny paused and lowered her voice—"was caught in bed with the mayor's wife."

"Goodness," Tucia said. No wonder they all expected her to fail. Such men were hardly representative of the profession, though. "We're not all like that."

"You're the first lady doctor I've met, so I guess we'll see." She slipped one more pin into Tucia's sleeve, then straightened and smiled down at her. "But my money's with yours. Now, let's see if we can fix this bodice."

Al arrived a short while later with the crinoline slung over his shoulder, its hoops bouncing with each step. The contraption was nearly as big as he was, and he presented it to his mother with a curious look.

"Is this what you were wanting?"

"Yah, thank you, *mäuschen*."

"What is it?"

"You'll see." Fanny handed the hoop skirt to Tucia. She reluctantly took it and slipped behind the screen. Despite its lightness, the hoop skirt proved an unwieldy garment, and it took her several minutes to fasten it in place. She nearly knocked over the screen trying to move around it.

Toby gawked when she finally emerged. Then, seeing Al was laughing, Toby did the same. Tucia couldn't blame them. Even without a mirror, she knew she looked ridiculous.

"She'll take up half the stage with that skirt," Al said between chortles.

Fanny hushed him. "Dresses like these were once the height of fashion."

"When?" Al said around another burp of laughter. "Five hundred years ago?"

"Enough." Fanny shooed him from the tent and turned back to Tucia. "It's not so bad as all that."

But Tucia didn't believe her. She felt like some dowdy old

widow from half a century ago. She might as well paint her face white and nose red like a clown. "He won't be the only one laughing. The entire audience will be in an uproar if I wear this. Huey can't seriously think this will work."

Fanny got down on her knees and began pinning the hem. "If there's one thing I'll say for Huey, he knows what catches a rube's attention. This dress certainly will do that."

Tucia did her best to stand still while Fanny finished with the hem but couldn't help herself reaching for a hair or two or five. When Fanny announced she was finished, Tucia hurriedly changed back into her normal clothes. Not only did the mourning dress itch and smell, it made her armpits sweat while her legs pricked with gooseflesh from the strange swirl of air inside the cage of her skirt.

"I don't suppose you could take your time with the alterations?" she said, handing over the dress.

Fanny smiled in earnest but shook her head. "I've got to answer to Huey, same as you."

"He couldn't blame you if your sewing machine suddenly jammed, though, or you ran out of black thread."

"Don't underestimate him. Once he's set his mind to something, that's that. He'd send you out in your underclothes before canceling the act."

Tucia plucked out another hair and sighed. "I guess I better get to memorizing, then."

13

For the rest of the day, Tucia held out hope that, despite what Fanny said, the god-awful dress wouldn't be ready in time. Or that a rainstorm would blow in. Or a plague of locusts. Something to halt the show or at least her part in it.

But soon after supper, just as the first townsfolk began to arrive, Fanny knocked on her wagon door again, dress and hoop skirt in hand. "It should fit a bit better now. Put it on, and let me have a final look."

Changing inside the wagon was no easy feat. No matter which way she moved, the hoop skirt was always knocking into something. Just getting through the door required her to press down on the sides, causing the front to balloon upward, giving anyone nearby a gander at her drawers. But, to Fanny's credit, the dress did fit much better. The sleeves fell perfectly to her wrists, and the front buttons no longer strained to stay fastened.

Tucia descended the steps of her wagon with care, fearful that the huge skirt might catch on something and trip her. After making it down safely, Fanny circled around her and smiled approvingly. "Good, yah?"

"As good as a dress like this can be."

The door of the neighboring wagon opened, and Huey stepped out onto the top stair. "Marvelous!" he said, eyeing her ridiculous dress. He jaunted down the steps and crossed to where they stood. "Excellent work, Fanny. It fits her like a glove."

Fanny shrugged at the compliment, but it was true: she had done an excellent job. If Tucia must perform in such a fusty dress, at least it fit well.

"But there's something missing." Huey stared at her a moment then exclaimed, "The weeping veil!" He turned to Fanny and asked her to check the supply wagon for a black bonnet and attached veil.

No sooner had Fanny left than Darl stalked by, a sledgehammer resting over his shoulder. He stopped when he saw her, pushing the brim of his hat away from his eyes.

Tucia flushed beneath his gaze. "It's too old-fashioned, I—"

"Nonsense," Huey said. "It's perfect. You look just like one of the Fox sisters."

She recalled the name but couldn't remember from where.

"The who sisters?" Darl asked before she could voice the same question.

Huey frowned at him. "They were spiritualists. Table-rappers. Some of the most famous men of the day attended their séances."

"If they're as old as that dress," Darl said with a snicker, "no one in the audience will remember them."

Tucia turned away from him, trying to shrug off his gaze, but it pulled at her with the same nagging weight as the damned dress.

"Don't listen to him," Huey said. He took a step back, appraising her with an admiring smile. "The older generation will remember. People are always foolishly sentimental about the past. At the very least, they'll see the dress and think of mourning and therefore death and therefore the spirit world. That's all any of this is"—he gestured toward the wagons and backdrop and the stage beyond—"a suggestion. A nudge toward a particular time or place or feeling. The imagination does the rest."

Even as she realized his unflagging confidence and the rich

timbre of his voice were their own sort of suggestion, the knot of unease inside her loosened. The audience wouldn't be seeing her, Tucia Hatherley, but someone else. Someone they'd cobbled together from their own memories and beliefs. All because of a few slick words and an old-fashioned dress. It was a strange sort of relief to have a persona to hide behind. And so long as she didn't cross that line between suggestion and manipulation, she wasn't doing anything wrong.

Tucia managed to hold on to that calm even as the lot filled, and the show began. She'd memorized the list and walked through the act with Huey before supper. Performing it onstage would be no different.

She leaned against her wagon and listened as Cal played a jaunty number on his fiddle. The star-spangled sky hung like a diamond canopy above. No matter what happened onstage tonight, this was far better than the life she'd left behind. In between songs, she could hear the soft clink of building blocks from within the wagon. Toby hadn't understood at first why the two of them couldn't watch the show again like they had the night before, and she hadn't wanted to admit—even to him—that she would be performing. But somehow, after watching her don that rank old dress, he knew not to protest when she bid him stay inside and play.

Hearing him now further calmed her. Her parents—her father and stepmother, anyway—would be mortified if they knew what she was about to do. In their day, women performers ranked just above prostitutes on the social respectability scale. Lady physicians not much higher. But her father was dead nine years now. And Tucia didn't care what her stepmother thought. In fact, the idea of further scandalizing her stirred a perverse delight.

But Tucia liked to think her real mother would understand. Would have made the same bargain. Toby was safe and well-fed, after all. No one was banging on her door, coming to take him away to some crumbling asylum. That was all that mattered.

Chief's war whoop pulled her from her thoughts. She, or Madame Zabelle anyway, was on next. She ran through the list of cues one more time in her head, then made her way to the break in the backdrop to await her entrance.

Chief's act ended, and he slipped backstage, nearly tripping over her sprawling skirt. His eyes widened—either on account of the dark or her awful costume, Tucia wasn't sure which. He shook his head and walked away, muttering something under his breath. Whatever it was, it wasn't "good luck." But Tucia didn't believe in luck anyway.

She peeked through the thin slit in the backdrop and waited for Huey to call for her.

"Ladies and gentlemen," he said from the center of the stage. "Tonight we have a special treat for you. A new and esteemed member of our troupe. A woman of international regard and astonishing skill. I give you, Madame Zabelle."

Tucia took a deep breath and pushed through the backdrop. She made her way to the stage, squinting in the bright glow of the torchlights, and slowly climbed the stairs. A few *ahh*s and whispers rose from the audience, but, thankfully, no laughter.

"To each of us," Huey continued as she came to stand beside him, "fate grants certain powers. Some are exceedingly brave. Some are kind beyond limit. Others have a gift with numbers and can calculate great sums in their heads. Still others possess incredible strength or the power to speak a multitude of languages. Madame Zabelle, dear audience, has been granted powers of a supernatural kind. The power to probe the thoughts of others and read their minds."

As he spoke, Tucia's eyes adjusted to the light, and the audience took shape before her. It was a larger crowd than the night before, and, to a person, they were all men. She blinked, pressure building in her chest. No, that wasn't right. There were several women and a handful of children too—a few in the front row. They stared down at her with pinched, disapproving expressions. No, not down. Up. They were staring up at her. And, if anything, their faces were happy and eager. She blinked again and tried to focus on Huey's words.

"The mystery of Madame Zabelle's skills has yet to be unspooled and explained. Some of the world's foremost scientists have come to scoff at the spectacle you're about to witness and have left baffled and bewildered."

He reached into his pocket and pulled out a scarlet-colored scarf.

"You, sir," he said to a man in the front row. "I invite you to examine this cloth." He tossed it down to him. "Inspect it carefully for tears or holes. Hold it up to your eyes and assure your countrymen it is of a dense and solid weave, impenetrable to sight."

The man examined the cloth carefully, turning it this way and that, holding it up to the light, fingering the weave. The rest of the audience watched him, and Tucia was grateful to be momentarily free of their scrutiny.

"Looks solid to me," the man said.

"Very good." Huey retrieved the scarf and folded it lengthwise several times. Then he tied it over Tucia's eyes. The crowd's needling gaze was once again on her. She didn't need to see their faces to know what they were thinking. *Imposter.* Just like in the operating theater.

She heard Huey hop down from the front of the stage and focused again on his voice, trying to push aside all her other thoughts.

"I shall now pass among you," he said, "and randomly select an article of clothing or adornment visible to all of us but unseen by Madame Zabelle."

He was silent for a moment, and she imagined him surveying the seated medical students, looking for the first object on the list. Sweat pooled under her arms and trickled down the back of her neck. No, that wasn't right. Not students. Townsfolk.

A cricket chirped from somewhere nearby, and Tucia latched on to the sound. She was standing on a makeshift stage in a vacant lot in the middle of farm country. Not in a hospital.

"Madame Zabelle," Huey called to her from among the crowd. Tucia startled.

"Can you see with your mind's eye what object I am pointing at?"

Tucia took a deep breath, forcing the air down her narrowing windpipe. She had to get a hold of herself. She couldn't have another hysterical attack and freeze here onstage.

"Think hard on the object, sir," Huey said to whatever dupe he'd selected from the crowd. "Without use of her eyes, she has only the connection between your minds by which to see it."

After another labored breath, Tucia brought her fingertips to her temples, as Huey had instructed earlier that evening. "Yes. Yes, I can see it."

"Louder, if you please, Madame, so everyone in the crowd may hear you," Huey said, his voice edged with annoyance.

"Yes, I can see it."

"And?"

The list. What was the first object on the list?

"A pair of spectacles," she finally said. A few in the audience gasped. Others muttered in puzzlement.

"And this?" Huey said after moving to a new spot in the crowd.

"A hat."

More murmurs of surprise and scattered applause. Tucia's racing heart began to slow. She could do this. It was just like her days at medical college when the professor would quiz them about the day's lecture. But instead of the bones of the foot or processes of digestion, she was listing off the type of objects one could buy in a Sears, Roebuck & Co. catalog. Watch chain. Handkerchief. Bootlaces.

Huey called out to her again, and she named the next item on the list, tie pin. *Oohs* and *ahhs* and scattered applause followed her response. But before Huey could move on to the next person, she heard someone call, "What kind of tie pin? If she can really read minds, she ought to be able to describe it."

The crowd went silent. And once again she could feel the prickle of their collective gaze. Just like that day in the operating theater.

The patient had been wheeled in and the ether administered. She and the other interns stood to the side of the stage while Dr. Addams presented the case history, peppering them with questions about the upcoming procedure: a *simple*—that had been his word—supravaginal amputation for fibromyomata of the uterus.

Then he'd held up a scalpel and said, "Dr. Hatherley will perform the procedure today."

Tucia neither spoke nor moved. She'd never performed anything more complex than a superficial wound exploration. Dr. Addams knew this well, but continued, "That is, unless you are unable to do so."

At that, the gaggle of onlooking medical students had gone silent. As silent as the crowd of townsfolk was now. Panic surged through her. What was she supposed to do? To say? Tucia fumbled with the buttons at her neck, unable to get enough air.

Huey answered for her, something about the connection between their minds being too weak, but Tucia could no longer focus. Her footing in the here and now felt tenuous. Her heart was again racing, and her muscles tight.

Huey called to her from the audience, "I've another object in my sights, Madame. Is it taking shape in your mind's eye?"

"A scalpel!" she cried, throwing her hands out and backing away. She wouldn't take it. Not this time.

"Surely you jest, Madame." Huey gave a nervous chuckle. "Perhaps it would help if I too focused on the item so that the mental picture is stronger."

His voice reached her as if through a cave, distant and echoing.

"I pray you try again, Madame. What does your powerful and mysterious mind see?"

A sharp, thin laugh escaped her. Her mind wasn't powerful. It was fractured. The list of objects she'd memorized hovered within her grasp, but she feared what else was there too. The scalpel. The gaping wound her own hand had cut. The blood.

She tore off the blindfold and hurried from the stage. The bottom hoop of her crinoline caught on the edge of the last stair, and she was momentarily pinned as murmurs and chortles rose from the crowd. In wrestling the hoop free, she lost her balance and fell facedown onto the ground, her damned skirt ballooning to reveal her underclothes. The audience responded with full-throated laughter as if she were a clown and this was all part of the act.

Tucia pushed herself up from the ground and escaped through the backdrop, the roar of the audience trailing behind her.

14

Tucia avoided looking at the others the following morning when she and Toby arrived at the cook tent for breakfast. She suspected at least one of them had been peeking around the backdrop watching last night, and by now, all would surely know of her disgraceful fall. They'd probably been laughing about it before she and Toby arrived and upping their wagers about how soon she'd leave.

She steered Toby straight to the back table where a vat of oatmeal and a steaming pot of coffee sat. Before she managed to fill their bowls, Darl appeared beside her.

"Heard you took a bit of a tumble yesterday," he said softly.

Tucia closed her eyes and exhaled. Of course they wouldn't make this easy for her.

"Did you get your dollar in too?"

"What?"

"Your wager. About how long I'll last. Cal's got a dollar— maybe more now—on a week." She looked up at him. "Where's your money?"

He hesitated, his dark eyes boring into her. "I ain't got time for such sh—" He stopped, glancing down at Toby. "Foolery. I only wanted to say I'll take a look at them stairs after breakfast. Make sure it weren't the head of a nail or something that caught your dress."

He looked as if he wanted to say more. To apologize for laughing at her costume yesterday. Or to speculate about the wager. Or perhaps only to comment on the weather.

Tucia waited, watching the tip of his tongue skate over his scar, then grew impatient. "You needn't bother with the stairs. I won't be going onstage again."

"I reckon Huey thinks you will be."

"Then that's between him and me." She poured a splash of cream into Toby's bowl, then set down the bottle with a thud.

Darl shrugged and walked back to his waiting breakfast. She hoped he wasn't right. Surely Huey would see she wasn't cut out for the stage.

She set the bowls down at the far end of the table and forced herself to eat, washing the oatmeal down with coffee. Toby took an interminably long time with his breakfast, his attention wandering between every bite, and a fair portion of it ending up in his lap.

At last she gave up waiting. "Two more bites, and then we need to get back to the wagon so you can practice your letters."

Toby stuffed two giant bites into his mouth, and Tucia whisked their bowls away to the wash basin. But they ran into Huey—the very person she'd most wanted to avoid—before they could escape the tent.

"Ah, Tucia," he said, placing an unwelcome hand on her arm and guiding her back to the table.

Last night, she'd fled to her wagon immediately after the act, tearing off her dress and scrubbing the dirt and blood from her scratched palms. Her entire body was shaking, but she refused to cry in front of Toby. The clamor of the show continued, and she welcomed the noise. The fall had been enough to jolt her senses, returning her squarely to the present. The sound of Fanny's dancing and Huey's lecturing kept her there. She fell into a fitful sleep alongside Toby. If Huey had come rapping on her door after the show, she hadn't heard him. Now, however, there was no escaping his censure.

He fetched himself a cup of coffee and, to Tucia's surprise, a cup for her as well, sweetened with a heaping spoonful of sugar. She drank her coffee black and never two cups back-to-back, but she accepted the mug with a polite, if fleeting, smile.

Huey sat down opposite her at the table. The others, she noticed, had ended their conversation and sat toying with their empty cups and bowls, as eager to hear what Huey had to say as she was dreading it.

"Tell me what happened last night, my dear."

Tucia bristled at the patronizing tone of his voice. "I told you, I'm not a performer."

"But you were doing so well in the beginning."

"I . . ." She wasn't about to tell him of her hysterical attacks. But what else could explain the way she'd acted? "I wasn't expecting any questions from the audience, and when the man called out about the tie pin, I . . . I got a little nervous."

"You needn't worry about the audience. When something like that comes up, I will handle it. The important thing is to stick to the script and listen for my cues. Do you think you can do that?"

Again with the patronizing. "The audience knows I'm a fraud."

Huey chuckled. "That's the beauty of show business, my dear. They won't see you as a fraud unless you see yourself that way."

"But I do!" Tucia hadn't meant to voice the words, let alone shout them, but she was still out of sorts from last night. "I can't. I just can't. It will happen again. I know it will."

"It may," Huey said. "And we'll try again. I've never known someone who didn't get over their stage fright eventually. Besides"—he inclined his head toward Toby—"you're a highly motivated woman. I'd venture there's nothing you wouldn't do."

The sweetened coffee curdled in her stomach. He was right. To keep Toby safe and beside her, there was nothing she wouldn't do.

* * *

That afternoon, she and Huey rehearsed the act again. In the daylight, with an empty lot in front of her, Tucia had no trouble running through the list of items. She kept up when Huey cleared his throat and skipped between items, and remained unfazed when he enlisted Al to heckle her.

Night came, and the lot filled. Tucia donned the widow's weeds again. She waited behind the backdrop for her cue, but when it came, she couldn't bring herself to join Huey onstage. It would happen again; she knew it would. Already she could feel her body tensing. And what if this time it was worse? What if she slipped away completely and froze?

Little Al, who was standing beside her, nudged her to go on. But Tucia shook her head. "No, I can't," she whispered. After Huey called for her again, Al sighed and trotted onstage himself. She watched through the break in the backdrop as he whispered in Huey's ear. Huey glared over his shoulder in her direction, then righted his expression and turned back to the audience. "I'm afraid Madame Zabelle has fallen ill. Reading minds and communing with the spirits is taxing work. Only the most sensitive among us possess such powers. It is a gift and a curse. But fear not, we've many more amazing acts lined up for you . . ."

The next morning, Huey slept through breakfast. He'd been surprisingly patient yesterday, but after ruining the act a second time, Tucia didn't expect such treatment again and was grateful he wasn't there. Without sidewalk cracks to count, she'd taken to carrying her pocket watch around in her hand. If she concentrated, she could feel the tiny secondhand pulsing in her palm, keeping her in the present. It served the secondary purpose of occupying her dominant hand, so she was less apt to pluck her hair.

Her hairpulling wasn't just a nervous tic, though that's how the alienist had seen it. Stress and anxiety certainly made it worse, but sometimes Tucia was merely bored. She'd catch herself with her fingers at her scalp, fondling a piece of hair, and it was all she could do not to pluck it. Tension built inside her like steam trapped beneath the lid of a boiling pot. Pulling her hair was the only release. The tension disappeared like steam into the air. But the calmness that followed soon gave way to shame. What kind of a woman plucked out her hair? And all too soon, the cycle began again.

She'd learned over the years having something else in hand helped break that cycle. At least some of the time. So far, the watch was working.

After hurrying Toby through breakfast—she couldn't stomach anything herself—they dropped his bowl in the wash basin and left the tent. They were halfway to their wagon when Tucia realized she'd left her watch on the table. When she returned to retrieve it, she heard the others talking. One of them—Cal, judging by his gravelly voice—said her name. She stopped outside the entry and listened.

"How hard can it be to remember a few dozen words?" Cal said. "Our Al could do it standing on his head."

Someone murmured in assent. Chief? Darl? Tucia's stomach knotted.

They were quiet a moment, and then Fanny said, "Once Huey gets the case-taking jamb up and running, she'll be earning her keep, you'll see."

"You're too trusting, love," Cal said, his voice surprisingly tender.

"I'm not. She's different from the others."

"Different or not," Darl said, "Huey ain't gonna redlight her. Not when he went to all the trouble of gettin' another doc here in the first place."

"He's fond of her, that's for sure," Chief said. "I'd be on latrine duty if I didn't show up onstage. That or worse."

They all chuckled. Then Cal said, "My money stands. As soon as the dope clears from Huey's head, he'll see she ain't worth a lick of trouble."

Tucia couldn't listen anymore. She straightened her shoulders and walked into the tent, hoping her flushed neck and cheeks didn't betray she'd been listening. She grabbed her watch from the table without looking at them and forced herself not to run but walk calmly from the tent.

She spent the day penned up in the wagon, fretting over what they'd said. It was like at the factory, where the other workers had gossiped and conspired against her. Fanny had been the only one to stand up for her. She expected Huey to drag her onto the stage and relentlessly rehearse like yesterday, but she didn't see him until that night when the lot was full and the show about to begin.

When her cue came, Tucia strode onto the stage, determined to prove the others wrong. But the day's worry had frayed her nerves. She was as afraid of failing as she was of having another attack. She winced when Huey blindfolded her and fumbled through the first few items, taking so long to recall the words the audience began to grumble. Her breathing quickened, and a feeling of light-headedness overtook her.

Rationally, she knew that if she slowed her rapid-fire breathing, the balance of oxygen and carbon dioxide in her blood would stabilize and her dizziness diminish. The same way she knew the next item Huey would find among the crowd was a necktie then a brooch then a sun bonnet. But the rational part of her was nothing but a distant echo.

She reached for something to steady herself, stumbling to the side and nearly swooning when her hand met with nothing but air. A moment later, someone was at her side. She clawed off the blindfold. Darl.

He kept his face averted from the audience and shepherded her offstage, his steadying arm around her waist. Huey made up some excuse and followed them backstage.

Once the backdrop closed behind them, Darl led her to a stool beside the properties table while Huey hissed for the others to carry on with the show. Cal hurried out, fiddle in hand. Fanny followed in her tulle dancing costume.

Darl made sure she was safely seated before letting go of her. "You all right?"

Tucia nodded, though the world still felt off-kilter. Some vague part of her missed the solidness of his arm about her waist. "How did you know I was about to fall?"

"Just happened to be peekin' out to check the torchlights," he said.

"Thank—"

A splash of cold water struck the side of her face. She turned and saw Huey standing there with an empty bucket.

Darl wrenched the bucket from his hands. "What the hell was that for?"

"Quiet," Huey said, and then to her, "Pull yourself together and see me after the show."

Both men walked away, though Darl returned soon after and handed her a towel.

"Thanks." Her drenched clothes clung to her skin, and a chill worked its way down her spine. But at least her head was no longer spinning.

He lingered a moment as she dabbed the water from her face. The towel smelled of soap and, faintly, of . . . sawdust. She breathed in again, finding the scent strangely calming.

"Good luck tonight with Huey," he said.

"Will I need it?"

Darl looked away from her. She followed his gaze to Huey's wagon. The large, scrolling words, *The Amazing Adolphus Medicine Company,* were barely visible in the dim backstage light.

"That's the trouble," he said. "With Huey, ya never know what you're gonna get."

15

Tucia waited until the show ended and the lot was quiet before climbing the steps of Huey's wagon. A halo of light slipped around the drawn window curtains, and the murmur of footfalls and clinking metal sounded from within. She knocked softly.

Tucia waited a full minute before he opened the door, her unease growing with each pulse of the pocket watch she carried in her palm. Darl was right. In the few short days since her arrival, she'd already seen how erratic Huey's mood could be. Angry, patient, impatient, grandiose, solicitous, conniving—Tucia wasn't sure which Huey to expect tonight.

If the water he'd thrown in her face was any indication, it was probably the angry side of him. But better that than something else. Darker sides than anger lurked in some men's characters. Darker sides she knew all too well.

To her relief, there was none of the lascivious glint she'd seen in other men's eyes when he finally opened the door. Nor did he appear angry but ushered her in with a smile. A silk brocade housecoat hung over his shirt and trousers. In contrast to the musty, broken-down interior of her wagon, Huey's was well-lit and richly furnished with a lacquered wardrobe, a desk and armchair, and a small tea table with polished stone top. Instead of a bed, there was a plush, velvet divan.

"Please, have a seat, my dear," he said, leaving the door open behind her so a gentle breeze wafted in. She remembered what he said about being a good observer of people and guessed he kept the door open to quiet her unease. It worked, if only partially.

She chose the armchair, and he sat on the far side of the divan closest to the table. Atop the table was a satin handkerchief draped over what she presumed to be a small tea set. But he removed the handkerchief to reveal not a pot and saucer but a silver tray with a small lamp. Beside the lamp was a brightly colored enamel box no bigger than a tin of shoe polish and what looked to be a silver knitting needle.

Huey lit the lamp, then dipped the needle into the box. "I imagine you feel rather foolish after tonight's little stunt."

"I hadn't planned for it to happen. I was breathing too quickly and became lightheaded as a result."

"Another bout of stage fright, then?"

Tucia nodded, watching him tinker over the silver tray. A dark, gummy substance covered the tip of the needle when he withdrew it from the box. He held the tip over the flame.

"And what is the cause of that fright, do you think? Surely you got used to speaking in front of others during your doctor's training."

Tucia shifted, the armchair creaking beneath her weight. "I had some experience, yes."

The dark substance on the tip of the needle had begun to bubble. A faint, sweet smell drifted through the room. Tucia wasn't sure what Huey was doing until he pulled a long, ivory opium pipe from beneath the divan. So this was what Cal meant when he said the dope needed to clear from Huey's head. It also explained why she hadn't seen him all day until showtime.

He worked the opium into a ball and pushed it into a hole in the bowl of the pipe. Then, after reclining on his side, he held the bowl over the flame and inhaled. His eyes fluttered closed, and he gave a contented sigh.

The watch in her palm ticked through several seconds. Had he fallen asleep? She knew opium, like the morphine used in hospitals, came from the unripened seed pods of the poppy plant. A dose of morphine injected beneath the skin could quiet a patient writhing in pain in less than a minute. Though opium was less potent, the lungs, with their vast surface area and natural permeability, ought to allow even quicker absorption.

She was just about to leave when he opened his eyes and offered her the pipe. Reluctantly, Tucia took it. She'd seen drawings of such instruments in newspapers and magazines alongside articles about the scourge of opium. But she'd never actually beheld one. The ivory was engraved with lilies and rambling vines, while the bowl, which rose from the pipe like a doorknob, was fashioned of molded silver. A beautiful object, to be sure, and one that must have cost him dearly.

"Go ahead," he said. "Take a puff."

Tucia nearly dropped the pipe. "What?"

"It helps."

"I don't need—" Tucia stopped. To say she didn't need help was a lie. That was the whole reason she was here, after all, her inability to function in the everyday world. But this—opium— wasn't the solution. She held out the pipe, but Huey didn't take it.

"Have you ever tried it?"

Tucia shook her head.

"Maybe a grain of the morphine you doctors keep on hand in your bag?"

"One-sixth a grain is the standard dose, and no, I've never taken that either. Legion are the number of physicians who've lost their practice to such folly."

Huey laughed. "Ah, but you have no practice to lose."

Tucia laid the pipe on the tray with enough force to make the lamp's light waver. "If this is all you wanted to talk about, then I'll be leaving now, thank you."

"I'm offering you a way out."

"A way out of what?"

"Your pain. Your fears. Your disappointments."

"I'm not in any pain. And as for being afraid, a few more shows and I'm sure—"

Huey waved his hand lazily and lay back against the divan. "I didn't call you in to lie to me. Either you perform or you don't get paid. It's as simple as that. And right now, your debt is moving in the wrong direction. I'm a patient man, Tucia, but not infinitely so." He glanced at the silver tray. "I'm offering you a solution. Take it."

Tucia looked to the open door, then back to the pipe. She tucked away her pocket watch and plucked a strand of hair, twirling it in her fingers. Her professors had warned her and her fellow students about the risk of morphine addiction. It was a lazy, incompetent doctor who reached too quickly for the needle. Medical journals were filled with similar warnings. Of course, they'd been talking about the risk to patients, who were perhaps, on account of their weakened states, predisposed to such addiction.

"You're curious," Huey said.

"I'm not." But she didn't move except to pluck another hair.

Huey picked up the pipe, warmed the bowl over the flame, and took another puff. "It's the ultimate medicine. All those worries in your head—I see them, swirling there behind your eyes—they fall away with a breath. It's as if there's nothing you couldn't do, and yet, you're totally content just to be. Flooded with a sense of quiet happiness." He took one more puff, then laid the pipe down, nudging the tray in her direction. "Tell me, Tucia, when was the last time you were truly happy, truly at peace?"

His eyes drifted shut again, and his breathing slowed. The lines of his face smoothed as if it had never known a frown or furrowed brow. She watched him through the smoky air, pondering his question. When *was* the last time she'd known such repose? When she'd slept without a care? Certainly not since that day in the operating theater. Perhaps long before that.

She let the hairs fall from her fingers and reached for the pipe. What harm could there be in one little puff? Just enough to ease her nerves. To quiet the memories.

A gust of wind rocked the wagon, and a far-off cry sounded through the open door. A coyote pup, perhaps. A kit calling for its mother.

Tucia stopped short and abruptly stood. Dear God, what had she been about to do? It wasn't just her own life at stake, but Toby's too. She left the opium lamp burning and rushed from the wagon. The sweet, alluring smoke trailed behind her, fading slowly into the night.

16

The following afternoon, Tucia went in search of Fanny. Toby shuffled beside her, clutching her skirt. A cold prickle skittered down her arms thinking how close she'd come last night to accepting Huey's pipe. Even in his dope-induced stupor, he'd made it clear if she wasn't performing, she wasn't making money. If she wasn't making money, her debt would never be repaid. Huey wouldn't long abide such a situation. Tucia had to find a way to manage her nerves enough to get through her act. A way that didn't involve opium.

She found Fanny behind the cook tent, standing over a small fire. Beside her was a folding table covered in empty tin boxes, each the size of a matchbook. Without their lids and labels, it took Tucia a moment to realize what the tins were for—Miraculous Corn-busting Salve.

She knelt beside Toby and gently pried her skirt from his grasp. "Can you go pick Mama some flowers?" she said, pointing to the nearby field. "But don't go any farther than that bush. You see it?"

He nodded and tottered away. They'd had another row that morning over his boots. He'd put them on the wrong feet and thrown a fit when she tried to switch them. At last, Tucia had conceded. Better to have his shoes on backward than no shoes at all.

Now, his straight-legged gait was all the more lurching. He stumbled every few steps, yet continued on, undeterred and smiling.

"Be careful of bees," she called after him. "And thistle."

Tucia watched him a moment longer, then turned to find Fanny frowning down at her.

"You coddle that boy too much, *schatz.*"

Tucia frowned too. This woman sure was nosy. "He's not like other boys."

"That doesn't mean you've got to keep him in your shadow all day long."

"He's got a weak heart and delicate immune system."

"Well, they're not made any stronger by keeping him cooped up all the time."

"I'm the doctor here, thank you very much."

Fanny's expression softened. "You're right. I don't know anything about heart or immunity troubles. But I do know about being different. Sometimes we just want to be left alone to be ourselves."

"I do let him be."

"He's a little boy. Let him be a little boy."

Tucia followed her gaze to the field. Toby stood amid a bunch of plumegrass, running his hands over their feathery seed heads. Was Fanny right? Had Tucia's own anxieties spilled over into Toby and how she treated him?

"I didn't come to talk about my son."

"I don't suppose you came to help either."

"Help with what?"

Fanny gestured to the table of empty tins.

"Oh."

"Here." Fanny nestled a steel pail amid the low flames of the fire, then handed Tucia a quart jar filled with a clear jellylike substance. "Add that to the bucket."

"What is it?"

"Vaseline."

Tucia looked around for a spoon. Not seeing one, she sighed, slipped the watch she was carrying into her pocket, and rolled up her sleeves. "I wanted to ask you about stage fright."

"What makes you think I know about that?"

"The way you dance. Ballet, is it called?" Tucia scooped a palmful of Vaseline from the jar and flung it into the pail. "You must have been doing it your whole life to be that good."

Fanny grabbed another jar of Vaseline and joined Tucia at the fire. "Yes, ballet. I danced my first *pas seul* when I was four. My mother had been a prima ballerina in Wien before we came to America. I could have been a prima too. If it wasn't for my size." She dove her thick fingers into the jelly and scooped out a large glob. She plunked it into the pail and sighed. "*Tja*, that was a long time ago."

"When did you come to America?"

"I was five."

"And when did you . . . er . . ."

"Become this?" Her lips flattened, and she made an upward gesture. "I was the same size as other girls until about nine. Then, Lord knows what happened."

"Some physicians speculate that it's due to a malfunction of the pituitary body in the brain. Others suspect the thymus gland."

"A problem with my brain?"

"The brain does so much more than help us think. It controls our breathing and our reflexive movements like blinking and swallowing. It houses our sensory centers and helps with balance. The pituitary body, well, we still don't fully know what role it plays in our physiology, but it's believed to be connected to the central nervous system and—"

"So I've got a problem with my brain *and* my nerves."

Tucia frowned. She wasn't explaining it well. "No. I only mean to say . . ." She glanced across the field at Toby. He'd found a yellow wildflower and was pulling off its petals one by one the way she plucked out her hair. "When I had my son, there were plenty who whispered that his condition was God punishing me for my sins. But I believe someday we'll discover it's just a difference of biology. Not the act of a vindictive God."

Even the doctor that delivered Toby had offhandedly remarked that such children were born to mothers with loose morals or those who overtaxed their minds. His words cut deep, despite their lack of scientific validity. Besides, what of the father's morals? If anything, he was to blame. But to accept that, she had to see Toby as some sort of punishment. And Tucia did not.

"I don't know if anyone ever said such things to you, about your condition, that is. But if they did, they were wrong."

Fanny was quiet for a minute, a smile working its way onto her face. She took their empty jars and gave Tucia a rag to wipe her hands. The jelly in the pail had begun to liquefy, hissing and popping. Fanny handed her a long stick. "You stir while I add the rest of the ingredients."

Tucia watched as she added camphor gum, menthol crystals, oil of eucalyptus, and turpentine. Then she sprinkled in a red powder.

"What's that?" Tucia asked.

"Capsicum. Red pepper."

"Won't that make the salve burn?"

"That's the point. Yokels think if it doesn't burn, it's not working."

Tucia shook her head.

"Keep stirring," Fanny said. "Now, about this stage fright business. Here's my best advice: The surest way to avoid stage fright is not to go onstage at all. Take your boy and get as far away from here as you can."

Tucia looked over her shoulder at the wagon and stage and rutted dirt road beyond the lot. If only it were that easy. "Any other advice? What do you do?"

"Me? I'm more comfortable on the stage than I am off it." Fanny grabbed a knife and began shaving paraffin into the bubbling mixture. "Habit, I guess. The more times you do something, the more confident you get."

Tucia sighed. How could she make a habit of something she couldn't do once? She switched the stir stick to her left hand and reached for her hair. Fanny intercepted her hand, but instead of smacking it away as Tucia's stepmother had often done, she wrapped it in her own and brought it gently back to Tucia's side.

"What are you thinking about right before you go on for your act?"

"How I don't want to mess up again."

"And when you're onstage?"

Tucia hesitated. "I have trouble keeping my focus. My mind slips back into . . . unpleasant memories."

Fanny nodded as if she, too, had memories she'd just as soon forget. "Here's what you must do. First, stop pulling out your hair. Can you imagine the wig Huey will put you in if you go bald?"

Tucia managed a small laugh. Stopping wasn't that easy, but she could tell Fanny meant well.

"Second, breathe. Nice and slow. That's a trick my mother taught me. Don't think about what's going to happen when you get up onstage. Try not to think at all. That's hard for you know-it-all types, but try. Then, when you go out there, before you climb up to the stage, get a good look at the audience. It's the only time the light won't be blinding you. You'll see that they're just everyday people. And they *want* to believe in what you're telling them." She tossed in the last of the paraffin, then took over stirring. "Once you're up onstage, you can't let your mind wander all over the place. Me, I'm only ever thinking of two things: the dance step I'm about to take, and the one after. That's it. The audience could be on fire, and I wouldn't notice." She stopped stirring long enough to point. "Fetch that kettle, will you?"

Tucia grabbed the large kettle resting beside the table. "I've tried focusing on the list of words Huey gave me. It doesn't work. I . . . I . . ." Even now, she could feel her chest tightening.

Fanny took the kettle and set it on the ground beside the fire. Using her apron as an oven mitt, she grabbed the lip of the pail, heaved it off the fire, and poured the liquid salve into the kettle.

Then she returned the bucket—still about half full—to the fire. "I'll keep stirring. You fill."

Tucia grabbed the kettle and began filling the small tins. The salve smelled faintly minty, its color shifting from clear to an opaque yellowish-white as it cooled.

"Try only thinking about the first two words on the list," Fanny said, refilling the kettle for her after it was empty. "And then the next two and so on as the act goes on. And I mean really think on them. I knew a dancer once who broke her ankle. When she got back on her points two months later, she knew the dance better than anyone else in the entire company. Didn't miss a step. How? She'd been practicing in her mind."

Tucia thought about Fanny's words as she filled the remainder of the tins. Breathe, get a good look at the audience, only focus on the very next thing she had to say—it seemed too simple to work. But then, hadn't she lectured Fanny about the wonders of the brain? The alienist she'd seen had diagnosed Tucia as having a nervous organization and an innate frailty on account of her sex. But what if her hysterical attacks were more like a sickness of the brain, something that could infect anyone under the right circumstances? Could these mind tricks Fanny suggested alleviate that sickness the way quinine reduced a fever? It seemed worth a shot.

"Anything else?"

"I knew a woman in my circus days who swore by this concoction of celery juice, coca, ground kola nuts, viburnum bark, and aromatics. She downed that nasty stuff every night before a show. Guess you could try that too."

That sounded about as useful as the corn grease they'd mixed up. If anything, the stimulating effects of the kola nuts and coca would make her anxiety worse. She was about to say so when her mind snagged on something else Fanny had said. "You were in the circus?"

The Giant's Story

Franziska Fink's parents could not explain it. She'd been such a pretty, petite girl and one of the best dancers in the company. She still danced well; it was true. But one couldn't dance the part of Giselle or the sylph if she towered over her partner and caused his arms to buckle when he lifted her for a grand jeté.

There *had* been that Russian dancer—a man of extraordinary stature—who'd toured with the company in Belgium before Franziska was born. Her father nurtured a secret jealousy of the man, and when Franziska wouldn't stop growing, that jealousy soured into suspicion, despite the many years and wide ocean now separating them. He never voiced his suspicions to Franziska's mother—who could have assured him she'd already been pregnant two months before the Russian's arrival—and instead took his anger out on his daughter, refusing her but one meal a day and relegating her to the back row of the ensemble.

Franziska, who'd dreamed of becoming a prima ballerina since her first chassé across the stage, couldn't explain her size any better than her parents. Day to day, she did what she'd always done—stretch, rehearse, perform. But then she'd catch a glimpse of a stranger in a mirror or stand beside a fellow dancer and find herself a head taller when only last season they'd stood nose to nose.

Different parts of her grew faster than others. Her hands and feet were enormous, while her chest remained flat. Her forehead had lengthened, and jaw squared. Ugly, she overheard her father say of her.

Franziska tried to forget what she'd heard. One didn't need a pretty face to be a prima ballerina. But one couldn't be too big. So she ignored her hunger pangs and took to sleeping on the floor, her head flush against the wall and a heavy sandbag at her feet, as if in meeting resistance, her bones might cease to grow.

They did not.

Still, Franziska practiced hard and laughed freely. She knew no other way to be.

By her fifteenth year, when she ought to have been dancing center stage, Franziska was too large even for the far back corner of the ensemble, and her father's chiding had grown commensurately more vicious.

When the calling card of J. S. Blum, of Danbury, Blum and Co. Circus, arrived for her backstage, Franziska accepted the invitation scrawled across the back to meet for tea the following afternoon.

Her life, until that moment, had largely been a cloistered one, filled with hotels, theaters, private train cars, and little else. Such was the life of a dancer. Especially when one's father went to great lengths to hide the object of his shame. And as she walked the five city blocks to the tearoom, Franziska realized she'd outgrown not only the ballet but common society as well. Not a single passerby—man or woman—could match her height. She was trailed by whispers and stares. A newsboy ran up to her and poked her legs, expecting wooden stilts instead of bone and muscle.

Franziska almost turned around and hurried back to the theater. Many times after, she'd wished she had.

Instead, at a prominent table in the tearoom, Mr. Blum regaled her with stories of the circus. *He* wasn't ashamed to be seen with her. On the contrary, he remarked several times what a singular, lovely woman she was. He praised her talent and promised Franziska her own leading act in his show.

And so, Franziska Fink became Fanny the Fantastic, trading in one dream for another. The theater for the circus big top. And for a short while, that dream came true. She danced to great applause alongside lion tamers and tightrope walkers and flying trapeze men.

But soon, she was relegated to the sideshow, where rowdies and drunkards paid an extra dime to watch her show off her long legs and lacy stockings. When Fanny complained of the men's rude talk and hooting and begged to return to the big top, Mr. Blum gave her an ultimatum: perform as the sideshow freak she was or leave.

Leave and go where? Her parents and their company would never take her back. And what would she do? Fanny the Fantastic could dance and sew and nothing more, Mr. Blum was quick to remind her. She might find honest work as a seamstress or milliner's assistant, but alas—and here he sighed dramatically—who would take on a woman of her size? No, she belonged here and nowhere else.

Fanny believed him.

Still, she practiced hard and laughed freely, even as her heart was breaking and her dream was dying. She had a single friend, a fellow immigrant named Lena, who swallowed swords and fire. Lena had the beautiful face and comely figure of the big-top starlets, but her left arm had been shriveled since birth, so she too was relegated to the sideshow.

Sometimes, when the act before Fanny's was running long, she'd slip out of the bawdy tent and sneak off to watch Lena perform. Each time Lena opened her mouth—her smooth, plump lips painted red—and slipped a flaming torch or sharp-edge blade down her throat, Fanny would wince and hold her breath. The tiniest misstep, and she'd be dead. Not until the act was over and the audience applauding could Fanny fully breathe again.

But Fanny wasn't the only one who cut out between acts to watch Lena perform. Bruno, one of the circus strongmen, could often be found hovering at the edge of the crowd too. Arms crossed and face screwed into a scowl, he watched not with concern or awe. He watched only to be sure Lena didn't let any of the rowdy men who'd bellied up to the stage touch her.

Why Lena thought that was love, Fanny never knew.

One day a musician joined the troupe. At first, Fanny paid him little mind. She'd learned as well as the others to be mistrustful and aloof. But one day as she was laughing at something Lena said, she caught the musician staring at her from across the cook tent. He was half Fanny's height, on account of his bowed legs, with a pronounced nose and kind gray eyes.

A few days later, he asked to sit at her table. With only Lena and, regrettably, Bruno seated there, there was plenty of room.

He sat beside her the next day too. And the next.

He wasn't much of a conversationalist, but his eyes said enough. She wasn't a giant to him but a woman, plain and simple. And even though Fanny's eyes still strayed to Lena, she enjoyed his company too. They'd talk—when Fanny could loosen his tongue—about quitting the circus and starting their own traveling review show. Lena, of course, would come too. But not Bruno.

Though Fanny didn't practice so hard these days, she still found things to laugh about. And she thought the musician's idea to leave the circus was just that—a lark, something to laugh and dream about before turning back to reality.

But they did leave. And when they did, there were three of them—her, the musician, and a newborn baby boy.

17

That night before the show, Huey offered to light his pipe for Tucia again, promising a small puff would melt away her fears. Though Tucia believed him, her convictions hadn't changed. He scoffed at her refusal, reminding her how thin she'd worn his patience.

The lot filled with a boisterous crowd, and the show began. At first, Tucia was calm, even smug. With Fanny's tricks, she'd prove to Huey and the rest of them she could pull her weight.

It wasn't just the tricks Fanny suggested but the story she'd told as well. Tucia wasn't the only one with shattered dreams. She still couldn't understand why, with all their talent, Fanny and Cal had come to work for Huey after leaving the circus. But whatever their reasons, for once, Tucia didn't feel so alone.

For good measure, she'd tied her pocket watch flush against her wrist with a length of ribbon so she could feel its gentle thrum. But as her act neared, a familiar pressure built in her chest.

What if Fanny's tricks didn't work? What if she failed again? What if she had a complete hysterical attack in front of all these people? No, she couldn't do this. She couldn't go on.

Chief's act was wrapping up. Another minute or two and Huey would call her onstage. What had Fanny told her? Her brain was turning to molasses again. Tucia stepped back from the break in the curtain. Before she could turn around and escape, she felt a hand on her back. A huge, thick, soft hand.

"Are you breathing?" Fanny asked from behind her. She began to rub slow circles over Tucia's back.

No one had touched Tucia like that since she was a girl, and her first impulse was to pull away. But Fanny kept rubbing, slow, steady, and Tucia started to relax. To breathe.

Her mind cleared. The pressure in her chest eased.

When Chief pushed through the backdrop, an echo of her old worries surfaced. She was up next.

"Remember," Fanny whispered. "Get one good look at the audience, then focus all your attention on the first words on your list." Before Tucia had time to argue, Fanny pushed her through the slit in the backdrop.

Tucia stumbled forward, blinking in the sudden light. Her eyes adjusted, and she glimpsed the crowd before ascending the stairs to the stage. Most of the locals still wore their work clothes— mud-stained overalls and cottonade dresses. Some were barefoot. Everyday people, like Fanny had said. Not one looked like the haughty medical students who'd crowded into the operating room that day.

She climbed the steps onto the stage and was once again blinded by the pan torches' flickering light. She pictured Huey's list in her mind, clinging to the first two objects—spectacles and a hat—as he tied the blindfold over her eyes.

"There are a few yokels here who saw yesterday's show," he whispered into her ear. "Start with number eight on the list so they don't get suspicious. And for God's sake, keep your wits about you for once."

As he hopped down from the stage, a wave of panic struck her. Her stomach twisted, and her skin grew sticky with sweat. She was ready to call out spectacles, not jump to halfway down the list. If she let go of the words she had, could she conjure the others?

Already her mind had the quality of the corn-busting salve she'd cooked earlier, clear at first, but quickly clouding as it set.

Huey called out to her from the crowd, but the only objects she could think of were the first two. That day in the operating theater, she'd known exactly what to do, had known every step of the procedure the way she knew every word on Huey's list. Dr. Mary A. Dixon Jones had successfully performed a panhysterectomy for uterine fibroids only a few years before—the first in America—and Tucia had put the case to memory. Performing it on a live patient in front of a gaggle of onlookers, however, had been entirely different from reading about the procedure in a textbook or hearing a surgeon's lecture. Not even her time spent with cadavers had prepared her for the feel of cutting into live human flesh. And instead of a *simple* case of fibromyomota, she'd opened up the woman's abdomen to find far more extensive disease—a web of adhesions, a strange brown cyst on the right ovary, and an apple-sized lesion protruding from the uterus.

Huey called to her again, his clipped voice reeling her back to the present. She felt the watch pulse against her wrist and focused on the sensation. Her heart slowed to match its rhythm. Spectacles were the first item on the list. Then Hat. Tucia remembered what Fanny had said about the woman who'd practiced dancing entirely in her head and imagined herself going through the list, shouting out each item to an awestruck crowd. Watch chain, handkerchief, bootlaces, tie pin, necktie.

"Brooch!" she shouted, just as she heard Huey begin offering apologies to the crowd. A few gasps and a trickle of applause sounded. Tucia did her best to ignore the noise, focusing instead on the tiny vibration of her watch and the next item Huey would look for in the crowd. She made it all the way through the rest of the list with little more than a moment's hesitation. She even had the wherewithal to jump back to the beginning when Huey pressed on.

When at last he said they must stop—to the grumbling of the

crowd—and carry on with the show, Tucia pried the blindfold from her eyes. She'd done it. Whether it was the steady tick of the watch or Fanny's tricks or some combination of both, she'd done it!

She squinted through the bright lights at the applauding crowd, so relieved she forgot to bow or smile. Then, almost giddy with exuberance, she hurried from the stage, her only care not to trip on the way down the stairs.

18

The next night, Tucia battled with her nerves again. But Fanny's advice, along with Tucia's trusty pocket watch, helped her win the battle again. And again.

After she went three straight days without flubbing her act, Huey gave her more to memorize. Not just new words but new cues to add specificity. If he said, "Can you tell me what this gentleman has?" she knew to add gold to whatever item was next on the list—gold ring, gold watch chain. The *g* in gentleman (or goodly lady if it were a woman) was the cue. If he said, "Can you *see* what this man has?" the object in question was silver. If Huey called the local a "fine" man or woman, the object was made of fur.

Like the initial list of words, Tucia had no trouble memorizing the cues. The first night she worried all the extra pieces would derail her careful routine. But she found she need only break her concentration momentarily to listen for the added cue. If anything, the heightened complexity helped keep her mind off other things.

Audiences delighted in the act and grew in size. But after a few more days, Huey declared medicine sales were down, and the town had dried up. They packed up the stage and loaded the wagons and buckboard.

It was strange to see the lot empty, the trampled ground a vast footprint in the field. In a few days' time, the weeds and grass would grow back and it would be as if the wagons and stage had never been there at all. They'd stayed a little over a week and a half, but it seemed to Tucia much longer. And yet too quick to be moving on.

She'd only just come to know their acts were all ballyhoo and when Al said they were running low on corn punk, he meant they needed to cook up more of the Miraculous Corn-busting Salve. A squawker was a complaining customer. The burr or nuts were expenses and velvet the profit. A red one was a night where they'd done good business, usually due to a push, or large crowd.

There was so much more to learn if she and Toby were to get by, but today she was looking forward to a carefree day of travel.

Everyone climbed into their respective conveyances—Huey taking the reins of his own wagon, Chief, the supply wagon, and the Trouts, the buckboard. That left Darl to drive her wagon. He climbed into the box, sandwiching Toby between them. With a click of his tongue and shake of the reins, he urged the mules into an amble.

Toby clapped as the wagon lurched forward and tried to make the same sound with his tongue. It came out more like a smacking noise than a click, but Darl gave him an encouraging nod.

Darl had spent the better part of the morning dismantling the stage, and when Tucia leaned closer, righting Toby's lopsided hat, she expected to smell the ripe scent of his labor. Instead, she caught only the whiff of soap, linseed oil, and wood. Much like the towel he'd handed her that night backstage.

A sideways glance revealed he wore a fresh shirt and collar. They stood in strange contrast to the days' worth of dark stubble covering his jaw and the dusty hat pulled low over his brow.

"They're good at following, these two," he said, and it took Tucia a moment to realize he was talking about the mules. "Shouldn't give you much trouble."

"Me?"

"When you're at the reins." He turned toward her and raised his chin so his dark eyes met hers. "You do know how to drive, don't you?"

Tucia straightened and looked away, giving her head a reluctant shake. She'd ridden a bit as a girl and knew the basics of horsemanship. But she'd never driven so much as a jaunty two-person buggy, let alone a hulking wagon pulled by a team of mules.

Darl *humph*ed as if he wasn't surprised. She hoped that would be the end of it. But once they reached a straight stretch of road, he handed her the reins.

In that spare, straightforward way of speaking of his, he explained the various parts of the mules' harness and how to handle the reins. Toby clamored for a turn, too, and Darl obliged him a lesson, pulling him onto his lap and working the reins together.

When Toby grew tired of the sport, he settled between them again, and the responsibility of driving fell back to her. Over the next few hours, when deep ruts or wide holes presented themselves in the road, Darl coached her how to steer the mules around them. Her first few attempts failed miserably, and she could hear their things clanking to the floor inside the wagon as it jerked and shuddered.

Once, after slipping into a particularly deep rut, the wagon lurched so badly Toby nearly flew off the bench. She dropped the reins and grabbed him. Darl lunged, reaching over the dash and snatching the reins before they slipped away. He guided the wagon out of the rut before handing them back to her.

"Don't let go of these," he said, his voice stern but not unkind. "If you lose control of the wagon, you're both likely to get hurt."

"Thank you. I . . . er . . . panicked."

"Don't panic. The animals can sense it."

Easy for him to say. It wasn't his son who almost toppled to the ground. And yet, she had no doubt his words were true. They called to mind something a professor had said. *People will come to you both sick and afraid. It does no good if you're afraid too. They sense your fear, and it will compound their own, making their illness even more difficult to treat.*

At the time, she'd blithely filed his words away as if fear and panic were something knowledge alone could vanquish. As if it were as easy to shed as one's coat or gloves.

"What if I am panicked, though?" she blurted out.

Darl was quiet for a minute. "Practice until you're not."

"That doesn't help much in the moment."

"Life ain't about a single moment."

Tucia worried the reins, one hand reaching toward her hair before she caught herself. Darl was wrong. Everything for her pivoted around that single moment in the operating theater. Perhaps life had not yet dealt him such a moment. Perhaps it never would. When you traveled around hoisting backdrops and fixing loose stage boards, what real harm could come to you?

"Careful with those reins," he said. "They gotta last us at least until the next town."

She loosened her grip, only belatedly registering his joke, and smiled in spite of herself.

Darl pointed to another large pit ahead in the road, reminding her how to steer around it. This time, she managed not to let go of the reins.

That evening, their caravan pulled off to the side of the road and they set up camp for the night. They didn't bother with the cook tent but ate a simple meal of dried meat and fried cornmeal around the fire. Toby delighted in the sizzling sound the corn dodgers made when they were tossed into the pork grease and scarfed down three of them once they'd cooled enough to eat.

Chief sat beside them, dazzling Toby and Al with the tiny lasso he'd made out of a length of twine. He spun the twine over his head with exaggerated show, then cast the loop end toward the salt shaker Cal had set down at his feet. To Tucia's surprise, it landed perfectly around the shaker. Chief cinched the loop and flicked his wrist, drawing both the lasso and salt into his hand.

Both boys laughed, and Toby shouted, "Again!"

But Cal stood and snatched back the shaker. "Last time you played around with that string we had to go without salt for a week." A smile tugged at his lips as he spoke, though, and when he sat back down, he tossed Chief the pepper. "Use this instead."

Chief demonstrated the trick again, then handed off the tiny lasso for the boys to try.

"Where did you learn to do that?" Tucia asked him.

"My father's ranch."

"Oh," she said, unable to hide the surprise in her voice.

"Thought all of us grew up hunting buffalo, did ya?"

"Well, I . . ." Tucia knew the buffalo were gone and Indians now lived on reservations, but beyond that, she had no idea about their lives. "Are you really a chief?"

He laughed, but it was a breathy, mirthless sound. "Are you really a mind reader?"

No more than she really was a doctor, but Tucia didn't say so. "Then, if you're not Chief Big Sky, what's your name?" She glanced sideways at him, then quickly away, embarrassed it hadn't occurred to her to ask before.

He paused a moment before answering. "Lawrence Hiya."

"That's your Indian name?"

"No."

When he didn't say anything else, Tucia turned to Toby, who was watching Al try his luck with the lasso. "You hear that, darling? This is Mr. Hiya. Be sure you call him that and not 'Chief' as Mr. Huey does."

Toby nodded.

She wanted to ask Lawrence more about his life—where he was from, what tribe he belonged to—but Lawrence had already pulled out a small, leather-bound notebook from his pocket and turned his attention to its pages. She'd seen him with the notebook before, scrawling something with the nub of a pencil. More questions fluttered to her mind. What was he writing and to whom? His family? A sweetheart? Why had he decided to join Huey's medicine show in the first place?

She assumed they'd all joined for the good money and easy life. Though that easy life was shaping up to be a lot more work than she'd expected. Adventure, then?

She glanced from Lawrence to Cal and Fanny to Darl. Something told her it wasn't just greed or slothfulness or thrills. They, too, had secrets.

19

After another day of bumpy travel, the troupe split. Tucia, Huey, and Toby took his wagon and headed north to the county seat while the others continued west to the town where they'd stage the next show. In the city, Huey took Tucia to register her license so she could legally practice medicine here. It felt strange after so long to make the application. Not to mention dishonest. She half expected the clerk to refuse her. He eyed her and her diploma with mild suspicion, saying only, "A lady doctor, aye?" Then, with a shrug, he wrote out the license. Huey paid him the fee, and they were back in the wagon traveling by moonlight well into the night until they arrived at the camp the others had set up.

Tucia woke in the morning to the clang of the breakfast bell, stiff from so much travel and groggy from too little sleep. She hurriedly dressed and helped Toby to do the same. When they stumbled from the wagon, she saw the camp for the first time in the morning light.

They were situated on a bald patch of earth only a stone's throw from a tiny train station. Farther on rose a few brick and wood buildings that formed the heart of town, and above that a rusted water tower. In the other direction stretched the narrow dirt road they'd arrived on, fringed by fields and a scattering of trees. Their horses and mules had found a small patch of reeds and clover that banked a small creek.

The camp itself looked little different from their roadside stops. Neither the cook tent nor the Trouts' large house tent had been unpacked but instead still sat furled on the dusty ground. The stage had not been erected either. The wooden poles that served as scaffolding for the backdrop lay in a heap alongside a few crates of medicine.

Tucia thought she recalled Huey saying they would begin performing tonight. The reason they'd split up, as she'd understood it, was so the others could prepare the camp. Perhaps she'd been mistaken. She certainly wouldn't mind a day or two's rest.

As she and Toby shuffled toward the cook fire, still rubbing the sleep from their eyes, Tucia heard Huey's voice raised in anger and looked up.

"I gave you one task! One simple task. Get the goddamn reader."

"We tried," Cal said, heaving a skillet of sizzling salt pork off the fire. "It's a closed town."

"'We'?" Huey turned to Darl, who stood with his arms crossed, leaning against the side of the buckboard. "You sent a cripple to get it?"

Darl shrugged. "You know I don't deal with the law."

Huey threw up his arms and huffed.

Tucia seated herself on an upturned crate beside Fanny. She lifted Toby onto her lap, but he wiggled away to sit beside Al. She listened a moment while Huey continued to rant, then turned to Fanny and whispered, "What's going on?"

"Can't get a reader here."

"A reader?"

"A license. Most towns require them to sell medicine."

"Who issues the license?"

"That's the first thing you've got to find out when you get to a new place. Sometimes it's the mayor. Sometimes the town clerk. Here, it's the sheriff, and he won't budge."

"Why?" Tucia asked, though she could think of several reasons herself, including that the medicine they sold was entirely fake.

Fanny only shrugged.

Huey continued to interrogate Cal, asking what the sheriff said and if he'd slipped him any coconuts—which Tucia gathered meant a bribe. Cal replied he had, and the sheriff still didn't budge.

"What now?" Tucia whispered to Fanny.

"Pack up and move on."

Tucia groaned. She hated the idea of another day's travel.

"You think it's bad for you? Imagine how I feel in the buckboard. My knees about hit my chin every time we go over a bump."

Tucia laughed, envisioning poor Fanny having to fold herself up to fit her legs inside. The sound drew Huey's attention. His violet eyes fixed her with a skin-prickling intensity. Tucia stopped laughing. After a moment, he cocked his head and smiled.

"Don't pack up," he said. Though he wasn't addressing her in particular, his eyes never left her face. "I have an idea."

Fifteen minutes later, Tucia and Toby were walking alongside Huey toward town. Magpies perched on the telegraph wire that ran alongside the road, squawking as they passed. The smell of salt pork and biscuits trailed after them, growing ever fainter, and her stomach rumbled. Huey had shooed her back to her wagon to change into her plainest dress—the grease-stained and threadbare suit she'd worn at the factory—without sparing her a moment for breakfast.

He, too, had tempered his flamboyant style, wearing a simple morning coat and mismatched trousers. He walked at a clipped pace, his gaze straight ahead, oblivious to Tucia and Toby's struggle to keep up. Despite its modest size and the early hour, the town was bustling. And yet, unlike city folk who seemed in a constant rush, the townspeople strolled in and out of the bank, the post office, the dry goods store with unhurried purpose. The buggies and wagons slowed to let people cross the road, and, despite her bedraggled appearance, men tipped their hats and yielded the plankboard sidewalk to her.

It took less than five minutes to traverse the length of the town. Beyond lay a scattering of houses, two spired churches, and a run-down saloon. They stopped across the street from a small square building with barred windows and a sign over the door that read, SHERIFF.

Huey turned to them. "I'll do the talking."

"You think you'll have better luck than Cal at getting a license?"

"Not me. Us." He reached up and, before Tucia fully realized what he was doing, repinned her hat so it sat slightly askew.

Tucia pulled away and felt along her head. He'd exposed one of the bald patches she'd been careful to cover.

"No, don't touch it," he said. "And take off the hair switch too."

Tucia's cheeks flamed, but she did as she was told lest he yank it off himself. As she carefully rolled the hair and slipped it into her pocket, Huey bent down and scooped up a palmful of dirt. To Tucia's horror, he smeared the dirt across Toby's cheek.

"What are you doing?" Tucia said, tugging the hankie from her sleeve.

Huey didn't answer. Before she could wipe away the dirt, he took hold of both their hands and tugged them across the street and into the sheriff's office.

It was cool inside and poorly lit, with only a single lamp hanging overhead. The twined smells of must, chewing tobacco, and urine made her wince. She guessed the two jail cells sectioned off with thick, rusty bars at the back of the room were at least partly to blame for the stench.

"Can I help you?" a middle-aged man said. He lounged behind a large desk to the left of the door and didn't bother to get up.

"I hope so, good sir," Huey said. "Are you the sheriff of this fine town?"

"I am."

"I'd be most obliged for a moment of your time. May we sit?" Huey gestured to the two ladder-back chairs in front of the desk. The sheriff nodded. Huey sat in one and Tucia the other. She pulled Toby onto her lap and tried again to wipe the dirt from his cheek, but Huey batted away her hand while the sheriff wasn't looking.

"My name is Mr. Corner, sir," Huey said. "And this is my wife and child."

Tucia turned to him and gaped, but Huey continued. "I run a medicine business. Nothing fancy, mind you. Simple, time-honored remedies that help with those pesky ailments so many decent folk suffer from."

The sheriff crossed his arms and shot a stream of tobacco out the corner of his mouth into a spittoon beside his desk. "We don't allow no quack doctors and circus types here."

"Nor, indeed, should you. A godly town like this only remains so because men like you enforce standards of decency. Why, we owe you a debt of thanks for that. Wouldn't you agree, my dear?"

Huey looked at her expectantly. Tucia sat befuddled, glancing between him and the sheriff. How transformed Huey was. His rich voice had taken on a thin, folksy quality. And he sat in such a way that made him seem even smaller than his true size.

His foot slid next to hers, and he pressed down on her toes until Tucia winced and nodded. The compliment seemed to please the sheriff, for he uncrossed his arms and leaned back in his chair.

"We've encountered many such quacks and hambones as you described," Huey said. "Deplorable, the lot of them. Not an honest bone in their bodies. I assure you, good sir, I am no such man."

"That so?"

"I am but a lowly salesman, sir. My wife, you see, is no great beauty. Our son, alas, a hopeless idiot. We profit little from what we sell and do it only for the greater good it brings to others."

Tucia's arms tightened around Toby. She turned and glared at Huey. "Toby is not an—"

Huey stomped down harder on her toes and said over her to

the sheriff. "A mother's love. As pure as it is unreasoning." Both men chuckled while anger burned through Tucia's veins.

"A gimp came by yesterday asking about a license," the sheriff said. "He with you?"

"Yes. He arrived ahead of us and took it upon himself to see you. Quite without my leave, I assure you. A bit of a simpleton, too, I'm afraid. But a virtuoso on the fiddle."

The sheriff frowned, and Huey quickly added, "We play only hymns, of course. Nothing vulgar. We're a family show, after all."

"A family show?"

"Yes, sir. All the entertainment is of a perfectly harmless and irreproachable character."

The sheriff spat again, then leaned forward, folding his hands on the desk. "You seem like a straight enough fella. And I tell you, we've had the worse sort of folk come through. Hucksters pretending to be doctors and princes and Quakers and old Indian scouts. Not to mention the freaks they bring with them. But a rule's a rule, and we don't give licenses to no one."

Huey rose. "I quite understand, sir. We won't take up any more of your time."

He eyed her askance and jerked his head toward the door.

They were leaving? Without a license? She hadn't known Huey long, but he didn't seem like the type who took well to being told no. Then again, what could they do? Besides, if the rest of the town were as gruff as the sheriff, she'd just as soon quit the place anyway.

She slid Toby off her lap and stood. Huey stepped between them and hoisted Toby into his arms. "Don't worry, dear," he said to her. "I needn't any dinner today. Give it to our son."

"I'm not your son," Toby said. "My father's dead."

Huey clapped a hand over Toby's mouth and gave a thin laugh. "His feeble little mind gets rather mixed up when he's hungry," he told the sheriff. "We haven't had a proper meal for going on five days."

Feeble little mind? How dare he! Tucia opened her mouth, a

flood of angry words ready on her tongue, but Huey waved her off and continued, "Don't worry about me. I'll be fine going without dinner again. I'm sure we'll work in the next town." He turned to the sheriff. "That is, unless this good sir can find it in his heart to give an honest man and his pitiable family a break."

The sheriff's lips flattened, and he sighed. "One show. And if it ain't as wholesome as you say, I'll escort you out of town myself. At gunpoint."

Huey dropped Toby from his arms and shook the sheriff's hand. "Thank you. There's a bottle of my special elixir with your name on it, Sheriff, if you come out tonight."

"I'll be there," he said, more warning than friendliness in his voice as he scrawled out a license on a slip of paper.

Huey hurried Tucia and Toby from the building the minute the sheriff handed over the paper. Once they were outside, Huey straightened, brushing off his morning coat with a self-satisfied air, and started back toward camp. Tucia let him go, kneeling and wiping the dirt from Toby's face.

"He's not my father."

"I know, darling. Don't you listen to a word he says." She scooped him up in her arms and started after Huey. They caught up with him halfway through town, but Tucia held back her fury until they'd passed the train station and their camp was in view.

She set Toby down and grabbed Huey's arm, waiting until Toby was several steps ahead of them before speaking. "What kind of a farce was that?"

"A brilliant one, I rather think."

"You have no right to involve Toby and me in your lies. You heard what the sheriff said, he'll chase us from town with a gun to our backs when he sees what kind of show this is."

Huey shrugged free of her hold and began walking again. "He'll do no such thing. Men like him are harmless, so long as you let them believe they're in control."

"You don't know that. I'll not put my son in danger over this stupid show."

"Need I remind you, this *stupid* show is our livelihood? Mine and yours."

"I never agreed to lie."

"Of course you did."

Tucia's step faltered. She hadn't known all she was getting into, but she had known, at least on some level, the dishonesty of it all.

Huey, now several steps in front of her, turned around. "Listen, my dear, no license, no show. No show, no money. It's as simple as that. You've a debt to repay, remember?"

Tucia closed the space between them. "I do, but not my son. If you ever use him in one of your schemes again—so help me, God—we'll leave. Our contract be damned."

Huey held up his arms as if to concede. She brushed past him and caught up with Toby, dreading that night's show.

20

The sheriff came that night, as promised, and with him, a few dozen curious townsfolk and both ministers. Huey didn't seem at all nervous nor put out by the small crowd. But despite the changes he'd made to the show, Tucia was worried enough for the both of them. She'd not plucked a single hair for days, but the urge to do so in the hours leading up to the show all but overwhelmed her. She sat on her hands or kept them knotted together. By the time the torchlights were lit, her fingers were stiff and numb.

Instead of his usual program of popular tunes, Cal opened the show with "Abide with Me" and "Unto the Hills Around" and other hymns Tucia knew from the church services she and Toby had attended in St. Louis. He played with the same breath-catching skill he always did, though Tucia hadn't heard him practice a note all afternoon.

Fanny wore an ankle-length skirt during her dance numbers, and Tucia, a silver pendant in the shape of a cross when she took the stage as Madame Zabelle. Huey's pitch for rattlesnake oil varied only slightly. Instead of a chance discovery of the medicine's recipe in an ancient Siamese cave, it appeared as a revelation after Huey converted the Siamese medicine men to Christianity. Lawrence's act needed no alteration, though the Amazing Adolphus took credit for converting him too.

After the show, Huey turned his considerable charms on the ministers and shook hands again with the sheriff. By the time they left, he'd secured a two-week extension on their license. "And tomorrow," he told Tucia, an unmistakable glint in his eyes, "we'll pitch the case-taking tent."

The next day, Darl began setup for the new tent alongside the stage. Tucia sat nearby, gluing labels onto newly filled bottles of rattlesnake oil. Toby had wanted to help but quickly grew bored of handing her labels and had taken to tearing up show fliers and gluing the bits together. Huey would likely object on account of the wasted fliers and glue, but he was holed up in his wagon, and the faint scent of opium perfumed the air.

She watched out of the corner of her eye as Darl marked out the diameter of the tent with iron bars he drove into the ground. His jacket sat discarded alongside his bag of tools, and his rolled-up shirtsleeves bared his tan forearms to the sun. And to Tucia's erring gaze. He'd shaven this morning, and his cheeks were flushed from his labor. It seemed only on travel days he didn't bother with the razor. As if he were somehow trying to obscure himself from those they passed on the road. Whatever the reason, Tucia found she favored him clean-shaven even though his scar was more pronounced.

Together with Lawrence, he unloaded a dozen stakes—each longer than Toby stood tall—half a dozen poles, and several roles of canvas. A shrill but rhythmic clanging filled the camp for the next quarter of an hour as the two of them drove the stakes into the ground, swinging their sledgehammers high in the air before bringing them down with full force to strike the stake.

Toby didn't like the noise and crawled onto her lap, covering his ears with his sticky hands. She rocked him as she continued to watch the men—the arc of their hammers, the heave of their chests, the contraction of their muscles.

When they were finished, their shirts were soaked in sweat, and their skin had a ruddy glow. These were just the body's cooling mechanisms, she reminded herself, tearing her eyes away from them. Sweat becoming vapor and carrying off the excess heat brought to the surface of the skin by dilated blood vessels.

That explained their current physiology, but what of the heat she felt? That warm, heavy throb in her core. She grabbed a flier and fanned herself, hoping to hasten it away. The sensation wasn't altogether new, though it had been years since last it stirred inside her. Nor was it unpleasant.

It was, however, unwelcome, and Tucia made a point to focus on the bottles of medicine, taking care that each label was perfectly straight and all four corners securely glued. She glanced up as the men raised the center pole, which stood nearly fifteen feet tall, not counting the flagstaff jointed to it at the top, and again as they unrolled the canvas. Otherwise she managed to keep her eyes on Toby and her work.

Fanny arrived with cups of lemonade half an hour later, just as the men were fastening the last swath of canvas to the tent's frame. They drank greedily, tiny rivulets of lemonade dripping down their chins, then refilled their cups.

"Thirsty?" Fanny called, though it took Tucia a moment before realizing the question was for her.

"Me! Me," Toby said and hurried over for a cup. Tucia followed.

She sipped her lemonade slowly and started toward the tent. Unlike the others, it was circular in shape. The canvas had a dusty, packed-away smell but was bright and in good repair.

"What d'ya think?" Darl asked.

"It certainly went up quickly."

"You should see how fast the circus men do it," Fanny said. "Our big top was two hundred feet long and over a hundred feet wide, with four center poles to bear the weight of the roof. Those men got it up in less than an hour."

Tucia had never seen a circus. Her stepmother had thought that type of entertainment vulgar and pedestrian. But after hearing Fanny talk of it that afternoon mixing corn buster, Tucia could imagine it clear as a photograph. And not just the snake charmers and strongmen and acrobats. The darker side too. The bawdy tent and sideshow acts.

A faint nausea stirred inside her. Was this tent so different? She wouldn't have to endure what Fanny had, but it would be its own kind of indignity. Its own sideshow version of the dream she'd once had.

What if she suffered another hysterical attack while inside? During her mind-reading act as Madame Zabelle, she'd come close and the only part that called to mind her days in medicine was the audience. But the case-taking tent would be much more similar.

Another attack would ruin her all over again. Ruin her and Toby's chances of a better life.

Without thinking, she reached for her hair. Fanny caught her hand and held it in her own. "It won't be so bad, *schatz*, you'll see."

Tucia nodded, wanting to believe her.

21

The next day before entering the case-taking tent, Tucia tried again to convince herself of Fanny's words. It wouldn't be that bad. And even if it were, Tucia could endure it. Every day Toby breathed fresh air and went to bed with a full belly. Already the cuffs of his pants were too short and needed mending. And she was two weeks closer to paying off her debt.

She took several deep breaths like Fanny had taught her, then reached for the tent flap and pulled it aside. Daylight followed her inside. The air reeked of musty canvas and grain alcohol. She tied back the flap in the hopes of letting in a breeze, but it did little to stifle the smell. The occasional weed pushed through the hard-packed dirt at her feet.

At first glance it looked very much like a country doctor's office. A makeshift examination table sat to one edge of the room draped in a sheet that had once, perhaps, been white but now looked pale yellow. A chair and a small table stood nearby. Anatomical drawings hung from the canvas walls. A miniature skeleton and a few specimen jars crowded a small, worn-out desk.

Her chest squeezed, and pulse ticked faster. She set down her medical bag and wiped her sweaty palms on her skirt, drawing closer to the desk. The skeleton, about two feet in height, was held upright by a pole and wire connected to its skull. After closer study, she realized he—for it had the narrow hipbones of a man—was missing three vertebrae, two sets of ribs, the distal phalanx of each finger, and both patellae. Instead of twenty-six distinct bones, each foot was a mere nub of plaster with groves presumably meant to be its toes. Whoever had crafted this skeleton had as much anatomical knowledge as a buffoon.

Beside the skeleton stood the tapeworm jar Fanny had mentioned. The alcohol had been replenished, and a long, bloated worm was coiled inside. The idea that someone would drink from the jar nearly made Tucia gag.

What appeared to be a liver floated in the jar next to it. A stub of both the portal vein and hepatic artery remained attached at the bottom. She bent down and peered at the jar, still confident the preserved organ was a liver, but not a human one. It was too small and more clover- than wedge-shaped, with four lobes instead of two.

The drawings on the walls were as inaccurately rendered as the skeleton. One depicted the organs of the abdomen—minus the spleen and pancreas—but the proportions were wrong, with the stomach, large intestine, and small intestine all the same size. Another was a sketch of the heart and lungs with the heart incorrectly positioned and no differentiation of the lung's five lobes.

Huey entered the tent just as Tucia was examining the last drawing—a cartoonish depiction of both a straight and crooked spine.

"Marvelous, isn't it?"

She turned to face him and gestured around the room. "This? It's a farce."

He smiled. "Yes, but a good one."

Tucia sighed and shook her head.

"You watch, Mrs. Hatherley. These yokels will be greatly impressed." He handed her a small bundle of white cloth. "Put this on. I had Fanny make it just last night."

When Tucia unfolded the bundle, she saw it was an apron and a puffy white hat. "A nurse's cap? But I—"

"I shan't refer to you as a nurse, only as my assistant. And you mustn't refer to me as 'Doctor.' Best, perhaps, if you don't speak much at all."

Anger sparked inside her. Mustn't refer to him as "Doctor"? Of course, she wouldn't. He wasn't the physician, she was! At least on paper. She hadn't fought her way into medical college to shuffle silently behind some quack and play the part of the nurse. She threw the costume onto the examination table. "Even if we don't say the words, you know exactly what people will think."

Huey shrugged. "I can't help it if people leap to incorrect conclusions. But if you'd like to play the role of doctor yourself, by all means. You seemed quite against it when I first broached the idea."

Tucia hated how he said that—*play the role of doctor*—as if she, too, were a fraud. But then again, isn't that what she was? Hadn't that day in the operating theater proven it? And if she did play that role, as Huey said, an attack became ever more likely. Her nerves had settled a bit, seeing how ridiculous the whole operation was, but she could feel the threat of panic at her back like a lion waiting to pounce.

She glared at Huey and snatched up the apron and cap.

"Did you bring your medical bag?"

"If neither of us is doing any real doctoring, I don't see what need there is for it."

He raised his arms and gestured grandly around the tent. "Why, for effect, my dear. Consider this our own little stage and these our show properties."

"Medicine is not pulling a rabbit out of a hat. It's science. And the instruments in my bag are not props." Here she made the mistake of glancing at her bag, still sitting on the ground a few paces away. Huey's gaze followed hers, and his violet eyes positively twinkled.

They both reached for the bag.

Huey grabbed it first, but Tucia caught hold of one of the handles and tried to pull it away from him. Huey held on and tugged back. "You forget, this is my medicine show."

"It's my bag!"

He pulled again, not as hard as she knew he could, but hard enough to jerk her forward, a sardonic smile on his face. Her spark of anger flared into a blaze, and she yanked with all her might.

The bag popped open, and a tearing sound rang through the tent. The handle Tucia was holding ripped free from the bag, and she fell backward, landing on her rear while her carefully guarded tools spilled onto the ground around her.

Her rage dampened as quickly as it had flamed, and a whimper rose in her throat. Not on account of the pain, though her bruised tailbone had only just healed from her fall on the train, but for her instruments. She grabbed the slender tube that held her thermometer and unscrewed the cap. Fragments of glass coated in mercury spilled out into her palm.

"Really, my dear, you ought to be more careful." Huey dropped the empty bag and plucked her stethoscope off the ground. "This will do nicely."

Before she could gather up the rest of her instruments, he'd snatched her tongue depressor and percussion hammer as well. He set them on the small table beside a roll of gauze, a jar of pills labeled Worm Killer, and a few bottles of the Amazing Adolphus's Catarrh Cure.

Just as Tucia had finished inspecting her instruments and repacking her bag, their first client arrived. Everyone from last night's show who'd purchased both a bottle of rattlesnake oil and a tin of salve also got a ticket for a free consultation with a bona fide medical doctor.

"Doors open at noon," Huey had told the audience. "Don't forget to bring your ticket."

Now, Huey ushered the man into the tent and closed the flap behind him. Enough daylight filtered in through the canvas to see by, but Tucia missed the sunshine. And the fresh air. The stench of the man's sweat overcame the must, mingling with the sharp alcohol scent of the specimen jars.

Huey took the man's ticket and handed it to Tucia, whom he introduced as his assistant. Then he gestured to the examination table. "Please, sir, sit down."

The man hesitated, glancing about the tent, before taking off his hat and seating himself on the edge of the table. He looked at Huey expectantly, and Huey looked back, neither speaking for several uncomfortable seconds. Then the man said, "I ain't been to a doctor never, but I got this trouble with my—"

"No, no, don't tell me. A thorough examination will reveal all I need to know." Huey drew close to the man and took hold of his wrist. "You've a good, strong pulse, so it's not a case of backward-flowing blood."

Tucia gaped. Backward-flowing blood! There was no such diagnosis. Huey hadn't even felt the correct side of the man's wrist to palpate his pulse.

Next he pulled back the man's eyelids and peered into his ears. He knocked on his breastbone and scratched a fingernail over the top of his hand. He pulled out a small measuring tape and measured the circumference of the man's ankle and the length of his pointer finger relative to his thumb.

Tucia had never witnessed a more absurd examination in all her life. The man endured it with grave stoicism, wincing only once when Huey touched his lower back. After Huey finished, he stepped back and stroked his chin. "Mmm . . ."

"Is it bad, Doc? I only came because—"

"No, not a word. My medical judgment mustn't be clouded by speculation."

Tucia snorted, then tried to cover the sound with a cough.

Huey shot her a glare and returned his attention to the client. "I know exactly what is wrong with you, sir, and I shall tell you presently, but first, I must discuss it with my assistant so she may ready the necessary remedies should you consent to treatment."

He tugged Tucia to the edge of the tent. "How much do you think he's good for?" he whispered.

"What?"

"We must seem to be talking about something. How many co-conuts do you think he can cough up?"

"Why must *we*? You're the *doctor*, after all."

"Yes, but if it ever came to it with the law, the diagnosis must have plausibly come from you."

It was all Tucia could do not to roll her eyes. "Well, he's got some pain in his back, possibly a misaligned vertebra from an old work injury or a—"

"Yes, yes. I've got this." He flapped his hand toward the desk where the liver and tapeworm sat. "There's a stack of small en-velopes in the drawer and a jar of salts on the table. Ready a few tablespoons for this man." He glanced over his shoulder at him. "Ten, I think."

"Ten tablespoons?"

Huey turned back to her. "Of course not. Ten *dollars*. That's what he'll pay up. There's a notebook in the drawer. Write him out a receipt."

"Ten dollars! There's no way a man like him can afford that."

Huey hushed her. "Just do as I say. Ten dollars for A. A.'s Re-vitalizing Crystals."

He started to walk away, but Tucia grabbed his arm. "What's in it?"

Huey eyed her like it were a preposterous question.

"I'm not going to write a prescription for something that could harm this man."

"Epsom salts, my dear," he whispered sharply.

"And?"

"And oil of wintergreen."

"And?"

"A sprinkle of sugar. That is all." He pulled free of her grasp and returned to the man. "My apologies for the delay. My assistant is new to this trade." He launched into his diagnosis, beginning with a lengthy and nonsensical preamble about the man's general body habitus, using words like *peristalsis* and *tumefaction* in the entirely wrong context. Then, at last, he told the man he suffered from a sluggish liver.

"A sluggish liver?" the man said. "But it's my back that's giving me trouble."

"Precisely." Huey withdrew a short pointer from his jacket pocket and gestured to the drawing of the abdomen. "Your liver is here. See where it sits relative to your other organs? Being of particular importance to the homeostatic regulation of the body and a host of other energetic and toxoplasmatic pathways, any trouble with the liver is bound to affect other parts of the body. Especially the back."

Tucia shook her head and went to the dresser. The salts wouldn't do anything for this man's back pain, but they wouldn't harm him either. At worst, he'd experience a day or two of diarrhea. She scooped a few spoonfuls of the salt into a small envelope and wrote out the receipt as Huey had instructed. Her hands were no longer sweating and her pen surprisingly steady. But a pang of guilt stirred inside her when she wrote out *ten dollars*.

"What's to be done, Doc?" the man asked when Huey had finally finished his lecture. Fear tinged his voice, and Tucia felt another stab of guilt.

"There is a remedy. An alkaline crystal you dissolve in water that has miraculously healthful effects. Not just for the liver, which it flushes free of sludge and poisons, but on the body's general vitality. I'm afraid it's quite costly, though."

"How much?"

"It's a proprietary formula, you see. Developed and produced at considerable cost to me. I usually charge twenty dollars for the complete course of treatment. But you, sir, I see, are an honest, hardworking man. I could perhaps go as low as ten. Just on this one occasion."

The man worried the brim of his well-worn hat. "These crystals will cure me?"

"Sir, I'm so certain of this remedy, if in two weeks' time you're unsatisfied with the results, I'll give you a full refund."

"I'll have to go home to fetch the money."

"My assistant has everything ready for you." He turned to Tucia.

She had both the envelope and the receipt in hand, but hesitated to hand them over to the man. It was one thing to charge a dollar for a bottle of snake oil alongside a free show, but this felt entirely different. Huey sighed and snatched the salts and receipt from her. He gave them to the man. "You can return with the money tomorrow. What's important is that you start on this treatment right away."

He explained that the man must dissolve the crystals in water and drink a dose each night before bedtime, then hurried him from the tent. A line ten people long had formed outside, and Huey ushered in the next client.

Tucia watched the man walk away, pocketing the envelope of crystals and rubbing his back. The sight of it made her stomach squeeze. She wanted to run after him and suggest a more sensible treatment, but Huey stepped in front of her, closing the tent flap.

The entire fiasco began again.

It occurred to Tucia after three more clients had come and gone, each with an envelope or bottle of medicine for some fictitious ailment, that her heart beat slow and steady. She hadn't once felt starved for air or flushed with panic. The entire operation was so dissimilar to real physician's work that it hadn't triggered any of her old memories or anxieties.

Relief swept through her. But in its place crept a bone-deep melancholy. Yes, she could do this without slipping back into the past and suffering another hysterical attack. She could play her part. Day after day until her debt to Huey was squared.

And the cost? Daily mockery of the dream she'd once held so dear.

22

That night, after leaving the stage as Madame Zabelle, Tucia sat on the steps of her wagon, staring up at the moonless sky. It hadn't been one of her better performances, and she was sure to hear about it in the morning.

She unbuttoned the itchy collar of her widow's weeds, listening to the muffled sound of Cal's fiddle and the thump of Fanny's feet as she danced. Tucia knew she ought to go in, change into her nightdress, and slip into bed alongside Toby. But sleep rarely arrived with any haste, and tonight she didn't expect its visit anytime soon.

The day's heat hadn't retreated with the sun but lingered in the still air like a fever that refused to break. She unfastened her bonnet, balling up its long black veil, and fanned herself with its stiff brim.

"Somethin' wrong?"

Tucia startled at the voice, turning to see Darl. Or the outline of him anyway. The only light Huey permitted backstage during a show was the dim oil lamp that illuminated the properties table, but Tucia recognized his broad shoulders and the boxy tool bag he often carried.

"Why would it be?" she said, resisting the urge to refasten her bonnet. Surely it was too dark for him to see her patchy, uneven hair.

"You don't normally linger much after your act, is all. You . . . er . . . want some company?"

Tucia looked back at the sky and shrugged, but she was grateful when Darl grabbed a nearby pail and sat beside her.

Huey had taken the stage now, his spiel audible through the backdrop. Soon Cal, Lawrence, and Al would rush out with jars of medicine in their arms. Yokels were more likely to fork over their hard-earned dollars to a man than a woman, according to Huey, so she and Fanny only sold when there was a whopping crowd. But why didn't Darl sell? The only time she'd seen him stage-front during a show was the night she almost fainted.

"How come Huey doesn't make you sell medicine with the rest of us?"

"I reckon he knows I'll say no."

"But how come you can do that—tell him no—when the rest of us are beholden to his every whim?"

Darl looked down, rubbing the palm of his hand with his thumb. "Don't always get my way with him. He's got things he lords over me, same as the rest of you."

What sort of things? she wondered. And what did he mean by *same as the rest of you*? Did the others owe Huey a debt of some kind too?

There was certainly something different about his relationship with Darl. But before Tucia could press further, he said, "Now, one for you. How'd you wind up a doctor?"

Tucia laughed in spite of herself. "It's not a profession one just stumbles into." She stopped fanning herself and laid the bonnet in her lap. "I always wanted to be a doctor. Ever since I was young."

"How come?"

"It was my mother's influence, I suppose. She'd volunteered with the Women's Nursing Corps during the war. My fondest memories are of snuggling up beside her and listening to her stories." Tucia could still remember the pride in her mother's voice when she spoke of her days at the field hospital. The fervor that lit her eyes. "I wanted to do something courageous and meaningful like that too."

"She musta been mighty proud of you, becoming a doctor and all."

Tucia's lips flattened, and she shook her head. "She died in a carriage accident when I was eight."

In some ways, her mother's wartime stories had prepared Tucia for death. But not grief. Both she and her father were lost to it. He took refuge in his work. She, her books.

"I'm sorry," Darl said.

She could see him better now that he sat only a few feet away. His expression was guarded but his voice sincere.

"My stepmother certainly wasn't proud. She thought the profession quite unfitting for a lady." Tucia picked at a stray thread in her bonnet's stitching. A poor substitute for her hair, but she dared not reach for a strand with Darl so close. That was when it had started—the hair plucking—with the arrival of her stepmother. "My father remarried when I was twelve. She had ambitions of being a grand lady, my stepmother. The sort who strolls about town in imported French silk, wielding a parasol and a smug grin. She worried my *unnatural* interests would diminish her social clout."

"What'd your father think?"

A smile snuck its way to Tucia's lips. Darl would have liked her father. Everyone did. He was a man of humble beginnings who'd run a steam sawmill alongside the Illinois River. Hard work and fortuitous investments made him rich—for a time—but he never lost his reputation as a man of straight goods. He deferred to her stepmother in domestic matters. Except on the point of Tucia's education. "I think he saw my mother's hand in my ambition to be a doctor, so he was . . . indulgent of the idea."

"You're lucky for that. My pap indulged me nothin' but a black eye now and then."

"How awful." Her hand reached out to him unbidden, but she

stopped short, wary of seeming too familiar, and swatted at an imaginary mosquito instead.

"Here," Darl said, pulling a wad of dried grass from his pocket. He handed it to her, then rummaged through his tool bag, plucking out a matchbox and empty jar. "This will keep 'em away."

"What?"

"The gallinippers." He took the grass from her and stuffed it into the jar, followed by a lit match. Warm light reflected in his eyes as the flame flared before settling into a smoldering glow. Curls of sweet-smelling smoke wafted up through the mouth of the jar.

"What's a gallinipper?"

"A mosquito," he said, as if it were obvious, and set the jar beside her on the wagon step. "Vanilla grass works best, but cedar or sage will do in a pinch."

"Thank you."

Darl shrugged. "How about the rest of your tale, then?"

"Tale? . . . Oh . . . There isn't much more to it. I was accepted at a women's college in Chicago, studied there for three years, and received my degree. That's it."

But there was, in fact, much more to it. She'd had to plead and fight every step of the way. When her father died halfway through her schooling, and her stepmother refused to continue paying for such an "improper and wasteful extravagance," Tucia had exhausted nearly all of her inheritance to fund the rest.

"Why ain't you out doctoring, then?" Darl asked.

"We may be more common now, but women physicians still face prejudice. It's nearly impossible to get practical experience at any of the top hospitals. And even if you do, when you put out a shingle or advertise your services in the paper, people think you're nothing more than an abortionist. That or you're pushing ideas like dress reform or women's suffrage."

She stopped and sighed. After the incident in the operating theater, Tucia had quickly been dismissed from her internship at Fairview. Of course, Dr. Addams had underplayed his hand in it all, telling the hospital board she had insisted upon performing the surgery when he had been the one to hold out the scalpel to her and insist. Tucia could have fought him on that point. There'd been at least fifty witnesses, after all. But she feared what else he might say, what else he might reveal. So she accepted her dismissal without contest.

Word spread quickly about the incident, hastened by the mere fact of her sex. See what happens when you let women into the operating theater? Were she a man, the whole thing might have been brushed off as an unfortunate misstep. Instead, it became an act of gross incompetence and appalling hubris. Tucia herself became a cautionary tale.

She applied to every other hospital in Chicago, but none would have her. It was the same in the neighboring city. She took tutoring jobs when she could get them to bolster her fast-dwindling inheritance. Not until she was a hundred miles away and a month beyond the incident did a small, crumbling women's hospital agree to take her on.

They'd not regret it, Tucia promised, and arrived on her first day flush with confidence. She'd worried over the incident in the operating theater for several days after it happened, oscillating between weeping and numbness. But that was behind her now.

The doctor she was to work with met her in the mud-tracked foyer and escorted her to the ward. He was an old man, white-haired and unevenly shaven. Considering how long ago he'd studied medicine, she doubted there was much he could teach her by way of modern remedies. But she didn't need education. She'd had three years of college and all her private study before. Tucia needed experience.

But she hadn't been prepared for the familiar creak of the floorboards beneath the nurses' to-and-fro footfalls nor the commingled scents of putrefaction and antiseptic. Her heart was racing before they'd reached the first bed. A woman two days postpartum with puerperal fever, the old doctor said.

Tucia tried to listen as the nurse rattled off the woman's vital signs but found her words muddled as if by an invisible fog.

"What treatment do you suggest?" the old doctor asked her.

The answer was easy enough: quinine, morphine, and tincture of veratrum viride. But when Tucia began her examination, she found her hands shaking.

Incompetent woman, Dr. Addams said over her shoulder. She startled and turned around, sure she'd see him standing behind her. But only the nurse and the old, bewhiskered doctor were there.

She rose on unsteady legs and followed the doctor to the next bed. In it lay an older woman, crippled by arthritis and suppurating bedsores. With the nurse's help, they rolled the woman onto her side and examined the wounds—each deeply pitted, ringed with necrotic tissue, and weeping pus.

"These wounds need a good debridement," the old doctor said, and sent the nurse for a scalpel, oakum, and carbolized water. "I'll demonstrate on the first, and you can do the others."

Tucia nodded, though she still felt out of sorts. They dosed the woman with morphine, and Tucia watched as the doctors scraped away the pus and dead tissue from the wound bed. It was a simple enough procedure and one Tucia was confident she could easily replicate. If only her damned hands would still.

The lighting in the ward was terrible, and the old doctor growled at the nurse to move away from the window so he might see better. As she did, a weak stream of light glinted off the scalpel's blade. Tucia blinked, the edges of her vision blurring. Her throat narrowed with each breath. It took all her will to focus on the woman in the bed.

The old doctor's procedure had occasioned much blood, and he mopped it up with a square of flannel, which he tossed onto a rickety steel tray. It landed with a wet clang, blood splattering.

In an instant, Tucia was back in the operating theater. Not just her mind but her body too. She could smell the carbolic acid and sweet, pungent ether. Feel the cold scalpel in her hand. See the splatter of blood all around.

Dr. Addams shoved her aside. But they both knew it was too

late. The spurt of blood from the nicked artery had slowed to barely a trickle.

See what you've done with your folly? he said, and then, loud enough for the whole theater to hear, *This woman is dead.*

His words seemed to suck the air from the room. Bile threatened in her throat, and her breath came in heavy pulls. Dr. Addams spun around and grabbed her by the shoulders, smearing yet more blood onto her smock. His fingers dug deep into her flesh.

For a moment, Tucia couldn't move. It had happened so fast. Her brain replayed the last few minutes in chaotic succession as if in doing so she might pinpoint her exact moment of error. But there was more than one error, starting with her falling into the trap Dr. Addams had laid for her. He leaned in and whispered, *I knew you couldn't do it. The operating theater's no place for the likes of you.* Then he let her go. Let her go to stand on her own and face the horror of what she'd done alone.

Even this she couldn't do. After a minute, an hour, a second— Tucia no longer had any sense of time—her legs gave way. She collapsed into a heap on the bloody floor and wept, only distantly aware of the medical students' whispers as they shuffled from their seats and out the door. A nurse took pity on her and handed her a hankie. Orderlies came and wheeled the body away. The washerwomen lingered in the doorway, waiting for Tucia to pick herself up so they could get on with their cleaning.

Then someone took hold of her shoulders again. "Dr. Hatherley, Dr. Hatherley! Pull yourself together."

Tucia swiped the tears from her eyes and blinked at the face before her. Dr. Addams? She lurched back in fright, batting away the hands upon her shoulders. Her brain scrambled to make sense of things. The operating theater had vanished, and she was on the hospital ward. But no ward at Fairview was this bleak and grimy. She glanced down at her dress. Where had all the blood gone? Her hands were clean too. She looked again at the man who'd spoken to her. Patches of gray whiskers stood out on his otherwise clean-shaven face.

Tucia drank in a deep breath. The old doctor. She wasn't at Fairview but at the women's hospital half a state away. An entire month had passed . . . but, no . . . only moments ago she'd been in the operating theater. Her heart was still thudding from the terrible ordeal.

"Perhaps you ought to take a moment to collect yourself," the old doctor said. "And then, I think it best you go."

Though her thoughts were ascramble, Tucia understood his meaning. "But I—"

He cut her off with a shake of his head and walked away. When her steadiness returned, she hung her head and left. The only time she ventured into a hospital again after that was to deliver her son.

She didn't tell Darl any of this—only that a bad case in the operating theater had changed her mind about the profession—and he didn't pry further.

"Well, I reckon you'd be pretty good at it if you ever changed your mind," he said, standing.

Act two of the show had begun, and she could hear the audience applauding as Lawrence twirled and slung his lariat.

"You hardly know me," she said.

"I've seen enough doctors come and go to know you're different."

Tucia watched him walk away, vanilla-scented smoke swirling around her. If only what he'd said were true.

23

The days passed, and the changing crowds and towns began to blur together. Soon everything from cooking up corn-busting salve to driving the wagon to reading minds and assisting in the case-taking tent became a role Tucia could slip easily in and out of. Whether she was Madame Zabelle or the doctor's assistant or even Mrs. Hatherley, she felt somehow separate from herself. She hadn't the words to describe the feeling—and wouldn't even if she had for fear of being thought mad—but it had that peculiar, dreamlike quality of both living a moment and watching it happen from afar.

The only time Tucia felt fully present was when she was with Toby, alone in their wagon or during the short walks they took around the camp. And sometimes, even then, she found herself drifting—not her mind but her entire body—as if she were merely a ventriloquist's doll and motherhood simply another role she played.

Even after the most grueling days at the factory, she'd always found a spark of joy coming home and seeing Toby, just holding him in her arms or listening to him recount the day's adventures. Now, even that joy was muted, like a wet match that couldn't quite catch aflame.

* * *

Two months into their travels, Tucia was readying the case-taking tent for their afternoon clients. Last night's crowd had been a push, filling the lot to capacity, and she expected at least a few dozen callers today. She only had a vague sense of where they were—somewhere in North East Texas, for they'd recently taken a detour to register her medical license in Dallas—but it didn't matter. One small town was so much like another that she'd stopped bothering to learn their names. Yokels crowded the lot and lined up in front of their case-taking tent whether it was Ames, Iowa, or De Witt, Arkansas, or Plano, Texas.

Today, as always, she'd left Toby with a picture book and his building blocks in the wagon and then fetched a fresh stock of medicine for the case-taking tent. The afternoons passed more smoothly when she didn't have to scurry to the supply wagon to replenish their stores. She donned her apron and was about to pin on her cap when the tent flap opened.

"I'm afraid we don't begin seeing clients until noon," she said, squinting in the flood of sunlight as she turned around. "Please wait out—"

"Dr. Hatherley, I presume."

The backlit outline of a figure took shape into a man as her eyes adjusted to the light. A man, but not one she recognized.

He was better dressed than many of the clients they saw, his worsted blue suit impeccably tailored to fit his small, round frame. A dainty pair of spectacles sat on the bridge of his nose, and gray hair peeked from beneath his hat. A hat he didn't bother doffing as he stepped farther into the tent and let the flap close behind him.

"How do you know my—"

"I contacted the district clerk," he snapped. "That's how."

"And you are?"

"Dr. Kremer."

"You're . . . a physician?" Her throat tightened around the words.

"I've been practicing in these parts for over forty years. Long enough to spot a fraud from a mile away. When I heard your little show was in town, I telegraphed the clerk right away. There's a stiff fine in this state for practicing without a registered license. But then, you know that, don't you?" He took another step closer, and Tucia retreated, bumping into the small table where her stethoscope and other instruments were displayed like curiosities in a dime museum.

"Most outfits like this don't bother with a real doctor," he continued. "So you can imagine my surprise when the clerk tele-graphed back that he'd just processed the registration for one T. M. Hatherley. A *lady* physician."

"There, you see? I've broken no laws," she said, trying to regain her composure. "Now, if you'll please—"

"Better if you had. Better if you were just a huckster. But a doctor, a real doctor! I never thought I'd see the day." He wagged a fat finger at her. "Have you no shame? No care for the disgrace you bring upon your sex?"

Tucia's hand tightened around her nursing cap. "My sex has nothing to do with it."

"And what about the shame you bring upon this great profession? What about the people lining up outside that you're about to bamboozle?"

She opened her mouth, but no words came out.

"That's the grift, isn't it?" he continued. "You lure them here with the promise of a free consultation, distract them with these absurd posters and phony specimens, and then sell them false cure-alls." He thwacked one of the jars with the back of his hand. "What is that anyway? A pig's liver?"

"Please just leave," Tucia said, her cheeks hot and tingling.

Dr. Kremer ignored her plea. "What you're doing goes against every principle of medicine. Every noble impulse a physician ought to have. Surely even a lady doctor can see that."

At this, her humiliation gave way to anger. He was just as cocky and condescending as Dr. Addams. She cast the damned nurse's cap aside and met his eye. "And am I to believe it was your noble impulses that brought you here today and not your greed?"

"Excuse me?"

"You're afraid we'll steal away all your patients."

Dr. Kremer gave an indignant huff, but she could see from the sudden flightiness of his hands—tugging on his collar, fiddling with his shirtsleeves—she was right.

"At least I have the self-respect not to stoop to this." He gestured to the specimens floating in their jars. "Hawking fake medicine with a troupe of circus freaks."

"The people I travel with are not freaks. Any doctor educated within the last century should know better than to call them so." She made a point of glancing at his graying hair. "Furthermore, nothing we prescribe brings these yokels any harm."

"Listen to yourself, Dr. Hatherley! They're patients, not yokels, and since when is the only requirement of a drug that it cause no harm?"

A cold sweat prickled her neck, but she refused to shy away from his gaze.

"The good people of this town can't tell the difference between true medicine and bottled-up bathwater," he continued. "Between a real physician and a quack. When this swill you prescribe doesn't work, they grow mistrustful of it all. Not harmful, you say? Well, there's harm in that."

"Have you never prescribed mercury chloride to a syphilitic patient only to watch his mouth ulcerate and kidneys fail? Or laudanum to a patient only to have her come back craving more? Or performed a hysterectomy knowing full well the cancer had already spread and the patient had only days to live?"

He gave her a funny look and said more softly, "Sometimes medicine presents us with impossible choices."

"Sometimes life does as well." She jabbed a finger at the door. "Now get out."

24

Tucia's work in the case-taking tent had become as automatic as her work in the factory. She'd come to know which clients Huey would prescribe crystals or deworming pills or cough cure or bladder bitters, and would have medicine and a receipt prepared before he asked. Sometimes Huey would change the cost of a particular product depending on how much he thought he could wring out of a man (women, as a rule, were harder to squeeze), so she filled the price in at the end.

But today, after her argument with Dr. Kremer, her thoughts were ascatter. How dare he sashay into the tent and berate her for decisions he knew nothing about. He was just a greedy, old country doctor. And yet, his words had sliced her like a scalpel.

She'd gone weeks without pulling out a single strand of hair but now felt the urge so strongly, she could scarcely concentrate. Four times she handed a client the wrong medicine only to have Huey snatch it back with a tittering apology and prepare the correct one himself.

Dr. Kremer's words wouldn't be painful if they weren't true. She was debasing herself and making a mockery of medicine. She was betraying the very principles she'd sworn at graduation to uphold. With each new client who entered the tent, she felt that betrayal anew. These people needed practical advice on hygiene, diet, and the laws of health. Not phony cures and false promises.

When the last client finally left, it was nearly dusk. Tucia untied her apron and tore off her hateful cap, wadding the fabric and chucking it into the corner. She didn't wait around for Huey to lecture her about keeping the medicines straight. So what if a client got dewormer instead of cough elixir when neither actually worked?

She trudged across camp to her wagon, hoping to coax Toby into taking a nap before supper so she could lie down too. But when she opened the wagon door, Toby was not inside.

It wasn't a big space, and even if he'd been curled up beneath the quilt on their bed or hiding behind the traveling trunk, she would have seen him. Still, she called his name, just to be sure. When he didn't respond, not even with the muffled giggle of one playing hide-and-seek, Tucia's heart faltered, one beat tripping over the next as it sped to a gallop.

She leapt down the wagon's steps. He must be playing in the supply wagon or under the stage. She checked both places, but Toby wasn't there. She banged on Huey's door and found him lying on the divan with his pipe. No, he hadn't seen Toby, he told her through a cloud of smoke.

Next, Tucia searched the buckboard and the cook tent, but there was no sign of her son. She was about to tear through the Trouts' tent as well when Fanny opened the flap.

"Is Toby inside?" Tucia asked, breathless.

Fanny shook her head.

Tucia choked back a sob. Someone had taken him, then.

"Darl and Al went off to play ball," Fanny said. "Maybe Toby went with them."

"Where?"

Fanny pointed down the road in the opposite direction of town. A few shaggy trees and a low hill were all Tucia could see.

"There's an abandoned field just beyond that hill. Lawrence takes the animals to graze there sometimes. I think that's where they went. Want me to come with you and—"

Tucia took off running toward the field. What would she do if Toby wasn't there? Before she reached the top of the hill, she heard a playful shout followed by a few muffled words, but neither voice sounded like Toby's. She should have checked on him halfway through the afternoon. Usually she did, but today she'd been so out of sorts she'd forgotten. Forgotten her own son. What kind of mother was she?

A shout sounded, followed by a happy squeal. Toby! She scrambled to the top of the hill and looked down at the field below. The three of them were there—Toby, Al, and Darl—a short distance off from the horses and mules.

She drank in a breath, watching as Darl tossed a baseball up into the air and batted it toward Al with a stick. Al shuffled a few steps to the side and caught it in his mitt.

"Good job," Darl hollered as Al tossed back the ball.

"Good job," Toby echoed. Hearing his carefree voice both relieved and vexed her.

Next, Darl batted the ball lightly toward Toby. He lifted his gloved hand—where he got the mitt, Tucia didn't know—but the ball was already drifting past him, his reflexes not quite quick enough to catch it. He scurried after it, swaying with that straight-legged gait of his. And that's when she noticed it, his bare feet.

She hurried down the hill toward them, ignoring the burs and bramble snagging on her skirt. "Tobias Hatherley! What are you doing out here?"

They all turned to look at her. Even the animals raised their heads and glanced in her direction.

The baseball slipped from Toby's hand and his mouth hung agape. "Uh-oh."

She made it to the foot of the hill and stomped toward him. Before she could reach him, Al said, "You're in for it now, Toby."

He said it gleefully as if they were still playing a game and she had come to join them. But Tucia was in no mood for games.

"Stay out of it, Al," Darl said. But it was too late.

Toby's gaze swung from her to Al and back.

"Don't you dare—"

Toby took off running. Tucia shot Darl a glare before following after him. He wasn't a fast runner, but had several yards lead on her. She'd had little chance to rest, and her lungs soon burned and side ached. "Toby, you stop running right now," she managed to shout between panting breaths, "or it's straight to bed without supper."

Toby replied with a giggle and an over-the-shoulder glance.

Like other little boys, he'd always had a mischievous streak, disobeying her in small ways just to test her reaction. But he'd never done anything as willful as this. He zigzagged through the tall weeds and feathery grass, sometimes disappearing completely save for the sound of his laughter.

Tucia's boot heel caught in a gopher hole, and she twisted her ankle. She freed her foot and took a step. Pain shot up her leg. It lessened slightly with the next step. Not broken, she decided, but damned tender.

Toby had stopped running and was staring back at her. It wasn't a game, after all, if she wasn't giving chase.

"Toby, you come here right now."

He didn't move. She took a hobbling step toward him, and he watched her, his expression uncertain. Another step, and he took off running again. Tucia cursed. She followed after him, hopping and lurching more than running. He showed no signs of slowing, and she began to worry about what so much exertion would do to his weak heart and lungs.

"Toby," she called again, an edge of desperation in her voice.

Darl, who hitherto had stood back watching with an unmistakable smirk, intercepted Toby as he ran past, scooping him up in a single-arm hold.

"Sorry, kid," he said and brought him to Tucia.

Instead of thanking him, she shot Darl another glare as he set Toby down in front of her.

"He just—"

Tucia made a slicing motion with her arm, cutting him off.

Darl held up his hands as if he'd been innocent in it all and walked away.

She bent down and grabbed Toby's shoulders. He, too, was panting, a slight wheeze accompanying each exhale. She searched his face for signs of cyanosis, but his lips were pink and cheeks flushed. She pulled him close and put an ear to his chest. It was less precise than listening with her stethoscope, but the strong, steady lub-dub of his heart was enough to reassure her.

She exhaled heavily and gave him a tight hug. Her worry subsided and, with it, some of her anger. But not all. She stood and looked down at him, noticing again the worn baseball mitt he carried. It was several sizes too large for his hand, and the stitching had come undone in a few places.

"Where did you get that?" she asked.

He followed her gaze downward to the mitt, then hastily hid it behind his back.

"Toby."

"Mr. Darl. He said I could play."

"Did you see them leave camp and follow them here?"

He looked away, shaking his head.

"So they came to the wagon and asked you to come play with them?"

"Yeah, yeah."

Tucia swallowed a sigh. He never could lie well. She reached behind him and grabbed the mitt, digging her fingers into the leather.

"And your shoes?"

He shrugged.

She closed her eyes a moment and shook her head. Damn this place! If only they could go back to the city. To the way things were before the accident at the factory. They hadn't much food or money, but it was better than here. Her work was honest, and at day's end, she could count on Toby to be right where she'd left him.

The sky was draining fast of color now. Darl and Al were already gone, leaving the animals to their grazing. She and Toby followed behind, a twinge of pain shooting from her ankle with each step.

"Mama, am I in trouble?"

"Yes."

"But I—"

"I've told you dozens of times not to leave the wagon without me."

"It's too hot."

"That's no excuse," she said, though he did have a point. The further into summer they got, the more insufferable the wagon became. She'd told Huey three times about the broken furniture and the window that wouldn't open. He said he'd get Darl to fix it, but as yet, had not.

"Al plays outside," Toby said.

"Al is two years older and doesn't have a weak heart."

He stopped, kicking at the dirt with his bare feet, and she could sense a tantrum coming on. "It's not fair! It's not—"

"Life isn't fair." She grabbed him by the upper arm and dragged him along. "I cannot be worrying about you on top of everything else. You must do as I say, and that's that."

He fought her grip and started to cry. Tucia felt the sting of threatening tears too. Tears of frustration. Exhaustion. Shame.

The supper bell sounded not long after they reached their wagon. She ignored it, even though Toby whined he was hungry. A few minutes later, a knock sounded at their door.

"It's me, Al. I brought your supper." He knocked again. Toby started for the door, but Tucia held him back. "Pa says I got to apologize too. I didn't mean to cause no trouble."

The anger storming inside her lessened, but still Tucia did not speak or open the door. She just wanted them to be left alone.

She heard Al set the plate of food on the top step and walk away. It was still there an hour later when she left to take the stage as Madame Zabelle. She stepped carefully around it, hauling up her ridiculous skirt so the hem didn't drag through the congealed, fly-covered gravy.

Toby had cried himself to sleep, and her anger had broken. That left only her humiliation and the echo of Dr. Kremer's words.

25

That night after the show, Tucia waited on the steps of Huey's wagon. He was always the last one to leave the stage, alert for any opportunity to make another sale. She hadn't wanted to wake Toby, so she still wore the scratchy widow's weeds.

The din of the crowd dwindled, and the pan torches that lit the stage, at last, went dark. She stared at the night sky, wondering how she had ever thought such yawning blackness beautiful. Huey ambled through the slit in the backdrop a few minutes later.

"You were sloppy tonight," he said, approaching the wagon.

She scrubbed a hand over her face. This would be easier if he wasn't in a testy mood, but she didn't have the energy to placate him. "I know."

"Anyone can recite a list of words onstage. The trick is making people believe." He shooed her off the steps and opened the door of the wagon.

"I told you from the start, I'm not a performer."

"We're all performers, my dear. Every last one of us."

Tucia gave a hollow laugh.

Huey spun around on the top step. Before she knew what was

happening, he struck her across the face. Tucia staggered back. Her cheek burned, and she tasted blood.

"You look foolish onstage, *I* look foolish onstage," he said. "And foolish means less velvet. The same goes for the tent." He turned and stomped into the wagon.

Tucia remained where she stood, a pace back from the steps. She cradled her cheek and worked her jaw. No one had ever hit her before. Not even the foreman, though he likely would have if he'd been able to pull his trousers up fast enough to chase after her.

It took her a moment to cobble her thoughts together. He'd left his door open, and she called in after him. "We're leaving."

He appeared in the doorway a moment later, undressed down to his pants and shirtsleeves. Her muscles tensed with the impulse to run or cower. But Tucia held her ground.

"What nonsense are you spouting?" he said.

"We're leaving, Toby and I. At the next train town."

"Don't be so rash."

When she didn't speak, he sighed and lumbered down the stairs.

Tucia flinched as he drew near, but instead of hitting her again, he wrapped an arm around her shoulder and shepherded her into his wagon. "I didn't hurt you, did I?" He seated her on the divan and withdrew his handkerchief. After daubing the tip in whiskey, he wiped the blood from her lip. "I had to make my point, didn't I?"

The swing of his moods was dizzying. Still wary and a bit stunned, Tucia pushed his hand away. She'd made up her mind before tonight's show had even begun, and she wouldn't let him derail her. "I've been with the troupe two months. During that time I've done whatever you asked—the silly mind-reading act, the case-taking tent. Eight weeks at thirty dollars a week is two hundred and forty dollars. More than a third of what I owe. I'm good for the rest. I promise. As soon as we're set up somewhere, I can start sending you money."

"All this because of a little slap?"

Her hand involuntarily went to her face. Not so little. Her skin was still hot, and her lip had begun to swell. But no, that wasn't the reason. "The show. The medicine. The case-taking tent. It's all unethical."

"Ah, but you knew what you'd be doing when we made our little agreement. I made no attempts at deception. You knew and were perfectly happy to come along."

What could Tucia say? That she been desperate? Naive? Not in her right mind? All were true. And while Huey may not have outright deceived her, he'd certainly been vague and coercing.

"I thought I could do this, and I can't," she said, eyeing the door in case he got violent again. "That's all there is to it."

Huey rose and paced the wagon, rubbing his chin the way he did when he wanted to appear thoughtful. She'd seen him do it in the case-taking tent to draw out the client's suspense and in the sheriff or town clerk's office when he was angling for a license.

"I must admit, that's very distressing to hear. And you would, what, take another factory job? Pluck chickens or wrap soap or stitch corsets ten hours a day, six days a week, all for a few dollars?"

Tucia hadn't thought about the specifics. The long hours and grueling work. But she'd done it before. She could do it again. "I'll take whatever honest work I can find."

"And what of Toby? Seems to me the fresh air has been good for the boy. The three square meals a day. Why, he's shot up like a stalk of corn."

She shifted on the divan, scooting forward so the steel hoops of her crinoline were no longer pressing into the backs of her thighs. There was no denying Toby's health had improved in the two months they'd been traveling. And she'd been able to look out for him herself without relying on a good-for-nothing caretaker like Mrs. Harsnatch. But she couldn't watch him all the time. And what if he wandered off or followed behind Darl and Al again without them noticing? He could get lost. Drown in a river. Be bitten by a snake. Tucia shuddered. "I know what's best for my son, and it isn't here."

"I see." Huey sat back down on the divan. He seemed rather nonchalant about it all, but Tucia, still wary, inched to the far edge of the seat beyond arm's reach.

"So, let me see if I've got this all straight. You propose to leave after only two months' indenture and will pay back the remainder of your debt incrementally once you find new employment."

"Yes. Every extra cent I have, I'll send to you."

"And what if you lose your employment?"

"I won't."

He looked at her incredulously.

"I won't," she repeated, ignoring the way her throat closed around the words.

Huey nodded. "All right, let's say you find work in a . . . a glue factory."

Of course he would suggest the most wretched of places, but Tucia played along, nodding.

"You would make what? Four dollars a week?"

"Yes." If she were lucky.

"Subtract from that the cost of food and rent, and you could pay back perhaps two dollars a week?"

Tucia nodded again. Two dollars was a bit optimistic. She'd have the caretaker's fee too. But if they lived quite modestly, she might manage it.

"But you'd need, of course, something to start out. Train fare and such."

"A small amount, yes."

"Twelve dollars, say?" He stood again, not waiting for her response, and crossed to the small desk. From within a drawer, he pulled out a ledger and an arithmometer. For several minutes he flipped through the ledger, moving the nobs of the arithmometer up and down and turning the handle. Tucia watched, absentmindedly rubbing her jaw.

She hadn't expected him to take the news so well. But then,

she hadn't expected him to slap her either. She'd not let it happen again. Reading his moods was like trying to read a newspaper written in another language. Another reason she'd be happy to leave.

He continued to scour the ledger and tinker with the arithmometer. Tucia couldn't see the figures he was tallying, but the math wasn't that hard. Unless he was adding interest. Or the type of fees that had made it all but impossible to pay down her original debt. When he'd first proposed the idea to her, he'd promised to assume her debt without interest. But was that in the contract? Tucia couldn't remember. Her hand traveled from her sore jaw to the nape of her neck where soft new hairs an inch or so long had grown. She fingered them one at a time before the urge overcame her and she pulled one out at the root.

Before she could pluck another, Huey turned to her. Tucia steeled herself. Whatever fees or interest he charged, it would be better than this—the slow death of her dignity.

"I'm afraid it's just not possible, my dear."

Tucia dropped the hair she was holding and rattled her head. She'd expected him to strong-arm her into paying more but not for him to outright refuse her.

"It would take far too long for you to pay back what you owe," he continued. "The show couldn't bear such a financial burden."

"Unless you mean to go against your word and commit usury, I can pay you back in full in four years. And don't pretend it would be a burden. You pocketed twice what I owe last month alone. All thanks to *my* physician's license."

He chuckled in that belittling way men did. "My dear Tucia, I have no intention of charging you interest. But your numbers aren't quite right. According to my calculations, you owe five hundred and eighty-two dollars."

Tucia stood and snatched the ledger from his desk. Five hundred and eighty-two dollars? Impossible! That was only seventy-eight dollars less than her original debt. She flipped through the pages, surprised at how tidy the entries were. Each week's income and expenditures were listed in separate columns. At the bottom, the sum of the expenditures was subtracted from the income and then added to the previous week's total.

Certain income was missing, however, including a large chunk of the velvet earned in the case-taking tent, making it seem like the show was barely profitable. But right now, Tucia didn't care how much Huey was siphoning off for himself, only how much she truly owed.

She found each performer's salary recorded in the expenditures column. Hers was listed as thirty dollars, like they'd agreed. She checked each of the eight previous weeks' entries. All showed the same thing. "It's here, in your own hand. A deduction of thirty dollars each week for the past two months. That's two hundred and forty dollars. My numbers aren't wrong. Yours are."

"Ah, but you've forgotten a few things." He took the ledger from her and laid it open on the desk. Then he reset his arith-mometer to a starting position of two hundred and forty and switched the reversing lever from addition to subtraction. After flipping back the ledger's pages to the week she started, he ran a finger down the expense column. "Twenty-five dollars for the new dresses I bought you." He moved the counting nobs to twenty-five and cranked the handle. "Three dollars for a new hat. Six for that hairpiece. Two for . . . underthings. And ten for new outfits for the boy." The arithmometer clicked and whirred as he accounted for these costs.

"But you never said you were adding the cost of those things to my debt. It was you who said I needed them. I never would have agreed to it had I known. I thought they were . . ."

"Gifts?" He flashed her a suggestive smile.

"No. An . . . allowance of sorts."

"My dear, I run a medicine show. Not a charity." He continued on down the list, deducting the cost of their meals and train fare.

"You got that fare back, remember? When you kicked the stool out from under me."

"Ah yes, rather ingenious on my part. You, if I recall, did nothing but sit there on your rear. But I suppose I could give you a small cut." He added two dollars back in her favor. It was quickly gone again when he subtracted twenty dollars for what he called a costuming fee.

"This rag of a dress isn't worth five dollars, let alone twenty!"

He ignored her, deducting another twelve before turning the page.

"What was that for?"

"Why, your room and board, of course."

"That wasn't in the contract."

"You're quite right. Had it read 'a weekly salary *plus* room and board,' your indignation would be entirely reasonable. But, alas, it does not."

"You led me to believe it was, said I needn't worry about it."

Huey held up his hands. "I cannot be held responsible for your misunderstanding of the matter. *Needn't worry* and *needn't pay* are two entirely different things. Had you wished for room and board to be included in your compensation, you should have asked." He returned to the ledger and continued subtracting away on the arithmometer. Seven more weeks' worth of room and board, a lost product fee for a bottle of medicine she'd accidentally dropped and broken in the case-taking tent, the train fare for each trip they took into the city to register her physician's license as well as the fee.

"This is preposterous," she said, backing away from the desk like his ledger were poison. "I'm not . . . you can't."

"Oh, but I can."

"I'll . . . I'll take this to a lawyer. A judge."

At this, Huey laughed—not a condescending little chuckle, but a full-throated guffaw. "And what will he do? He'll laugh. That's what he'll do. Just like me." He carried on a moment longer, clutching his stomach with one hand and wiping his eyes with the other. Then, without warning, his mirth vanished. A prickle skittered down her spine. "He'll laugh until he sees that you're nothing more than a degenerate trying to weasel her way out of her obligations. A degenerate physician. A degenerate mother. He'll take Toby and lock him up in an institution. You, he'll throw in the poorhouse. Is that what you want?"

Tucia's entire body went cold as if someone had plunged her into a bath of ice water. They did that—ice-water baths—to patients at asylums and institutions. That and worse. They'd do it to Toby if they ever got their hands on him.

"And don't think of running," Huey said, stepping so close the hoops of her crinoline flattened against the front of her legs. "You wouldn't get very far. You're nothing without me."

Tucia pushed past him and hurried out the door, Huey's renewed laughter following behind. She wanted to snatch Toby and leave that very moment. But Huey was right. They wouldn't make it far.

A pair of field mice scurried from the steps as Tucia neared her wagon. The plate of food Al had left them was nearly picked clean. She kicked the plate to the ground, heedless of the clatter, then sank onto the top step, covering her swollen face in her hands as she wept.

26

Tucia awoke the next morning as the night sky was beginning to lighten. She rose from bed with Toby still snoring and quietly dressed. A dull ache radiated from the left side of her face, and a spot of dried blood remained crusted at the corner of her lip. She dipped a square of flannel in the water basin beside her dressing trunk and pressed it to her face. The sudden cold was both a shock and a comfort.

She stood with her eyes closed, breathing steadily through the wet cloth, loathe to greet the day. At least it was Sunday and the case-taking tent was closed. The shame she'd felt after her run-in with Dr. Kremer remained an irretrievable bullet festering inside her. And yet she had no choice but to don her cap and apron, and return to the tent tomorrow. And the day after and the day after that.

She peeled the cloth from her face and wrung it dry over the basin, twisting and squeezing until her knuckles blanched and fingers tingled. *You're nothing without me*, Huey had said. But it had been another man's voice she'd heard.

Dr. Addams had seemed like a demigod when Tucia first met him—handsome, confident, brilliant. He'd studied in Scotland with the likes of Tait and Lister and performed one of the first successful appendectomies in America. Of the five doctors on the internship selection committee, he'd been the most vocal against her application, even threatening resignation should she be accepted. So it had not surprised Tucia on the first day when he made a great show of ignoring her. She may as well have been a ghost, and a ghost she remained. Until finally, on the fourth day, Tucia's patience snapped. He'd asked the interns about the causes of gangrene, addressing each in turn. Except Tucia. None gave a sufficient answer. He'd begun his usual chastisement, the prelude to enlightening them with the correct response, when Tucia interrupted him.

"The immediate cause of gangrene is the arrest or deficient supply of blood to a particular part of the body."

He continued as if she hadn't spoken, but she interrupted him again.

"Specifically, gangrene may be caused by localized injury, extremes of heat or cold, arrest of circulation, loss of nerve power, the introduction of septic microorganisms into—"

Dr. Addams silenced her with a steely gaze. "It is customary, Miss . . ."

"Doctor. Dr. Hatherley."

"Customary for interns to remain silent unless directly addressed."

"I should be silent forever, then."

"Yes. That is quite the point."

He turned back to the other interns.

"But I answered your question correctly."

"A lucky guess."

"Ask another, then."

The corner of his eyebrow twitched at her impertinence. "We are here to practice medicine, Miss Hatherley, not play parlor games."

"Then perhaps you can quit your game of pretending I'm not here."

Another twitch. A heavy breath. Tucia held his gaze even as her knees went soft. Surely now he'd bellow for her to leave.

But he did not. He continued lecturing where he'd left off. Tucia feared she'd been relegated to the status of specter again, but when they moved to the next patient—a woman recovering from an ovariotomy—Dr. Addams turned to her and said, "*Miss* Hatherley, what is the appropriate nutritional regime for a patient such as this?"

"Beef tea and brandy, as tolerated, for the first twenty-four hours following the procedure. Then plain gruel and a poached egg. Mutton and potatoes on the third day, provided the patient's bowel evacuations are of a normal character and frequency."

Dr. Addams *hmmph*ed, but a slight smile played at his lips. By the end of the day, he was addressing her as "Doctor."

Tucia had been elated. But looking back now, she could see that was the beginning, the first inconspicuous turn in the road to her downfall.

To the great annoyance of the other interns, Dr. Addams continued to call on her. He invited her to observe special procedures and discussed case notes with her until late into the night. He praised her skill and intellect in front of other physicians but also when they were alone, which more and more often he contrived for them to be. Alone in the laboratory so he could show her a particularly interesting specimen beneath the microscope. Alone in the hospital's library to read the latest medical journals. Alone in his office to discuss the coming day's surgery.

His attentions thrilled and flattered her. Legitimized her claim upon the profession. So she didn't object when he stood too close. Or casually brushed a hand against hers. Or complimented her lovely complexion and alluring eyes. Far better that than being ignored.

Or so Tucia thought.

And then, a month into her internship, when he'd pushed her up against the wall in his office and kissed her, she'd been too shocked to object. As his hands groped at her skirts, tugging them upward, her shock had morphed into fear. Not only fear of what he was doing. Fear of what would happen to her and her place at Fairview if she objected.

Her entire life had been one of action, of bucking expectation and seizing what she wanted. But here, pressed against the cold wall, Tucia couldn't move. Couldn't breathe. Couldn't scream.

Even when it was over, and Dr. Addams stepped away, breathing heavily as he buttoned up his pants, Tucia remained frozen. It wasn't until he sat down at his desk and took up his pen, going on as if nothing had happened, as if she weren't still standing there stiffly against the wall, that her body reanimated. Her limbs began shaking, and a sob built in her throat. She clamped her lips against the sound, smoothed her skirt with a trembling hand, and staggered out of his office.

For the next few days, Tucia kept to the back of the gaggle of interns, skittish of his gaze and silent to the questions he lobbed their way. And though she couldn't refuse when he called her into his office again, Tucia was ready with her objections.

But Dr. Addams was not a man accustomed to being denied. He tried to cajole her, coerce her, and then, at last, disparage her. *You're nothing without me*, he'd said. And two days later in the operating theater, he'd proven it.

Now Huey wanted to prove the same thing.

Tucia glanced at Toby. He was smiling in his sleep, yesterday's tears forgotten. There was so little of herself left. So little, it seemed, to salvage. But for Toby's sake, she must. They were trapped here under Huey's thumb for heavens knew how long. If they couldn't leave, she'd have to find some way to endure.

No, not just endure, but *live*. And recover what she could of her self-respect. But she couldn't do it alone. The others had never been her enemies, though they might have treated her coldly at first. Toby had been wise enough to see that. Why hadn't she?

For a moment yesterday, as he'd reached for the baseball, a look of pure joy had shone on his face. That was thanks to Darl. And Al. And a pair of discarded shoes.

Surely joy like that was worth bending one or two of her rules.

She grabbed the borrowed baseball mitt, slipped out of the wagon, and went in search of Darl.

He was an easy man to find, always making some kind of noise with his hands or tools. Today, he was in front of the stage where the nightly crowds had worn the grass down to a bald patch of dirt and dust. Half a dozen crates and various other bits of refuse lay scattered about. Darl picked up one of the crates and began prying apart the wood. Townsfolk brought them to sit on during the show, but Huey insisted a standing crowd bought more medicine. So every morning, those that remained were broken down and tossed into the cookfire.

If Darl saw her approach, he made no show of it and continued dismantling the wooden slats and tossing them to the ground. The sun was just peeking above the horizon, and a thin scrim of mist still hung in the air, but he'd already abandoned his jacket and worked up a sheen of sweat on his brow.

"Morning," she said, trying for that friendly lightness she heard in other people's voices.

Darl only grunted.

"I wanted to return this." She held out the baseball mitt.

He took his time prying apart the last few slats, then walked over. "That all?" he said, without taking the mitt.

Tucia sighed and lowered her arm. She hadn't fully worked out what she wanted to say to him beyond an apology, but now even the words *I'm sorry* seemed to stick in her throat. "About yesterday, I . . . Toby's not like other boys and—"

"You don't say."

"He's got a defect with his heart, and his lungs aren't strong."

"Strong enough to run. You, on the other hand . . ."

She scowled at him. "My point is, he needs careful minding."

"He followed us down to the field. When I saw he was there, I let him play along. That's all."

"Yes, but—"

"Listen, if you wanna lock your boy up like a circus animal, that ain't none of my business. I won't butt in again." He reached for the baseball mitt, grabbing it as Tucia tightened her hold.

"I do not keep him locked up like an animal!"

"No?" He pulled on the mitt.

She pulled back. "There are a hundred things out here that could hurt him."

He let go and jabbed a finger toward their wagon. "That wagon's a cage. Ain't right for anyone, especially not a young boy like him."

"You don't know the first thing about caring for a child."

"Maybe not. But I know what it's like to be locked up in a cage. And trust me, it ain't no way to live."

Tucia opened her mouth to speak but closed it again. Locked up in a cage? Did he mean a jail cell? For what crime? His stony expression told her it was better not to ask. She glanced at the wagon, then back at his dark eyes, hugging the baseball mitt to her chest. "I know. But how else am I supposed to keep him safe?"

"You can start by trusting that the rest of us ain't gonna do him no harm." His gaze traveled to her swollen lip. "'Cept maybe Huey."

Heat crept into her cheeks, and she turned her face away from him.

"He do that?"

"You needn't worry about Huey. I'll kill him if he touches my son."

Darl nodded slowly. "And the rest of us?"

"It did seem like Toby was having fun playing ball."

"He ain't that bad at it neither."

She fingered the mitt's unraveling laces and smooth worn leather. "I don't know what I'd do if something ever happened to him. He's . . . he's everything to me."

"I grew up with little mindin' and I turned out okay."

"That's yet debatable."

He grinned, and Tucia realized it was the first time she'd seen him smile. Thanks to his scar, the grin was somewhat lopsided, but handsome nonetheless.

She held out the baseball mitt again. "It was good of you to let him join you yesterday. And I'm . . . I'm sorry I reacted with such a hot temper."

"Keep it."

Tucia returned his smile. "But if he plays again, mind that he doesn't wander off. Or get bitten by a snake. Or fall into—"

"He'll be fine."

For all she knew, Darl might be a criminal. But somehow, she believed him.

Silence spread in the space between them. Darl glanced at the remaining crates but didn't move to pick one up. She ought to let him get back to work but instead found herself searching for something more to say.

The sudden clang of Cal's triangle spoke for her. Breakfast. Neither of them moved until it clanged a second time. And just like that, they were in motion again, Tucia turning and heading to the wagon to wake Toby, Darl bending to pick up the slats of wood. She glanced back as she reached the wagon's steps, watching him walk toward the cook tent with the wood, still wearing a hint of a grin.

27

Tucia kept her attention fixed on the doorway during supper, bracing for Huey's arrival. There was little left to say in last night's feud. She was here and had no choice but to remain. But she wouldn't put it past him to crow about his victory. Or browbeat her in front of the others for her poor performance in the last show.

She hadn't seen him all day and imagined him curled up in his wagon with his pipe. Usually, though, she'd catch a whiff of the smoke in the air—burnt sugar and decaying leaves. Today she hadn't. It was a relief not to smell it. Not to see him. But as the day wore on, her nerves had wound tighter. Did he have more hateful surprises for her? More vile words. More rage. Better to know and get it over with.

She caught Darl looking at her as she glanced away from the tent's door. An odd fluttering stirred in her stomach. Dyspepsia, no doubt.

He leaned toward her across the table, and Tucia found herself leaning forward too. His eyes, which she'd taken before to be a flat brown, had threads of gold and green. They were not arresting eyes like Huey's. Not the kind that caught you off guard or made you feel pinned like an insect in a display case. They were unassuming eyes. Deep and calming.

"He took the early train into the city," Darl said.

Tucia rattled her head. "Who?"

"Huey. Ran out of that crud he smokes."

"Oh," she managed, pulling back as she refocused her thoughts. That would explain Huey's particularly labile temper yesterday. "What about the show?"

"He'll be back for that. Always is."

She sighed. So much for a night's reprieve. She nudged the food around on her plate. Cal had made roast mutton with gravy, potatoes, and greens—an impressive feat considering he hadn't a proper stove. Delicious, too, if a bite or two were enough to judge. But Tucia had no appetite for the rest.

"Mama," Toby said. "Don't play with your food."

She looked down at the mess she'd made of her plate as he laughed. From across the table, Al laughed too. A flush crept into her cheeks. "Thank you for the reminder, darling," she said to Toby, and then to Cal, "It's a wonderful meal."

He replied with a snort. But she caught the twitch of a smile too. She managed a few more bites before Huey swept into the tent. He carried two brown paper–wrapped parcels under one arm and a box-shaped object draped in red cloth in the other.

"Good evening, my friends," he said, the cheer in his voice jarring after last night's encounter. "I trust you've had a restful day in preparation for tonight's show."

"What's under the cloth?" Al said.

"What's under the cloth?" Toby echoed.

Huey smiled. "It's a surprise." He set the object down on the table. "But first . . ." He removed the parcels from under his arm and handed the smaller one to Al. "A treat for everyone."

Al tore through the paper wrapping to reveal a box of chocolate bonbons. "Yum!"

The lid was off and two chocolates crammed in his mouth before Al noticed the sharp stare of his mother and set the box in the center of the table for the rest of them.

Toby reached out, but Tucia caught his arm before he could snatch a bonbon from the box. She hated the idea of Huey buying her son's affection. But when Toby turned to her with pleading eyes she let go of his arm. "Only one."

"And this is for you, my dear," Huey said, holding the larger package out to her. She met his smile with a glare. But, feeling the weight of everyone's gaze, she took the package. It was rectangular in shape, slender, and surprisingly heavy.

"Careful," he said, as she began to unwrap it. "It's fragile."

Her hand itched to shatter whatever was inside, but she didn't want to create more of a scene. Beneath several layers of paper was a pane of glass.

"Hold it up," he said. "See how clear it is."

Tucia obeyed, despite the sick feeling in her stomach. The glass was indeed clear. And smooth. And exactly what she would have wanted if it weren't a token of apology for the bruise on her face. For his refusal to let her leave.

"And how much will this add to my debt?"

"Nonsense. It's a gift. Now Darl can finally fix that window for you." He said it as if Darl were the one responsible for the delay. Darl snickered.

She pushed aside her plate and set the glass on the table. Part of her wanted to refuse. To shove it back to him. To let him know he couldn't buy her forgiveness. But then she and Toby would be stuck with a broken window for the rest of the summer. A chance for a cross breeze through their wagon was worth a little of her pride. But she'd not give him the satisfaction of a thank-you.

"What's the other surprise?" Al asked, his lips ringed with chocolate.

Huey grabbed the edge of the cloth, holding them in suspense for several more seconds before whisking the cloth away to reveal a rusty metal cage. Inside sat a stuffed monkey.

"Voilà!" Huey said as if this were an act and he'd just unveiled something spectacular. Then the monkey squeaked. Tucia startled, nearly falling backward off the bench.

"A pet monkey!" Al cried, and the animal squeaked again.

"A pet monkey," Toby said, clapping his hands.

"Monkeys are not pets," Tucia said, drawing Toby onto her lap and scooting away from the cage.

"A new addition for the show." Huey rummaged through his coat pockets and withdrew a miniature red vest. "The audience will love it."

"Can I touch him?" Al asked.

"That's not a good idea, son," Cal said at the same time Huey said, "Why, of course."

He unlatched a small door at the front of the cage. "I have it on good authority that the animal's quite docile."

The minute the door swung open, however, the monkey sprang out. It bounded down the table, knocking over cups and upending plates. Coffee spilled. Potatoes and greens went flying. Tucia's arms tightened around Toby as she stood.

The monkey leapt from the table onto the apple barrel and from there to the crates of canned goods and flour. It screeched and grunted as it scrabbled up one stack of crates and down another. Then it vanished from sight. When Al crouched down on the ground to look behind the crates, it jumped out from the shadows, using the boy's back as a springboard to bound onto the table again.

Lawrence tried to grab it as it scurried past him, but the animal was too quick. It climbed on top of its cage and from there made an astonishing leap upward, grabbing hold of the ridge pole that ran the length of the tent's roof.

There it cowered, screeching down at them.

"What the devil kind of animal did you buy?" Darl growled, looking around the tent, presumably for something to swat it down with.

"I'll get it," Fanny said. "Poor thing's just scared."

Toby wriggled free from Tucia's arms. She shepherded him to the edge of the tent, keeping him behind her. Scared the monkey may be—it was certainly shaking—but dangerous too. Who knew what sort of diseases it carried.

Fanny didn't even need to rise onto her tiptoes to reach the top of the tent. But just as her fingers drew close, the animal jumped onto her head. Fanny shrieked, batting it away. It scurried onto her shoulder and from there to the table, upsetting whatever cups and plates it had missed on its initial mad dash.

Now all the men were on the case. But as soon as one got close enough to catch it, the monkey fled in the opposite direction, scampering high and low to evade capture. Just when Tucia thought they had it cornered behind the water barrel, Cal said, "Damned beast's disappeared."

"Maybe it snuck beneath the canvas," Al said, running outside to check. Cal joined him while the others continued to search inside.

"Where's your lariat?" Huey said to Lawrence. "Can't you just lasso the thing?"

"A monkey? Here, inside the tent?" Lawrence shook his head as if he'd never heard such a ridiculous request.

"One way or another we've got to catch it. I paid good money for the thing."

The men rummaged through crates. They overturned the benches. After a glare in Huey's direction, Darl got down on his hands and knees and crawled beneath the table. Fanny searched up high. Tucia stayed close to Toby, peering around the tent in case she spotted it.

Cal returned to the mouth of the tent. "Find him?"

Fanny shook her head. "You?"

"Nah. Must'a run away."

"All for the better," Tucia said. "Monkeys can carry rabies. Not to mention worms and fleas and—" She stopped at the sound of Toby's laughter and turned around. He was cradling his stomach as if he were ill. But then he laughed again.

"Toby, what's wrong?"

"He's tickling me."

Tucia bent down in front of him. "What's tickling—"

Just then, the top button of his shirt popped off and the monkey peeked its head out through the collar. Startled, Tucia lost her balance and fell back onto her rear. The monkey gave a soft squeak as Toby continued to giggle. She scrambled forward onto her knees and reached out. "It's all right, darling. Don't move. It won't hurt you."

But her heart was pounding as she spoke. If the monkey bit Toby's neck, its teeth could nick his carotid artery. Or what if it were rabid? She moved slowly as the others gathered around, not wanting to spook it. But the monkey cowered back inside Toby's shirt as her hands neared.

"I'm going to unbutton your shirt and we'll get it, okay?"

Toby shuffled back. "He's my friend."

"It's not your friend, darling. It's a wild animal."

"He's my friend!" Toby cried, cradling the monkey close to him and taking another step back.

Tucia winced, afraid his loud voice would startle the thing, but the monkey remained still. She glanced at the others. Surely someone had an idea how to get this beast off her son, but they all stared at Toby in curious amazement.

"Go get the cage," she hissed at Huey, then turned back to Toby and inched closer. "I think it's tired, darling. We should put it back in the cage so it can sleep."

"He can sleep with me."

"No, it can't, darling."

The monkey stirred beneath his shirt, and Toby giggled again. "He likes me."

Huey grabbed the cage from the far end of the table and brought it toward them. The creak of metal made the monkey whimper.

"He's scared," Toby said.

"I know, but it will feel safer in the cage." Tucia reached toward him again. "Can you give it—er—him to Mama?" She unfastened the top buttons of his shirt and slowly reached inside. The monkey trembled as she wrapped her hands around it.

Huey was ready with the cage the moment Tucia turned around. She thrust the monkey inside, and he slammed the cage shut the second her hands were out. The monkey went wild, jumping and screeching. Toby started to cry and stomp his feet.

"He's scared! He's scared."

Huey draped the red cloth back over the cage but the monkey continued to wail. As did Toby, hollering between sobs, "My monkey! My monkey!"

Damn Huey for this mess. He grabbed the cage by the handle and began to walk away, but Tucia caught his arm. "What are you going to do with it?"

Huey shrugged. "The man I bought it off of said the beast was trained. I suppose I ought to have demanded proof. It can sit in its cage onstage before the show at any rate. Drum up some excitement."

"That will only frighten the monkey further," Tucia said, drawing Toby toward her. He wiped his nose on her skirt and continued to cry.

Huey gave another shrug and started again toward the door.

"He might bite someone," Darl said.

Tucia flashed him a grateful smile. "Yes. If one of the yokels gets too close or pokes a finger into the cage. An animal in distress is bound to bite. Think of how the audience would react then."

Huey sighed and turned around. "Very well." He walked back and thrust the cage into her arms. "It seems to like the boy. You keep it until it settles down."

"I wasn't suggesting . . . I only wanted . . ."

Huey reached down and ruffled Toby's hair. "Take good care of him, now, you hear? We need him for the show."

"I will!" Toby said.

"No, that's not what—" Tucia began, but Huey was gone from the tent before she could finish. Anger curled inside her. Damn that man! One look at Toby's overjoyed face, however, and she knew she couldn't hand the animal off to anyone else.

"You got a name for it?" Lawrence asked, looking down at Toby.

"It's not a pet," she said, at the same time, Toby said, "Kitty."

"Kitty the monkey?" Lawrence asked, choking down a laugh. Toby nodded.

"How 'bout Kit for short?" Darl said.

"Kit!" Toby echoed, his smile glowing even brighter.

"Come on," she said. "Let's go see if we can give him a bath."

28

In a week's time, Toby and Kitty—or Kit, as everyone came to call him—were inseparable, much to Tucia's chagrin. At least, after careful inspection, she'd assured herself he wasn't rabid or carrying fleas, lice, or worms. They kept his cage in their wagon, but Kit was seldom inside, preferring instead to travel around on Toby's shoulder, perch on his lap, or curl up in the nest of rags they'd made for him beside the bed. (He would not sleep with them *in* the bed—on that point Tucia remained firm.)

Kit was friendly with Al too. He tolerated the adults. All, save for Huey. Whenever he drew close, Kit hissed and screeched, and scampered out of reach. And though Huey promised one way or another he'd get that animal in the show, he still hadn't managed it.

Though having a pet monkey—and regrettably, he *was* a pet— went against all her physician's instincts, Tucia was grateful to see Toby so happy.

Soon after Kit's arrival, as they were settling into a new town, Huey stormed into the cook tent as they were finishing lunch. His lips were set in a snarl, and air wheezed through his flared nostrils. "Tonight's show is canceled."

"Canceled?" Darl said. "I ain't seen a cloud in the sky."

Tucia hadn't either, and rain was the only reason Huey canceled a show. And not just a little rain. It had to be a deluge.

Huey slammed a piece of paper on the table, rattling their plates and cups. "The damned Kicks have frozen us out."

Tucia glanced at the paper. Several colorful sketches adorned the page. A clutch of teepees. A lone Indian in a canoe. A group of braves with their bow-and-arrows drawn. The words *Kickapoo Indian Medicine Company* were stamped in bold letters across the top.

Another show had come to town? That explained the dwindling crowds the last few nights. And Huey's foul mood. She leaned toward Fanny and whispered, "I thought it was considered bad form to set up in a town where another troupe was already playing."

Fanny shrugged. "Big shows don't always bother with the rules."

Tucia studied the show bill more closely. *Free to all!* it read. *Indian Medicine Camp illustrating the wild, savage life on the plains. Picturesque Indian Village! Full War Costumes—Most Interesting Entertainment!* The names of several of the Indians were listed too, each with the appellation doctor. Dr. Eagle Eye. Dr. Poor Fox. Dr. Antelope. Dr. Lone Cloud. Dr. Swift Bear. She doubted greatly that any of them were really doctors, at least not in the traditional sense of the word. The profession was as unfriendly to men of other races as it was to women. And considering what Lawrence had told her, she doubted those were their real names.

Huey railed for an hour about the Kickapoos' second-rate show and the great slight they'd paid him by setting up camp in *his* town. Then he shooed everyone from the cook tent, telling them to wash up and don their Sunday best. Tonight they'd see this pathetic excuse for a medicine show themselves.

* * *

The Kickapoos had made their encampment at the opposite end of the town in a vacant lot beside the train station—a lot, Huey griped, refused to them when he'd met with the mayor to secure their reader. The camp sprawled the entirety of the lot, boasting a stage almost twice as large as theirs, a dozen more tents, and a ring of six teepees.

They tied the buckboard and horses to a split-rail fence at the edge of the lot and started for the teepees. Huey, dressed in his grand satin cape and top hat, took the lead.

As they drew near, Tucia noticed several Indian men dressed in fringed and beaded deerskin milling about the teepees. Before meeting Lawrence, she would have assumed this was their everyday routine. Would have assumed the brightly painted teepees were a faithful reproduction of a real Kickapoo village. Now she suspected much of it was for show.

On the surface, the village was an impressive display. A panorama of mounted braves chasing buffalo was painted across the white canvas of the teepees. A brewing potion of Indian herbs bubbled above a low fire in the center of the ring. But on closer inspection, Tucia realized the weathered canvas, the rusty pot, the shaky tent poles, and the shabby buckskin were all just worn-out props, the "picturesque Indian Village" advertised on the show bill just a set piece. The men themselves looked tired. No, not tired, vacant. As if they'd holed up somewhere deep inside themselves and weren't coming out for the ogling townsfolk.

Then one of the men's faces brightened. He strode to Lawrence and embraced him. A flurry of words Tucia didn't understand passed between them. It sounded different from when Lawrence was onstage recounting the Battle of the Little Big Horn—warmer, somehow, and more fluid—though she suspected it was the same language. A few other Kickapoos came over and the men switched to a pidgin blend of English and Indian.

"They're not all Kickapoo, are they?" she said to Darl, who'd come up beside her. He looked rather dapper in his Sunday suit, though she could tell by the way he kept tugging on his collar he didn't much like wearing a necktie.

"Reckon none of them is."

Then, suddenly, the group of Indians went silent and straightened. Tucia followed their gaze to a white man striding toward the village from the cluster of tents behind the stage. The fringe on his buckskin suit trembled with each powerful step. He looked the image of Buffalo Bill with his long blond hair, wide-brimmed hat, and hooked mustache.

The man growled something, and the Indians dispersed, their bright, animated expressions disappearing as they resumed milling about the village like wind-up figurines.

"Well, if it isn't the Amazing Adolphus and his ragtag band of performers," the man said, approaching Huey. "I didn't know you were in town."

Huey gave a tight smile and tipped his hat. "Texas Joe, what a surprise to stumble upon you and your little show here."

The man, Texas Joe, slapped Huey on the back as if they were old friends. Huey stumbled forward, anger flashing in his eyes. But his thin-lipped smile held.

"Do they know each other?" Tucia whispered to Darl.

He nodded, his jaw tight.

Texas Joe towered above Huey, his manner rough and feral. But both men had that oversized air about them.

"I see you've brought the whole troupe," Texas Joe said, his eyes sliding from Fanny and Cal to Lawrence, Darl, and lastly to her. He touched the brim of his hat. "And someone new."

His gaze lingered, sliding lazily over her like the wet tongue of a dog. Tucia pulled Toby closer to her side, not returning the man's slick smile.

Huey swept his arm in her direction. "May I introduce the esteemed Dr. Hatherley. She has been traveling with the show nigh three months now."

"A lady doctor?" He snorted. "What will you come up with next, Huey?"

"It's no gimmick. She carries a bona fide degree and license."

Texas Joe cocked his head, his leering expression turning to bemusement. "Well, I'll be. You must be making a pretty penny off her."

"Watch what you say," Darl said. "She's a doctor not a—" He stopped, his gaze flickering down to Toby.

"That's the most words I've ever heard you string together, Darl. Heck, I wasn't even sure you could talk on account of that harelip and all."

Darl's right hand curled into a fist.

"I rather prefer a man who knows the value of silence," Tucia said, watching from the corner of her eye as Darl inhaled slowly and relaxed his hand. "So many open their mouths only to reveal themselves fools."

Texas Joe chuckled. "You're quite right, Doctor. If you ever get tired of working for old Huey here, I'm sure we can find a place for you in our show."

"I'll stick with the devil I know, thank you."

"Think on it while you watch the show." He winked at her. "I guarantee you'll be impressed."

"Impressed?" Huey said, drawing back Texas Joe's attention. "The season's only half over and things are looking a little"—he cast a sidelong glance at one of the teepees—"threadbare."

It didn't surprise Tucia Huey had noticed too. He was nothing if not observant. And she enjoyed watching the flush that crept from beneath Texas Joe's collar.

"Yokels don't seem to mind," Texas Joe said, his voice tighter than before. "We don't usually bother with towns this small. Better for you lesser outfits. But we've had a real fine crowd these last few nights. You?"

Now it was Huey whose neck reddened. "We're having our best season yet."

"That so?" He looked again at the rest of them, the skepticism plain on his face. "Then I guess the first drink tonight's on you." He gave Huey another slap. "Bring your pretty little doctor along too."

He flashed her another sickening smile, then strode away.

It wasn't long before music sounded, and they made their way toward the stage.

"You didn't need to stand up for me back there," she said to Darl as they found a spot on the plank board benches to sit. "I'm perfectly capable of holding my own."

"So am I."

She crossed her arms and turned her attention to the band—a three-man outfit of only passable talent. When her gaze strayed back to him, she caught the flicker of a smile.

"I did rather like hearing you call him a fool, though," he said.

Tucia's posture relaxed as she fought off a smile of her own. "Well, he certainly fits the bill."

The band played a few more songs as townsfolk continued to arrive. Then they quit the stage, and Texas Joe appeared. He introduced himself to the crowd as a scout and fighter who'd licked enough Injuns to gain their obedience. Now, he acted as their agent. He called them to the stage one by one just as they'd been listed on the show bill—Dr. Eagle Eye, Dr. Poor Fox, Dr. Antelope, Dr. Lone Cloud, Dr. Swift Bear.

They were the same vacant-eyed men she'd seen idling about the teepees and cook fire earlier. They'd spruced up their outfits a bit, adding feather headdresses, beaded vests, and finely embroidered cross-shoulder bags. Two of them carried drums that they beat in a quick, steady rhythm while the others sang and danced in what Texas Joe called "traditional savage fashion."

After a few minutes, the dancing and drumming stopped. The men sat down in a semicircle onstage, facing the audience. One lit a peace pipe and passed it around to the others. Smoke rose into the darkening night while the rich scent of tobacco wafted over the audience. When each of the Indians had taken a draw from the pipe, one of them—the man who'd first spoken to Lawrence—stood and addressed the crowd.

He spoke with great solemnity in the same language Tucia had heard him use before. The audience listened with awe. Everyone except Lawrence. He was chuckling. She glanced at him, then back to the stage, noticing one of the seated Indians fighting back a smile. Another seemed to swallow down a burp of laughter.

Until now, their expressions had been as hard and unyielding as stone. But Tucia caught a flash of mischief in the speaking man's eyes. He continued on in his language, gesturing now with great force toward the sky, the ground, and then the audience.

Lawrence let out a full-fledged laugh. Standing at the far edge of the stage, Texas Joe's face darkened. His eyebrows pulled together and he threw a cutting glance at the speaker. But the Indian's monologue only grew livelier. Whatever he was saying, it had nothing to do with the peace pipe ceremony they'd just performed.

Another of the seated men choked back a peal of laughter, and Texas Joe cut in. "That will do, Dr. Lone Cloud." He shooed the men offstage.

Another musical act came next, then Texas Joe again, spieling about the blood-cleansing, life-sustaining properties of Indian Sagwa, a secret compound of roots and herbs. Available tonight for the very low price of one dollar!

Tucia only half listened as he boasted of all the ailments Sagwa could cure—constipation, liver complaints, dyspepsia, rheumatism, scrofula, catarrh. Her thoughts kept drifting back to the Indian's performance.

Whatever he'd said, it had been an act of defiance. Small perhaps, but potent. A way to show Texas Joe and the audience—even if they didn't realize it—that he was no one's man but his own.

Could Tucia find a way to do the same?

29

The next morning, Tucia stood watching Toby fill his breakfast plate. Wanting to be just like Al, he'd stopped letting her do it for him. He had to stand on his tiptoes to dip into the pots and pans, and more than once left a goopy trail of oatmeal and a pool of spilled milk on the buffet table, but it was a small price to pay to avoid a row.

Kit sat on his shoulder, chirping his approval of the second biscuit Toby had snuck onto his plate.

They'd only just sat down when Huey charged into the dining tent and announced they were leaving as soon as the camp could be packed up. No one was surprised. Even if their acts were better, they couldn't compete with a show the size of the Kickapoos'. In addition to the peace pipe ceremony, the Indians performed a medicine ceremony and a war dance. A contortionist, a blackface comedian, and the three-piece band also took turns onstage. Even Texas Joe had a fancy rifle shooting act he performed between hawking Indian Sagwa. The troupe sold penny candy between acts, too, and raffled off a quilt, a watch, and a cut-glass bowl.

Tucia was surprised, however, that Huey was awake so early.

After the show, he'd taken one of the horses and joined Texas Joe at a nearby saloon. Darl had gone, too, though he'd hardly looked eager, and Tucia suspected he was there to keep Huey out of trouble more than anything else. Thankfully, she'd been spared.

Before Tucia could take a sip of her coffee, Huey said, "Well, what are you waiting for?"

She looked around at the others. The Trouts had barely started eating. Darl and Lawrence weren't even up yet.

"We're eating our breakfast," she said.

"No, you're packing up camp." Huey's voice had a venomous edge.

"As soon as we're done we'll—"

He strode over and snatched her plate. "Not as soon as you're done." He threw it into the washbasin with a splash and clang. "Now!"

Kit gave a squeak and Toby scooted closer to her, leaving his own plate abandoned. Apparently drinks with Texas Joe had only further soured Huey's mood.

"What about the food, boss?" Cal asked. "You just want us to waste it?"

"You can shove it in your ears for all I care. We're packing up and leaving. Right now." He leered at them until they all stood and scraped their uneaten breakfast into the slop bucket. Tucia didn't even dare pocket the biscuits on Toby's plate for fear of further enraging Huey. He turned to go, but then spun around. "Where's Lawrence?"

Tucia had thought him still sleeping, but Cal said, "He stayed behind after the show. Said he'd be back this morning."

"And yet he's not."

"It's mighty early, boss."

Huey's expression darkened, but he shrugged as if it were of little consequence. "If he's not here to pack up his things we'll leave them behind. He can go without a tent for the rest of the season. Savage that he is, he might even prefer it."

Darl strode in then, bleary-eyed and unshaven.

"No breakfast," Huey snapped. "Get to work on the god-damned stage. We're leaving in an hour."

They broke down camp in record time, but it was still too slow for Huey, who strode around barking orders and doing little work himself. Lawrence didn't return, and when Darl made to pack up Lawrence's tent, Huey shouted not to touch it.

Tucia had brought very little with them from their flat in St. Louis. They'd had few possessions to begin with. But what she had brought—her mother's quilt, Toby's building blocks, even her old textbook—she'd be heartbroken to find gone. She kept watch on the road, hoping Lawrence would return in time to pack up his tent. But they were nearly finished and still he had not.

She passed Darl on her way to load a sack of flour into the buckboard. "If you create a distraction," she whispered, "I'll slip inside Lawrence's tent and grab what I can."

Darl hesitated a moment, then nodded.

A few minutes later, she heard a loud clatter followed by Huey shouting, "You clumsy ass!" She hurried to Lawrence's tent and dove inside without looking back to see what sort of mess Darl had orchestrated. Whatever it was, she wouldn't have much time.

Lawrence's tent was a small, wedge-shaped affair. But inside, it was spacious and surprisingly tidy. After a quick glance around, she grabbed the brightly woven blanket folded atop his bedroll and shoved it into her satchel. A paperboard-framed photograph sat propped up against the canvas wall. She slipped that into her satchel, too, along with the small leather notebook he often carried. There were other things—a knife with a carved handle, a beaded sachet, a book of Whitman's poems—but the noise outside had quieted and she didn't dare stay any longer.

Peeking through the tent flap, she saw Huey standing beside the buckboard. She waited until his back was turned before scrambling out. She'd gone a few steps before Huey turned and saw her. His eyes narrowed and he started to stalk over, when Darl called out that one of the horses had thrown a shoe. Huey spun back around and she hurried to her wagon, hiding the satchel at the bottom of her trunk.

Once Huey had determined the horse had not thrown a shoe and berated Darl for his harebrained mistake, they set off. They were almost to town when they came upon Lawrence ambling down the road. His face went ashen when Huey refused to let him take a horse and collect his things from their abandoned camp.

"I'll be there and back in under fifteen minutes," he said.

"We're already running late because you weren't around to help dismantle the stage and ready the animals."

"Late?" He glanced at the sky. "The sun ain't hung but nine o'clock high."

"Get in the wagon," Huey said, "or I'll head straight to the telegraph office and wire Agent Smithfield."

Lawrence glanced down the road toward their old encampment, then over his shoulder toward town, as if gauging whether he could fetch his things and still beat Huey to the telegraph office. But even with a horse, it was no contest. His shoulders fell and he climbed onto the driver's seat of the supply wagon beside Darl.

Later that night, after they'd pulled off alongside the road, scarfed down their supper, and turned in, a low knock sounded on her door. She opened it to find Lawrence standing on the steps.

"Darl said you might have some of my things."

Tucia glanced over his shoulder to make sure Huey wasn't about, then nodded. "Wait here."

She left the door open, and he sat down on the wagon's top step. Toby was asleep in bed with Kit curled in his nest of rags nearby. She opened her trunk slowly, glad when the hinges didn't creak and wake them. After grabbing her satchel, she sat down on the step beside Lawrence, pulling the door halfway closed behind her.

"I didn't have a lot of time," she said, handing him the satchel.

He pulled out the blanket and brought it to his nose, inhaling deeply. Then he retrieved the photograph. He held it in both hands, staring down at the image. Only a faint glow of light reached them from the lamp hanging inside, but Tucia could make out two people—a man and woman—standing side by side in the photograph.

"Who are they?" she asked.

Lawrence traced the outline of the figures with his finger, a smile pulling at his lips even as he blinked back tears. "My parents."

He seemed so young suddenly. He *was* so young, though it was easy to forget here on the road.

"And the man you were talking to yesterday before the show, was he family too?"

"A cousin." He swiped his eyes with his shirtsleeve and reached into the satchel again.

"I wasn't sure what to grab," she said when he pulled out the notebook. "There was your knife and that beautiful beaded bag, but I always see you carrying this and thought—"

"*Mvto.*" He pressed the notebook to his forehead and breathed a sigh. "Thank you."

"What's inside?"

He tucked the notebook between the folds of his blanket.

"Sorry, I . . . it's late and I've forgotten my manners," Tucia said, when he didn't reply. "I shouldn't pry."

"Poems," he said. "A few comedy sketches."

"For the show?"

He shrugged.

"You should—" Tucia stopped. She'd been about to say he should ask Huey if he could perform a few in the next town, but that was foolhardy. Huey was more apt to laugh in his face than let him perform them. "Toby and I, we're good listeners if you ever want to try them out on an audience."

"Thanks."

"Toby especially. You know he's always quick to laugh."

"There was a boy like him from the town near our ranch. They rounded him up like the rest of us for boarding school. But he wasn't there for more than a few weeks before they sent him away. Home, I thought. And I was jealous. But later I learned they sent him to an asylum in Kansas. He died of typhoid before his family even knew where he'd gone."

Tucia shuddered. How awful it would be to wake up one day and find Toby gone. Taken. Dead. She wrapped her arms around herself and stared up at the sky. It was a clear night, dark, the crescent moon just rising above the horizon. She was lucky Toby hadn't been taken like that. Lucky, too, she'd had a choice in coming here. A near impossible choice, yes. One with no good options. But a choice nonetheless.

She'd assumed Lawrence had a choice too. That he was here of his own volition. For the money perhaps. Or the novelty. The excitement. He was young, after all. And those were young men's pursuits. But maybe for Lawrence it hadn't been that simple.

"Huey threatened to wire a Mr. Smithfield if you disobeyed him. Who's that?"

Lawrence's hands clenched around the blanket, his knuckles white and bulging, before he drew in a breath and they relaxed. "*Agent* Smithfield. He's the man your government assigned to oversee our territory."

"Why should he control what you do here?"

He paused again. And she didn't pressure him to go on. There was plenty in her life she'd not want to share. But after a moment he turned to her and spoke.

The Indian's Story

Yaha Tustenuggee always had an ear for words, whether it was the *Mvskoke opunvkv* spoken at home, the English he learned at boarding school, or the *este charte*—red man—English bantered around town. He loved the way words sounded and the multitude of ways they could fit together. Their power to reach inside a man and pull something out of him—fear, anger, sadness, joy. But most of all, laughter. He loved the stories his grandmother told, the jokes spat back and forth between his father's ranch hands, the poems he read in school. And he dreamed someday of creating his own.

But Yaha Tustenuggee, who became Lawrence at school, also had a taste for politics. While he was reading Keats, Whitman, and Byron, he was also listening to whispers about allotment, statehood, and the dissolution of the Creek government.

Some, like Lawrence's father, supported the idea of dividing up the land and joining with Oklahoma Territory to become a new state. A new century's on its way, he told Lawrence, and Indian Territory has to change if it wants its share of progress.

Others thought differently. And though Lawrence held his father in high esteem, he found himself drawn to the fiery talk of a group of conservatives known as the Snakes.

Their leader insisted they hold fast to the Treaty of 1832, which guaranteed

Creek lands in Indian Territory. The United States, he said, had no business meddling in their laws and government. What had allotments and new deals with the United States brought their brothers to the north and west? he asked the crowd gathered alongside Lawrence to hear him speak. Poverty. Sickness. A plague of white men as thick as crows behind a plow.

Here was a man who knew the power of words.

In the leather-bound notebook his father had given him, Lawrence wrote down the Snake leader's words. They, too, were a kind of poetry. They reached inside him the way a sapling's roots reach into the earth, sucking up its medicine and giving life to something new. Passion. Conviction. A zeal Lawrence had never known he possessed.

Lawrence, his cousin, and a few of their school friends followed the Snakes to a small town along the Canadian River, joining them in establishing their own tribal government. A government dedicated to the old ways and treaties.

Young, eager, and comfortable in the saddle, Lawrence was made a light-horseman. He spread word through the area that those Creeks who signed up for allotments or rented out their land to whites or hired white laborers would be punished.

It was just words, though. Warnings.

But another word was spreading too: Uprising. It reached the ears of the Indian agent at Muskogee, who whispered it to the Inspector of Indian Territory, who wired it to the Secretary of the Interior, who called out the U.S. Marshals and cavalry.

Lawrence and many other Snakes found themselves locked away in the jailhouse in Muskogee. He sat for several weeks in a small, dank cell with only his notebook to occupy his time. He still believed the white man had no business telling the Creeks how to live, but the longer he sat, the less the Snake leader's words moved him. He missed his father and the ranch. He missed his mother and the boiled corn grits she made with pork grease and wild game. He missed the ranch hands and their raucous jokes. He missed his grandmother and her stories.

Lawrence never got a trial, but he did get a choice: two years at the federal prison in Leavenworth, Kansas, or four years performing with the Oregon Indian Medicine Company. Lawrence chose the medicine company. He'd already spent enough time locked up in a cell. His cousin and many other

Snakes chose the same fate. They were contracted out to other companies like the Kickapoos and Nevada Ned's Big Indian Village by the Office of Indian Affairs in exchange for a cash deposit.

The deposit, or security bond, was ostensibly to ensure the Indians were not mistreated and returned after their indenture ended. If it supplied the office with a little cash in the meantime, so much the better. But Lawrence only learned about the bond after the manager of the Oregon Indian Medicine Company lost it to another showman in the smoke-filled card room at the back of a saloon in Denver.

With over three years still left on his contract, Lawrence now belonged to the Amazing Adolphus, another man who had a way with words. But unlike Whitman or the Snake leader, his were false words, Lawrence soon learned. Empty of anything but poison.

Three days after her talk with Lawrence, Tucia waited in the case-taking tent as Huey fetched more bottles of medicine. They'd settled in a new town, one small enough the Kickapoos were unlikely to follow. The audience at last night's show had filled only half the lot, but nearly everyone had left with a bottle or two of rattlesnake oil. And they'd returned today for their free consultation.

The afternoon was only half over and already Tucia's feet ached. She took advantage of Huey's absence to sit down and prop her feet up on the examination table. The tent trapped the summer heat like an oven. Sweat dampened the thin chemise beneath her dress. She plucked off her cap and fanned herself.

A moment later, she heard the tent flap open.

"Please let's rest a moment more before you let the next client in. I—" Tucia turned and saw it wasn't Huey who'd entered. She hurriedly dropped her feet to the ground, tugging the hem of her skirt down to cover her ankles.

"I'm sorry, ma'am," the man said. "The feller over by the stage said this is where I could see the doc." The man doubled over with a hacking cough. His skin had a sallow tinge. When his cough subsided and he righted himself, she saw how sunken his cheeks were and the way his collarbone jutted out beneath his shirt. He fished through his pocket and handed her his ticket. "Got this at the show last night. The man said it was good for a sit-down with the doctor."

Tucia stood and gestured to the examination table. "Yes. Please take a seat."

The man happily obliged.

She started to say her partner would return in a moment, but stopped before the words left her mouth. "How long have you had that cough?" she asked instead.

"Goin' on two months, I reckon."

"Do you find yourself racked with chills?"

"Sometimes."

"Have you woken up at night to find your bedclothes soaked through with sweat?"

A flush rose in the man's cheeks as if such things were improper to discuss with her, and his gaze cut toward the door. "Shouldn't we wait for the doctor? He's coming, right?"

"I'll take that to mean yes." She grabbed the stethoscope from the small display table. The earpieces were cold and foreign as she situated them in her ears. She laid the drum of the stethoscope on the man's chest. "Breathe deeply for me."

It had been ages since she'd listened to a patient's breath sounds. Her hands trembled slightly but otherwise her hysteria remained in check. An experienced physician could differentiate between slight variations in a patient's lung sounds. The crackle of rales. The harsh squeak of strider. The low-pitched rattle of rhonchi. Tucia's practical experience amounted to a few weeks at Fairview and a single day at the women's hospital, but she'd heard enough to know this man's lungs were certainly not healthy.

She'd withdrawn the stethoscope from her ears and was about to ask the man if he ever coughed up blood, when Huey reappeared. He frowned, his eyes narrowing at her as he set down the crate of medicine he carried. But when he turned to the man on the table, his face was a mask of congeniality.

"I see my assistant wasted no time in beginning your examination."

"Doc, I've—" the man started to say but Huey waved him off and launched into his *Wait! Don't tell me* routine. Tucia tried to interrupt, first with a quiet *ahem* then with a louder clearing of her throat, but Huey ignored her. He began his phony exam, peering and poking indiscriminately. After a minute, Tucia finally managed to catch his eye and inclined her head toward the far side of the tent.

Huey straightened, "Sir, I know exactly what ails you and I've got just the thing for it. Give me a moment to consult with my assistant."

The man coughed in reply.

Huey grabbed Tucia's arm so tightly she thought her bone might snap and dragged her to the edge of the tent. "I run this show, remember?"

She wrested free of his grip. "This man has tuberculosis." When Huey didn't reply, she added, "Consumption."

"I know what it is," he said, glancing over his shoulder at the man. "Are you sure?"

She wasn't sure. It could be cancer or some other ailment she'd entirely forgotten. But one thing she was sure of: the man wasn't well. And his symptoms pointed to consumption. "Yes," she said, with as much confidence as she could muster.

"All right. Two bottles of catarrh cure and we'll send him on his way."

He started to turn back to the patient, but Tucia grabbed his sleeve. "No."

"No?"

"You said we wouldn't treat sick people. And this man is sick. May very well die without the right treatment."

Huey cocked his head, a bemused smile tugging at his lips. "Look who suddenly wants to play doctor."

"This isn't play." Her heart thudded against her breastbone, steady but insistent. "If this man dies, the weight of it would rest on us."

Huey's smile vanished and he glanced again at the man, who sat rubbing gooseflesh from his arms despite the tent's oppressive heat. "You're right. We could be held responsible if the law got involved."

That wasn't what she'd meant, but at least it had given him pause.

"Good sir," Huey said, turning around. "After speaking with my assistant, I've come to the conclusion that there's nothing wrong with you in the slightest."

"There isn't?"

"Not one thing."

Tucia gaped at Huey. It was just as unconscionable to tell a sick man he was well as it was to tell a well man he was sick. Worse, really, for this man needed care. May well die without it. Tucia didn't need another death on her conscience.

"But I got this cough and I'm tired as a dog and—"

"Actually," Tucia interrupted. "What my colleague was trying to say was, you're not ill in a way *we* can help with. But you are, I'm sorry to say, most decidedly sick."

The man glanced between them, confused. "But he said—"

"It's tuberculosis, I'm afraid." She walked up to the man and took his hands. His skin was clammy and rough. "Is there a doctor here in town?"

He shook his head, fear showing in his dark eyes. "No, that's why I came here." He looked to Huey. "Are you sure?"

"Sure enough we must insist you make a trip to the nearest town where a doctor resides and seek care," Tucia continued, even though the man was still not looking at her. "He may recommend you to a sanatorium, but perhaps you might stay here. There's great value in fresh air and the out-of-door life. With the proper medicine and sufficient nutrition, you may well recover."

His eyes brightened slightly at the word *recover*, and he turned back to her. "None of what you got here is the right medicine?"

"No," Tucia said even as she spied Huey from the corner of her eye reaching for a bottle of Catarrh Cure. She stepped in front of him, blocking him from the man's view. "You'll need Fowler's solution, and, perhaps a creosote tincture, syrupus codeiae for your cough. Those are best procured from a druggist."

Tucia was surprised how much she remembered from her schooling. She helped the man from the table and led him toward the mouth of the tent. "Best to stay away from the young and the enfeebled until your cough is better." She held the flap open for him, but the man paused and turned back to Huey.

"Thanks, Doc," he said.

Tucia ignored the slight and watched the man shuffle away. He'd only made the same assumption everyone else did. An assumption, a charade, they took pains to sow. And no matter if he thought her a nurse or assistant, for the first time since joining the show, a buoyant feeling filled her chest. She'd made a positive difference. Perhaps even saved the man's life.

She basked in the feeling until Huey came and stood beside her.

"We did the right thing," she said. "That man would have gotten much worse without proper care."

He pinched the back of her arm, his biting fingers cleverly hidden from the line of awaiting clients. "Don't ever contradict me in front of a yokel again."

31

The next morning after breakfast, Darl followed her and Toby back to their wagon to fix the window. Tucia still felt buoyed by a faint but pleasant lightness that outmatched the bruise Huey had left on her arm. Not only had she helped someone, someone truly in need, but she'd done it without the slightest flare of hysteria. Her hands had trembled, yes, but every other part of her body had remained steady. Present.

But perhaps best of all, in helping that man, she'd subverted Huey. A small act of defiance, just like Lawrence's cousin had done in the Kickapoos' show. And she longed to do it again. But how? It might be weeks before another truly ill person entered the case-taking tent.

She pulled herself from her thoughts as they arrived at the wagon, hesitating before opening the door. Their nightclothes were tucked away in the trunk and the bed made, but she still felt a prickle of discomfort at letting Darl inside. She doubted he was the type who'd notice dust in the corner or a few strands of monkey fur on the quilt. But it was more than that. Like they were crossing some threshold of familiarity. One there was no stepping back from.

Still, she couldn't keep Darl waiting on the steps while she scrubbed away any trace of her and Toby's private lives from the wagon. She took a deep breath and opened the door. Darl followed her inside with Toby and Kit bounding in after them. His head nearly scraped the ceiling, and between the tools he'd lugged inside and all three of their bodies—plus a monkey—the space felt impossibly small.

She followed his eyes as he glanced around.

"Can't say I've ever seen it look so homey in here. The only thing the last boozer brought with him was a jug of whiskey."

"You're forgetting the mouse."

Darl grinned and chuckled. It was the first time she'd seen him smile since the Kickapoos' show. He'd been almost as taciturn as Lawrence these past few days, though she couldn't say why.

"I see how come you've been pestering Huey about this window. It's hot as hel—er—hot as heck in here." He leaned the new pane of glass against the wall and looked at Toby. "Mind this now. Could hurt you mightily if it breaks."

"Yes, maybe we should take Kit and wait outside," Tucia said.

"I want to help," Toby said. "Can I help?"

"Okay by me if it's okay by your ma."

They both turned to look at her. Darl was right; it was hot as hell inside the wagon. Sweat had already begun to collect beneath her arms and at the small of her back. She'd much rather sit outside beneath the shade of a tree where they might be lucky enough to catch a breeze. But she nodded, looking around for an out-of-the-way place to sit. There was only the broken chair and the bed.

Her stepmother would have fainted at the mere suggestion of sitting on a bed in the presence of a man who wasn't her husband. She may well have blushed when that man *was* her husband. But Tucia had stopped being embarrassed by such things long ago. She sat on the bed and clicked her tongue for Kit to join her. He scurried from Toby's side and leapt onto the mattress.

"Got yourself a well-trained pet there," Darl said.

Tucia gave a wry smile and pulled the hankie from her pocket.

Inside were a few browning apple wedges. She gave one to Kit, who chirped with delight.

Darl chuckled again, a deep and pleasant sound, then squatted down and opened his tool bag. Toby crouched beside him.

"You listen to Mr. Darl, now," she said to Toby, and the two of them got to work.

Tucia grabbed a rumpled copy of *Collier's Weekly* from the makeshift shelf by her bed. Fanny had given it to her, and though it was a few years old, she enjoyed the stories and illustrations. But today, it served as little more than a pretense. Something to hold on to while she watched Darl and Toby work.

First, Darl laid out several tools, naming each and explaining their purpose. He didn't speak loudly or overly slow. Didn't incessantly repeat himself or use infantile words. Next, he pried loose the nails in the board that covered the missing pane, then handed the hammer to Toby, letting him give the final, freeing tug.

She expected Toby to quickly lose interest but he remained eager and attentive at Darl's side. Soon he'd learned the names of each of the tools and waited at the ready to hand over the hammer, the measuring tape, the screwdriver, the awl, the level at Darl's request.

Tucia delighted in seeing him so enthralled, eyes wide, mouth slack and smiling. And though surely Darl could complete the task in half the time on his own, he didn't seem to mind his little helper. He was careful, too, when the old windowpane was exposed, instructing Toby not to touch the sharp edge where it had cracked and broken.

Once they had removed the window sash from the jamb, Darl asked her to raise the flap table so they could use it as a workbench.

"It's broken," she said.

"It's broken," Toby echoed.

Darl frowned. He raised the flap and examined the damaged support beneath. "I can fix this, ya know."

"I told Huey."

"He look like someone that's handy with a hammer?"

"I thought he'd mention it to you."

"*Humph*," Darl said. He glanced at the broken table, then back to her.

"I didn't want to . . ." *Bother him*—that's what she'd been about to say. But he'd know it was a lie. "I didn't want to be indebted to anyone else."

"Do I seem like the kind of man who keeps score?"

"I assumed everyone did."

"That why you gathered up Lawrence's things for him?"

"No, of course not. I . . . I'd hate to have that happen to me, so I . . ." She shook her head. A man like him with no attachments wouldn't understand. "Never mind."

He gave another snort, then bent down in front of the broken table. "Hand me the screwdriver, kid."

In less than fifteen minutes, the support was fixed and the table worked good as new. Darl had even oiled the hinges so it didn't squeak when it was raised and lowered. He set the window sash atop it and began chipping away at the puttylike substance he called glazing compound holding the broken pane in place.

Before, the silence in the wagon hadn't bothered Tucia. Now, it felt as stifling as the heat. She tried to read the magazine—a new serial by Henry James. New when the magazine came out, anyway. But she couldn't stop stealing glances above the pages.

Her eyes first went to Toby. They always did. But he stared at Darl with such rapt attention, eager to help at the slightest command, that Tucia found her gaze straying there too. His movements were small, careful, precise. Almost graceful. His strong, roughened fingers moved as deftly as Dr. Addams's had when performing an operation.

Tucia shuddered at the comparison and trained her thoughts back on the story. But a few moments later, her gaze drifted to him again. "How did you learn to do that?"

Darl glanced up at her, and she was struck again by the handsome, variegated shade of his eyes.

"Fix a window?"

Tucia blinked. She'd almost forgotten she'd asked a question.

She gave a flick of her hand, hoping to seem only casually interested. "Well, all of it, I suppose."

He returned his attention to the window, scraping away the last of the glaze with his utility knife. "I learned on my pa's farm back in Tennessee."

"What kind of a farm?"

"Wheat."

"Your father taught you, then?"

"No."

"No?"

His knife slipped and nicked the pad of his thumb. Darl grimaced. "Dagnammit!" He glanced at Toby, then shot Tucia an apologetic look, sucking on his finger to staunch the blood.

"Ouch," Toby said.

"Here, let me see." Tucia held out her hand. Darl hesitated before placing his hand in hers. A prick of anxiety stirred inside her at the sight of his blood. Just a prick. A momentary quickening of her pulse. A single tight breath. Then it eased, and she became conscious of the warmth of his skin, the tiny tickle of his hairs against her palm, the slight wetness of the thumb where his spit had mixed with blood.

"It's not deep," she said. "But you shouldn't put it in your mouth. Toby, grab my doctor's bag, please."

"It don't need fussin' over," Darl said, but he didn't withdraw his hand from hers.

She cleaned the cut with a clean square of flannel from her bag. Darl winced.

"My father was a drunkard who never taught me a damned thing," he said quietly.

She wiped away a fresh line of blood, then wrapped his thumb in gauze. "There. Good as new."

He frowned at the gauze and gave another *humph*.

"Well, I can't have you getting blood on my new window, now can I?" Her smile managed to wrest a snicker from him.

"What about your mother?" she asked as he returned to work on the window.

"Died birthing me."

"I'm sorry." No wonder he'd listened with such understanding when she told him about her own mother.

Darl sheathed his knife and lifted the old pane from the sash. After propping it against the wall beside the new glass, he waved Toby over to help brush away the bits of glaze and dust from the sash and table. "Ought to have done this outside," he said—to himself? To Toby? To her?

And why hadn't he? It was so hot inside the wagon his brow shone with sweat. And so crowded they could barely move without bumping into one another.

But Tucia was glad he hadn't. She reached again for the magazine as Darl showed Toby how to measure the hole inside the sash where the new pane would go.

She'd taken for granted how smoothly things worked around camp. A wobbly stage step was righted before the next show. A cracked tentpole was replaced before it ever caused trouble. The buckboard and wagons never broke down. The torches always burned brightly. All that, she realized, was because of Darl.

He scored the glass, broke off the extra length, and placed the newly sized pane in the sash. It fit perfectly.

His old leather work bag seemed to hold an endless supply of gadgets and knickknacks, for next he withdrew a bottle of linseed oil, a chalky powder he called whiting, and a jar of lead. He looked the part of a chemist, adding careful amounts of each product into an old tin can.

"What are you doing here?" Tucia blurted over her magazine.

He looked at her with a raised brow.

"I mean, with Huey." She nodded at his bag. "Surely you could find work anywhere."

Darl handed the can to Toby along with a dowel. "Stir this, kid." He watched him a moment, then he turned back to Tucia.

"Your debt to Huey is the kind that can be repaid and forgotten. Mine ain't."

What did that mean? He looked away from her, and Tucia thought it best not to ask.

Once Toby tuckered out, Darl stirred the compound for another minute or two before asking Toby for the putty knife.

"My nana raised me," Darl said, scooping up the glazing compound with his fingers and smearing it along the edge of the pane where it met the sash.

It took Tucia a moment to realize he was returning to the conversation before. She set down her magazine and leaned forward. "Oh?"

"Until I was about Toby's age. Then my father came 'round and saw I was big enough to work a shovel and carted me off to his farm." He took the putty knife from Toby and began to smooth the glaze. His hand was steady, but there was a slight warble in his voice as he continued. "Didn't want to go. Cried for my nana every night for a month straight. Pa was just as mean sober as he was drunk. Said I couldn't have come from him on account'a my ugly lip. Other times he said it was the darkie blood in me. I said, why don't you let me go back then, and he said a boy who could pass had no business livin' among coloreds. I reckon he would'a brought me to the farm no matter what color I was so long as I could work."

Now it was Tucia who was silent. He hadn't said as many words to her in the entire two and a half months she'd been with the troupe. What had made him speak now? She hadn't realized he was Black. Or part Black. His skin was only a shade warmer than her own and she'd assumed it was the sun's handiwork. She supposed if she looked at him closely—the curl in his brown hair, the fullness of his lips—she might guess at it. He was certainly the handsomer for it. They were just traits, after all, passed down like tallness or baldness. She'd seen enough bodies splayed open on the dissection table to know what lay inside was the same.

"Is that why you didn't like the Kickapoos' show? Because of the blackface comedian?"

"That's one reason."

"And why we don't have a comedian who blackens up here?" It was more a realization than a question, but Darl nodded. She wondered again at the peculiar relationship he had with Huey. She certainly had no say in the show. Not even in her own act. Huey must know Darl's mixed lineage. Was that what kept Darl indebted to him? There were certainly those who thought passing a crime, especially here in the South. But that didn't seem the whole of it.

Tucia thought back to the Kickapoos' show. Had she laughed at the comedian's too-big pants and slap shoes? His heavy dialect and foolish jokes? She was certain she had.

"I'm sorry," she said. "I hate when people poke fun at those like Toby. Their quips about imbeciles and idiots. I never thought about it from a colored perspective. I shouldn't have laughed at that comedian's act."

Darl shrugged. He'd finished with the glaze and reseated the window in the jamb. "Most do."

"That doesn't make it right."

He screwed the sash in place and then began packing up his supplies. Toby scurried over to help.

"Don't open it for at least a week. The putty's got to dry."

"Thank you," she said.

He nodded at her, and ruffled Toby's hair. "Ya did good, kid."

Tucia couldn't help but smile, even as she wondered how a man with such a rotten father could be so good with children.

"What d'ya say tomorrow we fix up that broken chair?"

"Okay!" Toby said.

He wiped his brow on the sleeve of his shirt and left the wagon, glancing back at them from the top stair. The strange fluttering sensation returned to her stomach. Another bout of dyspepsia. Nothing a little pepsin wouldn't fix. But her smile lasted the rest of the morning and, for the first time in a long time, she found herself looking forward to tomorrow.

32

The following day, Tucia was rummaging through the storage wagon for more bitterroot to add to their latest batch of snake oil, when she came across a slender paperback book. The cover was yellow with a drawing of a man's hand, palm forward, the lines and creases shaded for emphasis. *Dick's Mysteries of the Hand*, read the title in big red letters. She snorted and chucked it aside. How could people believe in something so scientifically unfounded? Thank goodness Huey hadn't brought up the idea of her reading palms again.

She pulled forward another crate and sorted through its contents. There, at the bottom, was a dusty jar labeled *Bitterroot*. As she grabbed hold of it, an idea struck her. They used the root to mask the taste of alcohol in the snake oil and give it a medicinal flavor. Another one of Huey's tricks. Could she somehow use a similar trick on him?

In offering frank advice to that man with tuberculosis, she'd found a long-lost piece of herself. A piece she was desperate to hold on to. She'd foiled Huey's hopes of making a quick sale too. That was how they endured, Tucia realized. Fanny and the rest of them. How they survived. By hanging on to scraps like these. Lawrence had his poetry. Fanny, her dance. Darl, his forbiddance of blackface.

Tucia had medicine. Real medicine.

She needn't do any doctoring. Nothing that might trigger another hysterical attack. Only offer some basic advice. Hygiene, nutrition, the elementary principles of bodily functions. Dr. Blackwell had done the same in her lectures on health.

But Tucia couldn't do this in the case-taking tent. Not with Huey leering at her every time she opened her mouth. No, she'd need to mask her advice-giving behind something else. Find her own version of bitterroot.

Her eye snagged on the yellow book. Palm reading. Ridiculous as it was, it might be the perfect guise.

Convincing Huey that Madame Zabelle should expand her act to palm reading proved easier than Tucia expected. He'd suggested it, after all, when she first joined the show. She insisted on someplace private for the readings, and he agreed to let her use the case-taking tent for an hour each night after the show.

They quibbled however, on the point of money. Tucia wanted to offer the readings free of charge. But that would not do for Huey. The only reason to give something away for free, he told her, was to secure a bigger payout in the end. And before he could cook up ideas about how she could parlay fortune-telling into additional medicine sales, Tucia conceded and agreed to charge a small fee. They settled on fifteen cents, five of which she could keep for herself, paid in coin not ink-marked in his ledger.

With Huey's approval secured, Tucia began studying the little yellow book she'd found in the supply wagon. It wasn't as simple as looking at a crease or two on someone's palm, then blurting out some fake destiny. Palmistry, the book explained, was concerned not only with the lines of the hand, but the form of the hand and fingers as well as its mounts and other markings. Each were connected to astrological influences, which in turn coincided with a person's temperament.

Those whose little finger was proportionally longer and more pointed than their other fingers were of a nervous-bilious type and ruled by Mercury. They were known to be clever, eloquent, industrious, and prompt. Those with large, dry hands and knobby finger joints were of a bilious organization—wise, prudent, grave—and ruled by Saturn.

Tucia gave no more credence to palmistry than she did to mind reading. She chafed at the book's suggestion that palmistry was a *science*. But she'd need to be convincing—not only to fool Huey but to get the sitter to stay long enough that she might impart some useful advice. So she spent her free hours studying the book and its drawings.

She pestered Fanny and clumsily read the markings of her giant, doughy hand with the book open beside her.

"What's this about?" Fanny asked after Tucia finished. "Huey didn't feel like he was wringing enough out of you already?"

Tucia smiled, leaned closer, and whispered her plan. Fanny smiled too. "*Viel Glück.* Good luck."

Next, Tucia read Al's and Toby's hands. Unlike Al, Toby had only a single crease bisecting his hand instead of distinct head and heart lines. They giggled at the touch of her finger on their palms, but quickly grew bored as she flipped from one page of the book to the next. They insisted she read Kit's palm, too, though the monkey managed to sit still for only a minute before realizing she didn't have any food for him and scampering away.

By the time she read Cal's tobacco-stained hand she only had to open her book once. And Lawrence's palm, chafed and dry from the lasso, she read without turning to the book at all.

Tucia thought about pestering Darl, too, but couldn't muster the courage. It wasn't him as much as that spark she feared, that tiny fire she'd felt light inside her when she bandaged the cut on his thumb or watched him put up the case-taking tent. Surely the summer's stifling heat was to blame, but best not tempt such a feeling again.

After five days of study, Tucia knew the book cover to cover but still felt unready. How did she segue from talking about someone's lifeline or the influence of the mount of Venus to hygiene practices and nutrition? But that night when she appeared onstage in her widow's weeds, Huey announced to the crowd Madame Zabelle's prodigious powers were not limited to mind reading. She could also tell the future by examining the lines on their palms. For twenty cents each, he told them, they could have their fortunes told after the show.

Both anger and panic stirred inside her. She hadn't agreed to start tonight. Nor had she agreed to charging an additional five cents. But the hum of excitement that rose from the crowd told her there was no backing out now.

After her act, she readied the case-taking tent as best she could, throwing swaths of black crepe over the specimen jars and medicine bottles. She hid her stethoscope and tongue depressor, and moved the small side table to the center of the tent, draping it, too, in crepe. Tucia didn't really know what a palm-reading tent ought to look like, but at least her sitters wouldn't be distracted by the four-lobed pig liver.

Outside, she could hear the jaunty notes of Cal's closing song. She seated herself behind the table and tried to settle her nerves. If she mixed up the lifeline and heartline no one was likely to know, after all. But what if no one in the crowd decided to stay? It was late, after all, and twenty cents wasn't a trifle. Tucia knew that all too well. Or what if the sitter grew annoyed when she slipped in a few suggestions about weekly bathing and plenty of fresh air? What if—

The tent flap was drawn open by a ruddy-cheeked, middle-aged man. Behind him stretched a line of at least a dozen eager people.

"May I come in, ma'am?" he said, taking off his hat.

"Yes, please," Tucia managed. She gestured to the stool on the opposite side of the table. He sat down, but hesitated before presenting her his hand.

"Don't know if I believe in all this," he said. "But I thought . . . well, I reckon it can't hurt."

Tucia found herself smiling as she drew the man's hand closer. "That's all right. Skepticism is a worthy trait. But I hope you might find at least one or two things I divine of benefit."

And with that, she turned her attention to the man's palm and began the reading.

33

It was easier than Tucia expected to pass on bits of advice to the people who entered her palm reading tent. They were there seeking answers, after all. Ostensibly about their futures, but wasn't health part of that? To a man with a deep luck line and rheumatic knuckles she prophesied a fortuitous event was on the horizon while also suggesting that arsenic tonic and oiled silk wrappings might help his stiff fingers. To a young woman with a long heart line and blepharitis she foretold many great loves and casually recommended warm compresses and daily washing of her eyes. To an expectant mother with three lines on the outside edge of her hand beside her Mount of Mercury, she divined this baby would be the first of three. She also counseled plenty of rest and good nutrition in the coming weeks before the baby was born.

Tucia knew this didn't absolve her of what she did in the case-taking tent. For allowing her physician's license to lend credibility to Huey's nostrums. But it felt like something. A way to hold on to herself and maybe do a bit of good.

That's what she had wanted, after all, those many years ago when she'd set out to be a doctor. It fascinated her, yes, the body and its miraculous workings. But it wasn't just about satisfying her curiosity. It was about saving and bettering people's lives. The way her mother had done during the war. Nothing else Tucia could conceive of had the same impact. And to make such a difference as a woman, when everyone around her told her she couldn't and there were yet so few who had—that had only further fueled her ambition.

What she did in the palm reading tent was only a distant echo of that ambition. But it was more than she'd done in years. And though she'd feared it might awaken her anxiety, it had not. Even the desire to pull out her hair had gone all but dormant and the bald patches pockmarking her scalp had begun to fill out. When she slept, her dreams, though sometimes vivid and troubling, were not of her own bloody mistakes. Those nights she couldn't sleep, she pulled out her dusty copy of *The Principles and Practice of Medicine* and read, its words comforting her like a long-lost friend.

Two weeks after she'd begun reading palms, the troupe arrived at their next destination—a midsize town built along a lazy, clay-stained river where they'd done good business a few seasons back—only to find it busy with preparations for tomorrow's county fair.

The news enraged Huey, though he took pains not to show it in front of the yokels. But Tucia could tell by the flattening of his smile and sudden twitch of his eye. He left them, their caravan parked in the shadow of the tall brick courthouse, and stalked to the wide, bustling lawn where several stalls and a bandstand were being erected.

Tucia had never been to such a fair, though she'd heard tell of them, and imagined the troupe would just move on. After all, how could their show compete with such festivities? But when Huey returned, his eye was no longer twitching and his smile curved sinisterly upward.

They, too, would have a stall at the county fair tomorrow, he informed them, and they best sell their hearts out, for he'd slipped the mayor a hundred dollars for the privilege.

"A hundred dollars! Ain't it best we just move on?" Darl said, voicing the same shock Tucia felt but kept schooled behind a blank expression. If they were starting a hundred dollars in the hole, it wouldn't be easy to make any velvet. Not in one day with the competition of all the other vendors.

"Yeah, boss, shouldn't we head on to the next town?" Cal said, with Fanny and Lawrence nodding beside him.

"The next town? The next town! This is precisely why I make the important decisions. After tomorrow, the entire county will be dried up. We won't draw a decent crowd for fifty miles no matter which direction we head."

"How come we came this way?" Darl said.

Huey shot him a glare that could cut stone. "I was misinformed."

No one had the gumption to ask by whom, though Tucia wondered if it might have been Texas Joe. And they hadn't the time to press their concerns further, for Huey doled out a litany of tasks that kept them busy long past supper.

The sun had set and a fat moon was rising when Tucia and Fanny finished labeling the last batch of Revivifying Rattlesnake Oil they'd spent the evening mixing and bottling. That was after cooking up Miraculous Corn-busting Salve and painting a banner for the stall. Her lower back ached and she smelled of paraffin and bitterroot.

She said good night to Fanny and lumbered toward her wagon. They'd made camp on a narrow strip of land between the tannery and the river. It reeked of decaying flesh and swarmed with mosquitos and flies, but was as close to the fairgrounds as they could get without having to fork out any more money.

Before reaching her wagon, she took a short detour, following a narrow path to the river to wash the paint and glue from her hands. If the water weren't so cloudy and didn't have such a suspicious, rancid odor (no doubt thanks to the tannery) she'd strip down for a swim. A short ways upriver it might at least smell better, but tomorrow promised to be a long day and Tucia hadn't the energy for the walk.

A steady humming sounded from their camp—Darl still at work with his saw. Their stall would have to be assembled tomorrow at the fairground, but he'd kept busy with all the measuring and cutting and sanding. She passed him on her way to the wagon. He stood over a plank of wood stretched between trestles. A lantern flickered on a nearby stump, illuminating the flecks of sawdust dancing in the air.

"Need any help?" she asked. Her experience with a saw was limited to the surgical kind, but how difficult could it be?

"Nah," Darl said. "Few more and I'm done."

She glanced at the tidy pile of cut poles and boards beside him. It seemed like far more than they'd need, but then, she'd never actually seen a stall erected. "How big of a stall do we have?"

"Two," he said.

"Two?"

He drew a line across the plank with a pencil and straight edge, then looked up at her. "Huey didn't tell you?"

Her stomach sank and she shook her head.

He chuckled, though not unkindly. "Best get your widow's weeds ready."

Even for a county with only a few, far-flung towns and more cattle than people, the fair was a lively, gay event. Laughter and music rang out from every corner of the field. The smell of barbecue and freshly baked pies wafted through the air. Men wrestled in mud pits with pigs. Women clucked over prize-winning quilts. Children licked ice cream cones. And Tucia enjoyed none of it.

Seated in her scratchy costume with sweat bleeding through her underclothes, she read palms: dirty palms, clean palms, leathery palms, smooth palms, sticky palms, smelly palms, dark palms, light palms, and every shade and character in between. There was no time to assess her sitters and offer thoughtful health advice. She barely had time to pee or drink a glass of water.

Toby sat at her feet, playing with his building blocks beneath the table. Kit perched on his shoulder. The monkey's chirps and Toby's frequent interjections startled the sitters. He was hot. He was bored. He was hungry. He wanted candy, popcorn, lemonade. It broke her heart for him to have to sit there while other children skipped by, their arms filled with goodies.

She'd hoped Fanny might be able to take the kids around the fair, but Huey had her, Cal, and Lawrence all ballyhooing throughout the grounds to drum up interest for their medicine stall. Tucia's palm readings were meant to drive folks there, too, as each sitter received a ticket for twenty-five cents off a bottle of rattlesnake oil along with their fortune.

In the early afternoon, Darl stopped by Tucia's stall. He'd fitted it with an extendable canopy and helped her adjust it to block the sun. It was an impressive feature, considering he'd done all the work just last night, and a godsend in the heat. And she couldn't help but notice the main stall where Huey stood hawking medicine had only a plain overhead canopy.

"Thank you," she said, taking advantage of the quick break to stretch her back and gulp down some water.

"How 'bout a free reading?"

He said it with a joking lilt to his voice, but she wondered if he'd taken offense to her not asking to read his palm when she was still trying to memorize the book.

"You'll have to get to the back of the line," she said, more pleased than she ought to be when he returned her smile.

"I got one more load to fetch from the wagon, then I could take Toby 'round to see the fair."

Tucia hesitated, trying not to let her smile falter. The grounds were so crowded. What if he lost track of him? And with the river so close. Fanny had a mother's watchful eye, but Darl?

She pushed down her worry, fighting off the urge to reach for her hair. Toby deserved to enjoy the fair like everyone else. "That would be wonderful, thank you."

Darl returned half an hour later with Al in tow.

"Please keep an eye on him," she said to both of them.

Darl nodded, and Al grabbed Toby's hand. "Sure thing, Mrs. Doc."

Her chest tightened as she watched them slip into the crowd, but the line of waiting sitters forced her attention back to the stall.

The sun hovered near the orange-washed horizon when Darl and the boys returned. Chocolate ringed Toby's mouth and dirt clung to his sticky hands. He plopped down beside her, wearing an expression of dulled happiness. Kit's beady eyes had a similar glaze of contentment. Tucia was sure they'd both wake with stomachaches in the morning, if they'd didn't have one already.

Before she could hear about their afternoon of adventures, another sitter bellied up to her stall. She patted Toby's head, mouthed *thank you* to Darl, and got back to work.

Pan torches and strung lanterns lit the fairgrounds until well into the night. Toby and Kit fell asleep at Tucia's feet, neither stirring when the troupe at last packed up and she carried them to the buckboard. Her watch read ten to midnight when she laid them down in the wagon.

She stripped out of her widow's weeds and hoop skirt, but tired as she was, couldn't bear to don her nightdress with the day's dust and sweat still clinging to her skin. Instead, she threw on her work dress and headed upriver to bathe.

Not far above the tannery, she found a faint path through a tangle of oak trees, the wide, gently sloping river bank just visible through the low, sweeping branches. Frogs croaked and insects hummed. A faint breeze fluttered the leaves. The cool water, silty as it was, would feel divine on her sore muscles and gritty skin.

When she cleared the trees, Tucia froze, drawing in a sharp, silent breath. Darl stood with his back to her not ten paces away, drawing up his trousers. His wet hair glinted in the moonlight and beads of water rolled down his back, following the path of half a dozen long scars that crisscrossed his skin. Her eyes strayed downward, glimpsing the top curve of his rear before he hitched his trousers above his hips and buttoned them in place.

Tucia bit her lip and took a step backward, hoping to disappear within the trees before he turned around. But her foot landed squarely on a pile of twigs. They snapped and crunched beneath her weight, shattering the quiet. Darl spun around.

"Sorry, I just . . . I didn't see . . . I didn't know you were here."

Darl's eyes flickered from her to the trees and back, his shoulders and fists slowly relaxing. A scattering of dark hair covered his chest and the groove between his rectus abdominis muscles trailing down to the waistband of his trousers.

He cleared his throat and Tucia looked away, silently cursing the flush that swept into her face. "Sorry," she muttered again. "I only came for a quick bath."

From the corner of her eye, she saw him slip on his shirt. He fastened the buttons, leaving the top two undone, then sat down on a felled tree trunk facing away from her and reached for his socks and boots.

"What happened to your back?" The words were out of her mouth before her addled brain registered the indelicacy of such a question.

Darl glanced at her over his shoulder, then resumed tugging on a sock. "Prison."

Tucia moved closer, stepping over the trunk and sitting beside him.

"We was in a chain gang layin' railroad tracks."

"We?"

"Huey and me."

The Tinker's Story

Darl hated his pap something fierce. Most nights, he slept out in the barn with the field hands to avoid him. The hard ground was better than a bed if it meant he didn't have to dodge a belt or fist. Besides, Darl couldn't walk through the kitchen without being reminded of the time the doc came by to sew up his lip. His pap had given him a swig of whiskey, taken two for himself, then held Darl down by the shoulders, pinning him to the kitchen table as the doc wedged a piece of wood in his mouth to keep it open and started in with his needle.

Darl had been six years old.

Twice after, he tried to run away home to his nana's. She didn't call him an ugly cur or take the belt to him when he lagged behind in the field. Both times his pap caught him and beat him black and blue. Darl's lip hadn't yet closed, and the second time, his father's fist split the stitches, occasioning the old doc's return.

Eventually, Darl's mouth healed up, and he got quicker in the field. One of the old hands took pity on him, said he remembered his ma, that she was a fine woman, and it was a right shame Darl had never known her. He taught Darl all he knew, which was a mighty lot considering he'd been around since before the war and done just about every type of handiwork a man could do.

Darl took to it like a pig to mud. Tools made sense to him in a way letters and numbers and people did not.

When Darl was going on fourteen, the old hand died. Darl wept. But not in front of his pap, who'd call him a sissy and use his fist to give Darl something real to cry about. He took on all the fixing and building and tinkering the old hand had done.

He'd hoped—though he'd not admit it—his pap would be proud of him. Say for once, nice work, son. But his pap didn't spare so much as a nod.

A few years on and Darl got to drinking and fighting just like his old man. A cutty-eyed look or the wrong word, and Darl would lay a man out flat. He never struck his pap, though, even as the years made the old man all the meaner. But each time Darl's knuckles struck flesh and bone, he imagined it was him.

He'd have turned out just like his pap—was already well down that road—but a fateful night in a bar two towns over changed everything.

The kid—that's how Darl thought of him, though he himself wasn't yet eighteen and "the kid" a full twenty—said something about Darl's scar. Most nights, Darl ignored such drivel, but his pap had been on him all afternoon about the seed drill being jammed and the windmill not turning. Never mind Darl only had two hands, damn it, and was already at work fixing the hog cart. So that night when the kid pointed at Darl and said to his buddies someone musta mistaken him for a catfish and snagged him by the lip with a hook, Darl pushed aside his whiskey. He got up, walked over, and beat the kid senseless.

It wasn't the first man he'd roughed up, but this one happened to be the nephew of the town's mayor. So instead of being kicked out of the bar, he was thrown into jail.

The judge gave him six months' prison labor for disturbing the peace and six years for assaulting the kid, who—Darl learned at the trial—had gone blind in one eye as a result. When it came out Darl was part colored, the judge tacked on another two years.

Darl brought his cussing and fighting with him to prison, earning himself no friends and a few good lashings. But the guard's whip had a hell of a lot more bite than his pap's belt, and Darl soon settled. He didn't want to be like his pap, after all, and the hard days shoveling dirt, lugging rails, and driving spikes sweated the anger out of him, drip by drip.

He wouldn't return to the farm once he was released, Darl decided. Not then, not ever. He'd go north or west or clear across the ocean and make a new life for himself.

Seven years on, another prisoner joined the gang. Dozens had come and gone over the years—some lasted, some didn't. Darl could usually tell right from the start which it would be. He rarely bothered to learn their names, even the ones he reckoned would last. But he lent a hand when he could and warned them which guards were quickest to pull their clubs.

But this new fella baffled him. Darl gave him less than a month, owing to his scrawny arms and short stature, but when two months rolled around, the fella was still there. Darl had even learned his name—Huey—though he couldn't get straight what he was in for.

Huey didn't break the same sweat as the rest of them, but he sure worked hard with his mouth. He could talk the guy next to him into carrying half his load or convince the guard to give him an extra water break.

He had a knack for getting things, too—candy, tobacco, bawdy photographs, even liquor—and kept close track of the favors owed him.

Darl kept his distance. He liked the picture of a pretty girl as much as the next fella, but he no longer drank and didn't like the idea of owing anyone anything. Besides, there was something in those violet eyes of Huey's Darl didn't trust.

But somehow, Huey got to thinking they were friends. And before long, Darl got to thinking the same thing. By the time he realized otherwise, it was too late.

34

Darl stared forward, seemingly lost in the memory. The frogs and insects had gone quiet, as if they, too, had been listening. Only the murmur of the river filled the silence, lapping lazily against the bank.

A convict in a chain gang. That was the very sort of man whom mothers warned their children against and shopkeepers barred from their stores. But Tucia found she didn't fear Darl any more than she had that morning. He wasn't the only one with a dark past, and he'd served his time for it.

Still, it couldn't have been easy to tell her all that. To be so open. So trusting. She owed the same to him.

"Do you remember when I told you a bad case in the operating theater changed my mind about being a physician?"

He turned to her and nodded.

"That wasn't the whole truth of it." She looked down at her knotted hands. "I . . . I killed someone. A woman. On the operating table."

The words had been a constant companion for years, but she'd never said them aloud. She'd told the alienist a patient had died and it had been her fault. But even that was different. To have killed a person . . . there was no way to shed the weight of it.

She lifted her eyes, expecting to meet with a look of disbelief or scorn. That, or Darl's usual straight-faced reserve, leaving her to guess at what he might be thinking. But his expression—at least what she could see of it in the moonlight—was open and without judgment, so she continued.

"It was supposed to be a simple hysterectomy. I'd never performed such an operation, but I'd seen it done once, from the farthest row of the theater, and I'd read about it. So I thought . . . foolishly I thought I could do it."

Even now, she could recite the steps: transverse incision through the rectus muscle; ligate, clamp, and divide the broad and round ligaments; locate the cervix for ligation and amputation; removed the uterus; ligate the uterine and ovarian arteries; wash out the abdomen with normal salt solution; sew the patient up.

It hadn't just been hubris that spurred her on, though. A gauntlet had been thrown. Take up the scalpel or admit defeat.

"But when I reached the abdominal cavity it was grossly diseased." Tucia hugged herself, rubbing the gooseflesh from her arms, and continued. "I tried to be careful as I separated the adhesions, but my hand slipped and I cut too deep. I think it was the uterine artery I nicked. I couldn't even pinpoint it in time to see, let alone clamp it before she bled out."

"There was no one there to help you? To teach you?"

To ask Dr. Addams for help would have been tantamount to admitting defeat. To admitting he was right. Admitting she was nothing without him. "There was another surgeon there, but I was too proud to ask for his help. And he was too proud to give it."

Proud and controlling and manipulative. He'd presented it as a simple case, knowing full well it wasn't. Knowing she'd open up the woman's abdomen and find a web of disease. Knowing how easy it would be for an unskilled hand to cut too deep.

Tucia shuddered as tears built in her eyes. Dr. Addams had wanted her to fail. But that didn't change what happened. What she did.

She looked away from Darl, swiping at her eyes.

"What happened after?" he asked.

"I lost my internship." And her mind. "I never really practiced medicine again."

The riverside clearing drifted into silence again. Tucia's confession had left her hollow, and yet, somehow relieved. Relieved to have dipped into her memories like that without losing herself to them. Relieved not to be the only one who knew the truth of it. Relieved Darl was still sitting beside her.

She wiped the last of the water from her eyes and peeked over at him. "You must think it horribly unfair. You landing in prison and me not when mine was the worse offense."

He stared at her a moment then shook his head. "What you and I did ain't the same. I was angry and drunk and lookin' for trouble. You was tryin' to help someone." He turned back to his boots, taking up the laces again and tying them in a tight knot. "Besides, there's more to a person than the worse thing they done."

Tucia considered his words while he tugged on his other boot and tied the laces. He certainly was more than a barroom brawler. And more than the aloof lughead she'd taken him for at the beginning. Might there be more to her too?

"Let me see your hand."

Darl eyed her warily.

"I promised you a reading." She swiveled toward him, taking his hand in hers. It was just as she'd feared. Her body hummed like an electric bulb at the touch of their skin.

She turned his hand over and stared down at his palm, happy to have someplace to turn her attention besides his handsome face. She ran a finger over the lines and calluses, then gave a faint chuckle. A Saturnine hand. Of course.

"What's so funny?"

"Your hand matches your disposition quite remarkably. Prudent, grave, thoughtful, melancholy. Your life line is deep and rosy. That foretells good health and a long life. Your luck line is faint, here where it originates, but grows more solid as it reaches the mount of Saturn, suggesting you'll know greater prosperity as you age. Except here, where it breaks. That betokens a loss of some sort, financial perhaps, or an illness. Even death. Not yours but someone else's."

He snorted and tried to pull his hand away, but Tucia held fast. "I'm not finished. See the way your heart line is formed like a chain here where it starts?"

He leaned closer, the crown of his head nearly touching hers. "That suggests a number of undecided affections or small love affairs when you were young. But after a while it evens out, and stretches clear and pure across your hand. That's a sign of great affection and devotion."

Darl snickered. He pulled back, but only slightly, raising his gaze at the same time she raised hers. The heat she'd felt when she'd first seen him here on the bank, half dressed and glistening in the moonlight, returned, settling in her core. It was a pleasant, heady feeling after the cold she'd felt describing that day in the operating theater. Still, she retreated from his stare, turning her eyes back to his palm. "That's interesting . . ."

"What?" he said, his breath warm on her cheek.

"This star. It's here in your quadrangle. I've not seen this before. It seems to align exactly with the break in your luck line."

"What does it mean?"

"A disaster of some sort . . . Let me see your other hand."

She searched his other palm but, thankfully, the star wasn't there. Not death, then, just a great calamity. A sigh of relief escaped her, then a laugh. This wasn't real. Not one bit of it. She raised her head, but too quickly, smacking the top of her forehead into Darl's chin.

"Sorry," she said, rubbing her forehead.

Darl laughed. "Was this the disaster you were talking about?"

"I hope I didn't hurt you." She reached toward his chin, her thumb whispering over a dark shadow of stubble to check for bleeding.

"I'm fine." He drew her hand away but didn't let go. Instead, after a moment's hesitation, he leaned closer and kissed her. It began as a tentative brush of the lips, the line of his scar a faint tickle as his mouth hovered over hers. An invitation waiting for an answer, not a demand for submission the way Dr. Addams's kiss had been. He started to pull away, but Tucia closed the distance, kissing him back with hungry intensity.

Darl didn't need any further coaxing. He wrapped an arm around her, his hand resting on the small of her back, pulling her closer. His other hand cradled the back of her neck as Tucia cupped his bristly cheeks. It wasn't until his lips moved down her throat toward her collar that Tucia's muscles suddenly tensed, and she pulled away.

"I . . ." She wanted nothing so bad as to feel his lips travel further down her body. But her hands were trembling, and the urge to flee overwhelmed her. She stumbled to her feet and hurried from the riverbank toward camp, not daring even a single backward glance.

35

By the time Tucia made it to her wagon, she'd plucked out enough hairs to leave a bald spot the size of a nickel near the top of her head. She shut the door hastily and fastened the lock, sagging against the wood. From the bed, she could hear Toby's slow easy breath and tried to match it, even as her heart continued to flap like a panicked bird caged within her chest.

She sank onto the floor and pulled her knees close. A slight breeze stole through the windows, stirring the air. It carried the smell of rot from the tannery. Better that than the insufferable heat. She rested her head on her drawn-up knees, keeping her hands tightly laced while the urge to ravage her scalp lingered.

The pad of footfalls through camp told her Darl had returned from the river. She stiffened, even as part of her longed to go to him. Longed for another kiss. Longed to lose herself in his touch as she'd so nearly done.

He wouldn't hurt her as Dr. Addams had, but still she couldn't manage to stand, let alone to go to him. Maybe this was just another way she was broken.

* * *

The bushcrickets were still chirping when Huey roused them the next morning. The day was wasting, he said, and they best be on their way if they hoped to clear the county line before nightfall.

For once, Tucia was grateful for Huey's barked orders as it made it easier to avoid Darl. She ate a hurried breakfast with the same downcast gaze she'd perfected when she and Toby first arrived. She helped Cal load the cookware, Fanny fold the tent canvas, Lawrence hitch the mules and horses—anything to occupy her hands and keep a safe distance between them.

When their caravan was all packed and the animals ready, Tucia grabbed the reins for her wagon and climbed with Toby onto the driver's seat, spreading her skirt out around her so that it appeared there was no room left on the bench. Darl took the hint and climbed onto the supply wagon beside Lawrence.

By now Tucia was a passible driver, though she usually preferred (and suspected the mules did too) when someone else took the reins. Most days, that someone else was Darl. After a few strained and argumentative rides, she'd come to enjoy him as a traveling companion. He'd point out the various trees and animals to Toby as they passed—his knowledge of the land seemingly endless—but most of the time they sat in pleasant silence.

Today, Tucia feared that silence as much as she feared the alternative. It would lie open between them like a wound, festering and painful. So she and the mules endured the road, with all its ruts and divots, alone.

By early afternoon her fingers were stiff, her rear sore, and Toby and Kit growing restless beside her. Huey had insisted they skip lunch and though she'd snagged an apple and biscuit for them when they'd stopped to water the animals, Toby wanted another. He wanted a drink, but not the hot water sloshing in the jug at their feet. He wanted to run and play and catch the ball with Al. Tucia suspected it was the aftereffect of all the sweets he'd had yesterday at the fair, and tried to coax him to lay his head on her lap and nap. Toby was so put off by the idea he began kicking the underside of the bench.

"Darling, please," she said, turning toward him. "The mules cannot abide such a noise." That wasn't exactly true. The mules seemed unfazed by the sound. But Tucia, whose head had begun to throb, certainly couldn't. "You're liable to—"

A cracking sound split the air and the wagon lurched, listing to one side. Tucia whipped her head forward and pulled back on the reins like Darl had showed her. Once the mules were at a standstill, she turned back to Toby. His feet had gone still, and he gripped the seat rail like one approaching a cliff. Kit clung to his arm, squeaking.

"What's the damned delay?" Huey shouted from the front of their convoy, slowing his horses.

Tucia breathed a long exhale, then leaned over Toby and peered at the back right wheel of the wagon. Darl, who must have sprung from the supply wagon the moment he heard the sound, was already crouched beside it. "Cracked spoke," he yelled.

Huey cursed and climbed down from his wagon. "Everyone stay where you are."

No one listened. They sprang from their seats as quickly as he had, Lawrence fetching water for the animals, Cal stretching his back and bowed legs, Fanny scavenging the buckboard for a snack for the boys. Tucia, meanwhile, sheepishly joined Darl and Huey beside the busted wheel.

"I suppose that hole in the road appeared out of nowhere, did it?" Huey said.

"Let her be," Darl said, still crouching down, examining the spoke.

Tucia bit her lip, and leaned over him. "How badly damaged is it?"

"I've seen worse."

"How long till it's fixed?" Huey snapped.

"Couple hours, I reckon."

"Hours?" Huey glanced down the road in the direction they'd come. "That's too long."

Darl sighed. "I could brace it and fix it up tonight, but if the brace don't hold and it breaks clear through it could ruin the axle. That'd be trouble of a whole 'nother kind."

"You'd better make sure the brace holds, then," Huey said.

Darl fetched his tools from the supply wagon while Huey hustled everyone else back into their respected conveyances.

"You're going on without us?" Tucia said as Huey gathered up his reins. Before when there'd been a delay—a thrown shoe, an axle in need of greasing—they'd waited it out together.

"You ought to have been paying better attention." He glanced down the road again. "Go help Darl and hurry along as soon as you're done." With that, Huey flicked the reins and started off, the supply wagon and buckboard following behind. Cal handed her another jug of water as they passed. "We'll save supper for you."

Tucia sighed. So much for avoiding time alone with Darl.

She seated Toby and Kit in the far-reaching shade of a roadside oak tree, then rolled up her sleeves and joined Darl by the wagon. He'd already raised the wheel above the ground with a large wooden contraption wedged beneath the axle. His jacket was rumpled up alongside his tools, and a patch of sweat dampened his shirt in the flat plain between his shoulder blades. It called to mind the beads of water trickling down his back last night as he'd hoisted up his trousers. Tucia batted the thought away.

"Sorry for landing us in this mess," she said, then quickly added, "with the wheel."

Darl *humph*ed. "I told you to keep your eyes on the road."

"Yes, but we'd been traveling for so long and Toby was—" She stopped and sighed, sinking into a crouch beside him. "I know. I'm sorry. How can I help?"

He eyed her with a dubious expression, then said, "Hand me the measuring tape."

For the next several minutes he worked in silence, pointing at tools as he needed them. Tucia watched him, his clever hands, his muscled forearms, his focused gaze. He seemed entirely unperturbed by her presence. And yet the quiet that spread between them was as painful as she'd feared. Surely he felt it too. She tried to think of something to say, a way to step around what happened last night without seeming to do so. But every thought she had smacked of childish avoidance.

At last she gave up and muttered something stupid about the weather just as he turned to her and said, "I do something wrong last night?"

Tucia's mouth went dry. So much for banal conversation about the summer heat.

"I apologize if I was too forward," he continued. "But it seemed like you wanted to kiss me as bad as I wanted to kiss you."

"I did." *I do.*

His handsome face regarded her with such earnestness, it was all she could do not to lean forward and kiss him again. "But I . . ." She couldn't find the words for the mix of fear, shame, and longing she felt. How she dared not let him into her life for fear of further breaking. Or, more accurately, being broken by him. "It was a mistake."

Darl winced, and Tucia immediately regretted the words. "It has nothing to do with you. You're—"

He waved her off and turned back to his work.

Wonderful, she'd been about to say. Unexpected. Better than she deserved.

He grabbed another tool without bothering to point or ask.

"Let me help."

"I don't need your help. I can get things done faster on my own."

His raw, honest words stung.

"Darl, I—"

The sound of galloping horses made her stop. She and Darl stood. Two men rode toward them, reining back their horses as they approached. Tucia glanced back at Toby, happy to find him napping beneath the tree, and hastily rolled down her shirtsleeves. Darl didn't bother with his jacket, but wiped the sweat from his brow and pulled his hat low as the men drew close.

"Howdy, sirs."

Neither of the men smiled nor tipped their hats. One of them—a middle-aged man with sun-chapped cheeks and an overgrown mustache—wore a sheriff's star. He eyed them a moment then said, "You with that medicine show that had a stall at yesterday's fair?"

Tucia didn't speak. As much as the townsfolk liked their show, they tolerated her and the rest of the troupe like one tolerates a mangy cat, as quick to douse it with bathwater as to offer a pan of milk. But how could they lie? *Miraculous Cures!* and *Remedies for Everything!* were emblazoned across the side of the wagon.

"Yes, sir, we is," Darl said, stepping between her and the riders.

"Where's your boss man? The one with the funny eyes."

"Our wagon here had some trouble. He and the others rode on ahead while we stayed to fix it."

"How far ahead?" the other rider said. He had spindly limbs and a narrow face pitted with smallpox scars.

"A ways."

The men exchanged a frustrated look. Foreboding skittered through Tucia like a spider's egg had hatched beneath her skin. The muscles in Darl's back had grown taut beneath his sweat-dampened shirt and his fingers curled halfway toward fists before slowly releasing. When he spoke, his drawling voice was calm. "Somethin' I can help you with?"

"Y'all left without paying up," the lawman said.

"We paid upfront. A hundred dollars to set up a stall."

"The deal was a hundred dollars *and* a fifty percent cut of the profits."

Fifty percent! What kind of a deal was that? Tucia didn't know a lot about their overhead, but with a cut like that, they'd hardly make any velvet at all. Huey would never agree to such terms. Unless . . . Her stomach tightened. Unless he'd never meant to make good on them. No wonder Huey had woken them so early and driven them so hard to get over the county line.

She could see by the way Darl's hands flexed again he'd come to the same conclusion. "Afraid I don't know nothin' about that," he said. "But if you ride on up a ways, I'm sure my boss'll be happy to set things straight with you."

"Now, why would we do that when we can settle things here?" the pockmarked man said, his eyes flickering to Tucia.

"We ain't got the kind of money I reckon you think you're owed," Darl said, his voice sharper.

"We'll be the judge of that," the lawman said, dismounting from his horse. "You two just stay right where you are while we take a look around."

The other man dismounted as well. Tucia watched them as they prowled around the wagon, grateful their sinister gaze never strayed to the tree beneath which Toby slept.

"They're gonna want to go inside," Darl whispered to her.

"They can't." A fresh jolt of panic rushed through her. The wagon was her and Toby's home, or as close to a home as they had. The idea of letting these men inside sickened her. "I've nothing of any value."

"They don't know that, and we ain't in much of a position to tell 'em no. Besides, best keep their attention there than elsewhere." His gaze hung on her a moment, then cut to Toby.

"You think they'd hurt him?"

"Not likely, but I'd rather not find out."

Tucia nodded.

"Best we do as they ask. Within reason. If things get . . . ugly, you grab Toby and run. Ya hear?"

The men drew near again. "Mind if we look inside?" the lawman asked.

"Of course I mind," Tucia said, unable to hold back her spite. "But I'm sure that won't stop you."

"I hear you gypsy women line your petticoats with dollar bills and diamonds," the pockmarked man said, taking a step closer to her. "Maybe you'd rather us search there instead."

"I'm a doctor, thank you very much, and—"

"I'll lower the jack and you can go inside," Darl interrupted, stepping between them. He pulled her along with him to the busted wheel and gave her a look that told her to stay quiet.

He was right, of course. Maybe if these men saw there was nothing in the wagon worth taking, they'd leave. And she certainly hadn't liked the way the pock-faced man had leered at her. But men like him, men like Huey and Dr. Addams, men who thought the entire world and everyone in it was theirs for the taking made Tucia insensible.

"Don't worry, darlin'," he said over his shoulder to her as he climbed the wagon's steps and winked. "We'll be real gentle."

Gentle, they were not. Almost immediately Tucia could hear the thud and clatter of things hitting the floor. She started toward the steps, but Darl grabbed her arm and shook his head. His grip was firm, but his eyes apologetic. Next came the sound of shattering glass. A glance at her window revealed a jagged hole where the new pane had been broken. "Clumsy me," came a voice from within, followed by laughter.

"Mama?"

Tucia whirled around at the sound of Toby's voice. Darl let go of her arm and she hurried to the oak tree.

"What's that noise?" Toby said.

"It's nothing, darling. Everything's all right," she said, keeping her voice steady even as she saw Darl slip a knife from his bag of tools into the back pocket of his trousers.

The banging inside the wagon continued for another few minutes as Tucia imagined the men rooting through her underclothes and upending the contents of their trunk. She scooped Toby into her arms. Kit climbed up her skirt and onto her shoulder, squeaking softly as if he sensed the danger.

"He doesn't like the noise either," Toby said.

"Some men are just taking a look around in our wagon. They're almost done." Or so Tucia hoped. Her insides had twisted themselves into an ever-tightening knot, but she kept her expression impassive. Surely Toby could feel the anxious thud of her heart. He didn't need to see it in her face as well.

The ruckus quieted, and she heard the distinct rattle of coins. "Thought you said you didn't have any money." The lawman held up a glass jar full of nickels as he left the wagon.

It was the money she'd made in the palmistry tent. Five cents for every palm. In all the tumult, she'd forgotten it was stowed behind her spare boots beneath the bed. Six dollars and fifteen cents jingled inside the jar—a trifle to men like these, but the world to Tucia. Not just money, but freedom.

Still, Tucia kept quiet. If that was the price of getting these men to leave, so be it.

The lanky man loped out of the wagon next, swinging her pocket watch on its chain. She hadn't needed it in a while, but felt a jolt of panic at the thought of losing it. What would she use to keep herself grounded and present the next time hysteria overtook her? Then she saw the old flour sack swinging on its ties from the man's arm, its contents shifting and jangling with each step.

"You can't take that," she said.

"This?" he said, holding out her watch. "Perdy little thing, even if it ain't real silver."

"Not that, the toys, my son's building blocks."

"Oh, this?" He glanced at the flour sack. "Got me a boy too. He'll have real fun playin' with 'em."

Tucia set Toby down beside the tree and stalked to the lawman, as he seemed like the one in charge. "You've no right to any of this, not my money, not my watch, but if you try to take my son's building blocks, God help me, I'll . . . I'll . . ."

"You'll what?" the lawman said with a chuckle. "A deal's a deal and you're still coming up short. Be grateful we don't take you back inside and get payment of another kind."

Tucia's limbs went cold and rigid even as the flicker of rage inside her burned on.

"Bet a woman like you would like that," the pockmarked man said, pocketing her watch.

"That's enough," Darl said, moving between her and the men again. "Take what you got and go."

"I'll say when we're done here," the lawman said.

"Yeah, what's the hurry?" A grin spread across the other man's scarred face. He swung the old flour sack in a circle at his side the way Lawrence did with his lariat. "Maybe we could make a deal. How bad do you want your son's blocks back?"

Tucia's anger continued to grow. On her shoulder, Kit trembled and bared his teeth. She grabbed for the sack, but the man stepped back, swinging it beyond her reach. "Whooee. Got some fire in you. Have to try better than that, though."

Darl moved toward the man, but the sheriff blocked his way, his hand hovering near the pistol at his side. "You best stay right where you are."

Tucia wanted nothing more than to reach for the flour sack again. To wrest it free from the man and smack him upside the head with it. From the corner of her eye she saw Darl's right hand flex again and drift toward his back pocket. They couldn't battle these men. Not when all Darl had was a utility knife and Tucia her bare hands. But the part of her that was all rage wanted to try.

Then she heard Toby whimpering behind her. The rage poured out of her.

"Come on," the man said, moving closer as he swung the sack. "Try again."

Tucia shook her head, and looked away from the man's goading grin. "Take it."

"Aww, where's the fun in that?" He let the bag fall limp and dangle from his hand but kept coming closer. "Maybe I ought to check your skirts for diamonds after all."

Tucia shuffled away from him, stumbling over Darl's tools. She threw her arms out for balance. Another step back and she'd be flush against the wagon with nowhere to go. Toby started to cry. She could tell from the sound he hadn't strayed from where she set him down, thank God. Don't worry, darling, she wanted to call out to him, but the words stuck in her throat as the pock-faced man kept approaching.

"Don't you touch her," Darl growled.

"Or what?" the pock-faced man said. "You no-good hucksters come into our town selling your swill and think you don't have to pay up?" He turned his gaze back to Tucia. "That ain't how things work around here."

As Darl took a step toward them, the lawman unholstered his gun.

"Stop!" Tucia cried, her voice high and shrill. And they did. Neither Darl nor the pock-faced man took another step. The lawman didn't shoot. Toby ceased crying. Even Kit's trembling stilled.

Then the pock-faced man gave a dark chuckle. As he swaggered toward her, Kit leapt from her shoulder. He landed on the man's chest.

"What the—"

Before the man could say another word, Kit scurried up his neck and bit him on the nose. The man screamed. He dropped the building blocks and grabbed for the monkey, but Kit was too quick. He scampered up over his head and down the man's back.

"Get him off me!" the man cried as blood poured from his nose.

Kit jumped to the ground and dashed across the road. The lawman aimed his gun at him and fired. The sound was deafening. A spray of dust bloomed in the air where the bullet struck the road, but Kit escaped into the prairie unharmed.

"He bit me! That goddamned monkey bit me!" The man had a hankie to his nose. "You're gonna be—"

"I'd hurry back to town if I were you," Tucia said. Her entire body was shaking, but her voice came calm and authoritative. "You never know what kind of diseases an animal like that can carry."

The lawman snorted, but the eyes of the pock-faced man grew wide and restless.

"Rabies," she continued. "African sleeping sickness. Beriberi fever. Leprosy. Some monkeys carry a disease that causes the flesh to rot and suppurate. I've seen men with half their faces gone. It's dreadfully painful. Why, one man I treated at the hospital in—"

"That's not true. I ain't never heard of such a disease," the man said, still holding the blood-soaked hankie to his nose, but his voice trembled with uncertainty.

"No, I'd expect not. These are diseases of the tropics. Of the jungles. I hope the physician in town has read up on them. You'll need to begin prophylactic treatment right away."

"You're just trying to scare him," the lawman said, holstering his gun. "You wouldn't keep a diseased animal with you."

"He don't bite us," Darl said. "Only them he don't like."

"I told you, I'm a doctor," Tucia said, turning back to the pock-faced man. "It's not just your nose, but your very life is at stake."

"You got anything that can help me?"

"All our medicine is in the other wagon, I'm afraid." Boldly, Tucia took the man's arm, and led him back to his horse. "Tell the physician in town what I said. A dose of castor oil is in order. A tincture of eucalyptus. Hopefully he'll know what to do from there."

The man had gone pale. He nodded and climbed onto his horse. When his companion hesitated, he said, "Well, come on, Jim. You heard the doc. I could be dying!"

The lawman glowered at her but mounted his horse, and the two of them rode away.

36

It was dusk by the time they reached the troupe's roadside encampment across the county line. They'd ridden the entire way in silence, Darl's mood dark and brooding, Tucia anxious and alert for any sign the men might be after them again. Kit had scampered back when Toby called, and the two of them sat together still and quiet.

After parking alongside the others, Darl jumped down and stalked straight to Huey's wagon, entering without knocking and slamming the door behind him. His voice boomed from inside.

Tucia could only make out parts of what he said. *You greedy son of a . . .* and *we agreed not to cross the law . . .* and *I've half a mind to leave right now, you and your threats be damned . . .*

Lawrence came over and unhitched the mules from Tucia's wagon. "What happened?"

She shooed Toby and Kit toward the cook fire where Al sat playing with his ball and cup. Then she told Lawrence the story of their encounter with the men. Fanny and Cal drew close and listened too.

"Huey's never burned the lot like that," Lawrence said. "Not in my time with him."

Cal took a drag on his pipe. "Us neither. He's getting reckless. No wonder Darl's mad as hellfire."

"Not reckless. Plain old greedy." Fanny wrapped an arm around Tucia's shoulders. "Come on, *schatz*. You must be exhausted. Let's get you something to eat."

Tucia *was* exhausted, though she hadn't realized until that moment how deep her exhaustion had settled. Fear and vigilance had kept it at bay. Now she felt as wrung out as a rag. Fanny shepherded her to the cook fire, and Tucia managed a few bites of supper.

Not long after she sat, Darl stormed out of Huey's wagon. Did he mean to make good on what he'd said and leave? Tucia's chest tightened at the thought. He grabbed an ax from the supply wagon and stormed across the open prairie toward a small stand of trees about a quarter of a mile off.

A few minutes later came the faint but rapid *thwack* of his blade against wood. He wasn't running off, then. Not unless that lone stand of trees somehow stood in his way. The tightness in her chest eased. She gave Kit the rest of her supper—he'd saved the day, after all—then lit a lantern and went to clean up the mess the men left inside her wagon.

The next day, after the wagon's cracked spoke was replaced and her broken window boarded up, the troupe took to the road again, arriving at the outskirts of another small town by nightfall. Huey didn't apologize or repay the money stolen from her, insisting it was her fault for falling behind. As for the men who'd come after them, who'd taken their things and threatened their lives, Huey shrugged them off as hazards of the profession.

She wanted to get mad like Darl and threaten to leave, but where could she and Toby go when they had nothing? Where could they go where Huey wouldn't follow? Those hours hobbling slowly along on a braced wagon wheel, fearing those two men might return had worn Tucia raw. How would it be if she were always looking over her shoulder? Always afraid Huey might find them?

So Tucia choked down her anger, and the days proceeded much the same as they had before. They mixed new bottles of medicine, papered telegraph poles and shop windows with their brightly colored show bills, and performed nightly until the crowd thinned and sales dried up. Then they moved on.

Her palmistry was a favorite wherever they went. Sitters might be few the first night, but interest increased with each passing show. Most seemed positively grateful for the bits of health advice she wove into her readings, and some asked for it outright, having heard from neighbors and friends about her particular talents.

They came with infected splinters in need of removing. Boils in need of draining. Colicky babies in need of soothing. One woman had sought help from the local doctor for the crippling pain that accompanied her menstrual flow only to be told it was Eve's curse and nothing could be done. Tucia assured her that was absurd. She recommended hot water bottles and ginger root tea. Sometimes, she even grew so bold as to send her sitters to the local druggist when the pocket medicine case in her doctor's bag didn't have what they needed. And no, she'd tell them, Revivifying Rattlesnake Oil was not a viable substitute.

It wasn't doctoring. Not really. Just a little help here and there. Though Tucia had taken to reading her textbook every night, not just when she couldn't sleep. And if fewer clients showed up at the case-taking tent the next day, well, all the better. As long as Huey didn't find out what she was doing.

The tricks she'd cobbled together—Fanny's advice to breathe and the old army lieutenant's suggestion to latch onto something tangible in the present—were working too. She hadn't felt even the threat of a hysterical attack in months. And so long as she kept her hands busy, she could usually ride out the urge to pluck her hair too.

It was as if the storm clouds that had overshadowed her life for so long were thinning. Here and there a shaft of light spilling through. The squeal of Toby's laughter as he chased after fireflies.

The scent of Cal's peach cobbler as it cooked over the fire. The light in Fanny's smile as they chitchatted in the shade over cups of sweet tea.

Tucia doubted the clouds would ever fully clear, but maybe that was okay. Maybe *she* was okay. Imperfect, perhaps, but not irreparably broken.

Yet there was still the problem of Darl. She hadn't forgotten that night on the riverbank or the way he'd been ready to risk his life for hers with those men. But a coolness had settled between them again. He hardly spared a glance for her and kept to single word sentences like *pardon, there, nope, yes'm.*

Did he blame her for landing them in that mess with those men the way Huey had? Was their kiss so easy to forget? Tucia could scarcely go an hour without some remembrance of it—the hum of his touch, the rough calluses knitted into his palm, the dance of his lips over hers.

But perhaps it was for the best, this distance, this chill between them. She finally had a semblance of calm in her life, a few glimmers of light. Wasn't that enough? Yet each morning when she arrived at the cook tent and found Darl hadn't made good on his threat to leave, part of her rejoiced.

One Sunday a few weeks after the county fair, Tucia was hanging her laundry when she heard a sharp cry. A child's cry. Her heart stopped short, then thudded into double-time. Toby and Al had gone to play in the shade of the big cottonwood tree at the edge of camp.

She pushed through the hanging sheets and shirtwaists. The sound was no longer the sharp cry of sudden pain, but a loud, continuous wailing. She tore across the field toward the tree, even as her brain had already worked out the cry. Not Toby's. Al's.

Fanny too was running, outpacing Tucia with her wide stride. Cal followed, his seesaw gait slower but just as urgent.

When Tucia arrived at the base of the tree, Fanny was already kneeling in the grass, rocking a screaming Al in her arms. Toby crouched beside them, agog.

"He fell, Mama," Toby said before she could ask what happened. "He climbed the tree even though we weren't supposed to and he fell."

Al stopped wailing long enough to shoot Toby a glare. "Tattletale."

"His arm," Fanny said, her voice calm but eyes dark with worry. "I think it's broken."

"Let me see."

Fanny laid him gently on the ground and brushed back the hair from his tear-stained face. "It's gonna be all right, *mäuschen*. Dr. Hatherley is here now."

Panic flickered through Tucia at the word *doctor*, but it came and went quickly, no match for the concern driving her focus. Al curled like a possum around his left arm, crying anew. His shoulder was dislocated. She gently felt along his forearm, hearing the faint, telltale sound of crepitus. Al winced and pulled away. His ulna was broken, though thankfully it hadn't pierced the skin.

She turned to Cal, who'd just arrived and stood looking down on them. "I need my medical bag. It's in my wagon beside the traveling trunk."

Cal nodded and dashed away.

"I've got to fix his shoulder," she said to Fanny. "Hold him still."

Fanny drew in a breath and placed her huge hands on her son. "Try not to move, *mäuschen*."

Tucia acted quickly, raising and rotating his arm while applying steady traction. Al loosed another sharp cry, his body tensing, but he slowly relaxed and quieted once the ball of his humerus was back in its socket.

"You're doing so good," Tucia said to him. "Being so brave. As soon as your pa returns with my bag I'll fix your arm right up."

"It hurts."

Fanny scooped him up again and kissed his brow. "I'm sorry, *meine mäuschen*. I know."

As they waited for Cal to return, Tucia walked through the steps of resetting the ulna in her mind. Panic stocked at the edge of her thoughts. She could feel it there waiting to pounce. But if she kept her breathing slow and her mind focused maybe it wouldn't find an opening. That's what she hoped at least.

When Cal arrived flush and panting with her bag, Tucia sorted through its contents and pulled out a small bottle of laudanum. She fed Al three drops, then took her time arranging the rest of her supplies, knowing it would take several minutes before taking effect. Once he was drowsy, Tucia made quick work of resetting his bone. He still flinched and whimpered in pain, but was fast asleep by the time she was through splinting and bandaging his arm.

"There, all finished," she said after she'd tied off the bandage. "He'll need to keep it bound and immobile for at least three weeks."

Fanny nodded. "Thank you."

"We're lucky you're here, Doc," Cal said. "Can't imagine any of them other boozers doin' it half as well."

"It was nothing. Anyone with a little training could do it." But Tucia couldn't deny the lightness she felt watching the Trouts walk together to their tent, Al asleep in Fanny's arms. It was true, resetting a simple fracture didn't require great skill, but she'd done it. She hadn't panicked or frozen or slipped back into the prison of her memories.

Later as Toby napped, she stopped by the Trouts' tent to check on Al's condition. He'd woken from the laudanum but was still groggy. Fanny had made a sling for his arm, and a rubber ice bag rested on his swollen shoulder.

Tucia gave him another few drops of laudanum and promised to return again for another dose before bed so he'd sleep through the night. In the morning the arm would likely be stiff and sore, but the pain bearable.

Fanny sat beside Al's cot with a book of children's stories splayed across her lap. As Tucia turned to leave, she grabbed her hand. Fanny's eyes were damp but her smile bright. "You must know, as only a mother can, how grateful I am."

Tucia gave her giant hand a squeeze. "It's nice to do something good for a change."

"You do a lot of good."

Was that true? Perhaps with her small ministrations in the palmistry tent she did some good, though she doubted that fusty old Dr. Kremer would think so. Not enough to tip the scales in her favor anyway. But she wasn't doing it for him. And why should his opinion matter more than Fanny's? Matter more than that of the townsfolk who left her tent smiling and hopeful.

Perhaps even their nightly show did a little good. The yokels arrived at their lot tired, worried, weighed down by the struggles of their everyday lives. They left lighter. Happier. Who knew how long it lasted, but surely that was worth something.

Cal followed her from the tent and closed the flap behind him. "I was . . . er . . . gonna brew up some tea before starting on supper. Care for a cup?"

She'd seen him sipping tea and smoking his pipe dozens of times in the afternoon. Occasionally Fanny, Lawrence, or Darl would join him, but most of the time he sat alone, seemingly unbothered by the looming task of supper. He'd certainly never asked her to join him, eyeing her like a farmer eyes a crow whenever she came around the cook tent.

But he wasn't eyeing her that way now.

"Tea would be lovely," she said.

Tucia filled the kettle while Cal stoked the cook fire. They sat on upturned crates as the water heated, distant birdsong and the low crackle of flames easing the silence. Cal filled his pipe, but didn't light it. When the tea was ready, he poured her a cup.

"Sugar? Milk?"

She shook her head.

"I can rustle up a biscuit."

She smiled to know he had a tin of biscuits secreted away somewhere amid the sacks of potatoes and flour, but shook her head again. "Tea's fine."

He sat down beside her, balancing his cup between his knees as he lit his pipe.

Tucia sipped her tea distractedly, burning her tongue on the too-hot liquid. Fanny's words still played in her mind. "Do you think the good outweighs the bad? Of the show, I mean. We're selling fake medicine, after all."

Cal took a slow puff of tobacco. "Sometimes a smile's all these yokels need."

"Is that why you do it? Why you're here? You and Fanny could perform anywhere."

He was silent for a moment, then glanced at their tent. The lilt of Fanny's voice as she read from the storybook was just audible over the fire's crackle.

"Suppose you know he ain't really our boy," Cal said. "Not by blood anyway. We love him just the same, though."

Tucia had suspected Al wasn't their son by birth, but hadn't wanted to pry.

"Did Fanny tell you how he ended up in our care? How we came to work for Huey?"

"No."

Cal nodded. He took a sip of tea and stared at the fire. "Suppose you've earned the right to know the whole of it."

The Musician's Story

Calvin Trout never met an instrument he couldn't play. Those who heard his music said it must be in his blood. But neither of his parents—both workers at a sugar refinery in Brooklyn—had struck a chord, plucked a string, or even so much as tapped out a rhythm in their lives. Twelve-hour days at the factory and the rearing of eleven children left nary a minute for frivolity.

But Cal heard music everywhere. He heard it in the rainwater that leaked through their roof, plinking into the pan set out below. He heard it in the staccato cries of the newsboys and matchbook peddlers and fishmongers who called out their wares from the street below. He heard it in the swish of his mother's spoon as he helped her with Sunday supper. When he was six and went to work alongside his brothers and sisters and parents in the refinery, he heard music in the whirr and clink of the machines.

His first instrument was an upturned pot. Then a washboard and spoon. When he was twelve and fired from the factory on account of the trouble with his legs, he took his music to the streets.

At first, he earned only pennies. But he watched the other buskers and listened. Listened to their sounds and rhythms. Listened to their notes and harmonies.

He found a cracked recorder in a back-alley waste bin and patched it with putty. Its tone was thin and sharp, but it played well enough to double his earnings. Then he traded up for a harmonica. He rigged the harmonica to the washboard (much to his mother's dismay), added a horn, and soon came home with more coins in his pocket after a day's work than he'd made in a week at the refinery.

The owner of the music hall four blocks down from their tenement passed Cal on the street one day and brought him in to audition for the band. The hall was dark, and if they sat him at the back, no one noticed his bowed legs. His favorite instruments were the fiddle and banjo, but he learned them all, filling in whenever one of the regulars was too sick or drunk to get up onstage.

After his mother died of yellow fever, Cal left Brooklyn. He played in music halls and saloons and theaters up and down the eastern seaboard. Travel suited him, for he always felt himself to be searching. For what, though, he didn't know.

He'd been traveling for years, never staying with one troupe for more than a handful of months, when his path crossed with the Danbury, Blum and Co. Circus. He'd never played for a circus, never even attended a show. But they must need musicians, he figured, so he took his case of instruments and walked to the lot.

Cal had long since grown accustomed to people staring at his legs. He'd been called every name imaginable and been denied his share of jobs on account of his short stature and tottering walk. But here, his appearance was an asset. Talented musicians were common enough, Mr. Blum, the circus's owner told him. But a crippled virtuoso—that was a rarity indeed.

Cal, or Gimpy the Musical Genius, as he was billed, didn't like his deformity touted above his playing. And he didn't like the food. His mother's recipes, many of which she'd taught him over their rusty tenement stove, tasted far better.

He'd all but settled on leaving when he heard a woman's laugh one day in the cook tent. It was a deep, rich sound. Generous and unabashed. It struck him this was the sound he'd been searching for, the music absent in his life.

He looked up from his plate of boiled beefsteak and soggy greens and searched the crowded tent for the owner of the sound. It belonged to the giant. He spied her at the far side of the tent, seated with another woman and one of the big top strongmen. He'd seen the giant a time or two before. Someone of her stature was hard to miss. She had pretty gold hair and clear blue eyes, but it was her slowly spreading smile and the exuberant laugh that followed that truly did him in.

For several days he watched her. Watched and listened. Not just in the cook tent but when she performed too. In the big top, she danced the same way she laughed—full of heart and spirit. In the sideshow tent, her exuberance faded, and he hated Mr. Blum for it.

When he finally worked up the courage to ask to sit beside her in the cook tent, Cal was thoroughly besotted. She introduced herself as Franziska Fink but insisted he call her Fanny.

Fanny.

Halfway through his thirties, Cal was no longer a young man and had little to offer besides his music. But that and everything else was hers. He would endure his despicable stage name and the god-awful food to be around her however long she remained with the circus. He didn't want to be anywhere she wasn't.

Cal didn't say so, of course. Not during that first supper. In fact, he said very little, shyer around her than he was with most women, and contented to listen to her talk.

Her friend—Lena—was pleasant enough, too, though he hardly would have noticed her had it not been for Fanny and the tender way she regarded her.

Bruno, the strongman, noticed nothing. Not even Lena's swelling belly until she was several months along.

The night of her labor, Cal and Fanny were seated outside his tent. Fanny mended a show costume while he played his harmonica—the same one he'd bought with his spare pennies back in Brooklyn. They were friends as well as dining companions now and spent many a free hour dreaming up ideas for their own traveling show.

But Fanny would never leave without Lena. And Lena would never leave without Bruno. Certainly not now. And neither Fanny nor Cal could abide Bruno or the bruises he left behind on Lena's face and arms. So even as they plotted and dreamed, Cal never thought they'd actually leave.

Just after midnight, the circus's physician strode past them, wiping off his forceps. Fanny rushed after him and asked after Lena. Both mother and baby—a lusty nine-pound boy—were fine, he told her.

Cal knew it wasn't a man's place in a tent with a woman who'd just given birth, so he stayed behind as Fanny went to see them. She'd been gone only a minute or two when Cal felt a wriggling unease in his stomach. It could well be the chef's bad cooking, but he pocketed his harmonica and followed after Fanny just the same. He never liked her around Bruno, and it wouldn't hurt to wait outside and listen.

Bruno and Lena's tent was pitched a ways apart from the others so the sounds of labor and the baby's cries wouldn't disturb anyone. And sure enough, as Cal walked there, he could hear the little one wailing. The sound, though expected, caught him off guard. There was music in that cry. Music that touched his heart almost as much as Fanny's sweet laugh.

But as Cal neared the tent, he heard someone else crying too. Fanny. He hurried as fast as his bent legs could take him. The crying became shouting. Bruno, then Fanny, then Bruno again. Then the clatter of a table being upturned.

Cal pushed aside the tent flap in time to see Bruno strike her—a hard punch to the stomach that doubled Fanny over.

"Don't you touch her!" Cal hollered.

Bruno turned his mean eyes on Cal, but just as he did, Fanny straightened to her full, awesome height. She punched Bruno square in the jaw. It was an impressive blow, full of rage and sorrow, but hardly enough to down a strong-man like Bruno. It *was* enough, however, to send him staggering back, his foot landing on an empty whiskey bottle.

Cal watched as Bruno's arms wheeled and his balance faltered. He plunged backward, twisting as he fell, his meaty hand reaching out to absorb the brunt of the fall. Before his hand met the ground, the side of his head struck the sharp edge of the overturned table. The hair on Cal's arms stood on end at the awful cracking sound.

Bruno's heavy body hit the ground and didn't move. Fanny stared down at him, covering her mouth with her hands. From across the tent, Cal stared too. He didn't need to get any closer to know the man was dead.

"*Mein Gott,*" Fanny whispered, then more loudly, "Oh God, what have I done?"

Cal didn't move, noticing for the first time the wide stain of blood across the front of her dress. "What happened? Are you hurt?"

Fanny shook her head and pointed to the bed at the far edge of the tent.

The sheets and blankets were colored red. Lena lay among them, her skin that of a ghost. Her eyes open and unblinking. Her chest still.

"He let her bleed out," Fanny said between sobs. "She died right in front of him, and he didn't even notice . . . but I didn't . . . I didn't mean to . . . oh *mein Gott!*"

Cal could hardly hear her over the baby's cries. He looked around at the mess—the overturned table, the empty bottle, the bloody bedclothes, the bodies—and knew what he must do. He walked to the cradle and picked up the swaddled baby. How small and light he was! He laid the baby in Fanny's arms and told her to go. Take the baby and never look back.

At first, Fanny didn't move, her eyes locked on the body of her dead friend. Then, the baby's cry jogged her senses. She put her knuckle into its mouth, smiling through her tears as it suckled.

Cal told her again—go—and watched her cast a final glance at Lena before hurrying from the tent.

No one could know what happened here. Bruno's death had been an accident, but who would believe a pair of sideshow freaks? Cal had to protect them. Fanny and the baby. Let them get away.

He doused everything with gasoline—the gasoline Lena used to light the torches she swallowed—then hurled the oil lamp at the ground. The tent went up in flames faster than Cal had expected. Heat licked at his back as he hurried out.

To his surprise, Fanny stood just beyond the blaze, Lena's baby tight in her arms.

"You have to go," he said. "If anyone sees us here, they'll think . . ."

He didn't need to finish. Fanny nodded her head, her face screwed tight as she held back a sob. She swallowed a ragged breath and said, "You're coming with us, aren't you?"

Cal stared back at her, following her gaze to the baby.

"We're his family now," she said.

The fire burned hot and quick, its unfurling plumes of smoke awakening the camp not moments after Cal and Fanny fled. They left everything behind. Their clothes and money. Fanny's ballet shoes. Cal's instruments. Travel was slow with an infant. The baby needed milk and changing, after all.

Albrecht, they would call him, Fanny said. And even though they were fugitives now, with a hungry, fussy baby and not a penny to their name, Cal didn't regret what he'd done.

He hoped Mr. Blum and the rest of the troupe would think the fire a tragic accident. An exhausted new mother and her sleeping babe. A passed-out drunk. An overturned lantern. Anyone who knew Bruno could certainly believe it. As for Fanny and Cal's sudden disappearance, a mere coincidence.

Still, Cal was relieved when, on the second day after the fire, they passed a medicine show wagon on the road. The man in charge of the outfit—a small, strange man with violet eyes—offered them water. Al was fussing again, so Cal took out his harmonica—the only thing he'd had in his pocket when they left the circus—and soothed him with a tune.

"You're quite the musician," the pitchman said to him and asked him to play another song while his traveling companion, a harelipped man, rustled up some milk. When Cal had finished the second tune, the pitchman told him he'd just lost the ventriloquist who ballyhooed for their show and offered Cal the job. After a wary nod from Fanny, Cal accepted.

Cal had ballyhooed for medicine showmen a time or two before. If the man had a good spiel, the money was decent and the work not too demanding. They'd save up a few dollars and put a good hundred miles between them and the circus. Then Cal and Fanny and little Al would strike out on their own. Not quite the dream they'd imagined, but a new start nonetheless.

After a few months, when Al was finally putting on weight and Fanny just finding her laugh again, Cal went to the pitchman to tell him they'd be parting ways at the next train town.

Not if they wanted to stay out of prison, the pitchman said. He retrieved a newspaper clipping from his wagon. Cal couldn't read, so the pitchman read it aloud. The article spoke of a dashing circus strongman and his sweetheart who'd been killed in a fire with their newborn son.

"The fire chief ruled it an accident," the pitchman said, folding the newsprint and tucking it into his pocket. "But imagine what they'd think if I told them not ten miles away I picked up a giant and a cripple, both smelling of smoke, with a newborn baby boy."

Cal said nothing. He and Fanny never tried to leave again.

37

Tucia wiped the gummy yellow wax off the tip of her otoscope and returned the instrument to its velvet-lined case. The last of her sitters had just left the palmistry tent, a young man whose trouble hearing was the result of an accumulation of earwax and not a torn tympanic membrane as she'd first feared when he favored his other ear and asked her to speak louder. She'd suggested he rinse the ear with a mixture of warm water and castor oil, then sent him on his way. She was looking forward to stripping off her widow's weeds and crawling into bed when Fanny poked her head into the tent.

"Huey's wanting a meeting."

"Now?"

Fanny nodded, and Tucia groaned. What did he possibly have to say that couldn't wait until morning? No matter how seamless their acts went or how many bottles of medicine they sold, the man was never happy.

"I'll be right there."

She slipped the otoscope case into her mended medical bag and tucked it beneath the table. Huey hadn't found out about her nightly ministrations in the palmistry tent, had he? Her stomach clenched in panic.

In the week and a half since she'd set Al's arm, Tucia had grown even bolder. Helping a woman with the return of her menses. Pulling an old man's abscessed tooth. Townsfolk asked her openly for remedies—real remedies—without bothering to even lay their hand on the table for a reading. If word was spreading among the yokels, it was only a matter of time before Huey heard of it too.

She'd been lucky in the previous towns they'd visited that Huey declared the town dry and they'd pulled up stakes before he'd caught on to what she was doing. Perhaps now, her luck had ended. She'd come to look forward to her time in the palmistry tent. The advice she offered her sitters wasn't just an act of defiance. It was an act of redemption.

The rest of the troupe had gathered in front of the stage where Huey stood, looking down on them.

"Ah, at last," he said when Tucia approached.

She stood beside Fanny, her heart stumbling a beat when Huey clapped his hands to get everyone's attention. The pan lights that illuminated the stage during the show had been dampened and a single lamp burned at Huey's feet, casting long, fingerlike shadows over his face.

"I've important news," he said. "Tomorrow, we pack up and head to Galveston."

Galveston? Tucia had heard of the island city once or twice, but knew little of it aside from its seaside amusements. Why would they go there? More importantly, did this mean he didn't know of her doings in the palmistry tent?

"Ain't that a full-fledged city?" Cal asked. "What the devil are we gonna do there?"

"I've an acquaintance in Galveston who operates a museum with the recent addition of a theater. We're going to overwinter there."

It took Tucia a moment to shake off the panic she'd carried to the meeting and grasp what he was saying. Fanny had mentioned a time or two that when the weather turned too cold to draw an audience, the troupe migrated west to California, overwintering in Los Angeles. To Tucia, it sounded like a pleasant break from the constant travel. No setting up or tearing down the stage. No hiking a mile to bathe in a muddy river. No excursions into hostile towns to paper the lampposts with show fliers. No late nights and early mornings cleaning up the lot for the next show.

Huey would procure a license and pitch a few times a week from whatever street corner suited him, taking one or two of them along to ballyhoo up a crowd. Darl fixed up the wagons and stage for the next year's season. Fanny mended the costumes. Lawrence tended the animals. But otherwise, their time was their own.

Fanny hadn't spoken of it with much fondness and looked just as displeased about it now. Darl too, Tucia noticed, had gone stiff, his face lined with irritation.

"Overwinter?" he said. "It ain't but the first of September."

September. Already? Tucia had long ago lost track of the days. Some passed quick as a breath. But most stretched on, slow as sap leeching from a tree.

"It's still hot as hell," Cal said, after a glance at Fanny. "We got at least a month of good travel left."

"Three, I'd wager, if we keep to the south," Lawrence said.

Huey's lips flattened, and Tucia inched back, even though she was well beyond his reach.

"I know very well the month and what the almanac says about the weather," he said. "An opportunity like this is not to be missed. We'll make double in Galveston what we could have made in Los Angeles."

"We will or you will?" Tucia asked.

He smiled down at her, but his gaze was sharp. "All of us, my dear."

Darl snickered.

"Think of it," Huey said, speaking with his pitchman's fervor. "A bone fide theater. Not having to worry about rain or a license. Sleeping every night in a real bed. A break from the interminable travel."

"I don't know, boss," Cal said, reaching out and taking Fanny's hand. "We got a good spot in California. It ain't as easy for the rest of us to, you know, fit in at a new place."

"It's not a point up for discussion." Huey flung out an arm, pointing at the muslin backdrop behind him. "Whose name is there? Whose? Certainly not yours." His narrowed eyes hung on Cal, then ticked over the rest of them. "Or yours. Or yours. Or yours! I decide where we go and when. Understand?"

They all muttered their assent, Tucia noticed, but Darl. He stood with arms crossed and jaw clenched shut, glowering at Huey.

"Ingrates, all of you," Huey said. "Go. Go! And be ready to leave in the morning."

Tucia exchanged a wary glance with Fanny, then started toward her wagon. It would be nice for a break from all the travel and long days setting up for the show. The others' reluctance gave her pause, though. Out here on the open road they were free in a way they could never be in a city. Free from sidelong stares and whispers. Free from the noise and bustle.

And what of the troubles living inside her? Though they were quieter than ever before, they hadn't gone away. Not fully. Would this change bring them out again?

She'd reached the steps of her wagon when the sound of voices stopped her. They came from the stage, and though the backdrop muffled them, Tucia could just make out the words.

"This ain't smart," she heard Darl say.

So not everyone had heeded Huey's warning to go.

"What if someone recognizes us?"

"Don't be so paranoid. That was ten years ago and two states away," came Huey's breezy reply.

"You know them reward notices went out as far west as Colorado. It ain't the kind of thing one up and forgets."

"This is too good of an opportunity to pass up. Hide your face in a paper bag if you're so worried."

"I won't go."

"No?" Huey gave a spiteful laugh. "And what would you do

instead? Stay here? Wander alone? You're invisible thanks to me. One anonymous telegram and . . ."

"And what? If I go back, so do you."

"Maybe. Maybe not."

"You're bein' damned reckless, Huey. This Galveston idea, that stunt you pulled at the fair. I ain't the only one with a face people remember."

"Ahh, but yours looks so much more menacing on a wanted poster."

She heard Darl spit and stomp away.

"Don't forget, you owe your freedom to me!" Huey called after him.

Darl came into view, tromping toward his tent. "I don't owe you shit," he growled over his shoulder. Tucia snuck behind her wagon and watched him cross the camp. He threw open his tent flap and vanished inside. A moment later, a light glowed from within. Did he mean it this time? Was he packing up and leaving?

She climbed up the wagon's steps but hesitated in the doorway, glancing back at Darl's tent still alight against the blackness of the night. Cal's story from days before came back to her. He'd stayed with the circus despite hating it because he didn't want to be anywhere Fanny wasn't. Somehow, without fully realizing it, she'd come to feel the same for Darl.

Tucia glanced at Toby, sleeping soundly in their bed, then stepped back onto the stairs, easing the door shut behind her. Her feet carried her to Darl's tent before her brain could think better of the idea. For a moment, she stood there, uncertain whether to call his name or just walk in. She settled for a soft *ahem*, then pulled aside the flap and stepped inside.

The lamplight, though dim, was enough to make her squint.

"Tucia?" Darl stood in the center of the small tent. A low cot sat along one wall. A stool and an upturned crate, atop which the lamp sat, were the only other furniture. A bulging rucksack lay on the ground beside the stool.

"You *are* leaving, then."

He glanced at the rucksack then back at her. "That why you're here?"

"I . . . I overheard what you said to Huey and I thought . . . I worried you were . . ." She closed her eyes and took a deep breath. Part of her had been frozen, locked tight since Dr. Addams forced her against his office wall. But he'd ruled her life long enough. She opened her eyes and looked at Darl. "Please stay."

He held her gaze for a long moment, then sighed. "I packed that damned thing five weeks ago after our run-in with them yokels from the fair. Ain't been able to bring myself to go."

"No?" Tucia bit her lip, waiting through his drawn-out silence for a reply.

"You're like a splinter, damn it, under my skin. Even if I left I reckon you'd still be stuck there."

She closed the short distance between them. "Then stay."

After another steadying breath, she rose onto her toes and kissed him.

He hesitated a moment before kissing her back, the movement of his lips soft and light as if he were afraid of spooking her. She found his hand and brought it to her waist. Then his other. The clenching panic that had sent her fleeing before didn't surface, even as his kisses deepened. This time, when his mouth moved to her neck, she didn't pull away but relaxed into his touch. The only thought that crossed her mind was more. More of his mouth. His hands. His heat. They both fumbled with the buttons of her dress, then, once they'd reached her navel, he gathered up the fabric of her skirt.

"Lord, there's a lot of dress here," he said, finally reaching her hem and pulling the dress over her head as Tucia raised her arms and wriggled out of the sleeves. He tossed the heap of black fabric to the floor, then stepped back to look at her, his eyes stalling on her ridiculous hoop skirt. She'd forgotten she was wearing the damn thing. They both laughed, and the last of her unease fell away.

He hooked his finger through the waistband of her skirt and

pulled her close, kissing her again as he worked at the knot holding the crinoline in place. They laughed again when it fell away. Next came her corset. His shirt. Her shoes. His boots. Then they fell onto his cot, pulling off the last of their clothes in a mad rush. She lay back and opened herself to him. Darl took his time, his hands and mouth exploring her body, igniting a spark of pleasure within her and coaxing it to grow. And grow. And grow.

Afterward, Tucia lay beside him on the cot, her head resting on his chest, his fingers making lazy tracks across the small of her back.

"What did Huey mean when he said you owed him your freedom?"

Darl's hand stilled. She felt the slow, deliberate rise and fall of his chest. "I told you we was in a chain gang together. Me for lickin' that kid and Huey for . . . well, he told so many different stories about why he was in I never knew which was the truth. He saw I was good with tools and such. Started askin' how we might be able to pick the locks or split our chains when we was out workin'."

Tucia raised up onto her elbow. "You escaped?"

He held her gaze then looked away, nodding. "Huey can be mighty convincing when he tries."

Didn't she know it.

"So that's why you're tied to him. Either one of you talks and you both go back to jail."

He opened his mouth as if to say something, then closed it, still skittish of her stare. She lay back down beside him, leaving a sliver of space between their bodies. He and Huey, escaped convicts. Their odd relationship finally made sense.

"I shoulda told you the other night. Down by the river but I . . ."

"It's all right. There's something I didn't tell you too."

He rolled toward her, dredging up a playful smile that set her insides aflutter. "You a jailbird on the run too?"

"No," she said, managing a short laugh before the sound died in her throat. "Toby's father. He's not dead."

"You ain't a widow? Does that mean you're still married?"

"No . . . I mean, yes . . . no. I'm not widowed or married. His father and I, we were never . . . it only happened once and wasn't something I engaged in willingly. He doesn't even know about Toby."

Darl's expression turned to stone. The scant space between them seemed to widen. Should she have told him sooner? Not told him at all? Her stepmother's voice weaseled into her head. *Ruined.*

"I . . ." She started to roll away, but Darl laid a hand on her hip—heavy but gentle.

"You don't owe me any explanation," he said. "Though I have a mind to find that man and gut him."

Tucia drew closer until her body was once again flush with his. "It's in the past," she said, and for once, the words were true.

38

They reached the southern edge of Texas in three days' time. Nothing more was said about Huey's decision to overwinter in Galveston, but it was clear no one was happy about it. No one, except for Huey himself, who rose early every morning, humming and smiling and hurrying the rest of them along.

Though Tucia didn't share the others' misgivings about the island, she knew better than to believe Huey when he carried on about how wonderful their new situation would be. Still, she couldn't deny the kernel of excitement sprouting inside her. Instead of bracing for the day's dreary tedium, she found herself waking with a sense of anticipation.

The heat and mosquitos bothered her less. The sky seemed wider, bluer, clearer. She laughed more readily and caught herself smiling without cause. It wasn't just on account of Darl, though certainly, he played no small part in it. She'd opened herself a little wider to life and hadn't broken.

A thrill licked through her each time their hands brushed, or he leaned over to whisper something in her ear. That was as close as they dared come with everyone else around. In the moments in between, it wasn't just yearning she felt, but hope.

As they neared the gulf, shotgun homes and shops sprouted up across the flat landscape. A post office, a clapboard schoolhouse. A sprawling warehouse with a bank of high windows glinting in the sunlight. It was just the sort of place they would have parked their wagons for a week and papered with handbills: *Free Show To-night!*

But today, they stopped only long enough to water the animals. Huey, still in a magnanimous mood, surprised them with ice cream.

Tucia and Fanny stood in the shade of an elder tree while the boys and Kit sat on a nearby bench, legs swinging and melted ice cream dripping down their chins. Al finished his cone first, while Toby—much to Tucia's dismay—shared his with Kit. She'd told him countless times not to put anything in his mouth that Kit had nibbled on. Today, she only sighed and let them enjoy themselves.

"How long do you think Huey's good mood will hold?" she asked Fanny.

"Hmm?"

"Huey's good mood. How long do you think it will last?"

Fanny tore her eyes from the far horizon where green marshland blurred with the blue of the sky. She looked down at the half-eaten ice cream cone in her hand, then at Tucia. "What were you asking about Huey?"

"Never mind. Are you okay?"

"Oh, yah." Her gaze drifted back to the horizon as a stream of ice cream dribbled down her thumb.

Tucia grabbed the cone from her and handed her a hankie. "You're a bad liar."

She gave Al the rest of Fanny's ice cream, watching him finish it in four bites. Then she returned to the shade of the tree. "Do you really think overwintering in Galveston will be that bad?"

Fanny shrugged. "I've never liked it, being in one place for months on end. It's not in my blood. But at least California was solid. I don't like the idea of an island. All that water."

"Los Angeles is right on the ocean."

"On the ocean and *in* the ocean are two different things."

Tucia laughed, hoping to coax a laugh from Fanny, too, but her friend only managed a wry smile.

"I take it you're not looking forward to renting a swimming costume and spending a Sunday afternoon on the beach."

"We had a bad crossing, my family and I, when we came to America."

Tucia listened as Fanny spoke about the voyage—the wind and waves that had buffeted the ship, the icy rain that drove everyone from the decks into the hold, the countless days of seasickness.

"That sounds awful," Tucia said when Fanny finished.

"It was." She looked again toward the horizon. "Cal insists the gulf waters are much milder. Says I shouldn't be afraid."

Tucia reached out and squeezed Fanny's hand. "The mind may know something, but the body doesn't always listen. I know a helpful trick, though."

"What?"

"Breathe."

At last, Fanny laughed—that rich sound Tucia relished—even as it ended too quickly.

"I guess we'd better get back to the wagons," Tucia said. "I'm sure Huey's antsy to leave."

"Hold on." Fanny grabbed her sleeve. "Something's different about you."

Tucia felt a flush creeping up her neck and groped for something to say. "I . . . I've stopped pulling out my hair. See, it's growing back too."

Fanny waved her hand. "Not that." She eyed Tucia a moment, and it was all Tucia could do not to look away like a guilty child.

"There it is—*that*."

"What?"

"You're smiling."

"I smile all the time."

"Now you do."

"It's just nice to have a few days' break from the show."

"I'm not the only one who's a bad liar." Fanny glanced toward the wagons. "It wouldn't have to do with a certain tinker, would it?"

"Of course not," Tucia said, though she knew it was useless. Even his damned name made her lips curve upward.

Fanny winked at her. "Your secret's safe with me."

They corralled the boys and climbed back into the wagon and buckboard. Tucia did her best to keep her face impassive as she sat down on the bench beside Darl with Toby and Kit between them, but Fanny caught her eye, and she had to choke down a schoolgirl giggle. At least Fanny seemed a little more herself again.

"You all right?" Darl asked her.

"Yep," she said a bit too breezily and grimaced. Schoolgirl indeed.

A few miles past town, the trees parted to reveal a short expanse of feathery marsh grass. Beyond that stretched brownish-blue water for as far as the eye could see.

"The ocean!" Toby cried.

"It's not the ocean, darling. It's the Gulf of Mexico."

Insects buzzed around them, and pink-winged birds took flight from the grass. Dozens of small fishing boats bobbed in the water.

A wagon bridge—the longest Tucia had ever seen—stretched from the mainland to the island. Her stomach clenched as they started along it, even though the water around them was calm, lazy even, and she hoped Fanny was remembering to breathe.

Darl must have sensed Tucia's unease for he began recounting to her and Toby a conversation he'd had in town with a man about the bridge. Solid as they come, he said. Been in use for almost a decade. Longest wagon bridge in the whole world.

Knowing about the bridge's remarkable construction did less to calm her than his steady, drawling voice. As they reached the end of the bridge and turned down a long, broad lane, he quieted. Oyster shells paved the road, crunching beneath their wheels and blooming into a white cloud of trailing dust. A green sea of grasses and cattails surrounded them, giving way to wide mudflats where the island met with the gently lapping bay. Butterflies danced amid the vegetation, and birds swooped above.

Tucia couldn't recall a more beautiful place. But Darl seemed to see only the city taking shape in the distance, a vast grid of buildings crowned with smokestacks, church spires, turrets, and domes. His hands had tightened about the reins, and his shoulders tensed.

Was he regretting his decision not to leave? They hadn't had a moment alone since two nights ago in his tent. Did he miss her touch as much as she missed his? Hopefully tonight they could find time to slip away, and she could reassure him of his decision.

For now, she leaned back and admired the island stretching before them. Sunlight gleamed off the windows of the nearing buildings. A gentle breeze stirred the air, fragrant with the scent of brine and earth. Frogs croaked, and bees hummed.

What harm could possibly come to them here?

39

Lodging had been arranged for them by the museum's owner at a boardinghouse not far from the docks on a road called Post-office Street. Few towns would rent to medicine show folks. Tucia had learned that early on when they'd run into a string of particularly wet weather. Her wagon had leaked, and the tents were soaked. The local hotels and lodging houses all turned them away. They couldn't even find a yokel willing to let them stay in their barn. Performers and pitchmen couldn't be trusted, they said. Never mind they'd bought medicine at the show the very night before.

As their caravan traveled down Postoffice Street, however, she realized how the museum owner had managed it. Most of the surrounding homes—large, but somewhat outdated, with Greek columns and wide verandas—had been converted into brothels. If the boardinghouse abutted the red-light district, they wouldn't be too choosy about their lodgers.

Though it would be nice to have a proper room with a wardrobe and washstand and space enough to spread her arms, Tucia still felt a twinge of reluctance to leave their wagon. It was stuffy and crowded and creaky. But it was home.

The matron of the house, Mrs. Pitt, was a short, pinched-faced woman with strands of silver threaded through her red hair. She laid out the rules of the place: No drinking, gambling, or whoring. Leave that to the neighboring houses. Otherwise, they were free to come and go as they wished. Outhouses were in the back, sand needed to be shaken from their shoes before entering, and they could draw water from the cistern once a week on Saturdays to bathe.

Mrs. Pitt eyed Lawrence as if she didn't particularly like the idea of an Indian lodger but didn't say anything. Tucia imagined she'd think the same thing of Darl if she knew his parentage and had to check the urge to reach out and grab his hand.

Upon seeing Kit, Mrs. Pitt threw up her arms and shooed him from the house, insisting he stay in the backyard shed, despite Toby's tears. Thankfully, Tucia and Toby's room overlooked the backyard, and Toby was consoled he could press his face against the window and see Kit's shed. He also delighted in turning on and off the overhead electric light—a wonder he'd seen before but never been able to control—and soon his tears were forgotten.

Supper was plentiful but bland and lacking in their usual boisterous conversation. Tucia missed the jokes and laughter. But it would come. They were travel-weary, after all. Unaccustomed to being so penned in.

Only one other boarder was staying at the house, a salesman about Tucia's age with a neatly trimmed beard and a large mole on the side of his nose. He spoke little during supper except to begrudgingly offer his name, Mr. Wilder, and place of residence, Kansas, but she caught his eyes often flickering up from his plate, stealing wide-eyed glances at them all, particularly Fanny.

After supper, Tucia and Toby brought food to the shed for Kit and made him a bed out of rags and an old wash bin. He curled up inside and soon was snoring. Toby sniffled a little as they left but fell asleep as quickly as Kit had once they reached their room.

She pulled the mosquito netting around the bed, then returned to the small parlor at the front of the house. As she'd hoped, Darl was there, kneeling on the floor, examining the wobbly leg of a tea table. She watched him a moment, his skilled hands and steady focus.

"You can't help yourself, can you?"

He turned his head and smiled at her. "Gotta stay busy somehow."

"I've got another idea how you could occupy your time."

His smile widened. "Oh?"

Mrs. Pitt bustled into the room. Tucia turned toward the large window, taking sudden interest in the street and lamppost outside. Darl bumped his head on the underside of the table as he straightened.

"What the devil are you doing down there?" Mrs. Pitt asked.

"The leg of your table needs fixin', ma'am."

"That so?"

"Yes, ma'am. See how it wobbles?"

From the corner of her eye, Tucia saw Mrs. Pitt's pursed expression soften. "And you know how to fix it?"

"I do, but I . . . er . . . I'm kind of tired just now. Long day on the road and all." He cleared his throat, and Tucia bit her lip to hold back a grin. "How 'bout tomorrow?"

"That'd be fine," she said, and then, as an afterthought, "Thank you."

Darl stood and gave a yawn so clearly staged Tucia had to choke back laughter.

"Night, ladies," he said. As he walked past her, his fingers surreptitiously grazed the small of her back, sending a delicious shiver over her skin. Tucia waited for what seemed an interminably long time (five whole minutes according to the mantel clock), feigning to read a magazine while Mrs. Pitt sat across from her knitting, before declaring herself tired as well.

When she reached the second floor, she hesitated, realizing she didn't know which of the many rooms was Darl's. She tiptoed down the long hall, listening at each door. Snoring sounded from one room, Fanny's and Cal's muffled voices from another.

Complete quiet from a third. Mr. Wilder's pungent cologne water wafted from the next. As she approached the last room, she heard rustling from within. The door swung open as she reached for the knob, landing her face-to-face with Huey.

Tucia gave a start and stepped back.

"Sorry, I . . . er . . . I mistook this for my room. How silly of me."

He eyed her with suspicion. "Indeed." He stepped out and closed the door behind him. "I'm going for a stroll. Care to join me?"

"Oh, ah . . . no. Thank you. I'm quite tired."

"Of course. Rest up. Tomorrow we tour the museum and see our new stage." He reached out and took her arm, looping it through his. "I've big plans for us here."

Gooseflesh prickled her skin as he walked her down the hall.

"Us?" She hoped he meant the troupe, but something in his coy smile told her his designs were just for her.

"You'll see soon enough." He stopped in front of her door but didn't immediately release her arm. "I believe *this* is your room. I daresay I won't find you wandering the halls again."

"Thank you," she managed, her mouth suddenly dry.

"Sleep soundly, my dear." He let go of her arm and stepped back, watching as she opened the door and slipped inside.

Tucia listened but didn't hear his footfalls on the stairs. She silently cursed, imagining him standing outside her door, waiting to catch her sneaking back into the hall. He must suspect something. Part of her wanted to walk boldly out and straight back down the hall to the quiet room she was sure now was Darl's. It wasn't any of Huey's business, after all, what she did in her spare time. But nothing with Huey was that simple. He hated anything he couldn't control, and he'd find a way to make his displeasure known.

She slumped against the wall and sighed, letting the pleasant burn of anticipation leech out of her. Then, suspecting Huey was still listening outside her door, she noisily splashed her face with water from the washbowl, changed into her nightgown, and joined Toby in bed.

*   *   *

The next morning, Darl was absent from breakfast. She daren't ask if the others had seen him and suspected Huey had sent him off early to the livery to see to the wagons.

He still hadn't returned by the time Huey herded the rest of them into the buckboard to visit the museum. No chance to explain why she hadn't come to his room, then. Had he stayed up as late as her, waiting, hoping, too hot and bothered to sleep? Or had he given up on her quickly and slept soundly?

She tried not to think of it as the buckboard rattled down the city's busy streets. Tall stone buildings rose around them. Banks and restaurants. Grocers and dry goods stores. They passed a lavish hotel five stories tall with rows of arched windows and a broad flag flapping atop the roof. Farther on lay stately homes shaded by flowering oleanders and graceful palms.

Her worry lifted as they reached the south end of the island, and the sweeping blue-brown waters of the gulf came into view between stands of trees and sloping dunes. The briny air had a heavy, hazy quality, despite a stirring breeze, and the rhythmic beat of the surf sounded alongside the noise of the street.

She could see how a place like this would romance you, would settle like the salty air on your skin and be impossible to wash away. She pulled Toby onto her lap, pointing to the seagulls that circled overhead, delighting, as always, in his awe.

They turned down an avenue that paralleled the beach. The shops here—simple wooden buildings with large windows and brightly painted signs—catered to tourists and pleasure-seekers. There were beer halls and souvenir shops, soda fountains and candy stores. The smell of boiled clams drifted from the lunchrooms while a streetcar rattled past, ferrying eager beachgoers.

Toby stared in wonder, his mouth open and eyes wide, leaning so far out of the buckboard that Tucia had to hold the back of his jacket to keep him from falling. For once, she was grateful he couldn't read the words painted on the windows, or he'd be clamoring for taffy and chocolates and ice cream sodas.

A few blocks down, Huey halted the buckboard in front of a three-story brick building. A blue and red sign spanned the width of the facade. DARBY'S MUSEUM OF WONDERS, it read.

Al leapt down first and hurried toward one of two large windows framing the entry. Toby clambered down after him, with Kit chirping from his shoulder. Tucia quickly followed, fearful Toby might be swept up in the tide of people strolling down the sidewalk. A foolish impulse perhaps—how quickly she'd grown unaccustomed to city crowds—but her heart beat easier once she had hold of Toby's hand.

Each of the museum's display windows housed a different diorama with full-sized mannequins. One of the mannequins wore a turban and an Egyptian-styled costume. A bejeweled scarab on a gold chain (clearly fake) dangled from his outstretched hand. FIRST-CLASS ARTIFACTS FROM THE TOMBS OF GIZA, INCLUDING THE MUMMY OF A PHARAOH! read the accompanying sign. A mannequin dressed like a Wild West gunslinger stood in the other window, reminding her of Texas Joe. At his feet coiled a mechanical snake whose tail rattled and head swung back and forth as if ready to strike.

In addition to the dioramas, nearly every inch of the ground-level facade was papered with colorful handbills. *New Curiosities Arriving Daily! A Select Resort for Ladies and Children! Sterling Attractions! Astounding Oddities! Grand Performances Daily! Admission to See All, 25 Cts.*

Huey pulled them away from the window and ushered them through the door.

It was darker inside the museum than Tucia expected, and it took her eyes a moment to adjust.

"Look around," Huey said, an undercurrent of glee in his voice. "I'll go find Mr. Darby."

A velvet cord partitioned the foyer, directing her and the others through a doorway to the left. A sign above the door read CABINET

OF CURIOSITIES. Glass-fronted cases lined the room, their shelves crammed with knickknacks. Half a dozen people milled about, ogling the items displayed on the shelves.

She peered at a few of the cases as she passed through the room, keeping a tight hold on Toby's hand. There were Chinese coins, the sword of a Japanese Samurai, a papyrus scroll covered in hieroglyphics.

Tucia doubted any of it was real. One of the cases held a blue stone necklace, which, if the small placard beside it was to be believed, was made of lapis lazuli and worn by Cleopatra the night of her death. On closer inspection, Tucia could see flecks of blue paint peeling away from the stone. No wonder Mr. Darby—if that was the museum keeper's real name—kept the place so dark.

"How did Huey meet this man?" Tucia asked when Lawrence joined them beside a display of a black urn etched with dragons.

He shook his head. "I don't know. An opium den somewhere?"

That sounded about right. Or perhaps he'd wheedled Mr. Darby's name out of Texas Joe the night they went drinking. However Huey found him, they certainly shared a propensity for extravagance and deception.

The next room held much of the same, including the mummified remains of King Akhentutu II, famed pharaoh of the eleventh dynasty. It rested in a glass case at the center of the room, allowing patrons to view it from all sides. The lamp above was angled to cast an eerie shadow on the floor.

Toby tugged her toward the case and pressed his face against the glass. A group of young men joined them.

"Must smell something awful inside," one of the men said to his friends. "Seeing he's been dead some hundred years."

"Thousands," Tucia said, unable to help herself. "If you believe the placard. But likely, it's just a mannequin wrapped in bedsheets."

The man frowned at her. "How come it looks so old, then?"

"Tea would do the trick. It stains white fabric rather nicely. Turpentine, perhaps." She leaned over the case, peering through the smudged glass for a closer look. If Huey had taught her any-thing, it was how to spot a con man's tricks.

"The mummy is entirely real, I assure you," a silky voice said behind her.

A shiver prickled Tucia's skin, and she turned around. A man with an overly waxed mustache stood near the room's exit. He was the opposite of Huey in every way—tall and globe-shaped with dark eyes and a square chin. But he exuded the same gloat and charisma.

"I examined it myself when I acquired it from an antiquities dealer in Cairo," he said, turning his attention to the young man and his friend as he sauntered over. "And I can further assure you, if we were to lift this glass, you'd smell nothing more than the faintest scent of myrrh."

Unlike the flashy clothes and high-sheen fabrics Huey favored, this man wore a dark tweed suit and muted tie. The only glint was the gold chain of his pocket watch and the clip fastening his pince-nez to his lapel. Even his shoes had a matte polish.

He flashed her a placid smile—one that told her he'd been watching her from the shadows before making his appearance—then turned his attention back to the others. "It's quite a sanitary process, embalming. Are you familiar with how it works?"

When they shook their heads, he adjusted his pince-nez and re-galed them with a punctilious account of the ancient practice. He stood straight-backed as he spoke, one hand tucked in his jacket pocket, the other sweeping languidly through the air every now and then to emphasize a particular point. Tucia could tell the spiel was one he'd rehearsed and given a hundred times. The audience of young men believed every detail of his phony account.

"What'd they do with all the . . . you know . . . the innards?" one man asked.

"Ah, good question. But I'm afraid the answer is too macabre for present company." He glanced at Tucia and Toby, then smiled again.

The men *humph*ed and sauntered off.

"Mr. Darby, I presume," she said to him.

He bowed but without any of Huey's flourish. "And you must be Dr. Hatherley. Huey's told me so much about you in his letters, but he failed to mention how beautiful you are."

Tucia frowned at the thin flattery.

"This must be your son. Toby, is it?"

Tucia pulled Toby behind her, unnerved Huey had mentioned him too.

"What do you think of the museum, my boy?" he said.

Toby peeked around her skirt and stared up at him.

"Stupefied, I see," he said with a chuckle. "It does have that effect on people."

"Not stupefied. Shy. Especially around strange, officious men."

Mr. Darby continued to chuckle. "Huey said you were a spit-fire." His gaze snagged on something behind her. "And this must be Grazyna the Dancing Giant."

He stepped around Tucia and greeted the others. "Cal Crip Caboo. Chief Big Sky." He folded his forearms one atop the other out in front of him and said, "Haho!"

Lawrence didn't laugh or smile.

"The stoic type, I see," Mr. Darby said. "Yes, yes, that's good. Just as the audience will expect. It's so exciting to have you all here at last. Would you like to see the stage?"

When no one replied, he waved them onward. "Come, come. Huey's waiting for us there."

The theater sat at the back of the museum off a hallway between a menagerie of stuffed animals and PROFESSOR DARBY'S GALLERY OF ANATOMY, filled with disarticulated bones and specimen jars. To the right of the theater's doors was a dimly lit staircase with an overhanging sign: GENTLEMEN ONLY. Tucia caught Fanny staring at the sign and shaking her head.

"Wherever those stairs lead," she whispered to Tucia as they followed the others into the theater, "we don't ever want to find out."

The theater sat perhaps a hundred people with rows of velvet-upholstered chairs sloping toward the stage. Spotlights hung from the ceiling, their light pooling where Huey stood, inspecting the stage flooring.

"Solid oak," Mr. Darby said to him. "Even your giant here needn't fear it won't hold up."

"She ain't an elephant," Cal snapped.

"No, of course not, my apologies," Mr. Darby said without a trace of sincerity. He joined Huey onstage and waved for the rest of them to follow. The curtains smelled like they'd been scavenged from a cigar lounge, and the dressing rooms were no bigger than closets, but nonetheless, it was a vast improvement from the stage they lugged around on the road. Even Fanny seemed mildly impressed.

As Tucia listened to Huey and Mr. Darby speak of their plans—two shows a day with an extra matinee on Saturdays—she could picture the eager crowds filling the seats, snacking on Cracker Jacks and candy. Toby and Kit could curl up in her dressing room during the late performance, and though traveling to and from the boardinghouse every day would be a hassle, at least they needn't worry about pockmarked roads or hostile sheriffs. And if Huey paid them a fair share of the profits, she'd be free of debt by winter's end. Best of all, he made no mention of resurrecting the case-taking tent. No mention of her palmistry either. She'd have to find another way to offset all the bogus health advice Huey spewed during the show.

There were "a few more plans" in the works, Huey said, but the main show would start with a special matinee performance Sunday. They'd have dress rehearsals Friday and Saturday, but tomorrow was theirs to relax and acquaint themselves with the city.

"Seems too good to be true," Lawrence said as they left the theater. Tucia couldn't ignore the nagging feeling he was right.

40

After they finished touring the museum, Mr. Darby treated them to dinner at his favorite restaurant on the Strand—the city's main thoroughfare. It wasn't a fancy place, but the food was good, and the wine flowed freely. Tucia wasn't sure whether he was trying to impress all of them or just Huey, but Lawrence's words continued to gnaw at her. It did seem too good to be true. Besides, it didn't feel right dining without Darl. He wouldn't enjoy being out among so many people, but she doubted he much enjoyed suppering alone with Mr. Wilder either.

Dessert was served with another round of wine, but Tucia skipped both, giving her cake to Kit, whom Toby had smuggled in beneath his jacket. Afterward, Huey and Mr. Darby parted company with the rest of them, heading, she suspected, to an opium joint.

Back at the boardinghouse, she paid careful attention to which rooms Lawrence and the Trouts disappeared into after saying good night, then snuck back into the hallway after Toby was asleep and rapped softly on Darl's door. Silence was the only reply.

He must be asleep, she told herself, not wanting to consider perhaps he didn't want to see her. She raised her hand to knock again but let it fall. As she turned to walk away, the door creaked open.

Darl leaned against the jamb, his shirtsleeves rolled up to his elbows as if she'd caught him washing up for bed. A few tiny beads of water still clung to the dark stubble on his chin.

"Back from your night on the town, I see," he said.

Tucia couldn't read in his voice whether it was an observation or an accusation. "I . . . it's late, I'm sorry. I shouldn't have—"

He grabbed her hand as she started to step back, pulling her into his room. He kissed her deeply, hungrily, and whatever misgiving she'd had about the day melted away. The light was quickly off and their clothes cast to the floor—an easier task to accomplish without her gigantic hoop skirt getting in the way.

A dalliance like this had its share of risks. If she cared to, she could list them in her mind like a good scientist would do and weigh them against the benefits. But Tucia didn't care to do anything of the sort. In this moment, moving with him atop the mattress, she cared only that she felt something—something warm and wonderful—after feeling so little for so long.

She lay in his arms after they'd finished, nestling as close as she had on the cot in his tent, even though the bed afforded more room.

"Huey's given us the day off tomorrow. We're going to a bathing house. Even Fanny said she'd come. Will you?"

"I've got more work to do on the wagons, and Huey wants the costumes and properties unloaded at the museum."

"Tell him no."

Darl chuckled.

"You have more leverage than the rest of us."

He trailed a hand up her arm and along her neck, but when he got to her scalp, enmeshing his fingers in her sagging chignon, Tucia stiffened. Her bald spots now had a covering of fine short hairs, but they would feel strange, uneven alongside her longer strands and the hair switch still pinned in place.

He didn't pull back, though he must have felt her body tense.

Instead, he brought his other hand to her hair and began carefully unmaking her chignon. Slowly, Tucia relaxed. He laid the pins and hairpiece aside, then ran his fingers through her unbound tresses. The sensation was so pleasant Tucia actually moaned, then pulled away, embarrassed.

Darl drew her back, burying his face in her hair. His warm breath tickled her scalp. His arm tightened around her. "I want all of you, Tucia," he whispered. "Not just the parts you think I want to see."

The next morning, Darl was again gone before Tucia and Toby made it down for breakfast. She hoped he might return before they left for the shore but couldn't afford to wait. If they dallied, Fanny would lose her nerve.

Instead of crowding into the buckboard or paying the ten-cent fare for the streetcar, they decided to walk the dozen and a half blocks to the gulf. Mrs. Pitt had recommended a bathhouse where they could rent bathing suits and enjoy a soda or ice cream cone.

Postoffice Street was quiet as they walked, with only the occasional carriage or wagon rumbling past. The brothels' wide porches and balconies, raucous and crowded at night, were by daylight largely empty, though a few of the women sat outside in their everyday clothes playing cards or sipping coffee.

Tucia talked with Lawrence as they walked, trying to convince him to ask Huey about reading a few of his poems in the new show. Toby, carrying Kit, shuffled beside them. She agreed it was a long shot, but better to ask now when Huey was in a good mood rather than wait until he was back to his rancorous old self. They were about to turn down Twenty-Third Street when Tucia heard a shriek behind them.

She turned toward the sound, realizing that Toby was no longer beside her. Instead, he was running toward a house a block and a half back where a group of women were standing and screaming. Tucia raced after him, her heart pounding, trying to make out what was happening. She called for Toby to stop, but he didn't listen, scrambling instead up the steps of the porch where the women stood.

By the time Tucia reached them, harried and breathless, the women were laughing. One knelt beside Toby, pinching his cheek and ruffling his hair, while two others watched as Kit gobbled up the nuts scattered across the porch beside an overturned bowl.

"Is this your boy?" the woman beside Toby asked.

Tucia nodded.

"My, isn't he cute!" She turned back to Toby. "What's your name, sweetie?"

He glanced sheepishly at Tucia, clearly knowing he was in trouble. She nodded for him to tell the woman his name.

"Toby," he said.

"Is this your monkey?"

He nodded.

"I'm sorry," Tucia said, mounting the steps. "We didn't mean to disturb your morning."

"Not at all," the woman said. She extended a hand. "I'm Anna. This is Lucy and Mabel."

Tucia gave her name in reply and shook the women's hands. She'd learned about venereal disease in school and shared Dr. Blackwell's belief that prostitution reduced men to brutes and women to machines. But for all her notions on the matter, Tucia had not actually met a prostitute before. Certainly never shaken one's hand. Fresh out of medical school, she would have looked down on these women, and perhaps offered some trite and moralizing advice. Now, she found them little different from herself—women making the most of life's hard knocks.

"Kit wanted nuts," Toby said.

"I see that, darling. You've got to keep a better hold on him."

"But he was hungry!"

"No excuses. Come, let's clean them up."

With the help of the women, they picked up the scattered nuts as Kit squeaked and tried to hoard as many as he could in his arms.

"You one of them medicine show folks boarding with Mrs. Pitt?" Mabel asked when they'd finished.

Tucia nodded, brushing off her skirt.

"That stuff you sell any good?"

"No."

Mabel sighed. "Didn't think so."

"If you . . . er . . . need something, though, you can come to me directly, and I'll see if I can help."

"You a nurse or something?" Anna asked while Lucy took her turn clucking over Toby.

"No. I . . . I'm a doctor."

"And a good one at that," a familiar voice said from behind her. Cal.

She turned and found him and the others standing at the base of the steps. Al held up his arm. Only yesterday they'd removed the bandages. "My bone snapped in two, and she fixed it."

Tucia found herself fighting a blush. After another round of introductions, they parted ways and continued to the beach, Tucia keeping hold of Toby's hand the entire time, even as she surrendered to a smile.

When they neared the end of Twenty-Third Street the gulf waters became visible, and a welcome breeze fluttered Tucia's skirts. Fanny wore a tight expression, but she pressed on with the rest of them as they reached the sand.

The surf thrummed, and seagulls called from overhead. About a dozen yards from the water, they spread a blanket and sat down. Not far off stood Murdoch's Bath House—a long building raised on tall pillars above the sand. It was two stories with a wide deck overlooking the gulf. An American flag flew overhead. There were a few other such buildings farther down the shore.

The beach was crowded with groups much like their own—families picnicking, children playing in the sand, surf bathers enjoying the rolling water. Laughing, eating, soaking in the sun. Too caught up in their own amusements to pay their group of misfits much mind.

After a few minutes, Cal, Al, and Lawrence said they were heading over to the bathhouse to rent bathing costumes.

"Sure you don't want to come, love?" Cal said to Fanny.

"You think they've got a suit that would fit the likes of me?"

"Maybe they could stitch two together," Lawrence said. They all laughed, even Fanny.

"I'm fine right where I am, thank you very much, and not one step closer."

Cal turned to Tucia. "You?"

"I think we'll stick to the shore." She'd learned to swim as a girl—much to her stepmother's dismay—but had never taught Toby. Another day perhaps, but not today. The surf looked a bit rough, and he'd already got her heart racing once that morning.

Toby whined after they left, always wanting to do whatever Al was doing, but was consoled when she suggested they walk together in the surf and look for shells. After casting off their shoes and stockings, they left Kit with Fanny and marched toward the water, Toby giggling as his feet sunk into the sand. He cried with delight as the surf rushed toward them, submerging their feet. Soon, he grew bolder, racing after the waves as they retreated, then running back to her side, a new wave lapping at his heels.

Tucia drank in the warmth of the sun and the sound of his laughter. She couldn't remember the last time her breath came so easily.

"Mind if I join ya?"

Tucia turned to find Darl coming up beside them, trousers rolled up and feet bare.

"I thought you couldn't get away."

"Took your advice and told Huey 'no' for a change."

They walked side by side along the beach, Darl helping Toby

spot shells in the sand. She dared not take his arm, but every so often, their fingers brushed, filling her with a pleasant rush.

Last night that feeling had been like the breaking waves, all passion and desire. Today it was like the last reaches of the surf, gentle as it eddied around their feet. Tucia hadn't a name for it, except, maybe, love.

41

After they'd had their fill of the beach, they returned to Mrs. Pitt's languid and ruddy from the sun. While Toby napped, she and Darl made love in his room. Then, he returned to the livery to finish up work on the wagons. They couldn't go on sneaking around like young lovers forever. But for now, Tucia would be mindful of her monthly cycle and otherwise let things unfold as they would.

The next morning, Huey hustled them out of the house as soon as they finished breakfast. They spent several hours in the alleyway behind the museum mixing up rattlesnake oil, corn-busting salve, and a new medicine to be sold on the days Mr. Darby—or *Professor* Darby as they were instructed to call him in front of yokels—lectured between acts. Professor Darby's Proprietary Tropical Fever Reducer, it was called. It contained no true antipyretics. Instead, it was the usual mix of flavored water, aloe, and alcohol.

Huey's good humor had begun to fray. She noticed it at first as a general restlessness and distraction. By the late afternoon, as their first dress rehearsal wore on, he was back to snapping at them for any mistake. He released the others in time for supper but told Tucia to stay. She sent Toby, tired and cranky after a long day with little to do, back to the boardinghouse with them.

Unease settled in her stomach as she watched the buckboard pull away from the curb. It mounted as she returned inside the museum. Several guests milled about the halls, and Mr. Darby was waiting beside Huey at the door of the theater. His presence only worsened the knots twisting in her stomach.

"Did you want to run through the act again?" she asked, though she hadn't missed a single cue during rehearsal.

Huey shook his head. "Mr. Darby has a keen idea of how we can put your physician's license to good use without ruffling the egos of the medical men in town."

"Since when do you care about ruffling egos?" she asked, emboldened by fatigue.

"The situation is more delicate here. We cannot simply move on if a doctor or druggist starts bellyaching. And to pay them off would be too costly."

"With all the extra performances, surely the show is enough," she said, casting a sidelong glance at Mr. Darby.

"Not if you hope to make it through the winter without accruing more debt."

"More debt!" She took a step toward Huey, then stopped, remembering the sting of his fist. "You cannot mean to trump up my expenses such that they—"

"Please, please," Mr. Darby said. "Let's not quibble about it here where museumgoers might hear. At least listen to my idea before deciding, Dr. Hatherley. I promise it will be quite lucrative for us all."

Tucia drew in a steadying breath and unclenched her hands. "Fine."

Mr. Darby smiled and gestured up the stairs toward the GENTLEMEN ONLY section of the museum. Tucia hesitated, remembering Fanny's stories from the circus. But she'd agreed to hear him out, nothing more.

She followed him and Huey upstairs and through a narrow

corridor lined with medical photographs. They started out mildly titillating—a woman with a crooked spine stripped down to her petticoat and harnessed to a strange, back-stretching machine; another, entirely undressed save for a veil over her face, whose arms and legs were swollen to the size of tree trunks due to elephantiasis. Soon, however, the nature of the photographs included grotesque images of advanced venereal disease.

"This is a new section of the museum," Mr. Darby said as they walked. "The men think they're getting a peep show. Instead, they see these. A short lecture of the ravages of the disease and"—his voice took on a studious tone—"that gravest of sins, masturbatory self-abuse, and the men are clamoring for a bottle of Miracle Elixir."

They passed a small room with a few more pictures, specimen jars, and a small raised platform where he or Huey could stand over the frightened men and hawk their medicine.

The corridor continued beyond the lecture room, its walls bare of prints or photographs. It terminated in a hefty door Tucia guessed opened onto an outside staircase, giving the gentlemen, newly chastised from the lecture, a private exit.

"What do you need me for?" Tucia said. They could lecture and sell medicine all they wanted, after all, so long as they didn't purport themselves as physicians.

"Ahh, there's another room here," Mr. Darby said, opening an unmarked door halfway between the lecture room and the exit. "For a more select clientele. An examination room of sorts. Not unlike the case-taking tent you and Huey operated."

Tucia peeked inside. Red silk wallpaper with velvet filagree covered the walls. An examination table sat to one side of the narrow room, though it looked more like a bed with its white cotton sheets and ruffled muslin skirt. A vase of silk flowers adorned a lacquered side table. Otherwise, the room was empty.

"This isn't an examination room. There's hardly space to move around. Where would I put my medical bag?" It was always helpful to have around, even though the consultations Huey performed were entirely fake. You never knew when someone seriously ill might walk in. "And where will you put the medicine bottles? Presumably, that's the point. Sell these men more hogwash they don't need."

Huey and Mr. Darby exchanged glances. "You may leave the selling of medicine to us. This room is strictly for your . . . ministrations."

"I would be conducting examinations alone?"

Mr. Darby nodded.

For a moment, Tucia imagined herself continuing the work she'd done in the palmistry tent, only without the guise of fortune-telling. She could get right to the business of nutrition and hygiene and proper—

But wait. That didn't make sense. Huey Horn was not in the business of real medicine. She backed away from the room.

"Just what sort of ministrations do you expect me to perform?"

"Nothing untoward," Mr. Darby said. "But, in keeping with the purview of the lecture, men will expect your examination to include inspection of more . . . intimate regions."

The hallway seemed to shrink around her, and its air grew thin. She needn't further explanation to know the purpose of such examinations was not to assess the men's health. Her chest tightened, and her pulse thudded in her ear. She had to get out of here, as far away from this little room as quickly as she could. Dr. Darby's large body blocked the rear exit, so she turned and pushed past Huey in the direction they'd come.

"No," she said over her shoulder. "I won't do anything of the kind."

She raced down the stairs, slipping on the last few steps but managing to stay upright. The museum felt as cave-like as the hallway, and she pushed through the crowds of patrons until she found the exit.

At last outside, she drew in a ragged breath. The evening

air was hot and salty. Waves crashed against the nearby beach, louder than yesterday. But then, everything seemed different—the seagulls' call more shrill, the breeze more harassing, the lavender-colored sky void of beauty.

She looked up and down the busy street, disoriented. She needed to get back to the boardinghouse. But how? Was it left she turned or right? This morning she'd known, but now her brain couldn't latch on to anything except the sight of that room and Mr. Darby's words.

Breathe . . . breathe.

After a few moments, her mind settled enough to remember. Right, she turned right down Avenue Q, then followed Twenty-Seventh Street up all the way to Postoffice. But before she could move in that direction, a hand encircled her arm.

Huey.

His grip was not painful but firm enough to suggest it would become so if she struggled. He hailed a cab and bullied her inside. He gave the driver an unfamiliar address, and the carriage pulled away from the curb, merging with the line of wagons and coaches rumbling down the seaside avenue.

They drove several blocks in silence before Huey released her arm. "You've a tiresome propensity for the dramatic, my dear."

"I meant what I said, Huey. I won't be party to you and Mr. Darby's sordid little plan. I'm a physician, not a prostitute."

"Again with the dramatic. After our lecture, the mere suggestion of a private examination with a lady physician will be enough to excite these men. You need only hurry their release along with your inspection and hand them a handkerchief when they're through."

Bile rose in her throat. She crossed her arms and turned away from him, staring out at the rapidly darkening gulf with its pale, foaming surf.

"Don't play the part of the ingenue, Tucia. You're no stranger to the heat of a man's bed."

Tucia willed her cheeks not to color. Was he referring to Toby's father or his suspicions about her and Darl? Either way, Huey would make her pay.

"I haven't told you the best part," he continued. "Darby believes we can charge ten dollars for each examination. Ten dollars! Half of that is yours."

"It could be ten times as much, and I wouldn't do it."

"You'll do it, if for no other reason than because I say you'll do it."

Tucia shuddered. Dr. Addams had said something similar to her that day in his office when she'd refused to let him have his way with her a second time. It was as if saying no to these men made them all the more insistent she submit. Dr. Addams would have forced himself on her again—she'd seen the threat of it in his eyes—had a knock at the door and a summons from the head nurse not interrupted them. So instead, he ruined her career or, rather, goaded Tucia into doing it herself.

With Huey, she felt herself now on similarly perilous ground. "Is that what this is about? Proving yourself in front of Mr. Darby? Showing him how you lord over us?"

"Darby is a means to an end."

"Then tell him this idea has gone too far. You want to make money from my license, fine. Set up a case-taking parlor like we had before. Or, if you're worried about the local doctors, I can read palms."

Huey chuckled. "You'd like that, wouldn't you? You think I don't know what you were doing? Giving the yokels advice that kept them from returning to buy more medicine." Another dark chuckle. "My dear, I told you, I'm nothing if not observant. I know everything you've been doing."

As he said this, the wagon slowed in front of a hulking building. Iron bars covered the windows, even those three stories up, and a high brick wall surrounded the grounds.

"What is this place?" she asked.

"The county jailhouse. Rather grim, wouldn't you say?"

"Not half as bad as state prison, I imagine."

"Darl told you, did he? Good. It will make my job of explaining even simpler. You do as I say upstairs at the museum or this is where Darl will end up."

"If you turned him in, the both of you would be implicated."

"Yes, but not if someone *else* did. A respected business owner and member of the Knights of Pythias, say. Someone who could vouch that Hugh Hornby, Darl's partner, was long since dead. Then, Darl alone would be on the hook for murder."

"Murder?"

"Oh! Did he spare you that part?" The false shock in Huey's voice made her want to slap him. "There was an unexpected hiccup in our escape plans, you see, and an innocent guard lost his life. Really, I don't know how Darl's been able to live with himself all these years."

Tucia had sensed there was something else Darl had wanted to tell her the night she came to his tent. But murder?

Her stomach roiled. "You can't be . . . he wouldn't . . ."

"It's quite true, I assure you." He pulled the glove from his hand and examined his nails in the faint light as if bored with the discussion. "And he's not the only one at jeopardy of ending up here. Lawrence, Fanny, Cal . . . they all have sordid pasts."

Huey hollered to the driver, and the cab ambled on.

"You wouldn't. You'd have no one to ballyhoo in the show for you."

"Everyone's replaceable, my dear."

"Then replace me! Let me go."

"But you still haven't repaid your debt."

"I've repaid it twice over, and you know it. No matter what your little ledger says."

She reached up and pulled a hair and another and another. Huey grabbed her wrist with his bare hand, his nails digging into her skin. "You're much prettier when you aren't going bald. It matters more now, you know."

The cab turned down Postoffice Street, its familiar bars and brothels alive with customers. Tucia tried to think—there had to be a way out of this—but it felt like the world were trying to swallow her whole. The clomp of the horse hooves, the swell of music from inside the houses, the thud of her heart.

"Don't look so glum," Huey said. "It could always be worse. Think where you'd be if I'd left you in that squalid little flat where I found you. Toby would be in an asylum, and you'd be . . ." He glanced pointedly at one of the whorehouses. "Who knows where you'd be? Really, you ought to try and be a little more grateful." He squeezed her wrist and then let it go, tugging his glove back on as they arrived at the boardinghouse.

Darl sat on the porch steps beside a glowing lamp, whittling a piece of wood. Her chest tightened at the sight of him. What would happen if he were arrested? Would the lawmen send him back to Tennessee to work on the chain gang? Would they try him for murder and sentence him to hang?

His hands stilled at their arrival, and he glanced up, but Tucia couldn't meet his eye. Behind him, she could see Fanny in the parlor through a lighted window. Toby and Al sat beside her as she read from a book. What about her and Cal?

A sharp pain spread through Tucia's chest as if a horse had kicked her, cracking her sternum. Had she any food left in her stomach, she would have vomited.

Huey climbed out of the cab and held his hand out to help her down. "Well, are you coming?"

What choice did she have?

Tucia ignored his hand, fisting her skirts and stepping down on her own. Huey chuckled and left her standing there by the road. He and Darl exchanged a dark look as Huey passed him on the stairs. Only after the front door closed and Huey was gone could Tucia find the will to move.

Darl stood and met her at the foot of the steps. "What's wrong? He do somethin' to you?"

Tucia shook her head.

He reached for her arm, but she pulled away. "Don't. We can't."

"Can't what?"

"Any of it." She tried to mount the steps, but Darl blocked her way, grabbing her by the shoulders. He smelled as he always did of sawdust and linseed oil and soap, and she turned her head away lest she lose her nerve. "Darl, please."

"It's ain't any of Huey's business. If he got a problem with what we're doin' then he can—"

"It's not Huey!" She wrested herself free from his grasp. "It's me. I . . . I'm tired of carrying on like this. It was a foolish dalliance, and now it's done."

Darl stepped away from her and blinked. The wounded look on his face made the pain inside her all the sharper. She hated to lie to him, but the truth would only spur him toward recklessness. And he wasn't the only one she had to protect.

"You don't mean that," he said.

"I do."

"Well, it ain't no dalliance for me. I love you."

The words left her breathless, unable to speak. He loved her? Even with her frayed nerves and patchy hair? Her blighted past and interminable debt?

He loved her. And she loved him too. With every cell of her body.

She longed to fall into his arms and repeat the words to him, over, and over again. Instead, she willed her face into a mask of stone and spat out, "I don't love you." Then she brushed past him and up the stairs.

"Tucia—"

"Leave me alone, damn it!" She wrenched open the door and let it slam behind her.

As soon as she was inside, Toby called to her from the parlor. She couldn't look his way, not with the tears threatening in her eyes. He ran to her side, clinging to her leg and tugging on her skirt. *Mama, Mama*, he was saying, then something about supper and Kit and wanting to go back to the beach tomorrow.

Fanny appeared in the parlor doorway and said something too. Something about Toby being tired but refusing to sleep . . .

wanting to wait up for her. Tucia nodded. She reached down and patted his head, but he continued to paw at her.

From across the hall, Huey was watching, his expression smug. "Tomorrow, you'll apologize to Mr. Darby for your outburst, and we'll run through our little upstairs operation."

His gaze flickered to Fanny, then back to her, his violet eyes sharp and expectant.

Tucia forced herself to nod.

"Good. You'll see your first clients Sunday night." He smiled and started up the stairs.

Fanny spoke again, asking if she was all right. Toby bounced impatiently beside her. Mama. Mama. Mama.

How had she gotten here? So very far from the life she'd dreamed of having. It was a mistake. All of it. Believing she could be a doctor. Challenging Dr. Addams. Allowing Huey into her life. And not just Huey. Lawrence and Al and Fanny and Cal and Darl.

Darl.

The stinging pain spread from her chest to her arms, her legs, her head. She'd wanted too much. Should have stuck to her small little world right from the start.

Toby was pulling on her skirt, her hand. "I want to go to the beach again."

"Not tomorrow," she said.

"I want more shells."

"Another day."

Toby began stomping and shouting, the noise like needles to her brain. "The beach! The beach! The beach!"

Tucia pried his hands from her skirts and slapped him across the face. The sharp sound echoed through the hall.

Fanny gasped. Toby went silent. He stared up at her, his mouth open and pupils wide. Then he began to cry.

Oh, God! What had she done?

Tucia scooped him into her arms and carried him upstairs as he continued to wail. The sound blotted out everything else. She sat on the bed and rocked him, holding him fast as tears filled her eyes.

What had she done? Who had she become?

Eventually they both stopped crying, and he fell asleep in her arms, but the silence haunted Tucia as much as his crying, the emptiness of it keeping her awake long into the night.

42

Tucia awoke the next morning to the *plink* of rain against the window. Pale light streamed in through a gap in the curtains. What time was it? A heaviness clung to her body as if she'd slept too long and no time at all. It must be early if Toby hadn't woken yet. She rolled around to check on him, but found his side of the mattress empty.

Tucia bolted upright and looked around the room. He wasn't on the floor stacking his building blocks or splashing in the basin on the washstand.

She hurried from bed and threw on her robe, not bothering with shoes or slippers. He was probably downstairs eating breakfast or playing with Al in the parlor. But when she got to the parlor, it was empty, save for Mrs. Pitt, busy with her knitting.

"You missed breakfast, but there's coffee and a leftover biscuit or two on the table."

Tucia glanced at the mantel clock. Quarter after ten. How had she slept so long?

"Have you seen my son?"

"The older boy or the feeble-minded one?"

"Toby, the smaller of the two."

Mrs. Pitt thought for a moment, then shook her head. "Haven't seen him since last night. You might see—"

Tucia didn't wait for her to finish. In the dining room, she found Fanny and Cal seated at the table, sipping their coffee. A twinge of shame curled inside her. Fanny had seen her slap Toby last night. She'd never slapped him before. Not once. Not even in her lowest and most anxious moments. But now was not the time to explain. And when Fanny glanced up at her, there was no judgment in her eyes.

"Have you seen Toby?"

"No. We thought you both were still asleep."

"Where's Al? Could they be playing together?"

"Outside, but I don't think Toby's with him."

Tucia raced through the kitchen and out the back door. Outside, rain poured steadily down. Vast puddles covered much of the yard. She spied Al near the cistern chasing a frog. They were everywhere, the slimy creatures, hopping from pool to pool.

"Have you seen Toby?" she called, just as a gust of wind swept through the yard, pulling on the hem of her night coat and whipping her wet hair into a frenzy.

Al looked up but didn't seem to have heard what she said. Tucia yelled again. Al shook his head. Her ribs tightened. Her gaze snagged on the shed at the edge of the yard, its door cracked open.

Kit, of course! That's where Toby would be. She splashed across the yard and flung wide the door. The shed was cluttered with crates and gardening tools and empty paint cans. The nest they'd made for Kit was empty and Toby nowhere inside.

Tucia could barely breathe as she hurried back to the house. Fanny stood in the doorway, waiting for her. "He's not out there?"

Tucia shook her head, water dripping from her clothes onto the floor. "Oh, God, Fanny. What have I done?"

"He's probably about the house somewhere. Go change, and I'll help you look."

They searched every corner of the house, from the attic to the crawl space beneath the porch. Everyone, even Mrs. Pitt and Mr. Wilder, helped look.

No sign of Toby.

"Might be with Lawrence at the stables," Cal offered when they reconvened in the foyer. "Or Darl. I reckon he's still working down at the livery getting the wagons all shut up for the winter."

She plucked a strand of hair and rolled it between her fingers. Toby did like helping with the animals, but Lawrence would have checked with her first before taking Toby with him. Darl, too, even though he likely hated her now. Maybe Toby had tagged along without one of them realizing it or left with someone else.

Tucia froze. "Huey. Did anyone see him leave?"

"He stopped by the dining room during breakfast," Fanny said. "Told us he was off to the museum. That he'd see us there at noon for rehearsal."

Cal nodded. "Heard him leave out the front door, but didn't watch him go."

"Huey has him," Tucia said. He must. It was just the sort of stunt he'd pull. A reminder of how much she had to lose if she didn't go along with Mr. Darby's plan. She dropped the hair and plucked another. He wouldn't hurt Toby, though. Would he?

Fanny stepped in front of her and put a hand on Tucia's arm. "*Schatz*, last night, Toby kept talking about the beach, remember? Maybe he went there."

Tucia pulled away. "No. He wouldn't. Not on his own."

But what if he did? She brushed past Fanny and resumed pacing. What if he tried and got lost along the way? Or worse, what if he made it to the beach and strayed too close to the water? Oh, God, what if he—

Fanny grabbed her again, encircling Tucia in her arms and holding her still. "He's going to be okay. We're going to find him." She stared down at Tucia, holding her gaze until Tucia nodded. "Cal, *Mäuschen*, you go to the stables and see if he's with Lawrence. If not, check with Darl. We'll go to the beach in case he went there. We'll all meet up at the museum, yah?"

Mrs. Pitt sent them out with umbrellas and promised if Toby returned, she'd get him dry and fed and see that he stayed put until they returned. The storm, she assured them, was normal enough and would pass in a few hours.

Tucia hadn't even made it off the porch, though, before a gust of wind nearly ripped the umbrella from her hand. Gray clouds blotted out the sun, and rain continued to fall. Ankle-deep water swamped the yard and much of the street. How could this be normal? The thought of Toby out alone in such weather made her insides seize. Fanny tugged her onward.

When they turned down Twenty-Third Street, they found it crowded, as was to be expected on a Saturday morning, with carts and drays and carriages going about their usual business. The people passing by on the sidewalk moved through the water with resigned annoyance.

Tucia searched the crowd for Toby, hoping to see him hand in hand with some good Samaritan or huddled with Kit beneath some shopkeeper's awning, trying to stay dry. She scoured the face of every young boy they passed, none were Toby.

As they drew closer to the south side of the island, Tucia noticed two types of travelers braving the weather. One was eager beachgoers who'd heard from a neighbor or a friend of terrific waves and wanted to witness the sight themselves. The other, moving in the opposite direction, was families, carrying makeshift bundles and suitcases. Instead of eager, their expressions were wary. Neither group lessened Tucia's worry.

Shin-deep water greeted her and Fanny a block and a half before they reached the beach. It was as if the gulf were rising to overtake the shore. The roar of the surf was much louder than she'd heard it before. Her gut clenched.

Those around them were smiling. Laughing. Splashing through the water as if it were a thing of delight. But when she glanced at Fanny, Tucia saw a reflection of her own dread. They quickened their pace.

When they arrived at the gulf beach, the waves were as astounding as promised, rising far higher than she'd seen at their last visit and crashing with raging force. The water itself had swallowed the beach and nearby streets as far as the eye could see. The souvenir shops and restaurants shuddered with each new breaker. A few had already collapsed. Murdoch's Bath House stood like an island, waves besetting the thick pilings that raised it above the ground.

Wind blew stiffly at Tucia's back as she stared out at the gulf. She'd given up on the umbrella. Or any notion of staying dry. She took several steps forward before realizing Fanny hadn't moved. She walked back and took Fanny's hand. It was shaking.

"Stay here and keep an eye out for him," she said. "I'll look around."

She traipsed onward, asking every group of people if they'd seen a small boy about yea high, carrying a furry brown animal. Often she had to shout above the wind to be heard. *No ma'am, sorry ma'am,* or a quick shake of the head were the only replies. Each time she glanced out at the roiling water, her anxiety deepened.

She searched the bathhouse and a long stretch of beach beyond. Nothing.

By the time she returned to where Fanny stood at the far edge of the sand, the water had risen to her knees. The wind had strengthened as well.

"Any news?" Fanny asked.

Tucia shook her head. As much as she hated the idea of Toby being with Huey, she prayed when they got to the museum, he'd be there.

As they turned to go, a loud crack sounded.

She and Fanny whirled in the direction of the noise. Murdoch's pilings had given way, and the entire building crashed down into the water. Fanny gasped, latching onto Tucia's arm while she stood there, stunned. Tucia had been inside the building only minutes before.

The heap of wood that had once been the bathhouse churned

in the waves, boards splintering and clapping together. Had people still been inside? She didn't see anyone amid the wreckage, but likely they'd be buried, pinned beneath the wood, crushed and drowning.

Without thinking, Tucia hurried toward it, wading through the water. Before she could reach it, a fierce wave broke over the debris. The swell lifted her off her feet, the cold water rising past her waist and plunking her down a few yards up the beach. She froze, unsteady, as the surf ebbed back toward the gulf, sweeping with it the building's broken remains.

She found Fanny, and they locked arms, sloshing back toward the road. Neither spoke. Panic lodged like bile in Tucia's throat, impossible to swallow.

The museum sat a few blocks farther up the beach. She could barely make out its brightly painted sign through the rain. What if the waves grew fiercer? The water higher? Would the museum fall as well?

43

They reached the front entrance of the museum, but a sign on the door declared it closed on account of the rain. They knocked, but no one answered. The stage door off the back alley was also locked. Then Tucia remembered the second-floor exit she'd seen beyond the silk wallpapered room and found the stairs leading up to it. The second-story door was locked just like the others, but when they banged, Tucia first, then Fanny with her sledgehammer-sized fist, it swung open.

Mr. Darby stood in the jamb. "Oh, it's only you." He begrudgingly stepped aside and let them enter. "Mind your wet clothes."

"Is Huey here?"

"He left about a half hour ago when we closed the museum."

"Where'd he go?" Fanny asked.

Mr. Darby shrugged. "I presumed back to your lodging to call off rehearsal."

He walked down the hall and into his office. Tucia and Fanny followed.

"Was my son with him?"

"I don't know," he said, sinking into a plush chair behind his desk, his face pinched with annoyance. "The museum was packed to the gills before I decided to close it down. All those muddy shoes were set to ruin the carpets."

"I imagine they're more than ruined now," Fanny said. "The water outside is up to my shins."

He wandered his gaze down her body to the hem of her damp dress and back up again. "That *is* saying something. But this isn't the first time the island has seen a little storm. Besides, the building sits above the road by a good two feet."

"So you didn't see my son?"

"Mrs. Hatherley, I couldn't tell your son from Adam."

"But he's different. Small in stature. Round face. Narrow eyes."

"Oh, yes, the imbecile. No, can't say I saw him. But I was up here in my office most of the morning, and Huey was down in the theater."

"He's not an imbecile!" Tucia said, her voice at the edge of cracking. "He's kind and loyal and far more astute than a man like you could even begin to comprehend."

Fanny lay a doughy hand on her shoulder. "What about the others?" she asked Mr. Darby.

"The others?"

"The rest of our troupe. They were on their way here."

"You mean the Indian and that bowlegged man. Nope. You're the only two to come by since Huey left."

The worry in Fanny's eyes deepened.

"I can search here if you want to go find them," Tucia said. "We can meet back at the boardinghouse."

Fanny bit her lip, then shook her head. "No. We stay together."

As they started down the hall toward the stairs, Mr. Darby rose from his chair and followed them. He caught up halfway down the hall and grabbed Tucia's arm, pulling her close. He leaned toward her ear, his face so near the pointy end of his waxed mustache scraped against her skin. "Huey said you'd reconsidered my proposal. I can't tell you how glad I am to hear it."

She pulled away, her arm hair standing on end, but said nothing. She couldn't think of that now. The only thing that mattered was finding Toby. She followed Fanny down to the main level of the museum past the bawdy photographs. Mr. Darby remained at the top of the stairs. "Don't forget to mind your wet shoes," he called after them.

Fanny searched the theater while Tucia combed through the museum, calling her son's name. Panic hummed through her body, but she refused to let it overwhelm her. Breathe, she reminded herself. Breathe.

Several inches of water stood on the floor, and the building creaked in the wind. So much for Mr. Darby's blithe estimation of the storm. He'd be replacing the carpets for sure and half of the exhibits if the water continued to rise.

As she reached the final room, the electricity failed, plunging her into darkness. She managed to feel her way back to the base of the stairs, bumping into Fanny when she got there. Fanny shrieked.

"It's just me," Tucia said. "Did you find him?"

"No."

Tucia had suspected as much. Huey wouldn't have brought Toby here only to leave him behind. He was many things, but not careless. And Toby was no use to him lost.

"We should try to intercept the others instead of waiting here," Fanny said. "It doesn't feel safe."

Tucia agreed, not only on account of the lack of electricity but the steadily rising water.

They made their way up the darkened staircase and down the hall. A light flickered from within Mr. Darby's office, and they stopped at the door.

"We're leaving," Tucia said. "There's water downstairs, and Murdoch's bathhouse collapsed. We saw it happen right before our eyes."

He sat behind his desk, a candle burning at his elbow. If the news worried him, he didn't let it show. "You mainlanders. So quick to worry over a little rain and wind." He chuckled, but Tucia heard the faintest hint of unease in his voice. "We weathered the storm of 'eighty-six, we can weather this too."

"If the others come by, tell them we went back to the boarding-house and have them meet us there," Fanny said.

"Do I look like a damned telegraph clerk?"

Tucia itched to hit him upside the head with his candlestick but kept her anger schooled. "Please."

"Yes, yes, fine." He waved them away. "Take care not to let too much rain in on your way out."

They sloshed away from the museum, eager to be away from the beach and its roaring surf. The high water continued even as they reached Twenty-Fifth Street and headed downtown. Where had all of it come from? Surely it wasn't raining hard enough to raise the level of the gulf.

Tucia was no expert in flooding, but the way the water moved worried her, too, rocking back and forth as if under the sway of the tide. Should the ebb and flow grow strong enough, it might bring down the rest of the houses and smaller buildings near the beach. Maybe even the museum.

The rain and the wind showed no signs of relenting, but Tucia kept her fears silent. No need to add to Fanny's worry.

This part of the city was far emptier now. Shops were closed, and houses shuttered. Nearly everyone out braving the storm now was trudging away from the beach. They carried bundles of clothing, clocks, jewelry boxes, framed pictures, china teapots, and all sorts of houseware as if they feared the storm might wash away their homes.

Their expressions were graver than that of those she'd seen out that morning. Gone were the awe and delight. Gone was the casual annoyance. These people were sober, grim, some even frightened. Most walked in silence. Those who did speak were barely audible above the howling wind. She caught a few bits of conversation here and there. The streetcar had stopped running. All of the bathhouses, not only Murdoch's, had collapsed. Homes were swamped with seawater. Some had already fallen.

And then she heard someone utter a word that struck her dumb: hurricane.

Tucia had never been in such a storm before. Only heard tales. Frightening, horrible tales of roofs being ripped off houses and people being washed away to sea.

A gust of wind rent her from her thoughts, so strong it sent her staggering backward. Her hat flew from her head, taking her pins and hair switch with it. Another gust followed, this time from the side as if the wind couldn't make up its mind which direction to blow. Tucia lost her footing. Fanny reached out, grabbing her arm before she fell.

"Are you all right, ma'am?" a nearby man called. He was stout with a full beard just beginning to gray. By some miracle, the yarmulke atop his head had not blown away. Beside him stood a woman of equally solid build, carrying an umbrella. Its ribs must have been made of steel to withstand the fretful wind.

"Yes, thank you," Tucia said when she'd regained her footing. "I heard someone say this is a hurricane. Is that true?"

The man looked up at the sky and nodded.

"Are you sure?" she managed to ask. "Wouldn't there have been some warning?"

The woman frowned at the man and lightly cuffed his shoulder. "Leave the forecasting to the weather bureau, Moshe."

"Cline raised the storm flag yesterday," he said.

The woman turned to Tucia, smoothing away her frown. "They never can be sure of these things. But either way, it's not safe near the beach."

"How long will it last?"

The man and woman both shrugged.

Hurricane. They had to find Toby and the rest of the troupe.

"If it is a . . . a"—Tucia had trouble saying the word aloud—"a storm like that, where's the safest place to be?"

Before either of them could answer, a slate tile from one of the nearby houses broke free. Tucia saw it zip toward them from the corner of her eye, carried by the wind as if it were light as a pie tin. They all ducked and covered their heads. It splashed into the water, not two feet from where they stood.

"Inside, for starters," the man said. "You can come with us. We're headed to our rabbi's house. You'd be welcome there."

"Thank you, but we can't," Tucia said. "We've got to find our families first. We're staying at an inn on Postoffice Street."

The man nodded. "That's better than here. Might be all right so long as it's sturdy. I'd try to get closer to Broadway if you can."

"Highest ground in the city," the woman added. "The storm might blow over without much more fuss, but better to take care all the same."

As she said it, a fresh burst of wind struck them, and the ribs of her umbrella finally snapped. The wind rushed under the canopy, ripping the umbrella from the woman's hands and sending it careening through the air with other bits of detritus—leaves, wet newsprint, roof tiles—swept up along the way.

Tucia noticed more debris in the water, too, bobbing and swirling in what was now a steady current. Both forces—the wind and water—worked against them, making each step a precarious effort. She and Fanny said goodbye to the couple and continued onward, clinging to each other and whatever else they could use to steady themselves.

When they reached Avenue M, the water was waist-high and still rising. Three blocks away lay Broadway, its great stone mansions barely visible through the driving rain. It, too, was swamped.

The streets were mostly empty now. Anyone with enough sense, safely indoors. Tucia hoped that included Toby and the rest of their troupe.

The water's current, swift now, flowed westward—eager, it seemed, to sweep them from their feet and carry them along. They clung to fences and lampposts, inching down the street. The wind, meanwhile, harried them from the side, blowing with such force they both lost their footing on more than one occasion and would have toppled into the water were it not for the other's steadying hand. The rain struck them like icy pebbles.

"I'm sure they turned back hours ago when they saw the conditions of the road," she hollered back to Fanny, hoping to ease her worry. It was Tucia's fault, after all, they were out here, separated from them. If she hadn't slapped Toby last night, he might not have snuck out this morning while she was asleep, and if she hadn't made a deal with Huey, they wouldn't be here in the first place. If she hadn't—

A piece of siding several feet long came whirling toward her in the wind. It struck her shoulder before she could duck and knocked her off her feet. She careened into the water, going under as she was sucked along with the current.

Tucia flailed her arms and legs, at once trying to swim and stand. She managed to raise her head above the water, gasping for breath, but her feet couldn't find purchase. The current whisked her along, knocking her into debris—an upturned wheelbarrow, a broken crate, a lost suitcase.

Fanny rushed through the water toward her, but the current was faster. It pulled Tucia toward the center of the street where it flowed the swiftest, far from anything she might grasp.

Something softer than the other debris brushed past her. She turned her head to see the body of a drowned cow float by. Tucia screamed. She gave up trying to stand or grab hold of something and turned onto her stomach to swim.

She stroked her arms and kicked her legs, her skirt and petticoat fighting the effort. The current continued to carry her, but slowly, feebly, she was moving away from the center of the street toward the edge.

A fiery pain cut deep into her leg. Something had struck her as she kicked, slicing through her clothes and deep into her skin. A nail? A scrap of metal? A wedge of broken glass? Tucia knew she was bleeding but couldn't risk looking back. Forward. She must keep swimming forward.

Other objects knocked into her as well—the water was thick with them—trash barrels, chunks of wood, mangled umbrellas like the one the Jewish woman had lost to the wind. A bicycle sped past her, floating on its side, its handlebars snagging on the sleeve of her dress. It dragged her several feet off course until she managed to pull free.

Tucia's strength was flagging. Her leg throbbed. If the current swept her much farther, she might lose sight of Fanny and have to push upstream to get back to her. That was if Tucia managed to find something she could hold onto and get her footing again. About three yards ahead of her, the pointy tips of a wrought-iron fence stood above the water's surface, marking the bounds of someone's yard. She focused on the fence and swam with all her might.

Her fingers grazed the iron bars but couldn't grab hold. She tried again, this time managing to crook her wrist around one. She looped her other arm through the bars and, at last, could stand. Cold water rose to her armpits. Her breath heaved. Her spent limbs trembled.

She saw Fanny about a block away, wading through the rushing water in Tucia's direction. A broken tree branch flew at her through the air.

Tucia hollered and pointed. Fanny deflected the branch with her arm, but the end of it glanced off her head as it whipped past, leaving a long cut across her cheek.

When Fanny reached her, they embraced fiercely, both soaking wet and trembling.

"I'm not sure where we are," Tucia said, looking around when they pulled apart. "Or how much farther we have to go." She wasn't even sure what time it was. The dark storm clouds overhead made it impossible to tell.

Fanny nodded. She pointed to the house on whose fence they clung, a sturdy-looking two-story brick building that stood several feet above street level. "Maybe they can tell us where we are."

Floodwater blanketed the yard, reaching halfway up the porch steps. Though the current was not as strong here as it had been in the street, they crossed the yard with slow, careful steps. If Tucia lost her balance again, she'd not have the strength to swim back to safety.

A Black man answered the door when they knocked and welcomed them inside. The parlor was crowded with people of every color, who, Tucia quickly gathered, had come in search of shelter.

The man eyed Fanny, who towered over him by more than a foot but said nothing about her size. He introduced himself as Clive Baker and offered them refuge while the storm railed, but Tucia shook her head. "We're on our way to Postoffice Street. Is it far?"

"Too far to travel in this weather," he said.

"Our families are there." At least, Tucia hoped they were. "We have to get back to them."

"Well, it's about seven more blocks. But I can't say I recommend it."

Seven blocks. Surely they could manage it before nightfall.

Mr. Baker's wife came over with dry blankets and cups of warm tea. Tucia thanked her and drank hers quickly, ignoring the way it scorched her tongue.

"They're thinking of going back out," Mr. Baker said to his wife.

"What?" She spoke as if the idea were preposterous. "It's too dangerous out there."

Tucia handed her back the teacup. "Thank you," she said again. "We just came in to get our bearings."

The moment Mr. Baker unlatched the door for them to leave, the wind blew it fully open, nearly knocking the three of them over. Tucia glanced at Fanny, who took a step back, clearly shaken.

"Well?"

Fanny clenched her teeth and nodded. They stepped onto the porch. Mr. Baker followed them out. "If you find you can't make it, you're welcome—" He stopped. His jaw slackened, and his dark skin turned ashen.

Tucia followed his gaze to the yard. The muddy water that only moments ago had been level with the middle porch step was rising. It swallowed three more steps and was splashing at their feet in a matter of seconds.

The three of them hurried back inside, the water following them, seeping in beneath the door when they, at last, got it closed.

"Everyone upstairs," Mr. Baker called to the parlor full of guests, his voice steady but urgent.

Tucia's heart knocked against her breastbone. There was no getting to Toby now. She could only hope he was with the others at the boardinghouse. She tried to remember the look of the place. It was old and shabby, but hopefully the foundation was still solid, and had been built to withstand such a storm.

And the Baker's house? She prayed it, too, could endure the screaming winds and raging water the hurricane had loosed upon them.

44

Mrs. Baker, who only moments before had been serving Tucia and Fanny tea, now approached them carrying a crate of food. She thrust the crate into Fanny's arms. "Take this upstairs. We'll be right behind you." She motioned to Tucia to follow her to the kitchen and handed her a clutch of candles and a jug of water.

When they passed through the foyer on their way upstairs, Tucia hesitated. Water spilled beneath the front door at an alarming rate, already reaching above her ankles.

From the corner of her eye, she saw Mr. Baker come forward with an ax.

"Step aside," he said, raising the ax over his head and driving it into the floorboards. He loosened the blade from the wood and struck again.

"What are you doing?" Tucia asked, backing up until she ran into the banister.

"Water's coming in. It needs someplace to go out or it will find its own way and break the house apart." He heaved the ax overhead again and swung it down. The floorboards cracked, and water began to circle into the small hole he'd created. But it was coming in far faster than it was going out.

"Best get upstairs," he said, striking through the water to enlarge the hole.

Tucia didn't move, her heart beating at the base of her throat. Was the water rising this high and fast everywhere else on the island?

The din was suddenly too much for her—the roar of the wind, the clatter of rain, the splash and thwack of Mr. Baker's ax. She couldn't think or move or hardly breathe.

"Unless you aim to drown down here, you best get a move on," he said to her. The dark, cold water was up past their knees. He brought his ax down again, sending a splash of water into Tucia's face.

She blinked, coming to her senses. Her arms tightened around the jug and candles, and she carried them upstairs. Mr. and Mrs. Baker followed at her heels.

The second story was split into two bedrooms with a small washroom between them. Most who'd sought refuge in the house crowded into the leeward bedroom. Tucia found Fanny sitting on the floor in the smaller, windward room, her face aglow in the light of a quivering oil lamp. Many of those huddled there teetered toward hysteria, some crying, some arguing, some gnawing their fingers raw. But Fanny was stoic, her lips flattened and eyes fixed.

Tucia sat beside her and grabbed her hand, giving it a firm squeeze. How this must remind her of that awful storm when her family crossed the Atlantic. Fanny's gaze remained on the far wall, her fingers limp in Tucia's hand. Tucia didn't let go, as much for her own sake as Fanny's.

To keep her mind occupied, she examined the cut on Fanny's cheek and the gash on her own leg. Neither were severe enough to warrant concern. Not here, not now, when the house groaned and shuddered as if it might fall.

How scared Toby must be—wherever he was. She prayed the others had found him and were keeping him safe. She imagined him in Darl's arms or holding Al's hand as she now held Fanny's.

Darl would know what to do in a storm like this, and Toby would listen and follow him.

What if Toby wasn't with them but with Huey? Or lost and completely alone? What kind of awful mother was she to have let this happen?

It wasn't just that she'd slept late. Or forgotten to lock the door. Or let her frustrations get the better of her and struck him. Her life was a litany of mistakes—accepting Dr. Addams's challenge in the operating theater, borrowing more money than she could pay back, joining Huey's ridiculous show—and Toby would pay the price.

She closed her eyes and listened to the storm batter the house. Water seeped in through the roof, plinking onto the floor. A fierce gust of wind rattled the foundation. As Tucia opened her eyes, chunks of plaster fell from the ceiling, and a crack snaked up the wall. Someone in the room screamed. It was a shrill, unnerving sound like a screw twisting its way through a knot of wood.

A dark thought crossed her mind. What would happen to Toby if she died? Who would look out for him? Would he end up in one of those awful asylums?

Maybe he'd be better off that way. Better off without her.

The shutters covering the room's sole window blew open, banging against the side of the house.

Fanny freed her hand from Tucia's and covered her ears.

"Close them!" someone yelled.

They were right. If someone didn't close the shutters, the window could shatter.

Tucia rose at the same time as a man across the room did. He reached the window a step ahead of her and raised the sash. Rain lashed them both, carried on the violent wind.

She could see the dark floodwaters outside raging only half a dozen feet below. But it wasn't just water. Timbers and telegraph wires and wagon wheels churned with it. A shiver worked its way up her arms. The man reached out to grab the shutters, but before he could, the wind ripped them from the house.

"They're gone," he said, slamming the sash down. "We'll have to brace the glass another way."

Tucia looked around the room. "Maybe the mattress. We could prop it up against the window with the dresser."

As they moved toward the bed, the wind roared again, and something struck the window, sending a spray of shattered glass into the room. A piece sliced Tucia's arm. Painful, but not deep. The man suffered a similar cut to his leg.

Everyone else seemed unharmed, until she turned and saw Fanny, her eyes wide and face draining of color. Blood seeped from a gash in her side where a large splinter of glass was lodged. Though it was hard to tell in the dim light, it looked as if the glass had struck her between her lower ribs.

Tucia froze. Her heart quickened, and throat closed. Fanny needed a doctor. A *real* doctor. One whose mind wasn't fractured and hands shaking. Even as Tucia thought this, the roar of the storm began to fade. She felt herself slipping away. The smell of antiseptic stung her nose. The heat of the operating room lights beat down on her head. The rain on her hands turned to blood. She stood there, staring down at them as panic squirted through her veins. Fingers trembling, she wiped her hand on her skirt, but they came back even more bloodied.

No. No!

Well, what are you going to do now? Dr. Addams said from behind her.

"I . . . I . . ."

Keep standing there like a fool, Doctor, *and she'll bleed out before you can do anything.*

This wasn't real. She wasn't here.

Breathe, he said. No, not him. Fanny. *Breathe.*

She inhaled, forcing the air past her narrow windpipe deep into her lungs. Then a slow exhale, fighting off the echo of his smug voice.

The rain. The wind. That was real. She clawed her way toward them.

Slowly, the dark, drenched room came back into focus. Fanny lay slumped against the wall, her dress colored red, her eyes fluttering closed.

Tucia sucked in another breath. She had to focus. With that much blood, the glass must have punctured Fanny's spleen. If Tucia didn't act, her friend would die. Her rusty, imperfect skills would have to be enough.

Tucia turned toward two women huddled in the corner. "I need clean water, rags, and needle and thread." When they didn't move, she raised her voice. "Now!"

They hurried to their feet and scampered away.

Tucia grabbed the lamp from the center of the room. "You," she said to the man who'd tried to close the shutters. "Help me lay her flat. Gently. We can't risk the glass lodging any deeper."

Together they eased Fanny into position on the floor. Fanny winced and moaned. Her breath was shallow, her pulse thready and uneven. Careful not to jostle the protruding glass, Tucia ripped open the bodice of Fanny's dress. Her damned corset would have to be undone after Tucia removed the glass.

The women returned with the supplies she'd asked for. She sent one back in search of alcohol. The other, who seemed less squeamish of the blood, she commanded to stay.

"When I pull out the glass, I need you to unfasten her corset as quickly as you can. The bleeding will get worse, and I won't have much time to sew her up, so you'll have to move fast. Afterward, hand me rags as I need them. Can you do that?"

The woman knelt beside her and nodded.

It took Tucia three tries to thread the needle. Then she laid it aside and grabbed the edge of the glass. She could do this. She *must* do this. She just had to believe. In her schooling. In her skill. In herself.

"Ready?"

The woman nodded. Tucia drew in another deep breath, then pulled the shard free. A fresh stream of blood quickly followed. Tucia staunched the flow with a rag until the woman managed to unfasten the hooks of Fanny's corset. It sprang free. Tucia ripped apart the chemise beneath and studied the wound, pulling back the edges.

"Hold the lantern above me," she said.

The light revealed what Tucia had feared. Fanny's spleen had been pierced. She'd have to stitch it first, then the fascia and skin, all while working in the narrow space between her ribs. She wiped her hands on a clean rag, then grabbed the needle and thread. Blood was everywhere. Just like in the operating theater. But she steered her mind away from the thought.

Working as quickly as she could, Tucia sewed together Fanny's wound, mopping up the blood as she went. She was halfway through stitching the fascia when another blast of wind shook the house. Outside came a loud cracking noise followed by a sickening splash. Tucia didn't need to look up to know a nearby house had succumbed to the storm. It seemed only a matter of time before theirs did as well.

But she couldn't think about that right now. She had to focus on Fanny. Her pulse had grown weak, and her breathing labored. After tying off the final suture, Tucia doused the wound in alcohol and covered it with a rag. She found the driest blanket she could and wrapped it around her.

"Will she live?" the woman who'd been assisting her asked.

"I don't know."

The house groaned as more water poured in through the broken window and leaky ceiling. Would *any* of them live?

45

Tucia remained at Fanny's side through the long night. Sometime around midnight, the storm waned. The wind lost its terrible gusto, and the downpour of rain dried up. The floodwaters continued to buffet the house, cracking the plaster and stressing the timbers, until finally, just before dawn, it too lost its strength and retreated back to the gulf.

At first light, Tucia recruited the help of Mr. Baker and two other men. They made a makeshift stretcher, gently heaved Fanny onto it, and carried her downstairs. The water had receded from the house, but a thick layer of mud covered everything. Mrs. Baker opened the front door for them, and they emerged blinking into what seemed another world.

Galveston was ruined. More than half the houses on the block had collapsed, some reduced to a heap of rubble, most washed away entirely. Mountains of debris cluttered the yards and clogged the streets.

They had to find the hospital, but Tucia had no idea which way to go. The landscape was entirely altered.

Thankfully, even with little left standing, Mr. Baker knew the streets. Carrying the front end of one of the stretcher's poles while

Tucia took the other, he led them down one road and then another without hesitation. The two men at the back helped navigate too. A few streets were impassible, and they had to turn around or cut through yards or alleyways. But Mr. Baker's sense of direction never faltered.

They hadn't gone far when they saw their first body—a boy no older than ten, naked and twisted amid the rubble. Even from a distance, Tucia could tell it was not Toby, but her heart dropped nonetheless. They set Fanny down and picked their way through the wreckage to the boy.

Tucia checked for a pulse, then closed the boy's eyes. Mr. Baker said a quick prayer. He took his handkerchief and tied it to a nearby pole jutting from the debris so he could find the spot again and do right by the body. Soon they passed another body and another. Mr. Baker gave up trying to mark them.

A knot tightened in Tucia's stomach each time she saw a hand or leg or shock of hair sticking out from the wreckage, fearing the bruised and bloated body would be Toby's.

What seemed like hours later, they arrived at the hospital. A row of large cottonwood trees stood naked and listing before it. Heaps of rubble—timbers, bricks, broken furniture, doors, window casements—covered the sidewalk and affronting street. The roof had been stripped bare of its slate, and a fallen telegraph pole had crashed into the facade. But somehow, the great stone building itself was still standing.

They were not the only ones who'd come with their wounded. Dozens of others trudged down the cluttered streets toward the hospital.

Tucia expected mayhem when they entered, but though the floors were slick with mud, the halls filled, and staff harried, there seemed to be a tenuous order to it all. Wails and moans rose from the wounded, but no one pushed or shouted to be seen first.

A nurse was inspecting those who entered, then sending them off with orderlies to various parts of the hospital.

"My friend suffered a laceration to her spleen," Tucia told her. "I stitched it up, but she lost a lot of blood. She's in shock and may require whisky and ether hypodermically to sustain her circulation. She'll also need a fresh dressing, absolute rest, and to be watched closely for internal hemorrhaging and signs of infection."

The nurse stared at her a moment, then glanced down at Fanny, her eyes widening.

"Yes, she has gigantism," Tucia said sharply. "But that's not the issue at hand."

The nurse nodded and peeled back the bloodstained rag covering Fanny's wound, then instructed an orderly to take them to ward three.

Every bed in the ward was taken, many by two or more patients. The windows had blown in, and the blinds were gone. Bright sunlight streamed in, helping to dry the soaked walls and bedding. With nowhere else to put her, they laid Fanny on the floor at the far end of the room. Tucia thanked Mr. Baker and the other men profusely before they left, then waited beside Fanny for the doctor. She repeated her assessment of Fanny's condition when he arrived.

"You did this?" he asked, crouching down and examining Fanny's wound.

"Yes."

"And you're sure it cut to the spleen? A wound like this could bleed a lot without—"

"I visualized the organ myself."

"I see." He glanced again at the wound, then back at Tucia. "Are you a nurse?"

"No, I'm a physician. Woman's Medical College of Chicago. I graduated top of my class in 'ninety-two. But I . . . I haven't had much practical experience."

He eyed her not with derision but a sort of wonder. "The Medical Department next door graduated its first woman doctor just three years ago. A gentle lady but brave and independent. You seem like the same sort, and experience or no, we certainly need your help." He held out his hand, and Tucia shook it. "I'm Dr. Burns. I'll get a nurse to assist you and—"

"I can't stay. I have to find my son."

Dr. Burns tried to persuade her to stay, but after Tucia explained the situation with Toby, he seemed, if begrudgingly, to understand. She offered to take a bag of supplies—bandages, suture thread, morphine, a syringe, a tourniquet—and treat those she came across during her search. As soon as she found Toby, she would return and help.

Dr. Burns agreed and sent a nurse to pack a medical bag for her.

"You haven't seen anyone like my son today, have you?" she asked after describing him.

Dr. Burns shook his head. "Did you . . . er . . . check the morgue?"

Tucia winced at the word.

"Our deadhouse was destroyed in the storm, but I believe they're taking bodies to a warehouse on the Strand. You . . . you may want to have a look there first."

Her stomach clenched as she thought of all the bodies they'd seen along their way to the hospital. "How many do you think have died?"

"They're saying hundreds."

The room seemed to tilt and wobble before her eyes. Hundreds?

Dr. Burns reached out and set a steadying hand on her shoulder. "Have you eaten?"

"What?" Her brain struggled to parse out his words. Eaten? When had she last eaten? Not since before Toby went missing.

"Make sure you get some water and food before you leave too." He gave her shoulder a squeeze. "Good luck finding your son, Doctor. I'll be sure to take good care of your friend here."

The nurse returned with a bag of medical supplies and directed Tucia to the makeshift morgue on the Strand thirteen blocks west.

It was only a mile away, but it took Tucia, wending her way through the sludge and debris, over an hour to get there.

She hesitated before entering, then took a deep breath and pushed the door open. It may kill her, but she had to know if Toby were here.

Tucia had been in morgues before, but this was unlike anything she'd seen. It was a large room, empty aside from the iron pillars supporting its high ceiling. And the dead. The bodies lay on the wet floor in tightly packed rows, stretching from one end of the room to the other. There were hundreds of them.

Tucia buried her nose in her sleeve, thankful her stomach was empty. The condition of the bodies was nightmarish. Their clothes were in tatters—if they had any at all. Their hair was matted and tangled with bits of debris. Bruises, lacerations, twisted limbs, bloated abdomens—the storm's violence marked them all. Some were covered with sheets and rugs, only their faces exposed. Others had no covering at all.

The urge to hurry through the room and be free of the ghastly sights and smells almost overpowered her. It took conscious effort to keep her pace slow and steady. As awful as it was in here, it would be worse to wonder. Wonder if in her haste she'd missed the body of her son. Each face that wasn't his elicited a tiny swell of relief, even as she knew it was the face of someone else's son, mother, or husband.

Halfway down one of the rows, Tucia stopped with a gasp. Her stomach dropped. She crouched down beside the body before her, wishing for better light. But even in the dim, she recognized him. Mr. Wilder. His tidy beard and the large mole on the side of his nose made her certain.

Did this mean the boardinghouse hadn't withstood the storm? Were the others—Darl, Cal, Al, Lawrence—lying here as well? And Toby. If he'd been with them then . . .

Hysteria stirred inside her, and she strangled off a scream. Her legs were shaking when she stood. The urge to run up and down the final rows all but overcame her. She drew in a deep breath, wincing at the smell. Then another. A modicum of calm returned. She owed it to the others in the room—those, like her, searching for lost loved ones—not to fall apart.

With slow, deliberate steps, she searched the other rows. Mr. Wilder's face was the only one she recognized.

When she was sure she'd viewed all the bodies, she said a silent prayer and left the room. There were surely more dead buried among the rubble. But for now, Tucia would believe her son and the rest of the troupe were alive. *Had* to believe it. Alive and waiting for her to find them.

Outside the warehouse, the sun shone impossibly bright in the sky, illuminating the wrecked city. She guessed from where it sat high overhead half a day of light remained. She stopped a man passing by on the street and he pointed her in the direction of Postoffice Street.

Her progress was slow as she picked her way over and around heaps of rubble. Every so often, she stopped and called her son's name. She called for Cal and Al and Lawrence and Darl too. Even for Huey. Birds cawed in reply. Other searchers called out the names of their missing. Otherwise, the island was eerily quiet.

As promised, she stopped whenever someone looked ill or injured. Most had minor wounds that were quick to clean and dress. Others she stabilized with a tourniquet or sling and sent in the care of family or friends to the hospital. One man she found impaled on a fence post. After dosing him with morphine to ease his pain, she sat with him until he died.

Her bag of supplies was nearly empty by the time she neared Twenty-Seventh and Postoffice. Though battered and ringed with mud, most of the houses on the street still stood. The tightness in her chest eased a little, and she scrambled down the littered street to the boardinghouse.

"Toby!" she cried, slipping as she climbed the mud-slickened steps. "Toby!"

She kicked aside the flotsam cluttering the porch and hurried inside. The front door was gone, wrested from its hinges by the storm. "Toby!"

Mrs. Pitt rushed in from the kitchen. "What in the Lord's name— Oh, it's you. You're alive!"

"My son, is he here?"

She looked down and shook her head.

Tucia sank onto a chair. A layer of slimy muck covered the seat, but she didn't care. She felt hollowed out, like a doll who'd lost her stuffing. Her nerves exposed and raw.

"And the others? I saw Mr. Wilder's body at the morgue and feared the rest of you were . . ." Tucia couldn't bring herself to say the word *dead*.

Mrs. Pitt shook her head and crossed herself. "He left yesterday morning not long after you and the giant did to check on some goods he had down by the wharf. Never returned. Haven't seen Mr. Horn either. The rest came back just as the storm got bad and the power went out. We spent the night holed up in the attic."

"Everyone?"

"Well, the Indian fella and the cripple and his boy."

Tucia breathed a fleeting sigh of relief. Fanny would be overjoyed when she awoke.

"What about—"

The back screen door clattered, and footfalls sounded in the kitchen.

"I got that hole in the cistern fixed up," called a familiar voice. "But it won't do much good until it rains again. The water that's left in there musta mixed with the floodwater. Too dammed salty to—"

Darl stopped in the doorway and gaped at her. "Tucia?"

A jolt of happiness shot through her, giving her the strength to stand.

He crossed the foyer in three quick strides and pulled her into his arms, hugging her so tight she could scarcely breathe. "By Jove, I was so worried." He buried his face in her hair, and Tucia closed her eyes, letting the horrors that surrounded them disappear a moment. Then she pulled away.

"Toby."

"I know. Cal told—" He stopped. "That ain't your blood, is it?"

She followed his gaze to her bedraggled dress, stained a brownish red. It hadn't occurred to her what a fright she must look. "No. Not much of it anyway. Darl, we have to find him."

"We will," he said, his dark eyes steady and convincing.

"Where are the others?"

"Out looking for you and Fanny. Thought you mighta spent the night at the museum. I stayed in case you came back."

"And Huey?"

"Ain't seen him."

"I think he has Toby," At least, she hoped he did. The alternative—that Toby had wandered off on his own and endured the storm alone—was too much to bear.

"Let's go find 'em."

The assuredness in his voice buoyed Tucia's hope. She hardly deserved such kindness after the way she'd treated him.

"You will? You'll help me? Even though . . ."

Darl didn't hesitate. "'Course I will."

46

The floodwaters hadn't reached the second story of the board-inghouse, and Tucia was relieved to find her medical bag tucked in the corner where she'd left it. She changed out of her bloodied dress and switched out her boots, shredded to almost nothing by the shattered glass and splintered wood that lay everywhere.

Downstairs, Mrs. Pitt was waiting with the supplies she'd asked for—water, clean rags, matches, a cake of soap, and a bottle of alcohol. Between this and her own supplies, she should have enough to last until she could make it back to the hospital.

She explained Fanny's condition, and Mrs. Pitt promised to send Cal and Al to the hospital as soon as they returned. Dr. Burns had assured Tucia he'd take care of Fanny, and she hoped he had. Hoped her ragged stitches had held. Hoped the wound hadn't suppurated. As soon as she had Toby, Tucia would return and check on her. And if Dr. Burns still wanted her help, she'd stay as long as she could be useful.

Mrs. Pitt had heard from a neighbor that City Hall was badly damaged but the county courthouse had weathered the storm bet-ter. People were gathering there for news and aid.

It seemed as good a place as any to search, so Tucia and Darl started off in that direction. This part of the city was not as damaged as others she'd seen, and they made their way with relative ease, sidestepping large puddles and heaps of rubble.

Every few paces, one of them would call out Toby's name. Then they'd stop and listen. The wind and rain and clattering debris had raged for so long yesterday it was strange now to hear silence. Strange and crushing.

The silence between her and Darl felt much the same.

"Huey said you killed a man. A guard during your escape," she said, instead of the *I'm sorry* that hung on her lips. Right now, swamped with worry over Toby, she couldn't bear the added weight should he not forgive her.

"And if I did?"

Tucia stopped and faced him. "If you did, well . . . we're more than our worst mistakes, aren't we?"

She hoped he heard the apology in her voice. She owed him more than that. Far more, but she couldn't think on that now, and said the only other words she must. "I love you."

"You don't have to—"

"I love you."

Darl stared at her a moment with that guarded expression he wore so well. Then he pulled her into his arms, hugging her fiercely. Despite the grim destruction around them, hope swelled inside her. What lay ahead remained uncertain, but at least she needn't face it alone.

A few blocks on, they turned down the street to find a dead horse blocking half the road. Flies swarmed around its bloated body. The stench made Darl gag. They hurried around it, broken shingles and shattered window panes crunching under their feet.

"I didn't, by the way," Darl said once they were well past the horse and flies. "Kill that guard. Huey did. How he got that blade, I'll never know. Suspect it was meant for me."

He told her about their escape, how Huey had approached him one day during supper with the idea to run. He'd already planned everything. All Darl had to do was find a way to bust the locks on their shackles.

But even Huey's plans weren't infallible. The day of their escape arrived. Darl had sprung the lock on his shackle and was almost done with Huey's when a guard unexpectedly spotted them. Darl got Huey's lock open just before he reached them. Instead of running, Huey pulled out a makeshift knife and stabbed the man. Not just once but again and again until Darl wrested free the blade.

They'd planned to part ways once they'd got downriver to New Orleans, but now, with the guard's murder looming over them, neither trusted the other enough to let him out of his sight. They'd been stuck together ever since.

"He wouldn't hurt Toby. Not like that," Darl said when he'd finished as if he'd read her mind. "He's a bastard. But he's smart. Without Toby, he ain't got no leverage over you."

She'd been hoping the same thing. Once she found Toby, she'd get him as far away from Huey as she could, no matter what it took.

The county courthouse sat adjacent to City Park. Both were swarmed with people when they arrived. They split up and searched the crowds. Most people sat with blank expressions or moved as if sleepwalking. Several times she opened her medical bag, pulling out what she needed to dress wounds or reset broken bones. As she worked, she caught snatches of conversation that turned her insides cold. Everything on the gulf side of the island had been washed away. The orphans' home had collapsed. The bay side of the island was cluttered with overturned ships and floating bodies. The rail and wagon bridges were destroyed, cutting the island off from the mainland. The city's water main had broken, and they'd soon run out of drinkable water. Looters were robbing the dead. Martial law had been declared.

She asked over and over again if anyone had seen a young boy with Toby's features or a man with violet eyes. Some couldn't focus enough to answer. Others only shook their heads. One woman gave her a handbill the *Galveston News* had just printed. On it were listed the names of those believed dead.

Tucia held her breath as she scanned the page. Neither Toby's nor Huey's name were on it. But her relief was short-lived. Who besides their troupe and Mr. Darby knew them well enough to report their names to the paper? To most, they were unnamed strangers.

She was making her second pass through the main hall of the courthouse when Darl caught her eye and waved her over. He stood beside a short man whose dark hair was streaked with gray.

"This man reckons he mighta seen Huey."

"Really?" She turned to the man. "Was a young boy with him?"

"I'm not sure, *señora*," he said with a thick Mexican accent. He described how he'd taken shelter in the schoolhouse on Twenty-Fifth Street and Avenue P when the storm got bad, thinking it safer than his home several blocks closer to the beach. Dozens of people were already there when he arrived, among them a short man with violet eyes just like Darl had described. There were several children there, too, but he couldn't remember any of them well.

Tucia reached out and hugged the man.

"I must tell you," he said. "Part of the building collapsed during the storm. I can't say who survived and who didn't."

His words tempered her relief, but at least they had somewhere to look next. Another spark of hope to cling to. It was unlikely Huey and Toby would still be at the schoolhouse, but there might be someone in the vicinity who saw them too and knew where they went after the storm subsided. She thanked the man, and they hurried off.

As they headed south on Twenty-Fifth Street toward the school, Tucia saw that much of what she'd overheard at the courthouse was true. Roofs had collapsed or blown off completely. Homes lay on their sides. Entire blocks had been reduced to nothing but a vast pile of timber.

They stopped to help a man with a long gash running down his leg. And another frantically digging through the rubble, trying to unbury his wife. When they reached her, Tucia felt for a pulse, but the woman was long since dead.

The sun hovered close to the horizon by the time they reached the schoolhouse. Tucia could see why the man had fled here. It was a large, stone building three stories tall, raised on sturdy brick piles several feet above the ground. Even with its missing shingles and blown-out windows, it looked indomitable. But as they came round to the far side of the building, she saw an entire corner had collapsed, just as the old gentleman said.

Tucia had witnessed the storm's power for herself, remembered its dark, churning water and violent wind, but it was still hard to fathom such damage. Anyone who'd sheltered in this part of the school would have been crushed or swept away in the flood. She tried not to think of the terror they must have felt, those who hadn't died instantaneously. Had any of them been able to swim to safety? Not likely, considering the swift currents and perilous debris. Still, she vowed if she found Toby—no—*when* she found Toby, she'd teach him to swim.

They circled the school again, calling out, but no one answered. The steps to the main entrance had been washed away, but if she scaled the debris piled against the facade, she might be able to reach one of the lower windows. Darl caught her hand before she got far.

"It ain't safe," he said.

"But what if he's inside, too hurt or frightened to call out?"

"I'll go. Why don't you see if anyone's in them houses." He nodded to a nearby cluster of homes. Everything else for at least a block in any direction had been leveled.

He held fast to her hand until she climbed down.

"You'll be thorough?"

Darl nodded, and she knew he would. She'd never seen him do a slipshod job at anything.

"Be careful," he said to her.

"You too."

He scrambled up the wreckage and into the school. Tucia watched until he disappeared into the bowels of the building, then picked her way toward the houses. They were considerably more damaged than they'd appeared at a distance—windows shattered, siding blown off, roofs sunken. One listed heavily to its side.

A dead chicken and an overturned oil drum littered the yard of the first house she approached. The porch of the second collapsed as she tried to mount the steps, leaving her with another gash along her shin. The third house—the listing house—creaked such that she dared not go beyond its battered fence. All three appeared deserted. Had their owners survived the storm inside or sought shelter in the nearby school? What an awful irony if they'd been in the corner that collapsed.

She returned to the school just as Darl was climbing down, alone. Her stomach sank. Before she could ask what he'd found inside, the clomp of horse hooves sounded behind them. She turned to see three men approaching on horseback with several others—mostly colored men—trailing on foot. The mounted men, she noticed, wore shotguns slung across their backs.

Darl came and stood in front of her.

"Put down that bag and raise your hands," one of the men said. "Both of yous."

Tucia set down her medical bag and raised her arms. Darl did the same.

"What'd you take from up in the school?"

"We didn't take nothin', sir," Darl said. "We're here lookin' for her son."

"What's in the bag, then?"

"Medical supplies," Tucia said, stepping around Darl, even as he shot her a glare that said *stay back*. "I'm a doctor."

"A doctor?" The man laughed and dismounted. "I've heard some tall ones in my day, but a lady doctor?" He picked up her bag and peered inside. "Where'd you get all this?"

Tucia grabbed the bag from him. "I told you, it's mine."

"Why ain't you at the hospital, then?"

"Like he said, I'm looking for my son."

The man smirked. "Well, you best get along. The mayor's issued a curfew."

"Yes, sir," Darl said, grabbing her arm and tugging her away.

"Not you," the man said. "All able-bodied men have been conscripted to help with the cleanup."

"You don't have the authority to do that," Tucia said. Darl winced, and she realized these men could shoot them both and no one would be any the wiser.

"We've been deputized by the relief committee," the man said, hooking his thumbs beneath the strap of his gun. "Anyone who don't comply goes to jail."

"I'm glad to help," Darl said. "Let me get my friend here safely home, and I'll meet you wherever—"

The man with the rifle stepped closer. "That ain't how it works. You'll come with us and you'll come with us now."

Tucia clenched her hand around the strap of her bag. She opened her mouth to speak, but Darl shook his head. "Head back to the courthouse. I'll meet you there when I'm done helpin' these men."

She watched as Darl joined the group of men behind those on horseback.

"You heed what I said now, Doc," the deputy said as he climbed back on his horse. "No one's allowed out after dark, and we got orders to shoot looters soon as we see 'em. Hate for you to be shot by mistake."

The men rode off, the others following behind on foot. Darl glanced back, his expression grim. And just like that, Tucia was on her own again.

47

Tucia returned to the courthouse, hoping Darl would soon follow. They wouldn't work the men through the night, would they? Having him by her side had been an unexpected buoy. He kept her steady and hopeful. Kept the panic at bay. She itched to pluck a strand of hair. Just one. But one would turn into two and three and four. A night like tonight there'd be no end, no end until she was truly bald, her scalp raw and bleeding.

To keep her hands busy, she joined a line at the far side of the hall where food and water were being distributed. The flask of water Mrs. Pitt had given her was long since empty. She refilled it and accepted a can of peaches and some crackers, then found an out-of-the-way spot on the floor to sit.

Her first sip of water came back up with a hacking cough. Tucia tried again, more slowly, and managed to swallow without triggering another cough, but her throat burned as the water went down. The crackers were soggy and the peaches warm, but both tasted divine. She hadn't realized until then how hungry she was.

The food slowly settled in her stomach, bringing with it a tidal wave of fatigue. She curled up on the floor, heedless of decorum, and sleep quickly claimed her.

* * *

The next morning, she awoke feeling like a train had struck her. Her neck ached, and feet were sore. The gashes on her leg throbbed, but thankfully didn't appear infected. She made rounds through the hall, but got no new information about Huey or Toby.

Darl hadn't returned either. Where had those men taken him? How late had they worked? Certainly there was enough cleanup to do on the island to occupy ten times as many men as they'd conscripted. And the dead. They'd need to be buried. She shuddered and chased away the thought. As much as she wished Darl were with her, she couldn't wait for him to resume her search.

Outside, the morning sun was just rising. A fetid stench filled the air. A mixture of the sunbaked sludge the storm waters had left behind and rotting flesh. She'd seen piles of debris over a dozen feet tall. What lay beneath was now making itself known. Had anyone from the mainland made it to the island yet? If help and supplies didn't get here soon, the dead would multiply on account of disease. She pushed the thought aside, filing it away with the other things she'd worry about once Toby was found.

She stopped a passerby, who pointed her toward the hospital, and made her way there. When she arrived, she found Dr. Burns amid the bustle, and he updated her on Fanny's condition. Her wound had bled again, and he'd had to reopen it and reinforce the stitches. Not good news, considering all the blood she'd already lost. At least Cal and Al were at her side. She spied all three of them at the far end of the ward where Tucia had left her yesterday. Two beds had been placed end to end to accommodate Fanny's height, and a clean blanket covered her. Cal and Al were asleep—Cal slumped in a chair, and Al curled on the floor beside Fanny's bed.

Tucia didn't wake them. The next hours would prove critical for Fanny. Even at a distance, Tucia could see the pallor of her skin and the quick, shallow rise of her chest.

The hospital was running low on supplies with no word yet when more might arrive, but Dr. Burns gave her a few rolls of bandages and another vial of morphine. No children had been brought in since yesterday who matched Toby's description, he told her, but he promised to keep a lookout.

Though Dr. Burns didn't come out and say it, she could read from his tight expression he didn't expect her to find him. Time was running short, and Tucia knew it. She thanked him for the supplies and hurried out before he could try to dissuade her.

From the hospital, she headed south, hoping Huey might have returned to the museum. Progress was slow and grew slower the closer she got to the gulf. Long before she could see it, Tucia could hear the murmur of the waves, soft and lulling. So unlike the roar two days before. The air was different, too, the breeze barely strong enough to ruffle her skirt but heavy with the smell of death.

Almost nothing had been left standing here. She wound her way around the wreckage, careful of the glass and exposed nails and jagged wood. In some places, the debris seemed to stretch on forever, and she had to scramble over and across it, each step perilous. Her skirt caught on bicycle handles and stove pipes and broken-off tree branches. Through gaps in the rubble, she spied more bodies—cows, chickens, horses, pigs, fish. And people. At each, she stopped, but only long enough to be sure they weren't alive and their battered, bloated face wasn't one she recognized.

The sun was almost overhead when she finally caught sight of the gulf. Everything was gone—the streetcar, the bathhouses, the souvenir shops and restaurants, the museum—all swept to sea. The wooden piles of buildings once firmly on land now peeked above the surf as if the gulf had reclaimed the edge of the island.

A group of men labored nearby. Drawing closer, she saw they were unearthing bodies from the sand. Tucia turned away. Unless he'd left soon after she and Fanny had, Mr. Darby's body was sure to be among those buried here or crushed beneath the nearby rubble. Despite how odious she'd found him, how quick he was to use her for his own ends, he didn't deserve such a death. No one on the island did.

She wondered if Huey had come here after leaving the school

and seen the total destruction. Where would he go from here? Toby would be tired and hungry. If the buildings on this side of the island were gone, what did the bay side look like? If the storm had demolished the railroad trestles and wagon bridge, it likely had wreaked havoc on the wharf too. Their wagons had been stored only two blocks inland from the docks. Assuming they were gone as well, Huey would have no choice but to return with Toby to Mrs. Pitt's.

At least, that was Tucia's best guess. She hated not knowing. Trudging back across the island would take hours, and what if they weren't there? But better that than wandering aimlessly.

After several hours of picking her way around and over the wreckage, however, Tucia realized she'd done just that—wandered, perhaps not aimlessly but off course. With so few landmarks left standing, she found herself utterly lost. Every little while, she'd pass a group of people—men clearing rubble, women and children looking for food and clean water—and ask them how to get to Twenty-Seventh and Postoffice. They'd send her in one direction, then another, if they had any idea at all.

Late in the day, she saw Mr. Baker, walking alongside another colored man behind a horse-drawn cart. Tucia called out and hurried toward him. He'd known precisely where to go to get to the hospital. Perhaps he could direct her to Mrs. Pitt's as well. She thought the cart rumbling ahead of him was carrying debris, but as she drew closer, she saw it was filled with bodies. Her feet flagged and bile rose in her throat. When she reached Mr. Baker, he hardly seemed to recognize her. His eyes were bloodshot, and gaze unfocused. Sweat beaded his brow.

She offered him water from her canteen and tried to direct him to a patch of shade. He eagerly drank the water, then looked around before following her to the shade.

"Can't linger long, Doc."

"But you look unwell."

"I'll be all right," he said, his voice void of feeling. "You find your son yet?"

She shook her head, her gaze cutting back to the cart. "Were you . . . ?"

"Conscripted?" He nodded.

She remembered the armed men from yesterday. "Where are you taking the dead?"

"To the docks, to be buried at sea. We tried digging trenches, but the ground's so soaked they filled with water. And . . ."

"And?"

"There's just too many of them."

"What about their families? They at least deserve to know they're . . . dead." A flutter of hysteria rose inside her. What if she never found Toby? Never knew what happened to him? Never got to say goodbye?

Mr. Baker glanced at the cart. Though moving slowly, it was half a block away now. "I'd best be getting along."

She fished through her medical bag, wishing there was something she could give him. Something that could help with the awful task thrust upon him. Then she remembered a trick from her days in the dissecting room. She pulled the handkerchief from her pocket and handed it to him. "Here, soak this in camphor or whatever else you can find with a good strong odor and wear it over your nose. It will help mask the stench."

"Thanks. And good luck finding your son," he said. "Be careful, now. There's a good number of so-called deputies about, but I don't trust them any more than the next man."

As she watched him walk away, she couldn't help but think of Darl. Had he been saddled with the same dreadful task of gathering up the dead, or had he been spared on account of his light skin? She couldn't imagine anyone who'd endured the storm to be the same after, but men like Mr. Baker would have even darker nightmares to contend with.

Only after he'd gone did Tucia realize she still had no idea how to get back to Mrs. Pitt's. Her hours wandering hadn't been completely wasted. She'd set a few more broken bones, stitched a few more superficial wounds, eased a dying woman's pain with a shot of morphine. What had once been such a source of anxiety now became a fleeting retreat from the ever-present worry she felt over Toby.

By now, the sun had sunk toward the horizon. If she couldn't find her way in the daytime, she'd be even more lost at night. She turned north down another cluttered street. At least the setting sun offered her a clear sense of direction. But without knowing how far she had to go or whether she'd even recognize Postoffice Street when she got there, it was little consolation.

A block ahead, a group of armed riders came into view. She hesitated, remembering what Mr. Baker had said and her own unpleasant experience with the deputies the night before. Better to encounter them now than after dark when they might mistake her for a looter.

She climbed onto an overturned cart and waved her arms. One of the men trotted over.

"I'm looking for Postoffice Street. Can you tell me how far I have yet to go?"

He eyed her with contempt. "You work down there?"

"No, I'm boarding there." She realized that did little to clarify things, but she didn't care if he thought her a prostitute as long as he gave her directions.

He didn't press the issue and told her how many more blocks she had to travel, reminding her not to dally after dark.

Twilight had already fallen, but she didn't point that out, only thanked him and started back on her way.

She'd gone only a block and a half when she spied a man digging through a towering pile of rubble. Tucia hurried over to help in case he was trying to free someone buried and injured. He startled at her approach, then slipped something into his pocket, straightened, and turned around. Seeing his face, Tucia gasped.

Huey!

48

Huey's startled expression slid into a smile. "Tucia, what an un-expected surprise."

"Where's Toby?" She looked around frantically but didn't see him. Oh God, was he the one Huey was trying to unbury from the rubble? Tucia dropped her bag and fell to her knees. She heaved aside heavy timbers and dug through sodden scraps of fabric and shards of clay shingles.

"Help me!"

Huey didn't move.

"Help me! We've got to save him." Bits of glass and splinters of wood cut her hands, but Tucia didn't care. She flung aside tin cans and soggy newsprint and a mud-caked slipper. A fat moon was rising, and its pale light illuminated the rubble. She lifted a piece of wood siding to reveal a face, bloated and discolored. A woman's face.

"It's not Toby," she muttered, heaving a breath of relief. But a renewed panic followed on its heels. If this wasn't Toby, then where was he?

"Where's my son?"

"What are you talking about? I don't have your son."

"The day of the storm, you didn't take him?"

"Why on earth would I have done that?"

To manipulate her. To frighten her. To remind her of everything she had to lose.

Tucia stood, not bothering to brush the dirt and grime from her skirt. She had to go. To keep searching. But where? Toby hadn't been at the boardinghouse or the museum or the beach. He hadn't gone to feed the animals with Lawrence or been taken by Huey. He'd just . . . wandered off. That meant he could be anywhere in the city.

Anywhere amid the wreckage.

She fell back to her knees as tears flooded her eyes. All those bodies trapped beneath the rubble, tossed out to sea, buried in the sand—any one of them could be Toby.

She swiped at her eyes and tried to stand again. Her legs trembled but held. She couldn't give up. Not until she knew for sure. She grabbed her medical bag and turned to Huey. "We have to find him. You have to help me."

"You haven't seen Toby since before the storm?" He looked at her a moment, then reached out and stroked her cheek. Tucia flinched and pulled away. "My dear, I'm sorry, but your son is dead."

Hearing those words spoken aloud hurt worse than if he'd struck her.

"You're wrong."

He held out his arms. "Look around. How could a boy like him survive this on his own?"

Tucia brushed past him, but he grabbed her hand, his touch no longer gentle. "Where do you think you're going?"

"To find him."

"Come now, you must see reason."

She yanked her fingers from his grasp. "I'll find him without your help, then. Go back to whatever business you're about."

What *was* he doing here? She glanced down at the body. The woman's face wasn't the only part of her visible amid the debris. In her haste, Tucia hadn't seen the stiff, purplish hand also peeking out. Two of her fingers had been cut off.

"Did you do this?" She pointed to the woman's hand.

"It's not like she'll be needing them."

"Her fingers?"

"The rings she was wearing."

Tucia took a step back, tripping over a piece of lumber and flailing her arms to steady herself. "You're looting from the dead?"

"The storm took everything from us, Tucia. The museum. The wagons. The money I had secreted away."

Something else too. Tucia could see it in the sheen of sweat at his temples, in his watery eyes and dilated pupils. His opium. No wonder he seemed half mad. He stepped toward her, grabbing her by the shoulders before she could back away.

"Everything! This is how we take it back." He let her go and began to pace. "Yes, yes, it's perfect. With two of us looking, we'll find twice the gold. You can stand guard while I—"

"I'm not helping you, Huey."

"You're still hung up on that idiot son of yours, aren't you?"

"He's not an idiot. And even if he weren't missing, I'd never help you steal."

"You've been helping me steal for months, just in a different fashion."

"I'm done with that. No more Madame Zabelle. No more case-taking."

"What about a deal? I help you look for Toby, and you help me look for jewels."

Tucia shook her head. "I'm done making deals with you."

She started to walk away, bracing herself in case Huey tried to attack her. Instead, he laughed.

"Where do you think you'll go that I can't follow? And what will you do? You failed as a doctor. You failed as a factory worker. You failed as a lover. Why, surely you don't believe Darl actually cares for you."

Tucia kept walking. She was done with his lies.

"And you failed as a mother."

Her feet stopped of their own accord. Her chest tightened. Huey laughed again and strode toward her.

"Think of how frightening it must have been for the lad. All that wind and rain and water, and his mother nowhere in sight."

"Stop it!"

"Do you think he died slowly, pinned beneath the rubble? Or was he caught in the current and drowned?"

Tucia dropped her bag and covered her ears, refusing to turn around but unable to walk away. Though muffled, she could hear the crunch of Huey's footfalls as he approached, drawing so close his breath prickled the nape of her neck. With a sickening tenderness, he clasped one of her wrists and eased her hand away from her ear.

"Without Toby, you're nothing. Always were nothing."

A sob broke free from her throat.

Huey was right. She had no home. No money. And without Toby, she had no reason to care.

"There, there," he said. "Enough crying. Pick up your bag so we can be on our way. We mustn't be seen lingering too long."

Tucia bent down and picked up her medical bag. She'd come to like the weight of it. The feel of the leather straps in her palm. The sense of purpose it gave her even as everything else spun out of her control.

"Let's go."

Tucia's hand tightened around the straps. She might have nothing, but that didn't mean she *was* nothing. She'd saved Fanny's life, after all. Or done her damnedest trying. And not just so she and Cal and Lawrence and Darl could fall back into Huey's clutches. She'd had enough of men like him.

"I said, let's go."

Tucia whirled around and struck him in the head with her bag. As he staggered to the ground, she drew a deep breath and screamed, "*Looter!*"

49

"Looter!" Tucia cried again, hoping the posse of deputies she'd seen earlier was still within earshot.

Huey's eyes narrowed, and his lips curled into a snarl. "You bitch. Shut up."

She glanced over her shoulder and backed away. The street was empty, the moonlight casting a patchwork of shadows. She called out once more.

"Shut up!"

Before Tucia could turn and run, Huey reached into his jacket. The glint of metal made her still. A gun. Where had he gotten such a thing? She'd never known him to carry a weapon. Then she remembered Darl's story. The blade Huey had sneakily procured.

He pointed the gun at her and cocked the hammer. Tucia's entire body went cold. He hadn't hesitated to kill that guard. Would he kill her too?

"Where did you get that?" she whispered.

Huey smirked. "Jewelry isn't the only thing buried in this mess."

He'd stolen it from the dead, just like the rings and God knew what else. It was a small gun, the type a lady would keep in her reticule, but a gun nonetheless. Would it work after having been submerged in the storm? Tucia knew nothing about guns except they killed people. Perhaps its parts were too muddy and water-logged to fire. She dared not chance it and flee.

Huey's smirk grew into a sinister smile. She hated that smile. Hated the glint in his violet eyes. Hated the joy he got from controlling her. Her fear erupted into anger. Her anger, into rage.

He started to rise, momentarily looking away from her as he planted his free hand on the ground.

Tucia swung her bag and struck him again. The gun flew from his hand. It skittered across the street, coming to a stop several feet away beside a pile of bricks and timber. They both raced after it.

Tucia reached the gun first. Before she could do anything with it, Huey lunged at her, knocking her to the ground. The air rushed from her lungs, and her vision went white as her head struck the corner of a brick. Her medical bag slipped from her grasp, but she held fast to the gun.

Huey climbed on top of her, reaching for the weapon. He might not have killed her before, but if he got the gun back now, he surely would. He clawed at her arm, her fingers. Tucia felt her grip failing. With her free hand, she punched him in the ribs. Pain shot through her fist. Huey hardly flinched.

She balled her hand again and, this time, struck him lower, aiming for his kidney. Huey inhaled sharply and arched his back, his hands slackening a moment.

But a moment was all Tucia needed. Her index finger found the gun's trigger, and she squeezed.

Her hand jerked back with the force of the bullet's expulsion, and the resulting bang split the night's silence. Huey rolled off her and onto his back, clutching the left side of his stomach. Blood seeped between his fingers.

Tucia scrambled to her feet and gaped down at him, stunned. She'd shot him. She'd actually shot him. The gun dangled limp in her hand, surprisingly heavy for such a little thing. She flung it as far away as she could. It landed with a clatter somewhere amid the distant rubble.

"You'll pay for this," Huey said, writhing at her feet.

His hubris almost made her laugh. Judging by the location and amount of blood, his wound was serious, possibly fatal without immediate care. Her medical bag lay only a few feet away, but Tucia didn't move. If she let him die, Darl, Lawrence, the Trouts— they'd all be free of him. Tucia would be free of him. He wouldn't be able to prey on anyone else ever again.

"Do something," he groaned, his voice weaker than before.

The blood pooling beside him brought back memories of the operating theater. But not as they'd come before. Not as a deluge of sounds and smells and sensations. She saw herself in the moment as Dr. Addams must have seen her. Her once steady hands trembling. Her confidence shattered. Her bravado slipping.

He could have helped her. *Should* have helped her. Should have saved their patient. But he'd wanted Tucia to fail badly enough that he'd let the woman die. That was not the action of a doctor. It was the action of a small, petty, insecure man.

Tucia would not do the same.

She grabbed her medical bag and knelt beside Huey. "Move your hand so I can see the damage and fix you up."

She'd covered the wound with a lint dressing, followed by a wad of oakum, and was pressing down firmly with her hands when the posse she'd seen earlier rode up. The bullet, she'd left in place somewhere deep in Huey's abdomen—it could be removed later at the hospital with the proper tools and aseptic practices. One of the riders dismounted while the other two men trained their shotguns in Huey and Tucia's direction.

"What's going on here?" the man asked as he approached.

"She shot me," Huey said before Tucia could speak.

"It's true," she said, glancing at the men, then returning her attention to the wound. The bleeding had slowed, and she reached into her bag for a bandage.

"On accident?"

"No."

The man looked at her, confused. "Then why are you helping him?"

"I'm a doctor." She hefted Huey into a sitting position. He cried out as if she'd shot him anew.

"She wants me dead."

"Hush up and raise your arms so I can bandage your wound good and tight."

"That true, ma'am?" the deputy asked. "Did you try to kill him?"

"I only shot him so he didn't kill me first."

"That's a lie!" Huey said. "I was minding my own business when—"

"I'll have the lady's story first," the deputy said.

As Tucia wrapped the bandage around Huey's midsection, careful to keep pressure over the wound, she told the deputy her story—with more than a few interruptions by Huey.

"See?" one of the mounted men said when she'd finished. "I told you I heard someone hollerin' 'looter.'"

"That was me!" Huey said. He winced and grabbed his side. The damned fool would finish what the bullet started and shout himself to death.

"Be still and conserve your strength," she said. "Just because I've bandaged the wound doesn't mean—"

"That was me who called out," Huey continued. "*She's* the looter."

Tucia sighed.

"I'm inclined to believe the lady." The deputy turned to her. "But unless you got some proof, I'm afraid we'll have to take both y'all to jail." He nodded to one of the other deputies, who dismounted.

"Wait!" There had to be proof somewhere. Maybe if she let them search her bag, they'd believe her. They'd likely insist on searching her person as well, an indignity she'd rather not endure but—

"His jacket pocket!" she cried. "When I came upon him digging through the rubble, I saw him slip something into his pocket. It's there." She pointed to the bunched-up jacket beside Huey. "I took it off him so I could get at the wound."

Huey snatched his jacket, clutching it to his chest even as fresh blood bloomed on his dressing. The men pried it away. When they turned out his pockets, both of the dead woman's fingers fell out, along with another belonging to someone else and a host of other small trinkets.

Tucia had to dissuade the men from shooting Huey there on the spot. It took more persuading to get them to bring him to the hospital instead of the jail. At last, they agreed, but only if he were kept shackled.

She rode with them to the hospital and described to Dr. Burns what happened so he'd know what to do for Huey's wound.

"You're quite the field surgeon," he said with a chuckle once they'd found Huey a bed and chained him there while a nurse changed his bloodied dressing.

"And Fanny?"

"Your friend's made steady improvement today. No more bleeding, and her vitals are stable."

Relief washed over her.

"Did you find your son?"

Tucia looked down and shook her head.

"They're still digging people out of the wreckage," he said. "But . . ."

"I know." Her time for finding him, finding him alive, was all but up. She couldn't keep looking in vain. Not when there were people here who needed her help. "Tomorrow, I'll . . . I'll report first thing in the morning if you think I could still be of assistance."

"Yes. The entire city would be grateful."

With directions from Dr. Burns, Tucia was able to find her way back to Postoffice Street. Foolishly, she'd expected to hear music and laughter. To see crowded sidewalks and passing carriages. But the bars and brothels were quiet, their storm-ravaged balconies and porches empty. Candlelight flickered in a few of the windows, otherwise she would have thought them abandoned entirely.

Tucia hadn't seen Fanny before leaving the hospital. It was enough to know her condition was improving. Cal and Al were surely with her, keeping vigil at her bedside as they'd been that morning. She imagined Fanny awake, propped up with a mountain of pillows, Cal urging her to drink some broth while Al described how they survived the storm.

It was a lovely vision, and it made her sick. Sick and angry, ashamed and jealous. Tears streamed down her face, and snot dripped from her nose. The hope that had sustained her the last three days had evaporated, leaving in its place a heavy ache. One she'd carry with her for the rest of her life.

She dreaded reaching Mrs. Pitt's, though already she could see it beyond the next block. Dreaded climbing the stairs and opening her door to an empty room. Dreaded crawling into bed alone.

A squeaking sound made her stop. She swiped the tears from her eyes and looked around. One of the bottom windows of the nearest house was open and light glowed from within. But as best she could see, the room beyond was empty. The mud-crusted street and littered sidewalks were empty too. Tucia rattled her head and continued on.

The squeak came again. Louder this time, followed by a scampering sound.

Rats. The city would be infested with them soon.

Tucia quickened her pace as the sound drew closer. Then the rat was on her, climbing up the back of her dress. She tried to swat it away as it climbed higher. Tucia was about to scream when its brown face peeked over her shoulder.

"Kit!"

She grabbed the monkey and hugged him to her chest. He squeaked and purred. By what miracle had he survived? He must have remembered the nuts the women were eating on the porch that day and made his way there before the storm.

She glanced back at the house. If Kit had gone there, perhaps Toby had followed.

Tucia turned around and raced to the door, climbing up broken porch steps and over the thick trunk of a fallen tree. She banged twice, then tried the knob. The door was unlocked, and she hastily stumbled inside. Anna was on her way down the stairs.

"My son, is he here?"

Before Anna could say anything, a voice called from above. "Mama!"

Tucia looked up and saw Toby peeking between the balustrades at the top of the wide staircase. She raced up two steps at a time and swept him into her arms.

"My darling, my darling," she said, crying into his hair.

Toby hugged her back. "Where did you go?"

"I was looking for you."

"But Kit and I were right here."

She laughed and held him tighter.

Anna explained she'd found Kit and Toby on the porch the morning of the hurricane. "It seemed at first like any other storm, so I thought we'd wait it out and bring him home once the rain let up. Boy, was I wrong." They sheltered in the attic during the storm. Between the felled tree in the front and a mountain of rubble in the back, it had taken the ladies most of the next day to get out of the house.

"When we got to Mrs. Pitt's, she said you were gone. That we'd just missed you. She promised to let you know where Toby was as soon as she saw you again." Anna reached out and pinched Toby's cheek. "He and that monkey sure do liven up the place."

Tucia hugged and thanked her, sandwiching Kit and Toby between them, tears still streaming down her face.

Her son was alive! Not only alive but well cared for. His hair was combed, his clothes clean, and he even wore shoes.

Both Toby and Kit fell asleep in her arms before they reached Mrs. Pitt's. The moon glowed like a paper lantern in the cloudless sky, illuminating their way. Wherever Tucia looked, there were signs of the storm's wreckage. And she knew all around the island mothers and fathers and daughters and husbands and lovers and friends were falling asleep with empty arms. Her heart broke for them. She squeezed Toby tighter and promised to do all she could to help those who'd survived.

50

Tucia peeled back the dressing over Fanny's wound. In the three weeks since the storm, it had healed nicely. The edges were still pink and puckered—she'd carry the scar forever—but there was no heat, erythema, or pus. Over the past few days, she'd been up and about the ward with Cal's assistance, halting and grimacing at first, but soon back to her steady, graceful self. It would be weeks more before she was fully healed, months before she was dancing again, but all signs suggested she'd make a full recovery.

"Looks good," Tucia said. "Dr. Burns agrees you can be discharged today, so long as you promise to take it easy. And if you have any new pain or bruising or redness along the scar, you see a doctor immediately."

Fanny smiled and patted her hand. "I will, *schatz*. You'll be at the docks tomorrow to see us off, yah?"

Tucia nodded. Cal had secured them passage on a boat off the island.

"Are you sure you won't come with us?"

Now that they were free to strike out on their own, the troupe had begun parting ways. Lawrence had returned to Indian Territory. He hoped to start writing for the local paper and publish some of his poems. Cal and Fanny had decided to start their own music-and-dance company.

"What would I do in a vaudeville show?" Tucia teased.

"Anything."

"If I never step on a stage again, it will be too soon."

"I could teach you to dance."

"No dancing, remember? Not until after Christmas."

"Yah, yah, I remember."

"And don't forget to write. Toby and I will miss you."

Fanny squeezed her hand. "Us too."

For the rest of the afternoon, Tucia rounded on the other wards. Most patients were recovering from the wounds they'd sustained during the storm, though infection had claimed more than a few. Others, it seemed, simply lost the will to live. Tucia couldn't blame them. So many on the island had lost so much.

The dead they'd tried to bury at sea washed back ashore, leaving them no choice but to burn the bodies. Funeral pyres were still alight throughout the city, their smoke darkening the sky, their stench inescapable.

New patients were coming in now, though fewer in number, most with injuries related to the cleanup. She stitched cuts and reset broken ankles. She extracted nails, shards of glass, bits of metal, and slivers of wood from hands and feet. She treated lockjaw and dysentery. The Red Cross had recently arrived with much-needed help and supplies, making her work easier.

Huey had been among those earlier patients to recover, though his withdrawal from opium had slowed his progress and intensified his suffering. Tucia couldn't say she was sorry. He'd been discharged to the jail only three days ago to await trial. With all resources focused on clearing and rebuilding the island, he'd be waiting a long time.

After her rounds, Tucia stopped by the brothel to retrieve Toby. The ladies were more than happy to take turns looking out for him while Tucia worked at the hospital. She'd have to find a more permanent solution soon. Postoffice Street wouldn't remain quiet forever. Perhaps once Tucia was earning steady money—Dr. Burns had spoken to the hospital board about hiring her on as a house physician—she'd be able to persuade Anna to come work for her as a nanny.

With Toby and Kit now in tow, she collected the supper basket Mrs. Pitt had made for them and walked to the edge of the city where an encampment for the men rebuilding the railway had been erected. With two crews working twelve hours each—one by day, one by night—they'd already restored the bridge and gotten one of the lines to the mainland up and running. The next would soon follow.

Darl worked the night shift, taking up ties and rail from the switch tracks in the railroad yards and lugging them to the end of the line for the day shift workers to lay the following morning. It was grueling work, but better than what he'd been assigned before—excavating and burning bodies. No one knew for sure, but she'd heard death counts in the thousands.

They found Darl just as he'd finished shaving and washing up. He smiled at them in the tiny tin mirror above the camp's makeshift washstand. He pulled up his suspenders and uncuffed his shirtsleeves. They all wore mismatched clothing and shoes donated from across the country. Though his trousers were a little too short and his shirt a little too big, to Tucia, he looked handsome as ever.

With so much to do—here and at the hospital—snatches of time together were all they could afford. But they made the most of them. She'd apologized for how she'd treated him the night before the storm, and Darl forgave her. He made her repeat *I love you* a dozen more times, though, on account of how mightily he liked the sound. Tucia had happily obliged.

Now, they took the basket and ate their supper on a bench at the edge of camp.

"The Trouts are leaving tomorrow morning," she said.

"Fanny's out of the hospital?"

She nodded, and Darl smiled. It seemed ages ago she'd first met him at the train depot with Huey and wondered if he'd ever smiled a day in his life. Now, even with all they'd endured, she saw that smile often.

"I'll try to make it to the docks."

"They'd love that." Her hand found his, and she traced the thick calluses on his palm with the pad of her thumb. "I'm sure they'd take you with them if you wanted to go."

"You goin'?"

"No. They still need me at the hospital and . . . I thought maybe I'd stay."

"Here? In Galveston? There's hardly anything left."

It was true. Even with all the cleanup efforts underway, so much had been destroyed the city looked like a skeleton of its former self. But already, people were rebuilding. Starting anew. And Tucia liked the sound of that.

"Don't you like the idea of a fresh start?"

Darl squeezed her hand, then brought it to his lips. "I reckon I do."

Halfway through their supper, Toby dropped his sandwich and pointed up at the paling sky. "Look!"

A pelican soared above them, its wings outstretched, gliding toward the bay. One thing Tucia could say about the island, even in its current state, it still held moments of beauty. Perhaps other places could boast the same, but here, for the first time in a long time, Tucia could appreciate it.

The storm's ravages had not only opened her eyes, but her heart and mind as well. What mattered was the present moment. The people she was with. She may never be fully free of the past, and the future might bring more struggle. But the here and now wasn't a place to hide. It was hers to live.

AUTHOR'S NOTES

The inspiration for this book arrived in layers. First came my interest in medicine shows. They pop up now and then in movies, books, and songs, but always as an aside. A colorful detail. More myth than history. What exactly were these shows? I wondered. Did they really sell snake oil? I decided to find out, and that became the foundation for my story.

Traveling nostrum sellers have existed for centuries in many parts of the world. In nineteenth-century America, these pitchmen and entrepreneurs drew inspiration from minstrel shows, Wild West shows, the circus, vaudeville, and the patent-medicine craze. Some operated alone, hawking medicine on street corners. Others traveled with a cast of performers. At its height in the late nineteenth century, the Kickapoo Indian Medicine Company—one of the biggest and most successful medicine shows in history—had as many as one hundred troupes performing in the United States and Canada.

For people living in rural areas, these shows were often the only source of outside entertainment, and many eagerly awaited their arrival. That entertainment reflected the prejudices of the day and often included blackface and Irish comedy sketches as well as stereotypical and appropriated representations of Native Americans, Romani, and other cultures.

Several factors conspired to bring an end to the traveling medicine show, most notably the Pure Food and Drug Act in 1906, which prohibited the sale of misbranded food and drugs; increased education in rural America; and the rise of radio and TV. In 1964, the last of the big shows ceased operation.

Almost every aspect of the Amazing Adolphus Medicine

Show—from the case-taking tent to the rattlesnake oil to the ballyhoo—was drawn from historical accounts. I made up the names and little else. Licensed doctors—often those who'd lost their practices to alcohol or other addictions—sometimes traveled with these shows, providing legal cover and a veneer of respectability. Indian Medicine Shows like the Kickapoos' were very popular, and the Bureau of Indian Affairs contracted with these shows on occasion to provide Native American performers, whose participation was often coerced.

The next element of the book to take shape in my mind was the Galveston Storm. I first learned about it from a list pinging around the internet—The Ten Worst Natural Disasters in U.S. History. The Galveston hurricane of 1900, having killed between six and twelve thousand people, topped that list. I fell down the proverbial rabbit hole and read how a city, already one of the wealthiest in the U.S. and poised to become the most important seaport in Texas, was all but destroyed. Entire sections of the city were swept out to sea. Others were reduced to rubble. So many people died the city had to revert to burning the bodies. The smoke of funeral pyres choked the air for days after the storm. The city did rebuild, though it never regained its industrial prominence. A massive seawall was built following the storm, and for over a hundred years has protected the island from similar devastation. Some scientists worry, however, the effects of climate change will soon render the wall insufficient.

Tucia and Fanny's experience during the hurricane was drawn from several first-person accounts (letters, memoirs, oral histories, etc.). I found less to guide me about the days after, in particular the role of medical workers immediately following the storm. Where there were holes in the record, I drew from my understanding and experience of medical crises. One sentiment that came up repeatedly in the sources I did find was that the doctors and nurses of Galveston were exemplars of "courage and hope" in the aftermath of the storm. To that, I strove to be true.

In any disaster, there are those, like Huey, who behave unconscionably for personal gain. Fear and speculation about looters abound in primary-source accounts of the Galveston storm. But often, it was just that—fear and speculation (colored by anti-Black prejudice). Scholars of the storm and its aftereffects believe stories of looting were much exaggerated and only a few people were actually caught and executed for the crime.

When I first drafted the novel, Tucia was not a doctor, but a medicine show woman herself. Huey existed, too, though only as a minor character. Unsatisfied with that draft—Tucia in particular—I cast about for a more interesting approach to the story. That was how I learned of the considerable advancements women physicians made at the end of the nineteenth century. (I hadn't realized there even *were* women doctors at that time!)

It's true many people of this era did not believe women had the mental and physical capacity to be doctors. Most schools refused to admit them until the very end of the century. Women physicians faced considerable discrimination from hospitals, medical associations, and their male colleagues. Nevertheless, a surprising number persisted and succeeded.

In 1849, Elizabeth Blackwell became the first woman in America to obtain a medical degree. Several trailblazing women followed. As few schools were willing to admit them, several women's medical colleges were founded (nineteen in total by the end of the century). In 1870, only 0.8 percent of doctors in America were women. By 1900, that number had increased to nearly 6 percent! Unfortunately, growth slowed (and sometimes ceased) in the decades after. In 1970, women accounted for only 7 percent of doctors. Today, the percentage of active physicians who are women is around 38 percent.

Many of the struggles and prejudices Tucia faced as a physician were drawn from contemporary sources, although her experience with Dr. Addams in the operating theater was of my own imagining. As a healthcare worker myself, I can attest to the emotional toll mistakes—even harmless ones—have on you.

This brings me to the mental health layers of the story. Neither post-traumatic stress disorder nor trichotillomania (the overwhelming urge to pull out one's hair) are new disorders, though they were not always known by those names. Our mental health affects our lives just as much as our physical health. I was interested in exploring this connection and how it would play out in 1900, when little was known about either disorder.

Lastly, I did not set out with the intention of writing a character with Down syndrome. It arrived as a question during my research—what happened to people with intellectual disabilities in the nineteenth century? They seemed all too often absent from the mainstream narrative. That led me to learn about the institution model that arose in the latter part of the century, where people with such conditions were separated from their families and placed in schools and asylums. Of course, more questions arose, one in particular that stuck with me: What would it be like for a mother faced with the prospect of losing her child to such an institution? From that, the character of Toby was born. In creating his character, I drew from two sources: medical texts (both current and those of the late nineteenth century so I could understand how the condition was understood at the time) and personal experience (my own, albeit limited, experience with a family member as well as interviews with others). As with many things, the lived experience of people with Down syndrome varies greatly. The choices I made for Toby were both a function of my personal understanding and what seemed plausible in the context of the novel.

For those interested in learning more, here's a truncated list of the resources I used to craft this story:

Medicine Shows: *Step Right Up* by Brooks McNamara; *Snake Oil, Hustlers, and Hambones: The American Medicine Show* by Ann Anderson; *Four White Horses and a Brass Band: True Confessions from the World of Medicine Shows, Pitchmen, Chumps, Suckers. Fixers, and Shills* by Violet McNeal

Galveston and the 1900 Hurricane: *Isaac's Storm: A Man, a Time, and the Deadliest Hurricane in History* by Erik Larson; *The*

Storm of the Century: Tragedy, Heroism, Survival, and the Epic True Story of America's Deadliest Natural Disaster: The Great Gulf Hurricane of 1900 by Al Roker; *Through a Night of Horrors: Voices from the 1900 Galveston Storm,* edited by Casey Edward Greene and Shelly Henley Kelly; *Galveston: A History* by David G. Mc-Comb

Women Physicians: *Women in White Coats: How the First Women Doctors Changed the World of Medicine* by Olivia Campbell; *"Send Us a Lady Physician": Women Doctors in America 1835–1920,* edited by Ruth J. Abram, *Daring Women Doctors: Physicians in the 19th Century* (documentary film), directed by Valerie Scoon

Other: *Trichster* (documentary film), directed by Jillian Corsie, *The Body Keeps the Score: Brain, Mind, and Body in the Healing of Trauma* by Bessel van der Kolk, *We Had a Little Real Estate Problem: The Unheralded Story of Native Americans and Comedy* by Kliph Nesteroff, *The Fus Fixico Letters: A Creek Humorist in Early Oklahoma,* edited by Daniel F. Littlefield Jr. and Carol A. Petty Hunter

Acknowledgments

Sometimes, writing a novel feels like running an ultramarathon, the finish line far out of sight. Sometimes, it feels like running the fifty-yard dash—all you can do is put your head down and go as fast as you can. In both cases, it can seem like you're racing alone.

I am not a runner, though I've dabbled enough to know you're *not* alone. You have your coach, your training partners, your competitors (who sometimes are your closest friends), your cheering squad, your ride home when your legs are too wobbly to be trusted with the break. Writing is the same.

Readers, you are my cheering squad, the people whose praise and encouragement matter more than where I place in the race. You are the volunteers handing out cups of water along the way that keep me going when my lungs are burning and feet sore. You are my inspiration. My endpoint. Thank you.

John, Michael, you are my dear coaches. Thank you for helping me get to the finish line.

To all the assistant coaches and support staff at Kensington— Vida Engstrand, Michelle Addo, Lauren Jernigan, Alex Nicolajsen, Kait Johnson, Kristin McLaughlin, Carly Sommerstein, Lori Glick, and so many more—I'm truly grateful for all you do.

I would be nowhere without my training partners. In their brilliant company, I learn and grow and push myself to be better. Jenny Ballif, Angelina Hill, Wendy Randall, Veronica Klash, Reine Bouton, and Patricia Tudosa, thank you.

Thank you, too, to the experts who kept me on course: Dr. Brenda Harris, Christina Salmon, Alice Skenandore, and the patient and knowledgeable staff at the Galveston & Texas History Center and the Truman G. Blocker, Jr. History of Medicine Collection at the UTMB Moody Medical Library.

And Steven, you are my ride home and so much more. Thank you.

THE MEDICINE WOMAN
OF GALVESTON

ABOUT THIS GUIDE

The suggested questions are included to enhance
your group's reading of Amanda Skenandore's
The Medicine Woman of Galveston!